THE
AMISH
LANDSCAPE

THE
AMISH
LANDSCAPE

ROBERT HOLMAN

NICK HERN BOOKS
London

A Nick Hern Book

The Amish Landscape first published in 1992 by Nick Hern Books
A Random Century Company, 20 Vauxhall Bridge Road,
London SW1V 2SA

British Library Cataloguing in Publication Data

Holman, Robert, 1952–
The Amish landscape.
I. Title
823.914 [F]

ISBN 1 85459 114 2

Typeset by BookEns Ltd, Baldock, Herts
Printed and bound by T.J. Press Ltd, Padstow, Cornwall

I

Nakedness

1

I first saw Harry as he was walking across the quad on the open-ing morning of term. I was already thirteen and had never before attended school, let alone one with imposing ivy-clad stone facades and an impressive history, my mother having edu-cated me herself at home, alone in an attic room exclusively set aside for this purpose. I expect many boys in my position might well have had the pomposity of one not yet challenged by his peers. I did not; I felt uncertain and afraid. Three months earlier, following an interview, I had been offered a scholarship, so at least one of the adjudicators must have thought I would overcome these peculiarities, and this gave me enough confi-dence to ask Harry if he was a new boy too. He looked hapless, as if every decision he had made had always gone against him, and replied in the affirmative before walking away as if we had never spoken. I know many friendships are begun in far less aus-picious circumstances, but at the time I was most hurt by his rebuttal and straightway burst into tears.

The summer was over. My parents had brought me by train to Hampshire, and we had stayed overnight at a local coaching inn, where my father had even allowed me a small beer, much to my mother's chagrin. This sojourn must only have served to pro-long their agony. I particularly remember my mother's face which was drawn and white, as if the ghosts of her past had finally caught up with her: it was not her idea that I be sent away, and the arguments at home had been long and vicious. I had lis-tened, with a glass to the floor, from my room upstairs and had been both impressed by and a little frightened of my father's new resolve. It was on my mind to call down – it was me they were discussing and I should have a place in their argument – but I knew by then I had become irrelevant, and the bitterness between them would never be completely healed.

My father wore a moustache which twitched when he was sad, but his lips were still as we said goodbye on the gravel, although I could feel the doubt in his handshake. He looked towards my mother as if to apologize. She immediately glanced away. It was then his moustache quivered, not for me but for his marriage.

My mother's lessons in the attic had been brisk and formal, the politeness between pupil and teacher extending into every detail of our life together. So it was with her farewell.

'Remember, Daniel,' she said. 'You are a clever boy and can do well at your lessons. Remember you can be as clever as any boy here.'

Memory is illusive. If I think a little further, it is not Harry's haplessness I first recall, but rather that he was not accompanied by his parents. Everywhere about us were boys with their families, many standing listlessly by motorcars and chauffeurs, but Harry had the confidence of one by himself. It seems odd that even on that first morning I should have thought him unlucky or wretched, when all we had done was exchange a few words, and he had so clearly demonstrated his superiority by walking away in such a cavalier fashion. It seems even stranger that he should then have turned and walked back towards me.

'Stop crying,' he said.

Tears in themselves are not necessarily important. I was so shocked I did exactly as I was told.

'Look at those boys over there,' he said. 'Have you no shame?'

I turned and saw a group of smaller boys, younger brothers not yet old enough for the school. They were giggling at me.

'Their time will come,' he went on. 'You must learn to be an adult.' His voice had the edge of experience and expressed little sympathy. 'Don't ever cry again. You will make your own life a misery and everybody else's too.'

I have learnt that it is often the seconds in my life which have counted far more than the hours, for in the seconds our instincts hold sway, whereas the hours are governed by time and reason, and I have, for the most part, been instinctive in my choices. If I had had an hour to reason out his brusqueness, I might well

4

have run away and hidden my shame elsewhere. As it was, something in these first few moments of conversation, lasting perhaps no more than twenty or thirty seconds, told me I should accept his hostility and, what is more, be disposed actually to like him for it.

I am ever grateful for my instinct, for Harry's has been the single most important friendship of my life.

'You may carry my trunk if you wish,' he said.

The usual practice during all my years at school was for my trunk to travel ahead by train, where it was dealt with upon arrival at the local station by the porters and school valet staff. I therefore had no trunk of my own to carry. I picked up Harry's portmanteau and immediately felt its weight pull my arm from my shoulder socket, but I soldiered on, letting the smaller leading edge scuff across the gravel. It left behind a thin trench.

'What are you doing?' he said. 'This is not a battlefield. We are not digging-in.'

'Excuse me, but it's rather heavy.'

'Then you should not have volunteered to carry it.'

'I did not volunteer. You made me.'

'What on earth will you do when you have to serve King and Country. You are such a coward.'

Harry did not speak like an officer, but rather as I expect one might to an irksome younger sister, and it was not the loudness of his voice, for it was not loud, which made me pick up his portmanteau once again, nor its severity, for it was not severe: it was the reassurance he offered that all might be well should I really try. I recognized the tone from my father. My father had the same way of cajoling without ever being patronizing.

Harry kept himself ahead until we reached the stone portico, where the ivy was so well cut it fell like an expensive dress.

'Isn't this hideous,' Harry said. 'Nature should be wild.'

I was out of breath and my shoulder ached. It was then Harry turned and asked me the one last question I shall always remember from that morning. He asked me why I was so sycophantic. Today I might reply quickly, for I understand myself, at least a little, but at that time I had to battle for confidence, although for the moment I had fought enough. So I blushed and said nothing. Today I might hazard that between the ages of nought and thirteen I had been brought up to be humble, and that humbleness and sycophancy, in a young mind at least, often go hand in hand. It takes discernment and an older head to realize that humbleness is an admirable trait whilst sycophancy is not.

I have learned to believe in flukes. I do not mean luck, which on the whole one makes oneself. Harry and I were to share a room. It was there on the entrance-way noticeboard for no one to dispute.

'I thought I might have to relieve you of my trunk,' he said. 'But it now seems you may carry it up the stairs.'

The room was bland and cold, and so utilitarian it could have been prison. Harry immediately chose the bed by the window, so I was left with the other. I expect my own portmanteau was already there, because my memory is of both of us unpacking, hoping to bring a little of ourselves into these dismal surroundings. There was only one chest and one wardrobe, so some kind of division was required. Harry, as if feeling guilty about the bed, offered me the best of both. I accepted the top drawers of the chest whilst declining the wardrobe. The wardrobe was broken and had only one door, which Harry hung his shirts behind. I put mine in the chest.

'What are you doing?' he said.

'I fold my shirts like this. That's why I don't need much space over there.'

'Nonsense, they'll get creased,' he said. 'Hang them in here with mine.'

That night I lay in bed in my new cotton pyjamas. Indeed, everything I had worn that day had been new, from my underwear outwards. I still love that clean and crinkled feeling which comes from putting on an article of clothing for the first time and the confidence which it gives. I am not ashamed to admit I am quite feminine in this way.

I had not watched Harry change into his pyjamas, but had been deliberately preoccupied elsewhere. When I could occupy myself no longer I had stolen across the corridor to the lavatory and stayed there as long as I decently could, hoping that on my return Harry would have extinguished the lamp, which indeed he had. The relief of darkness was so great I could have cried again. I had never before been naked in front of another human being.

'Where've you been?' he said.

'The lavatory.'

'Does it take you that long?'

'Yes,' I replied.

I slipped into my pyjamas hoping that Harry was not thinking me odd. It took only a few moments. The bedsheets were cold and unwelcoming. I pulled them up to my chin.

'You are funny,' he said.

'Why?'

'You just are. Is this your first school?'

'Yes,' I said. 'My mother's been teaching me at home. She was a schoolmistress before she married my father.'

There was silence, and I thought Harry must be thinking of sleep.

'Why did they send you here?' he said.

'My father wanted me to go to grammar school. He thought it wrong for me to be in the house all the time. He said I should be with boys of my own age.'

'What do you think?'

'I don't know. I'm glad to leave for a while. They were arguing all the time. My mother said if I had to go to school, it must be to a public school like this. Really they both lost, because my mother didn't want me to go to school at all, and my father didn't want me sent away.'

I could hear Harry breathing and thought he must think me ridiculous, especially after what I had just said.

'They can't afford it either,' I continued. 'They are far from rich. My father did want a motorcar.'

'Don't tell that to the other chaps. Your life won't be worth living. Everyone has a motor.'

'How many schools have you been to?'

'This and my prep,' he replied.

The subject of nakedness is a difficult one. I was hoping to give it a less psychologically revealing place in my story, but now I find the topic is upon me without my fully realizing it. Those of you with siblings may find any need for discussion strange. I am an only child, and had therefore always bathed alone from the moment my mother considered it prudent and decent for me to do so. This must have been when I was six or seven. I know today many parents bath with their infant children, and I can see only good in this, but for my part I cannot ever recall seeing my mother naked, and what I know of her personality only confirms that my memory is correct. What is more, shortly before my father's death, as the advance of his cancer stimulated the need for confession, he told me he had only twice seen my mother fully naked, once before they were married, and again at her death when he had unclothed her himself. He said, 'Marriage in a woman like your mother produces prudery – she wasn't prudish before we married, but she believed it to be her duty to become so. It happened slowly, Daniel, but it happened nonetheless, as snobbery got the better of her. When she died I unclothed her myself to relieve her of that burden. That was not what she was like, and not what she truly wished to be.' And he added, speaking of himself, 'There is an energy in death which produces honesty. I must be honest now. We had intercourse many times before we were married, but I can count on the fingers of one hand the number of times since. I am not criticizing, I am still trying to understand. For many years, Daniel, particularly when you were small, I sought a schoolboy's relief. The shame I felt then is the shame I hope I have not passed on to you. I wanted to tell you this on the day you left for school, but I needed your mother's encouragement, and she would not give it. I expect you were as naive about your own feelings as your mother and I were about ours. I hope nakedness means nothing to you any more. I'd hate to think it did.' My father's head was on a monogrammed pillow in the hospital. He died two weeks later. I asked the authorities if I might undress his body myself, and did so, just as he had my mother's. I am still not fully sure why I asked, beyond my desire for symmetry, my belief in patterns, and my need for the security that comes from repetition. In fact, it made me miserable for weeks afterwards. I could fit his death into my life but not his nakedness, which was shocking and sad, for he seemed so to lack the dignity he had had when clothed. It was a mistake and I bitterly regret it.

When one is young one can never think of regret as a positive emotion, one sees it as dismissive, even hateful: a negative feeling one would rather be without. I have learned to treasure my regrets, they are the cornerstone of much of my thought and progress. It is said one learns more from failure than from success. I would like to put it another way: one learns more from what one regrets. I certainly regretted not undressing in front of

Harry on that first night at the school, for the ordeal would have been quickly over. Instead it was still to come, as come it must.

'Harry.'

'What?'

'Have you brothers and sisters?'

'Go to sleep. Three.'

'Brothers or sisters?'

'One brother, two sisters. Why?'

'I just wondered.'

'Have you?'

'No, I wish I had. Have you ever undressed in front of them?'

'I can't hear you.'

'I said, have you ever undressed in front of them?'

'When I was little, with Nanny. Why?'

'I just wondered.'

'You do a lot of just wondering, don't you?'

'Do I?'

'You're peculiar.'

'I know I'm peculiar. I never have, you see. Undressed in front of another person, that is. I knew I would have to today but I didn't. That's why I went to the lavatory. Harry?'

'What?'

'I'm pleased I've told you. Would you mind very much if I did it now?'

Harry lit the lamp, and I slipped out of my pyjamas.

I have only once behaved in a similar fashion since, and then for a completely different reason. I was travelling through Arizona on an American adventure I had been promising myself for a number of years. I had never been to a desert, but instinctively felt I might like it. My father's death had been a shock, and I needed an open landscape in which to sort through my thoughts.

The Arizona desert is a miraculous place; giant monuments of rock rise from the dry plains like vast European cathedrals. They absorb light and throw back awe. The plains bow before them like Islam at prayer. The religious similes are not erroneous, for who else could have turned such violence on the earth, and created such magnitude, but God. To look at these monoliths is to know that one is in the presence of greatness.

One such is Shiprock. It stands higher than the Empire State Building. The Navajo Indians have for centuries called it 'the rock with wings', and it is an apt description for it glows like a bird of prey and draws one to it with a mixture of terror and delight. A single spoke of volcanic lava, higher than the Great Wall of China, runs from the Cinder Coned Megalith into the distance further than the eye can see. As violence is fascinating so is Shiprock.

I parked my hired car and began to walk towards it along the spoke, my shoes kicking up dust from the scrub, my eyes searching the arid land for rattlesnakes. I was carrying a bottle of water with which to quench my thirst. The heat was prodigious. After two hours my car was the size of a matchbox and the rock no nearer. This is how big these Megaliths are, they look near but they are impossible to reach in a few hours. I climbed the spoke where this was made easy by smaller, less violent upheavals of earth and saw from the top how completely alone I really was. I had never felt so isolated. In every direction the circular plain of the desert stretched before me in a huge mirage, and the horizon, which might have put some limit to the infinity, had ceased to exist. It was unreal, as if I were floating on my own planet, yet the ground beneath my feet was solid and sharp. My heart was racing. I picked my way along the top of the spoke, letting the volcanic ash tear my shoes until I fell, luckily only a few feet but enough to make me change my mind. There was nothing and no one in sight. I found a boulder and stood on that and looked at the rock once again. It was challenging my imagination, and I realized for the first time the absolute power of landscape; how it moulds us and shapes us; how it defies us and makes us insignificant. There is a divine force in the earth which we will never attain; we inhabit it only for the small moment of life, and are mortal. I had only once before felt so humbled. I was so frightened by the rock that it was erotic. The more I looked the more erotic I felt. I tried not to take my clothes off because it seemed so foolish, but in the end I had to do so.

I realize I have said little about Harry. As the first few days of a new job seem to last forever, so did those early days at school. Harry remained aloof, and I learned little more about him than I had on our first morning. He had a shock of black hair, which made him look like a thistle, and such was his personality; whilst he was always cordial and polite, there was a prickliness about

him which caused one to step back and keep one'?
was good at the nuances of conversation, and adep
it should it become too personal. I rather envied t
did other children. Slowly he became a mysterious
the school. Boys thought him unique if a little odd
were so suspicious that they refused to come near
ever anyone felt, I was his friend and was consequen ͵ ͗appier
than I might have expected.

Harry's parentage still baffled me. Beyond knowing he had a
brother, two sisters and a nanny, I had no information whatsoever. On those nights when I could not sleep, my mind ran the
gamut of possibilities. I asked other boys in the house, but in
return they pumped me, and I realized they knew even less.
There were times in the evenings when he would ask to be alone,
so I would leave him to go and play chess. I often returned to
find him asleep, a book covering his face as if he might be hiding, and I would search the room for clues. My chess playing
improved so rapidly with such frequent practice that soon no
one would challenge me, so I took to secluding myself in the
library where I would sit and read in one of the comfortable
armchairs. I read Dickens here and Trollope, and ceased to
wonder about the mystery upstairs.

One evening Harry joined me, and we sat in silence. If I think
back, I realize that on the day I had so nervously slipped out of
my pyjamas I had been revealing myself both literally and metaphorically, for the fear of my literal nakedness was so great that I
no longer had anything to hide. For Harry, who had been first
into a tub when we had to bath communally, the opposite was
true: his apparent lack of fear hid everything. Had I realized
this, I might well have found a way of approaching him on his
level, but unfortunately I did not. I have learned to worship
silence but could not bear it that evening. It was not even the
silence between friends; so I left him and returned to the games
room where chess was in full swing. I played one of the many
elderly masters there – and won easily.

In truth, I was enjoying the security and the glory of Harry's
enigma but was too naive or selfish to be grateful to him. He was
good at all the multitudinous aspects of school, both in and out
of the classroom, and he was there when I needed him; on the
rugby field he taught me not to be afraid in a scrum; on the

arade ground he showed me how to march in step; in the schoolroom he tutored me in etiquette, and lessons became a joy because I knew how to shine. If I had known Harry's confidence to be a sham, I might have thought less about myself. If I had been more generous, I would have realized how lonely he was. If I had recognized his solitariness, I might well have seen that he was unhappy. All this should have been obvious to me, but Harry had given me such confidence and bravado I no longer noticed.

One night, shortly before the end of term, I got out of bed to go through his jacket pockets. I had not done this for a while, having decided that my inquisitiveness was wrong, but Harry had been morose all day and curiosity as to its cause was keeping me awake. He was moaning in his sleep. I found nothing that might not have been in my own pockets and climbed back between the freezing bedcovers.

'What are you doing?' he said.

'I thought you were snoring.'

'I don't snore.'

'Yes you do, Harry.'

'You still haven't answered my question.'

'I went to the lavatory,' I lied.

'I thought you'd stopped going to the lavatory now.'

'Ha, ha,' I said.

I heard the rustle of a match, and Harry re-lit the lamp. The room was suffused in its orange glow.

'If Matron catches us, I'll take the blame,' he said.

His cheeks were puffy, the colour of butter. The knuckles of his hands were clenched white. He pulled himself up like an exhausted climber. I had never seen him like this.

'What on earth's the matter?' I said.

'I can't tell you, Daniel. I have bad dreams sometimes, that's all.'

He lay still and quiet, his head resting in the crook of his arm.

'Should I go and get Matron? I think you're ill.'

'No. I wanted the light, that's all.'

He pulled himself further up so that he was sitting. His pyjama top was unbuttoned and for the first time I realized how thin his chest was, his ribs without flesh like a fledgeling. I must have shown this on my face.

'You look as though you're pitying me, Daniel,' he said. 'Don't pity me. I'd hate that.'

12

'You'll get cold. Pull the blankets over you.'

'No. I'm hot.'

'There's frost on the window.'

'I don't care.'

'I was searching through your pockets,' I said. 'I want to help. Please tell me what's the matter.'

'I have bad dreams, Daniel. I can't help them, I can't stop them, I can't do anything. They come when I least expect them; when I'm happy as a matter of fact. I've been happiest here at school and yet the dreams still come. I'm so frightened because they're getting worse.'

'Don't be frightened.'

'I do try not to be.'

'I hope you know you can rely on me. I mean, I've relied on you, haven't I?'

'You're pitying me again,' he said.

'I'm not. What's wrong with pity anyway?'

'I don't want to be felt sorry for.'

'Harry,' I said, 'I'm your friend, please trust me.'

'Yes, friends should be able to trust one another,' he said. 'But it isn't that.'

'What is it then?'

'I don't trust myself, Daniel.'

'You'll have to explain. I don't understand.'

'I have this feeling, deep down inside me, which wants to be really terrible to other people. To be really awful, to be wretched, to punch and kick them in as hurtful a way as possible.'

'But you're not like that. You don't behave like that.'

'Not at the moment, no. But the way I see it, it's just a matter of time.'

There was silence. Harry's face was beaded with sweat.

'The terrible dreams,' he said, 'are when I actually do do it. When I take my fists to people. When I knock them senseless and enjoy it.'

I did not realize then how obsessive an animal man is, and how it is our compulsions which largely dictate to us our destinies. I see it now as a matter of chance which of us has the greater control over his emotional desires, and it has taken me a long time to learn to be careful about apportioning blame. I have come to liberalism late in my life.

13

2

Harry's ravings continued that night so I tiptoed out for Matron. I did not tell him I was going but waited until his eyes were closed. His body was coursing with perspiration, and I knew he had lost control of his feelings and become disturbed. Matron, to my utter relief, took him straightway to the sanatorium. Harry did not complain. I sat on my bed, and after Matron had returned to tell me he was comfortable I fell shivering into an exhausted sleep.

I awoke in the morning to find snow on the ground. Harry did not appear for chapel. In Europe a war was raging, and the roll call of the newly dead was as sombre as any I can recollect; Henry Turner, Edward Griffiths, John Hazeldeane, ordinary names, old boys of the school killed on the battlefields of the Somme. I sat and somehow expected Harry's name to be among them; Richard Lightfoot, Joey Askew, Christopher Colfax. There were six that morning. I observed the row of elderly masters, who must remember their faces, and who must know how good or bad each boy had been. I tried to think of Harry as bad, tried to see him doing what he said he was capable of, but it made no sense. Outside the snow was melting, and I prayed someone would tell me of his condition. I had not told the other boys, for I knew it had to be a secret. No one, master or boy, spoke to me. In Latin, I watched a boy carve his initials in the wooden desk. There were hundreds of initials there already, the master too old to notice. In Greek, a group of boys held a farting competition. By lunchtime the word was about that Harry had run away because he knew he was hated, his aura already vanished, his mystery already reviled. By mid-afternoon it was said

14

that he had joined the army, that he had taken the King's shilling, that he was now in uniform and on his way to France. Another version had him being shown the white feather and being humiliated for despicable cowardice. The boys laughed, and in chess that evening I fought as I had never fought before. I wanted to beat them, and hurt them, and show them how wrong they were. When I lost, I threw the chessmen across the room and upturned a table. I spent the night alone, and still there was no word. In the morning it began again; Thomas Wilson, Angus Blair, Jimmy Lichfield. I saw their faces in the mud of Europe, and Harry's face too, squashed and bereft of all dignity. I hated him.

The day was cold. It had snowed again during the night, deep snow that looked as if it meant to stay. One or two boys began to fashion toboggans from odds and ends of wood. It was a Sunday, a free day, and we might do as we wished. I watched them through the window of my room. The hill was about ten minutes' walk away on the edge of the school grounds, and when I joined them their makeshift toboggans were already in pieces and a snowball fight was in progress. I tried to repair one of the toboggans, hoping I might find favour, but in the end gave up, making snowballs of my own, but no one seemed bothered whether I was there or not. In my mind I kept wondering which of them might be a friend, and decided on the boy with spectacles because he had often seemed interested in me. He was a weakling, which was not a point in his favour, but he had a sharp mind and a quick tongue. I hit him with a snowball, pulled his gabardine and apologized for my misbehaviour.

Later in the afternoon I went with him to the library and we sat by the fire with our books. It was the first time that day that either of us had been warm. We were allowed to toast muffins on Sundays, and this we did, spreading them with butter.

'What do you think of the school?' he asked.

'I don't know,' I replied. 'Sometimes I like it, sometimes I like it less.'

'It's falling apart. My brother was here. It never used to be like this. The headmaster's too old,' he continued. 'He's dropping asleep most of the time.'

The boy cleaned his spectacles with a napkin, and we took off our boots to warm our toes. I finished my book and went to the shelves in my stockinged feet to select another volume, closing

15

my eyes, letting it be chance which one I chose. We sat on until it was nearly dark and time for the evening service.

'Shall we go together?' I asked.

'I have a letter to write first. It doesn't matter about us sitting together.'

The local village joined the school for Sunday prayers, where I expected to hear Harry's name amongst the roll call of the dead. Afterwards, I walked to the sanatorium where a single light was burning behind closed curtains. I waited, hoping to hear voices. As there were none, I tapped on the glass as quietly as I could. I imagined Harry alive coming to the window, but he did not. I tapped again, this time with more force so that he would definitely hear but it was Matron who appeared. I ducked down and saw her peering out. She stayed there for several moments looking left and right, perhaps wondering if a starling had struck the glass. She must surely see me. I held my breath and leant close to the wall, pushing my knees up to my chin, my heart pounding against my thighs. All I could see was her face because of the angle I was at. She closed the curtains, dismissing the sound as unimportant, but I had recognized the voice that had asked her if anyone was there. I relaxed and let the air from my lungs. Harry was alive, and I knew where he was.

The headmaster asked to see me in the middle of Latin the following morning, so I was excused and dashed across the snow to his cottage, forgetting my overcoat. His wife opened the door. I liked her because she was always cheerful. She was also less eccentric than her husband.

'Goodness, you must be frozen,' she said. 'Come in and get yourself warm.'

'Thank you. I'm not really cold,' I said.

'I feel I ought to take something from you, but you've nothing to take. Do go through. He's in the sitting-room. He's waiting for you.'

The sitting-room was fogged with smoke from his pipe. His opening remark was not what I expected.

'You knocked over a table in the games room on Saturday evening,' he said. 'Did you do it on purpose, or was it an accident?'

'I did it on purpose, sir.'

'Why should you do anything like that?'

'I was losing, sir.'

16

'It's not a very correct way to behave now, is it?'

'No, sir.'

'Have you apologized?'

'In part, sir.'

'In part. What does that mean? You have either apologized or you have not.'

'I've apologized, sir.'

'I was upset when I heard. I dislike self-pity, it's most unbecoming. Sit down. I expect you had other things on your mind.'

'Thank you. Yes, sir.'

'If it happens again, it won't pass in this way.'

'No, sir.'

'I've been speaking to your father. I have his telegram here.' He was holding a piece of white paper.

'I beg your pardon, sir?'

'I sent your father a telegram. He has replied.'

'Yes, sir. Why?'

'I needed his permission for you to go to London. Your father's very slow. Is he dim-witted?' He had a habit of asking forthright questions.

'No sir, I don't think so.'

'Good, good. That's it. You're to go to London. I expect you'll be glad to get away.'

'Why, sir?'

'Why what, boy?'

'Why am I to go to London?'

'You are to go to London with your friend. He is your friend, isn't he? Don't you want to go?'

'No, I'd like very much to go, sir.'

'Then what is your problem?'

'I haven't a problem, sir.'

'Well done. Go and pack. You're to leave by motorcar within the hour.'

Harry was pale and drawn as if he had not slept at all during the intervening days, his eyes dark and concave, his pupils over-dilated so that he squinted at the light. There was no mystery about him now, there was no energy within him to recreate his former aura: it was a shocking sight. We walked to the Mercedes, Harry hunched and stooping. The chauffeur put a blanket around us both, and Harry sat with his knees almost touching his chin as I had done the previous evening by the sanatorium window. His cheeks were hollow, his face all bone. He shivered, his lips turning blue.

It was a sombre journey to begin with. Motorcars, let alone chauffeurs, were an unusual experience for me, and I tried hard to lift his spirits with my own excitement, but he hardly reacted or responded, so in the end I let him be taciturn, and we remained quiet for long periods. As Harry gradually became more animated, pointing out odd landmarks, I responded myself, letting him make the decision about whether we talked or not. I was still guessing that he lived in London and that we were in fact heading for his home; for some reason I could not bring myself to ask, fearful that his quietness would return. It seemed unfair that everyone was taking my cooperation for granted without telling me what my role was to be, if indeed I had a role at all. The snow was deep in many places, and the motorcar struggled up the hills: I felt I was struggling too.

'Come on,' Harry said, 'let's get out and push.'

'Pardon?'

'Let's get out and push before we stop completely.'

The chauffeur turned round and explained that we were approaching the summit.

'No, I'd like to,' Harry said. 'It'll be fun.'

We pushed the Mercedes towards the brow of the hill. It seemed incredible to me that Harry could behave in this way.

'Harry, this isn't fair,' I said. 'You must tell me something about what's been going on.' I had never felt so young, or been so perturbed by my innocence.

'Nothing's been "going on", as you put it. We're going home. We're free. You with me. Aren't I clever?'

'No, Harry, you're not clever at all. I liked it at school.'

'So did I, but this is much more fun.'

'You must tell me. I shan't come with you if you don't.'

'My mother's expecting us both.'

'Well, at least I now know that,' I said.

'Where would you go? London's fifteen miles ahead of us, school forty-five miles behind.'

'This is blackmail.'

'Yes, you're correct. I'm sorry. I needed you with me, Daniel.

18

I hope you don't mind?'

'I suppose I don't mind,' I said, 'but please don't lark about when I need an answer. I can get upset too, you know.'

'I know you can. That's why I like you.'

Harry lived in Mayfair in one of the large town houses which bordered the Park. By the time we arrived it was late afternoon.

'Shouldn't you at least pretend to be ill?' I asked.

'No, Ma and Pa only care about themselves,' he replied. 'In any case Pa is away.'

We entered the grounds through a heavy wrought-iron gate, which the chauffeur had to open and then close. When we stopped on the gravelled forecourt Harry gave him a ten-shilling note. It was so superior and arrogant an action. I had never seen so much money, nor felt so demeaned for another person. Harry's age and bravado made me shudder.

'From us both,' he said. 'Come on, Daniel. Home at last.'

There was no irony in his voice, no history: it was as if the events of the previous days had not taken place. I did not then understand why no recollection tempered his words, or slowed his pace, which had become as quick and as deft as anything I had previously witnessed. In a three-hour journey he had gone from one extreme to the other. This rapid alternation of moods was to be a feature of his life, and there were many times I was almost to detest him for it.

That Harry was a manic depressive might have been obvious to me. It is my adult experience that obdurate people often are, but I was thirteen and had not yet read Freud or Jung or any of the great psychoanalysts of our age; nor had I yet studied for my own medical degree in which psychoanalysis played a small part, though I could have wished it larger since I was fascinated by the subject. That Harry, at a similar age, had learned to control his temper (he used the word violence: he would never, for instance, have upturned a chess table) says much about the differences between us. Many years later, when he too had read Freud, he told me one of the several regrets of his childhood was that he felt he had forever been holding himself in check, that he had never fully discharged himself emotionally as had been his brute instinct. He was, of course, talking about anger. Harry had every right to be angry, and it was the check he placed on his anger which was at the root of his depression. He had told me as much on that night in our room at school. That Harry had great self-knowledge is important: it was the means of his survival.

The Mayfair house had two staircases such that one could run round in endless circles without ever having to disturb the servants, or 'helpers' as Harry insisted upon calling them, whose rooms, which were airy and afforded more space than I might have expected, were in the basement. Indeed, Harry spent a great deal of his time there, often without me, my having excused myself to read some novel or history book I had found in the library, where his mother would sit catching up on her correspondence. Finishing each book offered the opportunity of meeting her again and so I raced through them to this end. She was a petite woman with nimble fingers, and I liked her quietening gaze and voice.

'Another book, Daniel?'

'Yes please, Mrs Treffgarne.'

I went to the shelves, pretending to look through the glass at the myriad titles, but in fact intent upon her reflection. It was difficult to stay too long without my stratagem becoming obvious.

'Would you like me to choose something for you?'

'No thank you, Mrs Treffgarne. I've something here. I'll take this one if I may?' I picked a book at random and only looked at the cover when walking back.

'Let me see your choice,' she said. 'You know there is a saying that you can tell a man by the books he reads.'

I gave her the title, shamefaced.

'The History and Development of the Modern Undergarment,' she read.

'Yes, Mrs Treffgarne. I thought it looked interesting.'

'Are you sure there is nothing more suitable to your taste?'

'I'd like to look at it for half an hour, and then put it back if I may?'

'Then sit here with me,' she said.

I took my embarrassment to the leather armchair.

'I wonder if there might not be another reason for your coming to the library so often?' she asked.

'I beg your pardon, Mrs Treffgarne?'

'It's becoming such a common occurrence. I wondered if

there might not be something more to it?'

'Well, I like unusual books. That's probably the reason.'

'Harry's a funny boy, isn't he?' she said.

'Harry once told me I was funny,' I replied, relieved that she appeared to be changing the subject.

'All people are funny when we get to know them, Daniel.'

I looked through the pages whilst Mrs Treffgarne took up her nib. She wrote quickly in staccato fashion, searching her mind for the correct sentence then swiftly committing it to paper.

'I hope I will not embarrass you by talking about Harry,' she said, looking up after a short while.

'No, not in the least, Mrs Treffgarne.'

She folded the paper and ran her thumb nail along the crease.

'Harry would not come home without you,' she said. 'I feel we owe you an explanation, Daniel. You've been very patient not to ask. Would you tell me what happened at school, and exactly what Harry talked about?'

I told her. I could not help it. When I had finished, the library was silent.

'Thank you for being so honest, Daniel,' she said. 'You are a delightful child, we're all very grateful you're here. Take your book if you wish. Or would you prefer to talk for a little while longer?'

'I'd prefer to talk,' I said, captivated by her ease.

'I will end up telling you what I should not, as you have told me.'

'Is Harry pretending to be happy?' I asked.

Mrs Treffgarne picked up the small bell from the desk in front of her. The maid soon arrived.

'You will take tea, Daniel, and not lemonade?'

'Yes, please. Tea,' I said.

'Would you bring three cups, Bridget? And ask Harry if he would join us.'

I had thought her as delicate as the family's porcelain, but now began to see her pithy hidden strengths.

'I should not ask you to keep a secret, Daniel, but I'm going to.'

Mrs Treffgarne was wearing pale white, the bodice of her dress so exquisitely folded and cut that when she stood it seemed to lift her from the desk as though rising required no effort on her part. There was nothing about her which one would ever doubt or question. As she walked across the room towards me, I followed her with my gaze and began to play with my fingers, fearing she might suddenly find me young and useless. I stood, letting her sit first.

'I must tell you, Daniel, that what I'm about to say must never leave these four walls.'

I blushed. 'Yes,' I said.

The library door opened and Harry entered with Bridget. I stood again, this time watching Harry as he sat beside his mother, feeling a little envious of his closeness. Harry looked casually towards me, as if taking tea with his mother were normal at this hour of the afternoon, though it was not. Bridget left, snapping the door closed. Her going created a silence which Mrs Treffgarne made ordinary by giving us all a cup and saucer.

'What is it, Mama?' Harry asked, quietly. I noticed that he was playing with his fingers like me, but less agitatedly, as if he were both conscious of his action and what was to be said. I put my own hands by my sides. When the tea came I held the saucer as an excuse to be still.

'It's Earl Grey, Daniel. I hope you like Earl Grey?'

'Yes, thank you, Mrs Treffgarne.'

'Have you been well and content?' Harry asked me. 'I'm sorry if I haven't seen very much of you.'

'Poor Daniel's been so much on his own,' Mrs Treffgarne echoed.

To cover my unease I picked up one of the small biscuits. Harry sat back as if deciding the conversation was not going to bother him. It was a strange meeting because little was out of the ordinary, yet beneath it lay so many secrets and untruths.

Harry's tea had ripples running across it. He leant forward, putting his saucer on the table, steadying his forearms on his knees. I looked towards Mrs Treffgarne and felt her calmness; there was such delicacy and grace in her manner, such poise and dignity. She took her son's hand, fully aware that he was nervous and in need of reassurance: they were so completely together, so at ease in one another's presence. Harry smiled at her. I felt my envy rise again, and it was so strong that I might have run from the room; it was all so different from my relationship with my mother. My saucer began to shake so I put it down on the table

22

as Harry had put his.

'The tea is delicious,' I said.

The tension in the room was close to unbearable, but Mrs Treffgarne lessened it by saying, 'I was telling Daniel how many people are funny when we get to know them well.'

'What book have you been reading?' Harry asked.

I showed him. 'It was a mistake,' I said. 'I thought it might be enjoyable, but it isn't. I don't know that I'm particularly interested in undergarments.'

Harry reminded me of my love of Dickens.

'Well, it certainly isn't *Oliver Twist*, Daniel.'

'No,' I said, 'if you'll excuse me, I think I'll put it back. May I do that, Mrs Treffgarne?'

'Of course,' she said.

I stood and went to the shelves across the parquet flooring, relieved to be out of their circle for a moment, but catching their reflections in the glass. I adjusted the angle of the door so that my view was perfect. They were still, their faces impassive, their hands steady, almost as if they were an audience at the theatre awaiting an actor. I turned, thinking the glass was deceiving me.

'Is anything the matter, Daniel?'

'Nothing, Mrs Treffgarne. I shan't be a moment.'

I busied myself in the bookcase. My own mother would have used the opportunity for silent communication or a quiet word. I realized the secret, whatever it must be, needed no further explanation between them. It was this which was strange, for Harry's distress at school had been so great it could not possibly be right. A tiny part of my innocence was vanishing. One or two of my ideas were becoming clearer. I was learning enough from Harry to begin not taking people at their face value, and I found myself wondering about Mrs Treffgarne's tranquillity, and what might be concealed behind it.

'Daniel', she called.

'I'm coming,' I said.

I returned to my seat much relieved, determined to leave my fingers alone. But it was only a few seconds before I was playing with them again. My toes curled, too. When Mrs Treffgarne spoke, it was with such apparent normality that I knew it to be a lie.

'Harry killed a boy,' she said. 'By mistake, in an accident. In the boxing ring. The other boy had a weak heart.'

'I killed my brother, Daniel,' Harry went on. 'My father liked us to box together. I was eight years old at the time, my brother ten. I hit out and hit out because he was beating me. I didn't mean to hit him that hard. He was bigger than me. Unfortunately, I didn't know what I was doing.'

This then was the secret, but I somehow knew I would have to wait for the truth.

The house was grand and imposing, and Harry and I had separate bedrooms. In some ways I was grateful for this, although at night, when, inevitably I could not sleep and my thoughts were constantly drawn to the strangeness of my situation, I longed for company and a voice that would take me away from myself, as Harry's voice had done at school. I was beginning to realize how great was his ability to shoulder a burden, and, through seeing it in him, I was becoming able to understand and develop my own proficiency in this respect. Being essentially naive I have always been the pupil. I lay motionless in bed and pondered all that was the house and Harry, trying to build a picture from the jigsaw pieces. A few months ago I might have cried, but I knew my crying would not help him. Hoping movement would bring clarity, I tossed and turned, until the bedsheets were rucked and uncomfortable. It was a simple matter to set them straight and once out of bed to put on my slippers.

I picked my way cautiously down the least accessible of the stairways, trusting the eerie stillness was not deceptive and that there was no one about. I was looking for an object, still believing then that adults hid evidence ineffectively as many children do. The house was at bay in the darkness, as though time had stopped some years ago. It was not the sombreness of the building, the bleakness of the walls, or the over-reverent furnishings which disturbed me: it was their lack of joy. I do believe houses retain life, so even a family fallen on hard times will leave traces of the exuberance that once made them happy. Here there was no contentment. The house had shouldered a lie and was unforgiving. I stopped looking for an object and began listening for an atmosphere. It had suddenly dawned on me that truth lay in nuance. Harry and his mother had wished to fool me, but Harry had been too nervous to bring it off. The coldness of the house reflected their lies. My thoughts switched back and forth until my head was bursting. I crept back to the bed and did not sleep at all.

The following day was one of the most unsettling of my life. I did not see Harry but was told he was visiting relatives for the day in Chelsea, which I believed, knowing he had cousins locally. The doctor had called earlier in the morning, but they had convinced me he was to see one of the maids. Mrs Treffgarne was sitting in the library when I was summoned in the afternoon. She made no mention of Harry and instead talked of India where the family had large investments, both in tea and in cotton. All this was new to me. She talked of the coloured people who she always felt might riot one day, and the fears she had. She herself had once picked tea with them, this despite her situation and standing, and had struggled through the half-day believing in the value of experience. Once again I was enthralled by her poise. She was a woman beyond my experience, cultivated and daring. As I listened I knew just how beautiful she was. When she excused me and I was given tea alone, my schoolboy's mind was filled with wonder, and that night, as I tried to push her from my mind and sleep, she would not go but lay beside me. I had no doubt I was wrong about everything I had previously thought.

'Who's there?' I said. It had taken me a few moments to realize my door had opened.

'It's me. Harry,' he whispered. 'Where's your light? I want to turn it on.'

'Let me do it. I've a switch beside my bed.' I turned on the electric light. Harry was half into the room, fully dressed.

'Haven't you been to bed?'

'I've been in bed all day,' he said. 'I've just got dressed. Do you mind if I sit beside you?'

'No.'

Harry closed the door. He was worse than I might have expected, in the bare light of the room he looked shadowed and broken. In an instant all my old doubts returned.

'You look ill, Harry.'

'No, I'm better now.' He sat beside me.

'Pull a cover round you, you'll be cold.' I placed a blanket across his shoulders, and he kept still as if relieved to be in my presence, but I had never seen such despair. There was no decision in his short life that had ever gone in his favour. His face was a ring of thin spots, and he stayed hunched, like one of Shakespeare's older men. There was no joy in his life, but bitterness and blackness. I had acted Shakespeare at school but this was real.

'My mother's been talking to you,' he said. 'Bridget told me.'

'Yes, all afternoon. About India.'

'I was born in India, but that's not what I've come to say. We returned from India when I was four, so I can remember just enough to believe what they tell me.'

'Move closer, Harry, I can't hear you.'

'I'm sorry I'm whispering,' he said, 'but I don't want anybody to hear us.' He moved closer, tilting his head so that I could see his face. 'I didn't come to talk about India,' he continued. 'My mother talks about India because she knows how much it fascinates boys like us.'

'Yes,' I said.

'It's her way of dispelling doubt. What she was telling you was probably the truth, but she wasn't really talking about India, she was talking about what we said yesterday, and convincing you that it was true.'

'Gosh, Harry.'

'Daniel, we lied to you yesterday.'

'I thought I knew, and then I didn't know,' I said.

'I kept trying to warn you, but you didn't seem to notice.'

'I didn't know what to look for. I just knew something was wrong.'

'It's my fault, Daniel. I should never have brought you here. It's this house, it's swallowed by lies.'

'It's as if the walls are lying,' I said. 'I hate it, I wish I'd never come.'

'I needed you here so badly. I'm sorry.'

'But you've hardly seen me, Harry.'

'I know.' He pulled the blanket across his shoulders. 'You've saved my life. I might have killed myself.'

'You didn't kill your brother, did you?' I said.

'No.' He moved closer, a little light coming into his eyes. 'My father killed him, Daniel, in a fit of rage. I watched him do it.' He lifted his head a little so that he was looking straight at me. 'He didn't mean to, of course. He just hit out, and my brother fell.'

26

'How old were you?'

'Eight. My brother, ten.'

'Did he have a weak heart?'

'No, that was part of the story they made up, and they paid a doctor to corroborate it.'

'What is the rest of the story?' I asked.

'We did have a boxing ring, Daniel. They put his body in there and dressed him in shorts. I put my own shorts on.'

'Did they ask you to take the blame?'

'Yes,' he said.

I let the silence enfold us, not knowing quite what to say.

'My father is a violent and hateful man, Daniel. Please believe that what I'm telling you now is the truth. I forget it myself sometimes. If I ever forget completely, I want you to remind me.'

I moved from inside the bed and sat beside him. 'You didn't do it, Harry,' I said.

'I know. But it sometimes feels as if I did.' The sparkle had gone from his eyes. He was beginning to shake.

'Harry, you didn't do it.'

'You don't understand Daniel.' His voice was shaking. 'It doesn't matter whether I did it or not. I feel that I did it and that's all that's important.' He could barely get the words out. 'This is how much they've convinced me.'

'Harry, listen to me. It is not your fault.'

'I'm sorry to make you as dirty as me.'

'I am not dirty. You are not dirty. I know, Harry, I know you would never do that. I knew yesterday. Of course I knew. It's the last thing I'd ever see you doing. You haven't even a temper.' I pulled him towards me so that he was leaning against me and put my arm across his shoulder. 'Please Harry, you are asking me to believe you. Then you must believe me. I know you are innocent. We must never be untruthful with one another again.'

I could feel his exhaustion through the blanket. The energy drained from his body and he became still. I let him fall asleep in my arms and we sat there for some while until it became so cold I dared to move him. I placed him beneath the covers and lay down beside him. We both slept.

In the morning I awoke first and re-adjusted the coverlet, making sure he was still warm. The day was chilly, a deep frost having settled either side of the window. I had until then forgotten it was nearing Christmas. I found my dressing gown and washed in the small hand-basin. It had become my habit to wash in cold water, but why carry on the ridiculousness of school when hot water was available? I watched Harry all the while, checking that he was still comfortable and realizing I no longer envied him. Trying to rid myself of the pity which he so loathed was a more complicated matter. I actually saw nothing wrong in pity, but to Harry it was patronizing, and I knew I must try.

I towelled myself dry and set about brushing my teeth; at home we used salt but here a chalky white powder was provided. I used to be given a chalky drink by my mother whenever I felt bilious and the tooth powder tasted somewhat similar. I had once stolen into the pantry and rubbed this chalk into my face, trying to feign illness. But my mother was not fooled and smacked me with such ferocity that I peed myself. I tried to remember what punishment or potential humiliation I had been trying to avoid. Harry's boxing ring came into mind. It was my mother who was responsible for discipline, and I could not recall a time when my father had ever laid a hand upon me. I thought what a peaceful, sedentary man he must be, and how he was so different from Harry's father. I did my best to picture the unseen Mr Treffgarne. I swilled my teeth and then cleaned the basin where a thin sediment of chalk had settled around the plug. I was still looking at Harry, keen that he be there and this not be a dream.

I was, of course, from a very different class. My father was a grocer, who sold tea. It occurred to me we probably sold Harry's father's tea. I was looking at Harry, feeling guilty because there was something pleasurable about his being asleep in my bed. I sat beside him for a moment and watched his thin face, trying to banish this contentment: I knew it to be wrong and that pity was the correct reaction. I pulled a stray hair from between his lips, fearing he might swallow it. I studied the puckered curve of his chin.

My father's grocery store was in Yorkshire in a small market town at the foot of the Cleveland Hills. What little money he had made had come from an ingenious system of discount: he gave a penny back for every shilling spent, but not until a guinea's worth of items had been purchased. It had become known as the 'week-free' shop because a family could live for a week on the one and ninepence accumulated. I tried to imagine Harry in the shop, picking out his purchases from carefully stocked shelves and spending his discount. But the image was at odds with the ten shillings he had given to the chauffeur. I touched his eyelid where another hair had strayed. He seemed so childlike, it was as if for the first time I had realized he was my own age. I touched his lips with my fingers. They seemed more bulbous than my own.

So it was I sat on beside Harry far longer than I intended, contemplating our similarities, if indeed there were any apart from our ages, and worrying about our different parentage and circumstances. Eventually, as the frost slowly ebbed from the window, I stood to dress, fitting my arms through my trouser-braces and deliberately letting them snap noisily onto my shoulders. In imitation of my father, I pulled the elastic up and down, adjusting their tightness for comfort, and then looked at myself in the tiny mirror, trying to believe that the image there really was 'me' and that it was 'I' who was in this predicament, not someone more adult or experienced. In fact, it was to take me many years before I was fully to understand Treffgarne history, and even now I cannot be absolutely certain that I have penetrated every nuance and facet of their lives, or that I have come to the right conclusions about their motives. In a world which exhibits free will there will never be perfect understanding, but only degrees of correctness according to the individual. Long may this be so, for in debating our diversities we become moral. I am only sorry I did not realize much earlier in life that the truly moral person is one who listens. Listening, I have found, is an art, and the antidote to bullishness. But I have digressed. I fastened my shoelaces and re-tied the looser of the two again, looking for something to do until Harry awoke. It occurred to me I could go and see 'the helpers' – the reasons for Harry spending so much time with them were becoming clearer – but that meant traversing three corridors, a landing and two stairways where there was every chance of my meeting Harry's mother. I resolved instead to sit down and continue the discourse running through my head, and to ponder again the image of a bullish, self-righteous Mr Treffgarne which I cannot shake. I would like to see some good in him. I have his photograph in front of me at this moment, it is brown and creased from my constant handling; and every time I take it from the bureau, even today, I see a slightly different figure, as if the changing knowledge and experience I have brought to it over the years has been as important as the image of the man himself. It pains and tests my liberalism that I cannot find a redeeming feature, yet I hope more fervently to find one each time I take the photograph from the bureau. I never met Mr Treffgarne, so much has to be left to imagination and conscience. He is not bullish in frame or stature, but there is the decided air of a man who is certain of his own infallibility, an arrogance about him that history teaches us can be neither natural nor moral. His eyes are small like a pugdog's; his nose turns to one side as if already answering back; his mouth is pushed outwards as if to deny the pity he feels for himself. It is the face of a man who dislikes himself, but who would never be honest enough even to countenance the thought; it is the face of a man who believes cowardice to be the worst of sins, but who walks weakly away from any truth; it is the face of man who bullies because he has no inner strength; it is the face of a man who will not listen, nor ever understand another's vulnerability; it is the face of a liar and a cheat. I want so badly to be generous. Please, someone, help me, for I still cannot see good in Mr Treffgarne.

I have put his photograph away and must force myself to see Harry in bed, where he is peaceful and without trouble. The frost on the window is ebbing towards infinity and, from where I am sitting, I can see the trees outside in the garden, denuded because of winter and Christmas. I can see Bridget putting one or two candles onto the branches, some white, some coloured, and studying the pattern she is making in the sycamore.

'I asked you once not to pity me,' Harry said, breaking into my reverie about the young maid. 'I'm asking you again now.'

'I'm not, I'm watching Bridget. I thought you were asleep.'

'I was until you woke me.'

'I didn't wake you. I've been spending hours here not waking you, Harry.'

'Bridget will show you her mushrooms, Daniel.'

'Pardon?'

'Bridget will undo her blouse and let you see her mushrooms,' he reiterated, as if talking to a simpleton.

'If I knew what mushrooms you meant, I might have understood you the first time.'

'Not the sort that grow in soil.'

I climbed down from my place by the window. 'I'm glad to see you're better,' I said.

'Much. How long have I been asleep?'

'All night, and half this morning.'

He threw back the eiderdown and jumped from the bed still fully dressed from the previous evening. 'I must stink,' he said. 'We must do this more often.'

'Harry?' I was disturbed by his frivolousness.

'What, Daniel?'

'Please let neither of us forget what was said last night.'

'Don't be sombre. I'm better now. We won't forget.'

'I've an idea . . .'

'No ideas until we've seen Bridget's mushrooms.' He was pulling his arms from his braces and unfastening his shirt.

'I'm being serious, Harry.'

'Sometimes, you are far too serious for your own good,' he said.

'All right, I shan't tell you.'

'No, tell me, I'd like to know.' He put his shirt on my bed.

'It's this: why don't we go to Yorkshire for Christmas? I've been thinking about it a good deal.'

Harry considered for a moment: 'They'll never let me.'

'Yes, they will. We'll stay with my parents.'

He walked to the hand-basin. His excitement had abated. His face was pensive. 'They'll never let me. I'm sure they won't. What would I say?'

'We'll say my parents have invited us. It's as simple as that.'

'I'd really like to, Daniel. Wouldn't your parents mind someone like me?'

'We're not as posh as you. But of course not.'

He was looking straight at me: 'Will you come with me when I go and ask her?' He seemed frightened.

'That's my other idea, Harry. She can't really refuse if I'm there. It wouldn't be normal.'

'Normal?'

'Yes.'

'You are brilliant, Daniel.' He turned on the cold tap and

31

splashed water across his face and the tops of his shoulders.

My plan worked better than either of us could have expected. We were excited and packed immediately, but then had to wait three days for a reply to the letter I had sent home.

On the train journey to Yorkshire I asked him about Bridget and all the other servants of the house, really desiring to know of them as individuals, but Harry returned to the events of five years ago.

'They know nothing,' he said. 'My father changed all the servants.'

'What about your Nanny?' I asked.

'She was sent abroad. Well, as a matter-of-fact, she went to India, with my father. My father was having what is called 'an affair' with Nanny.'

'An affair? You mean they were lovers?'

'Well, I think so, Daniel. I'm not certain, but that's my guess.'

'Your poor mother,' I said.

'Yes.' He ran his finger along the collar of his shirt. 'I think my brother must have known what was going on, somehow.' He looked down. 'I should only state facts: I don't know it as fact.' He looked up again and put his hands on his knees.

'You're so lucid like this, Harry. I wish you always were.'

'So do I,' he said. 'I'm sorry about when I'm not.'

The train rattled on through Lincolnshire, and at Grantham Harry dashed from the carriage to purchase chocolate, only scrambling back on in the nick of time. We ate the chocolate like fugitives.

'I shouldn't have told you that about Nanny and my father,' he said. 'Only it helps sometimes, when I'm really depressed, to find a reason for it all. It's the only way I know I'm not culpable, when I can find my own logic. Will you forgive me if they were not lovers? It might be my own fantasy.'

'Of course,' I said.

'I need it to be true, you see. Sometimes we need to create our own reality in order to survive. I'd hate to think of him as a purely evil man, Daniel. You see, if he is evil, then so am I.'

'Is that because you sometimes believe yourself to be guilty?'

'I suppose so. I can't really explain myself very well.'

'You're not depressed now, are you?' I asked.

'No, Daniel, I'm with you. This chocolate is delicious.'

We opened another bar.

'By the way, you were brilliant with my mother. You were right, she couldn't possibly refuse me Christmas with you. It wouldn't be normal. I hadn't realized that before.'

I have learned that, sometimes, what we imagine we have done or might be capable of doing is as powerful an influence on our lives as any reality. That Harry was innocent was often of no consequence because he believed himself to be guilty. The human mind is fallible, and our fantasies are as important as the truth.

My father met us at our local station in a motorcar. He was meant to have been on the railway platform to help us with our bags.

'Where is he?' Harry asked.

'I think that's him, standing over there.'

'You think? Don't you know your own father?'

'I thought I did. He's gone and spent my school fees.'

'Oh, don't be silly, Daniel.'

My father advanced upon us as we left what served as the concourse for the station but which was, in fact, little more than a small meeting place, built of rough cut stone. I introduced Harry, who politely took my father's hand, whilst other passengers bumped and manoeuvred around us, some cursing.

'We'd better move,' I said, 'we're in the way here.'

'Some people are rude, aren't they, Mr Hinton?' Harry said, smiling.

My father leant an ear towards him: 'I beg your pardon, my lad?'

'I was saying some people are rude, Mr Hinton. Aren't they?'

'Are they?' my father said. 'I don't know.'

'Is your father deaf?' Harry whispered.

'Wax,' I said.

'Mr Hinton,' Harry called to my father who was racing towards the automobile, 'I didn't mean to be rude myself.'

I caught them up.

'Here she is, Daniel. A Wolseley single-cylinder, chain-drive.'

'It's a motorcar, Daddy.'

'Old, but in tip-top condition. Well, nearly tip-top. She will be when I've finished working on her.' He was wearing leather driving gloves. He put down Harry's case. 'What d'you say, Daniel, isn't she the most beautiful thing you've ever seen?'

'No,' I said.

'I thought you boys might like to help me with her over Christmas. Between us, we might really sort her out.' He was running his fingers along the chrome.

'Daddy,' I said, loudly, 'what does Mummy say?'

'Oh, she's a bit reticent at the moment, but she'll come round, you know how she does. I'm pleased you like the car, Daniel, we don't want you giving her further ammunition.'

'I agree with you, Mr Hinton. She's the most beautiful motor I've ever seen.'

'Don't be a liar, Harry.'

'Have you ridden in a motor before?' my father asked him.

'Daddy, they have a Mercedes. I wrote you all about it.'

'I'm only asking Harry himself, I'm only being polite.'

'You are far too excited to be polite,' I said, quietly.

'Your father's wonderful,' Harry whispered, 'he's completely crackers.'

'Stop sniggering you two boys, and help me with these bags.'

We lifted our cases onto the back of the Wolseley, Harry taking charge.

'You are disgruntled, Daniel. What about?' my father asked when we were alone for a moment. 'I've been longing to show her off to you. You know what your mother's like. She doesn't these days get excited about very much.

'Daddy, I am not disgruntled. How are we affording all this?'

'You will be worrying about your school fees, is that it?'

'Daddy, I am not selfish.'

'No, but you are right to worry, I can see that. Jump beside me whilst I drive.'

Harry sat behind us, enjoying himself rather too much for my liking. It was a short way home and one we could easily have walked. My father wore racing goggles.

'Your mother says I look like a frog. I don't, do I?'

'You do,' I said.

'You will tell her you agree with me, won't you?'

'Pardon, Father?' The machine was rattling along.

'Yes, she is rather noisy. I find she tends to make me a little deaf. I'll tell you all this evening.'

On Christmas Eve, three days later, I sat with my father in front of the fire in the sitting-room, whilst Harry helped my

34

mother in the kitchen surrounded by pots and the detritus of the meal we had just eaten. My father lit a cigarette and set his chessmen on the board; they were an old set, one he had carved himself as a child from hickory, and they still had a rough feel which made playing the game a pleasure. Harry and I had spent the previous days working on the Wolseley, mostly by ourselves, but occasionally with my father when he felt he could leave the shop at such a busy period. Harry and I were ignorant of the workings of the machine, tinkering with this and that, using it as an excuse to escape both the house and my mother, who was rather too dour in her rectitude. In truth, my father could not afford the boneshaker and had bought it out of spite, but I began to see that it was churlish to maintain my moral indignation.

'The boy who went to school a boy has returned a young man,' my father said, moving his first pawn.

'What a funny way of putting it.'

'Oh, I'm not complaining. I like you so much better now. I'm not a great one for young children, as you know.'

'No, I didn't know that.'

'These are troubled times, Daniel.'

'Yes,' I said, moving my own pawn, following his gambit.

'I'm glad to see you've sided with me over the Wolseley. I think your instinct was not to do so.'

'I'm concerned about school.'

'Of course you are, quite rightly. I haven't told your mother yet, but I'm going into partnership.'

I played a waiting game, avoiding central pawn exchanges. My father eventually underestimated the latent energy coiled up in my position.

'I'd like to know your views on the matter,' he said. 'Because it will concern you when you're older. In short it's this: have you an interest in ever running the shop, or not? It may be hard for you to say.'

'I don't know, Father. I haven't given it much thought.'

'You called me Daddy at the station. I prefer it when you call me Father.'

'What is this partnership about?' I asked.

'It means my selling half of the business. To be honest with you, Daniel, irrespective of all other considerations, I may have to anyway, because this ghastly war is taking its toll. I don't just mean of those men who are dying, although goodness knows that is bad enough, but of the town itself, where people no longer have any money. These are difficult times for us all. I take it you want to stay on at school?'

'Yes, very much.'

'It's as well to ask. By the way I like Harry. I should have told you that. Therefore, if you have no interest in the shop, I think I will do as I plan.'

'I don't think I have,' I said.

'Good. I wanted you at a school which would make you change your mind. It's as well to leave the area we're brought up in and do something different. It helps us learn, you know.'

This was a sentiment he had never expressed before, and it surprised me.

'I think, perhaps, I'd like to be a doctor.'

'That sounds good to me,' he said.

When Harry and my mother returned from the kitchen we all four sat by the fire, and Harry and I were given a stocking each, which we hung from the mantelpiece. I let my father win the game out of recognition of his generosity, though he touched me on my shoulder as he rose from the table to show he knew that I had needlessly sacrificed my queen. Harry impressed us all by the intelligence and keenness of his questioning. My mother in particular, seemed to grow fonder of him by the moment, and I was reminded of that fateful day in the Treffgarne library when nothing, too, had been out of place and everything had appeared to be ordinary. I had, indeed, grown up a little.

3

I lived then in a town surrounded by trees. Mine was a small world and it was a benign walk from the cobbled high street, with its frontages of butchers and cobblers, bakers and ironmongers, to the thick oak woods, where children played war games and young adults courted. Harry and I went to the woods carrying small bags of potato skins, which my mother curled in the oven, making them brittle and sweet. It was a childish idyll made stronger by the secrets we both shared. When we were alone together Harry seemed determined to be a child, rather as if he had not been one before, and I began to find his insistence on doing childish things a little irksome, particularly when he suggested we build a treehouse in the uppermost branches of an oak, whose height really frightened me. I was becoming bookish and priggish and he accused me of this, so I covered my doubts by joining in his games. It was one of the happiest times I remember: Harry sitting in our treehouse dropping acorns onto the odd courting couple, closing the hessian door when they looked up, and whistling, to demonstrate our innocence. If it had not been for the cold we might have spent our lives there.

Harry borrowed my father's now redundant bicycle and we toured the district. I took a noble delight in showing him my childhood places, and he wanted to know what I had done and felt in each and who my friends had been, though I had been a largely solitary child until Harry had come along. I explained this to him, and the restraints between us vanished. I suppose, in time, we became so exhausted by our knowledge of one another that I began to be able to tolerate silence, the silence which today I love between close friends.

But I am again digressing, and my story proper is now ready to begin. Suffice it to say that from my new-found confidence I was developing a priggishness, as Harry had pointed out. There will be time for confession later, when I enter my own dark period and flirt with Fascism. I was not yet the self-righteous, insufferable man that I later became. I still go to bed feeling guilty, as only the old can.

Harry brought my father's new road atlas to the treehouse and sat with it open on his lap. We were eating potato skins and I asked him to be careful because of the thin smudges of beef-dripping on his fingers, fearing he might transfer them to the maps.

'What's at Whitby, Daniel?'

'Fish, I imagine, it's a fishing port. Why?'

'Ever been?'

'No.'

'You live twenty miles away and you've never been? There's an Abbey on the map, we could pitch our tent there and stay overnight.'

It will not, I expect, be hard for you to imagine my mother's reluctance; her initial enthusiasm for Harry was beginning to wane, and she was tolerating his adventures like one wishing to be thought modern, but in secret they pained her a good deal. The truth was, Harry's presence in the household had completely altered its balance – we were now three men to one woman – and there was little she could do. For his part, my father enjoyed this new imbalance and rejoiced at the idea. My mother swallowed her common sense, and the worry left a lump in her throat. It was my notion we set off early in the morning and that my father follow us later in the day in the Wolseley, bringing the tent, which we could pitch on the grass by Whitby Abbey as Harry had suggested: I had this card up my sleeve and managed to play it at the moment when her doubts appeared least. To her credit, she did not realize how much I was learning the adult art of manipulation; I played along with her worries giving the impression of making them my own. She, of course, agreed, and even smiled at me. I smiled back; the deception was complete.

There are two roads to Whitby and we tossed a coin as to which we might take. The moorland route won: and so, with the dawn light slanting across the hedgerows, we set off on our bicycles to climb the first hills, zigzagging back and forth on the empty road until we had to dismount and push, then racing down the other side, Harry ahead with his legs splayed in imitation of the wings of an aeroplane: until he almost hit a sheep and went careering into the bracken. I bicycled between the torpid animals, ignoring him, waiting for him to catch me up.

'The sheep sit on the road where it's warmer,' I said. 'I should have warned you.'

'Oh, I'm glad you didn't. It's much more fun not to know.'

We bicycled side by side.

'These bare winter trees, Daniel,' he said, 'they look like dead men on poles in India.'

'No, they don't, they look like depressives in a mental hospital.'

My father helped us with the tent and then generously took his leave as the sun died and the first signs of a frost began to appear on the grass. We both shouted at him more than was truly necessary, Harry laughing so much behind his back I might have been embarrassed had not his mischievousness been so infectious. Inside the tent we had covers and blankets, all labelled by my mother as to where they should go. When the beds were settled we went into the town and bought fish and chips, eating them outside with our fingers, listening to the sounds of the harbour, which seemed to increase in resonance as the moon waxed, each separate sound becoming sharper and more identifiable from across the water. We must have looked a peculiar sight on our own by the fishing boats, Harry licking the grease and salt from beneath his fingernails. It was a glorious feeling to be marooned like this, for Harry created islands in which no one else existed, the bitter cold and unlikeliness of it all only adding to the atmosphere. It occurred to me we had come to Whitby so that Harry could eat fish and chips outside.

'You adore the low life, don't you, Harry,' I said.

'You're sometimes very slow, Daniel.' He was ferreting in his newspaper for another piece of fish. 'Of course I do. It's the best life.'

'Is that why you prefer "the helpers"?'

'I don't want to talk about home.'

A lone fisherman working on his boat gave us a glance. Harry nonchalantly raised his hand as if he had been to Iceland many times, which was where these boats trawled.

'I dislike superiority, Daniel. Commonness is better.'

'Is that why you like me?'

'Oh, you're not common at all.'

'You like commonness from the distance then?'

'You're becoming very particular these days, Daniel,' he said.

'As you like commonness, I like accuracy.'

'I would watch that, it can become a habit. Not a good one.'

'Why's that?' I asked.

'Because complete accuracy lessens feeling, it narrows thought. The pompous and self-opinionated take comfort from that, but you shouldn't.'

I ate a piece of fish myself. 'You have a way of saying things, Harry, that cuts quite deeply.'

'You like my cutting deeply though, don't you?'

'In a funny way, I do, yes.'

'You shouldn't listen to me, Daniel. I'll say anything. Mostly it's out of my mouth before I've even thought about it. Often I've surprised myself by what I've said.'

'But you remember, don't you? You go away and think.'

'Yes.'

'I do, too,' I said.

The tide was high and the fisherman was able to step from his boat without using the ladder. Harry waved, and the fisherman waved back; I was envious, manoeuvring my fish and chips to wave only when he had gone and it was too late.

'What would you most like to do in the whole world?' I asked.

'I don't know, yet.'

'What would you change if you could change anything?'

'You're talking about my parents again.'

'I suppose we'd all change our families if we had the chance.'

'I wouldn't change yours.'

'Wouldn't you?' I was astonished. 'Because they're low life?'

'No, because they care about you all the time. You are becoming incredibly disdainful, Daniel.'

'Was that from your lips before you'd thought about it?'

'No, quite the opposite. I've thought about nothing else.'

'Even this afternoon, when we were racing into Whitby?'

'I'm not going to answer that, it's too literal.'

'This has become bantering,' I said. 'It's ceased to have meaning.'

'It might have for you, it hasn't for me, Daniel.'

I could no longer tolerate his insinuations, so turned and walked away from him, following the fisherman's brisk pace along the quay towards the main body of the town, where small terraces of houses stepped the hillside and, up above, the Gothic shape of the Abbey could be seen in outline against the night sky. Harry ran and caught me and placed his arm across my shoulders. It was the first time he had done this.

'Gosh, I'm sorry,' he said. 'I'm always accusing others of what I'm guilty of myself.'

'No, you're not. Stop lying.' I was increasing my pace.

'Please, slow down.'

'Why? So you can tell me over and over again how right you are?'

'No.'

'I sometimes wish I was as clever as you,' I said. 'Only I'd go further because I'm more sensible.'

Harry kept his arm around me, ignoring my protests, and slowly I began to calm down.

'I'm sorry, Daniel,' he said, 'I'll never do it again.'

'Do what?'

'Oh, I don't know. Be so bloody hopeless.'

'Be so bloody honest, you mean?' I said, looking at him.

'Be so bloody myself. Friends?'

'Friends,' I said.

We walked back through the narrow streets where gas mantles lit the sash windows and the only other sign of life was the noise from a public house, drifting upwards towards the Abbey as we returned to our tent. The couch-grass was now brittle with frost, snapping with each footfall, sending faint echoes across the sea below. At the crown of the hill we intuitively paused. Harry kept me close. My arm was now across his shoulder as well, with our free hands in our pockets to keep them warm. We looked down at the pinpricks of light which were the town. It seemed in that moment as if the rest of the world did not exist but was, rather, an extension of ourselves.

'There's an infinity about solitude, don't you find, Daniel?' he said.

'I think so, I think I know what you mean.'

'It's as if we care about no one, except one person. It's as if no

41

one cares about us, except one person.'

We walked back to the tent and both our worlds changed, irrevocably and forever, although in my case it was to take almost forty years before the full effect was complete: for inside, lying across the beds, was the figure of a young man. He was so startled he jumped up, obviously not expecting our return quite so soon. Harry threw himself at him apparently intent on throttling him; the young man flailed his arms and legs this way and that in a non-violent attempt to remove Harry's bulk, muttering all the while, when breath would allow, about explanation. In a confined and flimsy space the effect was almost comical, and it seemed at one point we might become airborne, such was the movement and flapping of canvas. Eventually it dawned on Harry it was a peaceful contest, and so he stopped. The tent was sagging, one of the centre poles having been twisted in the struggle. The young man adjusted his clothing. He appeared bemused, which ought to have been our reaction, not his. We all three sat still, each of us taking a blanket for warmth. I thought his age to be not much more than my own.

His name was John Bell; he had watched from the distance as we pitched our tent, even smiling at our antics, and had been relieved when my father had left; he was sorry to intrude on people younger than himself, but it had been so cold he crept inside when we ourselves were gone, meaning to warm himself for only a few moments, but once inside he instinctively responded to the atmosphere we had created and felt he should stay; he had much to risk, but decided to trust us; he had received his call-up papers from the army and had never gone; he was a Quaker from York, a pacifist, as were all his family; his elder brother had been court-martialled as a deserter and executed by firing party, the year before, at Ypres for refusing to carry a gun; as a consequence his parents had tried to help him to safety in America, but without success; informed of his whereabouts by coded letters, they had sent him money through a series of post offices; he was on the run, living where and when he could; he had talked to no one in four months.

'No one at all?' Harry asked him.

'Well, no one apart from shopkeepers.'

If I am not really describing the alarm all this gave us, it is because the alarm was soon over. As do many fortunate people, as did Mrs Treffgarne, John Bell had the ability to behave normally in a crisis.

'Take my hand,' Harry said. 'I'm a pacifist, too.'

'If you are,' I said, 'it's the first I've known about it.'

'All decent people are pacifists, Daniel.'

'Oh, how romantic, Harry.'

'I don't expect John to find it romantic, do you?'

'No, not in the least,' he said.

The truth is, Harry was immediately enthralled by this new presence in his life and I, if I am honest, which I must be now, was more than a little suspicious. It often took Harry no longer than seconds to make a judgement, we were similar in this respect, and he did so in this case in John's favour; whilst I wished to, but could not. It is a paradox to say I respected Harry for siding with this young man against the system which had kept him in such a wretched condition, but respect him I did, while at the same time being rather repulsed by their joint demeanour and ease of conversation. It must be remembered I came from a family where respecting one's country was the first rule of living – this was 1916 – and the second was being ordinary, if my mother were allowed her way. No one in my family had ever made their point in public, let alone taken action when it had been ignored.

'We must get you to Liverpool,' Harry said, 'and onto a boat.'

'Why?' I asked.

'Oh, don't be naive, Daniel. To get him to America.'

'Harry, the Lusitania was sunk by torpedoes. There is no Atlantic shipping.'

'Yes, there is. Cargo boats, across the southern Atlantic. My family run them.'

'I didn't know that,' I said, apologetically. I was trying to keep my counsel and to pretend an excitement as great as Harry's. I still did not know the full extent of Treffgarne investments and wealth. 'You mean your family is in shipping, too?' I asked.

'Yes. This war is losing the company tens of thousands of pounds, so they cheat here and there.'

'Might you be able to help me?' John asked.

'Harry, this is impossible, you are making promises you cannot keep.'

'No, I'm not. It's easy. You yourself showed me how, Daniel.

My mother can refuse me nothing.'

It was a simple statement, but a true one. It had never occurred to me that Harry might go this far, nor, I think, had he entertained such thoughts of power until that moment.

When they were both asleep I walked to the police station but did not dare go in. It was an act of cowardice for which I have been eternally grateful.

John Bell is an undistinguished name and, perhaps, one of the most popular in Yorkshire, particularly in the old North Riding where Bell's proliferate. However, he was and is the most unusual of men, although that is the last accolade he would ever wish upon himself: indeed, he would reject any honour, deny any good reference, for that would be worldly and his life has been given to God, and to humbleness. He has lived in America now for seventy-four years. I had a letter from him yesterday which is as spirited and vital as anything he has previously written; he talks of the fields around his farmhouse in Pennsylvania where he has lived for all but nine of those years; and of the pacifism which has made his life what it has been; he recalls, for the first time I can remember, his fight with Harry in the tent and says, quite simply, if he is allowed one wish it will be to meet Harry in heaven. I shall reply that he will, but I myself must go to Pennsylvania when I have finished writing this account, for it is clear to me that John is dying.

In 1916 I had no such thoughts of death, nor could I have written that the two of them might meet again in an afterworld that is better than this one.

Inside the police station I could hear two constables talking, their chit-chat so ordinary and unconcerned it was frightening. I walked away slowly along the wintry streets where every house was shuttered against the night. A cat followed me until I picked her up. She began to purr, pumping her claws into my topcoat as if she had found home. I kept her with me, not once wondering if I was taking her into an area she did not know, or caring myself whether I was now lost. When I caught sight of a constable on his beat, I let her go, pushing her from me to distract his attention, hiding my small frame in the shadow of a wall as I had done by the sanatorium in Hampshire. The animal rubbed at his legs, her tail erect, her brassy purr distilling the cold and darkness. I thought how fickle cats are. He picked her up and strolled on, his boots beating a rhythm into the distance. I thought how fickle I, too, had become.

The first phase of our plan of action was this: we would tell my parents that a freak gust of wind had blown our tent into the sea during the night. This would have three effects; one, it would give John permanent shelter; two, it would prove my mother's fears correct (there is no greater pleasure than to be proved right, and any tincture of doubt as to the truth of our tale would be instantly dispelled); three, it would give Harry, who would pretend to be hungry and depressed, the excuse to return to London where the second phase could be put into operation. John was to move nearer my home, and I was to keep in touch on my bicycle. But phase two, essentially, belonged to Harry, who would write or telegraph when he had succeeded.

'You'd better write,' I said, 'on second thoughts, a telegram will look suspicious.'

Thus it was that John Bell left Liverpool on a merchant ship bound for the Gulf of Mexico and New Orleans, two months before America entered the Great War, in the February of 1917.

The following spring and summer Harry and I continued to learn the routines of school, where a new headmaster was being appointed and the gossip was of change under a stricter regime. No boy was under any illusion as to how the school had progressed, and most actually welcomed any further restrictions on their freedom. Harry and I seized our last opportunities to pedal into the countryside together on his brand new bicycle, taking it in turns to sit astride the cross-bar, in one of the most uncomfortable positions known to man. When my own bicycle arrived by train we went further afield towards the South Downs, finding the isolated streams where we were able to bathe without our clothes, and observe at leisure the changes taking place in one another.

The news from France was gloomy and depressing; in letters from the front and from newspapers, we learned of the stalemates that were trench warfare; of the Somme, of Arras, of the bloody battles at Ypres. In chapel, the roll call of the dead became almost routine. The new headmaster arrived and, on the day of British victory on Passchendaele Ridge, began by flogging three boys for insouciance, and the impact reverberated through the school to both master and pupil alike. Harry and I, being scholarship boys, worked harder than most. At first Harry regretted accepting his bursary but changed his mind when he learned that it gave him unlimited access to the new music room. The autumn passed in a daze as the school was transformed and we hardly had time for one another outside the classroom. In the spring, during British naval raids on Zeebrugge and Ostend, a new House was inaugurated, exclusively for scholarship boys, of which the headmaster assumed absolute charge. Our liberties were further curtailed, although certain privileges once denied us were now restored, permission to keep a bicycle being one of them. This immediately created enormous friction throughout the school, but, as the headmaster informed us, he was creating an elite of which we all should be proud to be part.

That summer, I found Harry practising Chopin at the piano. As I entered the music room he was slamming down the lid.

'Thank goodness, Daniel, I'll never be any good. Let's get our bicycles out and annoy the peasants.'

So we did. An hour later, settling ourselves on the grass by a stream in the heat of the afternoon, Harry still seemed distracted.

'That night in the tent, in Whitby . . ?'

'What of it?' I asked, innocently interrupting him.

'Why didn't you like John, Daniel?'

'I did.'

Harry rolled over onto his stomach, looking away from me towards the farm where a few cows were finding their way to be milked. I picked up a blade of grass and ran it between thumb and forefinger, deliberately making the annoying sound which often results from that action.

'I do so dislike you when you lie and become aloof,' he said.

'I'm sorry, I don't mean to.'

He jumped up, and before I knew what was happening he was sitting astride me with my arms pinned to the earth, his thighs against my hips. His weight emptied my lungs for a moment.

'It was a shock. John's being there, I mean,' I said.

'No, it wasn't. It's more than that and you know it. You disagreed with him, didn't you?'

'Let me go, Harry. It's too hot. You're crushing me. Why bring this up now?'

'No, I'll never let you go. Never.' He released my hands and sat upright across my chest. 'I have you now. I'm stronger than you. You'll never get away, Daniel.'

I tried to move to prove him wrong, but as usual Harry was right. His steadied eyes were piercing my conscience. 'Yes, I thought him wrong. Where would we be if we all felt as he did?'

'In a gentler, more sane world.'

'Life's a game for you, Harry. You'll do anything no matter what, in whatever circumstances, if you think it may prove exciting. You're immoral. I dislike saying so, but you are.'

Harry lifted his thin frame and stood above me, gently kicking at the sides of my stomach with his toe. 'Maybe so,' he said. He sat down close to me, his long fingers splayed on the grass beside my leg. 'But even the most immoral person will sometimes do what is right by mistake.'

'What are you saying, Harry?'

'I'm saying what I did was right for John. It might not be right for every person. For you, for instance, obviously not. But that is what human beings are: different.'

'In that case,' I said, 'there is no morality and no immorality. Everyone may do as they wish. There must be absolutes in right or wrong, otherwise all we have is anarchy and selfishness.'

'That is not what I'm saying and you know it. What about individual conscience, isn't that important?'

'Not here, no.'

'The fact that I get a vicarious pleasure from helping someone is neither here nor there. It's a bonus, maybe. Maybe it is selfish? But it was still the right thing to do. Both for John and for me. I need you to understand that, Daniel.'

'I don't,' I said.

He jumped up and sat astride me again without holding my hands, his eyes looking at me as if the conversation were not really about John at all. 'If we'd been swimming, we'd be naked now,' he said. 'I hate your morality. Why d'you have to be so serious all the time?'

'It's the way I am.' I could feel my heart beating through my shirt. He leant forward and kissed me on my lips. 'Please, Harry, don't.'

'Why?'

'This will spoil everything.'

47

'No, it won't. There's nothing to spoil, there's nothing we agree on.'

'Yes, there is, don't be silly.'

'What?'

'Our friendship,' I said. 'The love between us is more than this. I don't want to be like those rats at school. I want us both to be the best we can.'

'The elite, you mean?'

'If you like, yes.'

'Well, I hate the elite.'

'I know.'

We returned again and again to that same place by the river, where a dry 'V' had been cut into the earth by a long-gone tributary, and lay there on our elbows unseen by the world in the coarse grass, talking of morality and politics. On occasion we swam without our clothes in the fast flowing water, and for Harry this seemed enough.

When Harry was eighteen and I was nearing that age, and the Great War had ended with the peace conference at Versailles, one Sunday he reached across and took an envelope from his trouser pocket, opening the thin paper as if it might soon crumble and become dust. The letter was folded in three, but Harry refused to open the creases fully, so that to read the letter completely he had to keep altering the angle of his head.

'Who's it from?' I asked.

'John. It came this morning. This is why I was insistent we come here today.'

'John Bell? I'd almost forgotten about him.'

'I know we agreed to differ about John, Daniel. I'd like to ask you to change your mind.'

I could tell how much he revered what was written by his refusal to make it easier to read. Harry was not usually so meticulous, and I was immediately suspicious.

'Have you been writing to one another?' I asked.

'Yes, I should have told you, but chose not to.'

'What does he say?'

'Here, read it.'

And so I read of New Orleans, and of the sinking delta of the Mississippi and the docks, and of the poverty of the blacks who worked the water's edge; here were the paddle-steamers of Tom

48

Sawyer and Huckleberry Finn like ghosts, John wrote, on the ever widening plane of the river; here were the plantations where the purity of the white cotton was so mercilessly pitted against the blackness of the labour. John wrote of his job teaching in a school where no pupil had shoes and his schoolroom was a shack built on stilts flooded frequently by the rising Mississippi; when it rained it rained in torrents, and several times the school had had to begin again because the shack had actually floated away. He wrote wittily of the one occasion the old black slaves had rowed the shack back up-river, and of the songs which had accompanied their efforts ringing out across the swamps; and of how, once home, the classroom had had to be moored some distance from the bank, but he had insisted that lessons resume immediately, so that the children had to swim to and fro to attend their classes. He wrote of his life, of this place he now called home; of crocodiles, of bayous, of po-boys, of Cajuns; of the eccentricity of the black people, whose humour and resolve had made the delta what it was.

'How many other letters have you received?' I asked. 'This reads as if there have been many.'

'Quite a few.'

I gave the paper to him. Harry held it for a moment as if uncertain how to proceed.

'Harry, why show me this one?'

'I have an idea, Daniel. We finish school in three weeks, forever. Let us take ourselves to New Orleans for the summer.'

It was another of Harry's crazy, maddening schemes. I thought of my parents and the money it would cost.

'I know what you're thinking,' he said, 'but I've squared it with my father. He'll pay for us both. And give us both an allowance.'

'Is he back from India?'

'Yes, he's at home.' He returned the letter to its envelope, and the envelope to his trouser pocket. 'If we went for a year, Daniel, we could enter university on our return.'

'But you said just the summer?'

'I know we'll like it, so best be prepared to stay.'

The scheme was maddening in every dimension. It both perturbed me and thrilled me. 'What would my parents say?' I asked.

'Only you can know that. But at least you're taking me seriously?'

49

'I think so, yes.'

'Gosh, and I thought I'd have to persuade you.'

'You're a hedonist, Harry. A complete and utter hedonist.'

'We've worked hard. We deserve our excitement. We're the elite. If it gets you to New Orleans, I'll be anything you say.'

'Will you ever take me seriously though?'

'Of course. Left to ourselves we'll become staid and conventional before we know it.'

'Don't you mean I might?'

'No, not only you.'

'Perhaps that is the sort of life that will suit us both?'

'Come to New Orleans first.'

'All right,' I said, 'I will.' But there was some sombreness in my affirmation which I felt but did not show. For the first time I knew my life was not wholly my own, as no single life is or can be, for we are all influenced by and dependent upon others.

The two weeks following the end of school were as hectic as any I can recall. I travelled home to Yorkshire and lived with the consequences of the letter I had posted ahead detailing our scenario of itineraries and dates. My mother faced me across the tea-table.

'We don't like your friend Harry,' she said.

'Well, I do.'

'Your mother doesn't quite mean it that way, Daniel.'

'I mean it exactly that way, Henry. His family have money, so what? It doesn't mean they can throw it at us as if we're nothing.'

'They're not throwing it at us. They're giving Daniel an opportunity he'll surely regret if he doesn't take.'

'They could ask our opinion.'

'They asked Daniel. It's Daniel they're helping.'

'We are his parents, Henry. These people with money, they think they own the world.'

'They do,' my father said.

I was relieved when the argument so quickly became one between them. In due course it was settled in my favour and, as if to prove her point about wealth, my mother set about buying me a new wardrobe: I would have needed clothes for university, so perhaps, regardless, the money was available. She took me shopping with a vengeance, choosing the clothes for me as if she were to wear them herself, and pummelling the tailors when the

50

cut was only slightly imperfect or the style did not completely suit her taste. They were clothes for a young man at home, not abroad, but I did not argue.

One night I put a glass to the floor as I had done as a child and listened to them fighting below.

'He doesn't need all these clothes, Edith. New Orleans is a tropical city. He doesn't need worsteds.'

'He's my child. Whilst he's here he'll do what I want. When he's left home and is independent that will be a different matter. Until then, I won't have him shabby.'

'He's never been shabby. You are jealous.'

'I am not jealous, Henry.'

But my father was correct. If I had not been an only child, my departure might have been easier for her. As it was, it was no use my father telling her all that she was doing was merely postponing the inevitable, and when we sailed from Southampton she was there by herself on the quay, my father having refused to close the shop for the day. His four-year business partnership was already in ruins, and what little savings they had were now spent and in my trunk. It was the worst farewell of my life. Once on board Harry and I looked down at my mother on the quayside. Amongst one of the largest crowds I had ever seen, many of whom were throwing coloured streamers, she seemed a figure of fun, so ridiculously forlorn did she appear. I knew, but could not see, that she had tears in her eyes. I kept thinking, 'Please hide your face, please hide your face', but she would not, so I cried too, averting my own eyes and praying that the vessel set sail. Today, of course, I regret the banality of this leave-taking, and only later understood how much my mother was upset by my never asking her opinion, which I might easily have done. The human being is made comfortable and secure by the asking of his advice.

Harry had insisted we sail third class, so in our cabin in the bowels of the ship I did my best to forget my mother and to hide my continuing doubts about the voyage. As Harry unpacked his trunk, he clearly had no such doubts. I felt a little as I had on my first morning at school; the events which had brought me to this strange place flooded into my consciousness as the ship's engines throttled into gear, the fears which possessed me then uppermost in my mind now. I have been lucky to travel a good deal since, and always, hours before exodus, I have experienced the same minatory foreboding, which makes me almost cancel the adventure and stay at home where all is safe: I might have done so now had not the ship been tugged from her berth, had her propellers not been grinding through a heavy sea, the noise vibrating in third class where every lower-life passenger was jostling his neighbour to establish a routine. The liner ploughed on into the Atlantic. Our cabin had no fresh air or porthole so it became impossible to know when the boat might lurch. I left my own trunk unopened and listened instead to the dive and swoop of the liner's pitch, feeling her bow rise, then dig deep, sensing her cleaving a path through the water, the rivets seeming to shake in her hull. The engine noise altered but only when the ship was riding back up so that it was no guide to the initial fall and it required constant vigilance to remain upright. At all times we had to have a steady hand either on the bunks or the small lockers provided for our personal effects. There was no lavatory in our cabin , which was even more annoying, nor a handbasin to wash in. These were down the passageway and communal. The walk became such an effort that I began to allow my bladder to fill until it seemed I would go involuntarily, the discomfort of wanting to pee only relieved by my memories of the vomit in the lavatory bowls and on the bathroom floors. Luckily, Harry was seasick too. For thirty-six hours he lay on his bunk as if he should shortly die.

'What's that other noise, Daniel?'

'What other noise?'

'It's a Scotch noise of some kind.'

'Oh that, it's the Scotsman playing his bagpipes.'

'Well, go and tell him to be quiet.'

'I have. He won't.'

'Who else is out there?'

'People down on their luck. Apart from me, Bagpipes is the only other passenger not ill.'

'Please, Daniel, please get me out of here.'

'But, Harry, this is so romantic,' I said.

'No, it's not, it's hell.'

I found the purser smoking a cigarette, drinking whisky with the kilted Scotsman, and within an hour we were guests in first class. Here we had light, air, space, and the facilities of the vessel at our disposal, including a Turkish bath, the first I had ever taken. Although Harry's sea-sickness did not much improve, he at least gained colour. I would bring him books from the library, where there were well over ten thousand volumes, and tell him of my discoveries, such as the chandelier in the state dining-room, which had upwards of one million separate pieces of glass (I exaggerated, but only a little), and of Mary Pickford, the Hollywood star, who was definitely on board.

'My father met her, Daniel.'

'What?'

'Yes, at a reception at the American Embassy in London, with her husband, Douglas Fairbanks.'

'Harry, I sometimes feel I don't know you at all.'

'Why?' he asked.

'Because you give me these titbits of information as if I should know them already, when I don't.'

'This happens in friendship when familiarity takes over.'

'Oh, don't be pompous,' I said. 'Just how grand is your family?'

'Quite grand.'

'How grand is 'quite', Harry?'

'Daniel, I'm ill.'

'Why were you at such a crummy school?'

'It wasn't crummy. We passed our matriculation with flying colours, as I recall. That is all schools are for.'

'No, they're not, they're much more than that, and you know it.'

'Well, my father was at Harrow, it's true.'

The penny dropped. It clattered to my feet. 'Gosh, I'm sorry, Harry.'

'My name was down for Harrow, but obviously I couldn't go. You see, it is one thing for someone like you inadvertently to learn the truth, quite another for a Harrovian. I avoid these conversations because they lead to judgements of class. Daniel, I love you, I so dislike making you feel inferior.'

'But you don't.'

'Or making it appear you've been manipulated, which in a way you have.'

'Yes, I can see that.'

'All I want you to know is that it matters not one jot to me.'

It was the first time in almost three years that Harry and I had talked about his secret, but I knew it to be ever present in our lives as the ease with which we had slipped into this conversation had just demonstrated.

'I sometimes wish you didn't love me quite so much,' I said.
'Why?'
'Because I don't deserve it.'

I left Harry for my meals, eating in the stateroom where the food was exquisite and where I tasted many delicacies for the first time in my life. Of seafood there were oysters and smoked-eel; of the game birds quails, widgeon, guinea-fowl, peacock; of the meats venison, which was served with roasted sweet-potato and Jerusalem artichoke garnished with avocado; of the veget-ables fennel, choko, lady's fingers, capsicum, kohl rabi; of the salads, endive and chicory; but my favourites were the Marsala puddings which lay on the centre table below a white swan, or an Empire State Building carved in ice. All this extravagance Mr Treffgarne paid for, and I tried to visualize him as I signed the cheques. In our rooms his son lay quietly by himself, leaving untouched the tossed salads I had ordered for him.

On deck I met a Mrs Copeland, who told me one woman on board ship had had all the skin removed from her face and shoulders so that she might be more beautiful when her skin grew again; also with her were the doctors who had performed this operation. Mrs Copeland spoke to me as if I might be her son, which, ordinarily, I would have resented but on this occa-sion did not, for she was already a widow and childless and I could see that my company gave her pleasure. I had thought her a New Yorker and expressed surprise when she disclosed that she, too, would be changing ship in New York, before coasting down the eastern seaboard to her home in the Garden District of New Orleans, where, every spring, she and her husband had held a May Ball for upwards of eight hundred people. Now she would be organising these social affairs alone, guests travelling across the city in their limousines, her home welcoming their hedonism, a danceband and marquee on her lawn. I reported to Harry, who scoffed, but I found her quietude engaging and was pleased to dine with her on most occasions. When the captain joined us at our table one evening I was left in no doubt as to her powers.

Next day Mrs Copeland invited me to her suite for tea. I left

Harry early to await the appointed hour on my own. On the table was a vase of lilies and a thank you card from the captain. Mrs Copeland pointed out that it also mentioned me; so I stole a further glance, and read of my 'charming additions' to their discourse. As with many women of her age – I thought her, perhaps, thirty-one or thirty-two – Mrs Copeland delighted in my naivety without once drawing attention to my youth. I let slip much of my own history and circumstance while never being fully aware of how precisely she was questioning me, so circumspect was her manner. She offered me tea, and as she leaned forwards towards the silver salver I could see the dark, freckled crevice at the top of her dress.

'She wants something, Daniel.'

Harry had dressed when I returned, his pallor much improved as was also, unfortunately, the sharpness of his tongue.

'Oh, don't be silly, Harry. What could she possibly want from me?'

'Daniel, I've often marvelled at your simpleness, but now you're being naive in the extreme.'

'I suppose you've met her? I suppose you know what she's like?'

'No, but I know how you are drawn to women of a certain age. I'm asking you to remember how you were drawn to my mother. Let me tell you, women of a certain age are all the same.'

'You're a misogynist, Harry. It doesn't befit someone of your intelligence.'

Taking tea with Mrs Copeland became a regular occurrence. Afterwards we strolled on deck where the cold breeze added bite to our conversation.

'Have you many friends of my age?' I asked her.

'I hope you are not embarrassed to be seen walking with me, Daniel?'

'Oh, no, not at all. I was wondering if you weren't beginning to find someone like me a little unexciting?'

'It's expedient for us both to have a friend on a voyage such as this. What else is there to do when travelling, but to find a companion who is different from oneself? That is what travelling is for.'

'I trust I'm not so different, Mrs Copeland.'

'I was drawing comparisons, Daniel, not making judgements. I tire of my own company as I do of somebody who is similar. Harry, for example, he sounds very different from you?'

'Yes, he is.'

'Why don't we ask him to dine with us? I might see for myself.'

'Oh, no, he's ill, Mrs Copeland. He hardly eats anything at all.'

'What are you hiding?' she asked.

I played with my fingers as I had in the Treffgarne library in Mayfair. I lacked imagination even then.

'I am not one of those women,' she continued, 'who finds a young man attractive in a sexual way.'

'Gosh,' I thought. 'No,' I said, and the two words mingled somehow as I spoke them.

'But I do like to think myself liberated, which is why I am able to use such a word.'

'Americans are liberated. Judging by you, that is, Mrs Copeland.'

'Have you met many Americans?'

'Oh, no, only the one, only you.'

'I hope what we've been saying will not change our relationship, Daniel. It is true you've been wondering about me, haven't you?'

'It was Harry who wondered more than me,' I said.

'You know, in future, I would let Harry do his own wondering. He's probably good at it.'

'Yes, he is.'

'You're a sensible boy. It's a pity to be so influenced. Harry is clearly far too excitable. You know, I think we should return to our previous topic of conversation.'

'I was telling you about my father's shop.'

'One last word about Harry. Is he by any chance related to the Treffgarnes?'

'Yes, he is.'

'I heard how you had moved from steerage.'

'Third class,' I corrected her.

'Gossip on a ship travels like dust in a wind,' she went on.

'Harry has a thing about the lower classes,' I said. 'Do you know the Treffgarnes?'

'Only by reputation. I know they are one of the richest families in London. Money – and this recent war – is making the world a smaller place.'

As the voyage went by and Harry was bobbish enough to venture on deck, Mrs Copeland became more remote, and I began to notice her with an older gentleman with whom I presumed she had a rendezvous in New York, because I did not recognize him from The Olympic, our previous vessel. It was clear to me Mrs Copeland did not care for Harry and that he felt likewise towards her, although it is difficult for me now to remember exactly how their exchanges degenerated into mutual derision, such that a steely contempt developed between them which I, because of my charlatanism, was unable to affect for the better. Whenever Mrs Copeland found me alone we continued our discourse as before, but our friendship had changed, and on one occasion the older gentleman disturbed us, at which point she excused herself to leave with him. When Harry returned with his sweater, for we were sitting on deck where the air was still cool, he asked me why the old witch had disappeared.

'She's promenading,' I said.

'Who with?'

'The old man, the one with the pipe who fills the dining-room with smoke.'

'Oh, such a pity. I was rather enjoying myself.'

'Harry, please stop.'

'You are annoyed.'

'I am not annoyed.'

'I think you are infatuated, Daniel.'

'I am not infatuated.'

'If love produces the same sort of misery in me, I shall have to avoid it.'

And so I hit him. I smacked him across the face with my fist as hard as I could, drawing blood from his upper lip. For the first time in my life I struck another person, and shocked myself with the ferocity of my anger. As I brought my fist back, I hit him with the back of my hand too, his head stilled in the canvas of the deckchair, his eye now marked as well with blood streaked across the left side of his nose. Harry was quietened. I took pleasure from having taken him by surprise and walked away in as dignified a manner as I could, quite slowly. But I heard Harry begin to laugh and could only turn and yell, 'You're just jealous, Harry', before running into our cabin and dissolving into fits of tears on my bed. I cried until my shoulders ached and I wished I were at home.

When Harry came in several hours later I knew by his silence that he was contrite, so I ignored him, keeping my face buried in the pillow. My upset must have abated a little because I consciously determined not to help him. I felt one corner of my mattress sink as he sat beside me.

'I'm sorry, Daniel.'

I, of course, said nothing.

'When we have a friendship as close as ours it does mean that events will get out of hand occasionally. I am sorry and I want you to know that. It's all my fault. If it's any consolation I have an eye as red as an apple from where you thumped me.'

I hoped my continuing silence would punish him further. After a while I heard him stand and leave the cabin. But when I lifted my head he was still there.

'You see, you're doing it again, tricking me,' I said.

'I had to know how bad you were. I had to know if you were really ill.'

'Ill? Why would I be ill?'

'Ill, as I used to be ill at school. Don't you remember?'

My face must have registered incredulity.

'Don't be surprised, Daniel. The illnesses I had then were real: when it felt as if my life were not truly my own to decide what I might do, or what I should feel. It seemed, then, as if my life belonged to somebody else, as if I had no private thoughts whatsoever. I think you are in love a little, but it was wrong of me to say so. And yes, I am jealous, for I still love you, and I still believe that woman wants something from you.'

Harry sat on his bed; I was opposite him on my own.

'You see, Daniel, no one has ever trusted me before as you do. Until someone else does, I will always be jealous of you.'

'When you talk of love, Harry, are you talking of love in a sexual way?' I remembered Mrs Copeland's expression.

'No, I'm not bothered by sex.'

'I need to be clear in my mind.'

'Daniel, it is enough for me to have your trust. I cannot tell you what strength I have taken from that over the years. Without it, goodness knows where I might be.'

'Yes.'

'Now, regarding sex: at the moment I could love either of the sexes. But I am not a fool and I know that you much prefer women. And I mean women too, not girls of our own age.'

'Yes,' I said again, and added, 'Harry, when we love someone and our love is not answered, it can be torture, can't it? I hope you don't feel that about me?'

'Only sometimes, Daniel. But it soon passes.'

I stood and went to the bathroom to sprinkle cold water on my face. When I returned Harry was not there, so I spent the rest of the day alone reading Chaucer, missing much of what was written because my thoughts, quite naturally, were elsewhere. When the dining hour approached I ordered a cold buffet, which was brought to the cabin by the youngest of the waiters. We were of similar age, and I thought of asking him to stay and talk but always sensed an unease when he was in my presence. So I let him go and chewed the thick cuts of meat which seemed as dull as my mood. It was a blend of pride and self-pity – I have often found these two emotions to be inexorably linked – which stopped me seeking out Harry to say that all was forgiven.

When he did come in it was after midnight and he was drunk, the first time I had seen him so. I left my own bed and went to his, where he had fallen asleep within seconds, fully clothed and without saying a word. I looked at him for a few moments, feeling pity, before pulling off his shoes and undressing him. I sat on the mattress, studying his nakedness in the warmth of the cabin. Harry was thin, his long arms and legs unfleshed, his rib cage all bone, his pectoral muscles concave like those of a small child. He was as cadaverous as the day we had first met. I saw his penis, which was the size and shape of a walnut, and when I ran my finger along it, it bobbed up and down like a champagne cork in water. I continued with my finger along the line of his thigh, trying to imagine what it was that he found so attractive in me. Our bodies were so unlike, for I was small for my age and already plump. My finger rested in the crook of his knee. I touched his neck.

It was, perhaps, inevitable that the journey we thought would

bring us together actually ended by pulling us apart. On the following day, our last on board ship before our arrival in New
Orleans, neither of us spoke of our fight or its aftermath.
Instead, we set about the business of disembarkation without
ribaldry or pleasure. Harry repacked, and I had to sit on his
trunk so that he could fasten the lid, just as I had done in London
and New York, but the atmosphere was stilled, as if we were
both refusing to find the energy needed to be honest. I deliberately suppressed my own apologies when occasionally they effer-
vesced to the surface. When I told him I was going to find Mrs
Copeland and accept her invitation to stay with her in the Garden
District, he showed neither relief nor regret. When my purpose
with Mrs Copeland had been successfully achieved, I came back
and gave him her address which I had scribbled on a slip of
paper. I expected him to plead with me to stay but his pride prevented him.

'What about money, Daniel? The bank needs my signature on
withdrawals so it won't be possible for you to draw money on
your own.'

'I have the money you gave me. I shan't need much because I
plan to return to Southampton within the fortnight.' Once more
I expected him to plead with me not to be so foolish.

We parted on the dock in a monsoon-like rain, which was
spitting from the wooden planking, curling in eddies around
our shoes. Umbrellas were superfluous; Mrs Copeland's white
parasol quickly became flaccid and absurd, so she gave it to the
black boy to carry. He was so small he had to trot to keep up
with his father, who was portering our hand luggage. As I
turned, I saw Harry negotiating with another father and son, but
he did not see me for he was busy making the arrangements.

The Garden District of New Orleans is like no other. Its avenues
of bevelled, cobbled streets, bordered by closely planted, moss-
hung trees, sing of such riches and affluence that it is easy to
understand why its inhabitants believe no other world exists. In
Mrs Copeland's limousine I marvelled at the splendour of it all,
at the wrought-iron and the antebellum houses with their land-
scaped gardens whose lavishness and elegance seemed timeless,
as if the possessors of this grandeur were the owners of time,
too. It had stopped raining, so Mrs Copeland wound down the
windows. The motor turned by Lafayette Cemetery, where the

sun was beginning to slant across the raised tombs. It was late afternoon and the sky had cleared in seconds. I put my face into the stream of hot air coming in through the window and saw steam rising from the pavements. On many of the lawns black men were sweeping away the water. By a picket fence I saw a child with a hand pump, the Greek Revivalist mansion behind him built well above ground to protect it from flooding, the child's shoes fastened to a nail. Inside the limousine, Mrs Copeland talked of her return after a year in Europe, speaking with such inattentive passivity that I thought this wonderland of New Orleans must bore her. I kept my eyes to the open window, and she admonished me for my inattention.

'I'm sorry, Mrs Copeland, but I have never in my life seen anything as miraculous and ostentatious as this.'

She had been telling me of Florence, another world new to me, where a young man had introduced himself on the Ponte Vecchio. He had begun by buying her a gold pendant, but had later asked her for the money back because he was poor. In recompense, she had given him more than was necessary. I tried to listen but could find no connection with the story.

'Are you sad to be home?' I asked.

Mrs Copeland looked away, her eyes misted over, and I saw in her attitude how lonely she must be without a husband.

'Did you not enjoy the May Balls?' But Mrs Copeland did not reply, so I returned my gaze to my surroundings. She had successfully dampened my enthusiasm, if that had been her purpose.

When I saw her home it was a palace. On the boat I had thought her guilty of exaggeration but now I saw the opposite was true, for nothing had prepared me for this, and I began to understand what a quiet, modest woman she must be. Her staff were assembled on the lawn. They comprised, perhaps, twenty or twenty-five black men and women ranging in age between eight and seventy-eight whom she proceeded to greet individually. One of the young girls was obviously new to her because she spoke to her at some length, the girl curtseying at her every question until Mrs Copeland told her to desist. But her legs still twitched instinctively until Mrs Copeland kneeled down on the grass to hold them still. Elsewhere, standing on a waterlogged section of ground, I noticed the garden boy with a water pump, his shoes also hanging beside him on a nail in the wooden fence.

When Mrs Copeland went to meet him she splashed him with water, and he had the courage to splash her back, so that they momentarily looked like children at play.

'Who was that?' I asked, as we entered the house.

'Jeremiah. He had an accident as a teenager. He fell from a ladder. Unfortunately, it left him simple-minded, but we keep him on rather than let him suffer.'

If the exterior of Mrs Copeland's mansion was sumptuous then the interior, with its pine floors and crystal chandeliers, was even more so. She pointed out without affectation the hand-painted murals in the lobby which she had commissioned in Italy: I thought one of the panels slightly ridiculous for it was set around an Italianate marble fireplace and smoke had bruised the colour.

'I've engaged another artist, Daniel, in Florence to redo it, and we shall have electric heating. But I like them because they remind me of Tuscany and the country I most love. Italy is uninhibited and free.'

I was taken up the circular stairway by one of the servants to my room, which was, in fact, a three-room suite, where it seemed as if my arrival had been anticipated, for in the lounge was a vase of sweet peas and a copy of that day's newspaper, which I sat down to read until my portmanteaux arrived. I had expected to unpack myself, but this was done for me by the servant who, earlier, had shown me upstairs. I realized he must be my personal valet. He spoke with such a relaxed southern Louisiana drawl that I found him difficult to understand, so I ceased hovering by his side and left him alone with my wardrobe. I could still see him occasionally through the open, mahogany door, his white hair and stately bearing moving from closet to closet. I picked up the newspaper but was so discomfited that my eyes would not focus on the print. When Mrs Copeland arrived to check on my progress, I asked her about the house and its history.

'It was built in eighteen seventy-two, Daniel, in a style called Renaissance Revival.'

'Hence, the fluted columns,' I said.

'America has no past, so we take from Europe. We believe we can buy history, when, of course, we can't. You will find this makes us insecure, even afraid, which is why we'll never admit we're wrong. America longs for reassurance and to be told it's right.'

I asked if I might have a Bourbon from my drinks cabinet and stood to pour the liquor, adding ice.

'These rooms will be adequate?' she asked.

'Thank you, yes.'

'I am sorry about my mood in the Oldsmobile this afternoon.'

'Why,' I said, 'there's no need to be.'

'I know many people see the district's grandeur, whilst I alone see its poverty.'

'I saw no poverty, Mrs Copeland.'

'I'm talking of the spirit, Daniel, where so much is assumed and taken for granted that there is nothing left to fight for. You will see I speak my mind about the situation of the Negro, and am therefore not liked in many quarters.'

Mrs Copeland accepted a Bourbon. I fixed it for her whilst my valet hovered uncertainly as I had an hour earlier. I realized I had made him redundant.

'You may go,' she said, and waited for him to leave before saying, 'Daniel, you must dismiss your boy when all is done.'

'I didn't know that was the form, Mrs Copeland.'

'To be fair to you it isn't always, but it is in this house.'

I sat opposite her, content the black man had withdrawn and that I now knew a way of discharging him without awkwardness.

'Do you like your own company?' she asked. 'I think you are a watcher and a listener. You don't give yourself away easily, Daniel. You are very English. We Americans are clear and uncomplicated; we don't have a European sense of irony: we say what we mean. Is this why you argued with Harry, because neither of you expressed your true feelings?'

I sipped my Bourbon, which was hot in my throat. I had not expected any reference to Harry Treffgarne. It made me blink.

'I was wrong about Harry,' she said. 'We spent the last evening together on the boat; he took rather too much drink. I know you will be piqued to hear this.'

'Yes,' I said, 'I am.'

'But he apologized for his attitude. He told me you had been his courage.'

'I don't know, Mrs Copeland. If I am or was, it's been a fluke. Circumstance brought us together. I'm not really a very nice person. It's just that Harry is one of those people you get carried along with; he always manages to get what he wants. He's terribly good at it, too. I want my way sometimes. I'm a person myself, not a cipher,' I said, rather grandly. 'But it's his money, so what can I do?'

'Money is not all, Daniel.'

'It is when you have none of your own, and someone suggests you do this or that.'

'I do understand.' She slipped the gold pendant from around her neck with a quick forward movement of her head. 'I told you of the Italian boy on the Ponte Vecchio in Florence. This is what he bought me. He was a sneak-thief, but I fell for him. When I found out what he was I gave him money. Money cannot buy love or happiness. I was pleased to see him pleased, which is all Harry wants for you. Don't become a snob, Daniel.'

'A snob?'

'Yes, you have that within you. Secretly, you are impressed and envious of those with money. Tell Harry what you want and he will do it.'

When Mrs Copeland withdrew shortly afterwards I lay on my bed, an English fourposter, my head ringing with alcohol and her words. I had no doubt that her inviting me into her home had been for the sole purpose of this one conversation. It greatly annoyed me that I could have been so duped, and picked up a pillow, which I kicked around the room like a football. It was a game I had never played but only heard about. I made a goal between the closet doors and derived sadistic pleasure from wrecking the neatness of the room, though I later called in the black man to set it straight, apologizing to him. I offered him Bourbon, but drank the bottle on my own. He dismissed himself, for by then I was incapable of doing so.

I spent a miserable two days and on the third morning asked Mrs Copeland if I might take her limousine and chauffeur to the bayous of the Mississippi, where I knew John Bell lived and where I hoped I would meet Harry. Mrs Copeland surprised me by suggesting I take her motor part-way on my own, but she also chided my innocence and explained that the bayous were mostly inaccessible by land and that I would require a motorlaunch to reach the creeks, where shallow water, submerged cypresses, and alligators made river traffic dangerous. It seemed an impossible task, but I was given lessons in the Oldsmobile along the quiet streets. It was as if I were a puppet and Mrs Copeland knew which strings made me secure or in-secure, so that by turns she could play with my candour or flatter my reserve. To drive on my own was a crazy, wonderful, over-whelming experience. It was an act of genius on her part, which I obstinately chose to regard as an apology for her plain speak-ing the evening before.

On the fourth morning I departed alone for a rendezvous with a river pilot who was to take me across the swamps, my sense of elopement so ravishing that I almost failed to notice the first cotton plantations whose broad fields quickly superseded the outskirts of the city. The car rattled along the metal road, where white men took avarice to such a degree that their covet-ousness could only be explained by their ignorance. But in Mrs Copeland's Oldsmobile I was spellbound by this Never-Never Land of luxury, whose fairy-tale euphoria I entered with ease. I slowed the motor as the symmetrical white fencing began to fog my vision, forgetting that the plantation homes were monu-ments to the great wealth of a few and that only a half-dozen miles away poverty rolled along the river as a testament to the iniquity of greed.

I found the boathouse and was soon aboard a small craft, the skiff sliding through the murky reaches of swamp overhung with thick canopies of subtropical vegetation, while ancient gnarled cypresses with greying shawls of Spanish moss rose from the still water. Passage was slow and difficult. My captain, a black man, seemed to know his way through this never changing terrain almost by instinct, although he told me with evident fear of a monster, a 'critter said to be seventeen feet tall' who inhabited this area. At the top of the bayous were the rough, single room homes built from whatever was available which Mrs Copeland had warned me about, all on wooden stilts so rickety it seemed impossible they should remain upright. On their sloping verandas sat black men with roughly made fishing rods. Even at distance, their eyes pierced mine, although their true countenance appeared stoical, lazy and withdrawn. I was pleased I had my captain, for it was no journey for an ignorant white Englishman. Indeed, the more we progressed into this wilderness, the more uncertain I became. The homes with their roofs of tin-sheeting, walls of what resembled scrap-machinery and bamboo, seemed to reflect the lethargy and pointlessness I had earlier witnessed in the faces of the black men, as if their lives were a commodity at another's discretion. I became fearful, both for my own safety and for that of Harry. It seemed impossible he could have found this way on his own. But as the black captain cut the engine and took up the oars I saw the school shack on stilts that John Bell had written of in his letter. It was larger than the homes, with a rope ladder descending to the mud, the whole edifice of the schoolroom at an angle so that no child could possibly be sitting upright inside. A rectangular opening faced the river, which had it had glass might have been a window, but unglazed it allowed me to hear muffled voices from inside. The shack was built of wood, its planking waterproofed with tar, but in places both had rotted away to be replaced by cloth, which stretched across the holes held taut by nails. The shiny nail heads had not yet rusted and were reflecting the sun. It seemed crazy but also exhilarating, so I hooked my feet through the rope ladder and climbed up, for no one told me I should not do so.

Harry was teaching, three feet lower at the front of the class than those black children at the rear. Their faces turned as I held the open door and Harry introduced me without pausing as if I had been expected all along and my entrance had come as no surprise. He then resumed his lesson. He was speaking of London, his voice so mesmeric I found myself listening to him as though for the first time. John, who was seated by the door as if he were a pupil, clutched my hand and asked me to sit, which I did quietly on one of the two vacant chairs, whereupon a penny coin rolled from my trouser pocket. As it bounced past the children down the incline each one made a grab for it, but Harry caught it on its final hop and irreverently tossed the coin high into the air. Several children fell forward in an attempt to seize it, upturning their cane chairs behind them. In reaching forward each child fell on top of the one in front like collapsing dominoes. This might have been amusing – the children in fact were laughing – but for the cracking sound which oscillated from the schoolroom floor, suddenly stilling the mayhem. I felt the floor tilt and saw Harry by the blackboard drop another foot. The abruptness of the movement registered uncertainly on his face. John, beside me, speaking with great calm told those children who could move to make their way towards the door. The change from revelry to stoicism was incredible to behold in their young eyes. As I pulled a girl past me, the walls rippled as in an earthquake, and I heard shouting outside where the older boys had abandoned the rope ladder and were encouraging the younger children to jump. When the last girl was discharged, John held his arm to Harry, who was busy throwing chairs through a hole which had opened in the wall, and we all three jumped down ourselves. The stilts snapped and the schoolroom jack-knifed across the mud towards the Mississippi, where it floated away upended on its roof. In two minutes it was gone from our view.

I would have expected the children to be dismissed, but there were enough chairs for the lesson to be resumed by the river, and so it was, until it became apparent that swimming was a more attractive option. I watched them splashing through the water. The children were naked and unconcerned. John brought me a milky Cajun beer, and we sat together, while Harry dived from the branches of a low tree, joining us later when the afternoon light had begun to wane.

In truth, I had anticipated that Harry would have missed me as much as I had him and hoped he would be contrite and conciliatory. It was a shock to find he was neither and had no intention of being so. I do not know whether this was a calculated attitude or whether he was simply allowing his natural instinct to dictate his behaviour and therefore the resumption – almost – of our friendship. I was frightened by the straightforward manner with which he spoke to John, and hurt too, for it was clear he no longer needed me.

'I'm so sorry,' he said to John.

'Oh, don't be,' John replied, 'it wasn't your fault.'

'Yes, it was,' he said. 'I was showing off when I threw that penny. I'm forever at the mercy of my own fallibility.'

'Isn't that what being human is?' John asked. 'It is our fallibility which makes us good, and decent, and kind.'

'Yes, perhaps, but not when I destroy.'

I should have told Harry it was not his fault, as I had promised I would that night in Mayfair when I first learned the truth of his father's brutality. But I said nothing for I had not yet sufficient guilt of my own fully to comprehend it in another. As he left to fetch more beer I thought I saw again the boy I first met on the quad at school. I now have age on my side and can see it was Harry's energy which, throughout these years, had lifted our intimacy beyond the mundane. It was he who found dignity from being honest, and when his goodness was no longer forthcoming any rancour was purely my own. As he returned and we sipped our Cajun beer, I did not realize how narcissistic I had become. How I wish I had been wiser and less egotistical, for as it was, Harry had a new friend with whom he could be truthful, and that friend was John.

II

The
Prime Minister's
fathers

4

I booked a passage, setting sail from New Orleans within the fortnight. I had spoken without thought when I had declared this intention to Harry on our arrival, but the Solent was real and the sight of Calshot Castle, as we entered Southampton Water, brought home to me the full consequences of what I had said in pique. The liner edged towards her berth below a metal-grey sky, and it felt discordant to be back in England, as it often does after a long journey when one momentarily discovers little affinity or kinship with what was once so familiar.

On the quay I bade farewell to Sir Christopher Salisbury, who had been my companion for much of the peregrination from New York, not knowing what an influence he was shortly to have on my future. Sir Christopher, once a professor at Trinity, had recently lost his young wife in a bicycling accident in Cambridge. In fact she had been practising riding a unicycle on a high-wire for a circus act. I had listened to Sir Christopher's account of her eccentricities in the hope that he would go on to talk about the House of Commons, where he was now an under-secretary in the Foreign and Commonwealth Office – hence his visit to the United States. He had, quite incidentally, a son my age, whose friendship I later enjoyed at Cambridge myself, so Sir Christopher became a part of my life in a way I would never have anticipated. Indeed, I lodged with him in his Regency home in my final year, when I was by then vice-president of the Cambridge Union and he in the Home Office after Ramsay MacDonald's unsuccessful first Labour administration. So much of what happens to us in life is a fluke, and the arguments we entered into at weekends informed my political philosophy.

Christopher delighted in fine claret, and I would sit by his fire with a glass of a good vintage much in awe of his skilful reasoning, knowledge, and influence. I took his thinking and erudition to the Union whenever I myself was invited to debate on a topic of the day, which was often.

Meanwhile I hobnobbed with his son Giles, who I now recognize had much of Harry about him, as if I were replacing one with the other. Giles was an oarsman, Eton-educated, who rowed stroke in the Putney-Mortlake race the year both crews sank by the Fulham football ground. As had been the case with Harry, Giles and I shared little in common, although at the time such ideas seldom entered my consciousness. It is only recently I have fully perceived how for much of my early life, particularly during my twenties, I intuitively encouraged friendship with individuals who were so dissimilar from myself that there was always a tension between us. I can only presume I found gratification in the discomfiture which this created, as if from the unease I hoped to exert some kind of power. Harry had an obsessive anarchy which in several ways Giles mirrored, but where Harry was temperamental, Giles was sensitive; I was able to play on his inner feelings by becoming aloof or withdrawing favour whenever it appeared I might not get my own way. I had great capacity for engendering feelings of wickedness within others, and I did this many times with Giles, castigating his impartiality, attempting to produce a rift between him and his father, although, of course, never in Sir Christopher's presence, for he was far too sagacious and would have diagnosed my tactics immediately. I was, in short, becoming a manipulator.

This is a selective account of my life and I wish to mention, for my own ease of conscience today, that I subsequently apologized many times to Giles. He became a surgeon and was offered a knighthood – he pioneered much modern work in skingrafting – which unlike his father he declined for reasons Sir Christopher would never have fathomed but which Harry implicitly understood: both were modest men who did not seek worldly success for their own sake. Giles died in 1953, ironically of skin cancer, but with so much achieved. I was proud to know him, as I have been proud to know many friends whose behaviour has often been better than my own.

I wrote to Harry Treffgarne throughout my university days,

exaggerating my accomplishments, dismissing my failures. He would reply, and our correspondence continued on a regular if erratic basis. It was no surprise that he determined to remain in New Orleans upon completion of his initial year, and I was too busy myself to be very perturbed by his decision, but answered saying I was pleased he was happy. In my penultimate term at college I wrote again to Mrs Copeland, and she responded with a money-order large enough to fulfil all my needs. I penned a last letter to Harry explaining I would be in New Orleans for the summer before taking up a junior doctor's post in London in the autumn.

John Bell had gone. Harry was in charge of the school now with a new assistant whom I recognized as Jeremiah, the imbecile garden boy whom Mrs Copeland had splashed with water on my first visit seven years earlier. When I returned to the Garden District, I asked Mrs Copeland about this transformation, which was one change among many.

'Yes, it was Harry's idea to have Jeremiah, Daniel. He does the caretaking and odd jobs. I haven't seen him so happy. Who was I to refuse?'

'And Harry. How did you meet up with Harry again?'

'I went to see him shortly after you left.' We were eating an hors d'oeuvre of prawns with cucumber in her dining-room; she poured Tuscan white wine. 'I felt guilty, Daniel, for it was I who had driven a wedge between you. I shall never forgive myself for doing that.'

'Perhaps you are right', I said, when I should have answered that the schism in our friendship would have been inevitable. 'And Harry told you all about his past, Mrs Copeland?'

'Yes, eventually, as we got to know and love one another. It was not my choice he write to his family and sever all connection with them. I did try to stop him.'

'Harry embellishes,' I said. 'His mother is really rather nice. And I cannot quite accept that Mr Treffgarne behaved as badly as Harry would have us believe. In fact, I met him. We spent a pleasant evening together,' I lied.

'What was he like?' she asked.

'Well, I found him meek and mild, Mrs Copeland. Rather polite, rather tender.' I added untruth upon untruth as the chimera within me grew. 'I found him a sensitive man, a little dour,

73

but not at all the brute I had expected.'

'Brutes don't look the part,' she said.

'When he died last year he had a glowing obituary in The Times,' I replied, momentarily ending the falsehood, 'which I could only agree with, Mrs Copeland. I was rather sad to learn of his death, as one is with a friend.'

'Harry wasn't sad, Daniel. His mother wrote to tell him, but Harry refuses to even acknowledge her letter. So I have written. I hope I did right?'

'I wouldn't worry, Mrs Copeland. They are a family who do not take kindly to interference in their private affairs, but I'm sure you are different. Harry won't forgive her?'

'No,' she said, 'but I'm hopeful he will in time.'

Mrs Copeland slowly drew the blade of her knife across the table linen leaving a crease. As with many Americans, her desire to be loved made her vulnerable. Inwardly I rejoiced at the wound in the cloth.

'It's no way to behave, is it, Mrs Copeland? One must learn forgiveness.'

'I do beg your pardon, Daniel,' she said, looking up. 'Forgive me, I was distracted for a moment. You are quite right. But I have long ago stopped trying to live other people's lives for them, and Harry must do as he wishes.'

'Is that fair on you?' I asked.

'Perhaps not. Let us change the subject.'

'It was you built the new school, Mrs Copeland? When the Treffgarnes stopped Harry's money?'

'Yes.'

'Then I think Harry owes you much. You are being far too kind.'

The door opened, and her anxiety dissipated with the arrival of four Negroes with silver tureens, a fifth behind them with a platter of dressed teal and Canada goose. I ate capsicum, mung bean, and sweet potato with the gamebirds, declining the chestnuts, which tasted acerbic.

'You are very quiet, Daniel. I wonder if our conversation has not disturbed you?'

'Mrs Copeland, you are very generous,' I said. 'It has a little, because I worry about Harry.' I put down my knife and fork.

'I've spoilt your meal, Daniel. I'm sorry to be so self-absorbed.'

74

'But you haven't been, I'm only pausing.' I picked up my cutlery and could see that Mrs Copeland thought me noble, which had indeed been my intention.

'It is lovely to see you again,' she said.

'You are not eating. May I offer you something?' I said as I served myself with a little more teal. As was her custom, the Negroes had been dismissed, and we were dining alone.

'No thank you, Daniel. I'm not hungry.'

'Mrs Copeland, Harry has a way of eliciting pity from all those about him,' I interjected, which was the antithesis of the truth. 'You must not blame yourself.'

She poured wine into her glass as if determined to be drunk. 'You know Harry has asked me to marry him,' she said.

'Yes,' I replied. 'He told me this afternoon whilst we were sitting on the verandah drinking beer.'

'He so wants me to accept.'

'The children were fishing, Mrs Copeland. He told me as we were sitting watching them. One of the girls caught the strangest fish I've ever seen.'

'Is he in love with me, Daniel? Because I am in love with him.' She folded her napkin and placed it beneath her glass, where she had spilled a little wine on the white cloth. 'I think where love is concerned we often have no choice.'

'Then why are you sad?' I asked.

'I'm not sad, I'm uncertain. I love Harry so much I need to be sure it is right for him. If I thought he were not revenging himself on his family, I would have no doubt. But you say Mr Treffgarne was not a tyrant, so perhaps I am wrong. Harry has little to revenge, and he does love me. I must thank you, Daniel.'

I squared my own napkin and watched the niggers clear the long table. A negress left a meringue dessert.

'You will have some of this?' she asked. 'It was made especially. Everyone remembered how you were partial to meringue on your last visit.'

'Shall you marry him, Mrs Copeland?'

'My name is Stella. Yes, I shall marry him, Daniel.'

When the meal was finished I asked to be excused and walked the four miles to the Vieux Carré where I found a wooden seat beside the Mississippi, the gaslight of Jackson Square behind me. Thin streaks of a cotton mist drifted down river. I found myself crying shamelessly despite being asked for money by passing vagrants. I sensed a figure sit down beside me and knew at once it must be Harry, but when I looked up it was a black boy of about eleven years old. He had no shoes and tucked his bare legs underneath himself as though he wanted to become smaller and disappear.

'I behaved despicably at dinner,' I told him, 'with lie after lie and it got me nowhere.'

The boy inclined his head towards my lap, peering upwards into my eyes whereupon he remained stilled and peaceable, as if checking my sympathies.

'I'd forgotten how much I loved them both,' I said. 'They are both so unselfish. All I do is manipulate, and I can't even do that successfully. Harry was so happy this afternoon sitting by the river. It's so unfair.'

The boy had undersized fingers which he raised towards my cheek, afterwards running them along my lapel where the jacket was buttoned. It was a warm night; the child was wearing an old woollen jumper and gingham shorts. He unfastened my top button, his forefinger crooked so that I could see it had once been fractured.

'I have a friend in England,' I told him, 'called Sir Christopher Salisbury, who is self-righteous.' He gazed vacantly, almost imperiously towards me as if mine was a face he could not quite remember. 'I like him because he's influential, but really he's an awful man full of self-opinionated indignation.' I held the boy's hand where the skin around his nail was calloused and the broken bone had reset itself at an eighty degree angle.

'Whereas Harry is content. When I saw him teaching this afternoon, he seemed simple and straightforward.'

The boy lifted his hand from mine, brushing open my jacket in the same movement and giggling so that I heard his voice for the first time.

'I'm so mixed up. I don't know who is right, or what is proper anymore. I don't know what to think.'

The boy transferred his hand to my inside pocket without altering his expression, his tongue between his lips in concentration. He was tiny, so defenceless and vulnerable. Any imperiousness he might have had had vanished.

'I'm not a very moral person,' I said. 'In fact, I rather despise myself. I'm no help to anyone.'

'Are you from England?' he asked, my wallet now sitting on his knees. 'Did you come on a paddle-boat?'

'No,' I said, 'I didn't. England's too far for that. I feel a long way from home today.'

'Bye,' he replied, uncurling his legs which did not quite reach the towpath so that he had to jump from the bench to reach the ground. He fumbled with my wallet, as he slipped it into the torn pocket of his shorts.

I followed the boy a short distance as he scampered through the Vieux Carré until I lost him by St. Louis Cathedral amongst a mass of late-night churchgoers who were gathering on the pedestrian mall, the young women in pure white surplices forming a strong contrast to the unwashed child who had just stolen my billfold. I found a place amongst the crowd and entered the cathedral through a stone arch, waiting under the tympanum for the young women to be seated in the chancel. They were coal-black, their vestments so immaculate it was sublime. I chose a bench in the ambulatory where my view was unrestricted and watched as they whispered occasionally to one another until the liturgy began, with incense being dispersed across the transept by several altar-boys, the priest with them so resplendent he might have been a deity. He spoke in Latin, which I was able to follow, but, my not being a Catholic, the course of the Holy Communion was new to me. At the Eucharist I went forward and knelt, taking the consecrated bread and wine, which prickled on my tongue, for even I understood my partaking of the host defiled the sacrament. But I was so distressed I needed God's forgiveness. I hoped the body and blood of Christ would make me less immature. As I returned towards my pew the choir began to sing a cantata, the descant of the young women's voices rising to fill the whole Cathedral, nave and aisle, pulpit and confessional, with the most beautiful sound I had ever heard, their voices so rich I was choked with tears as I had been outside before the sneak-thief had made off with my wallet. I walked on and stood beneath the campanile, turning to see their white surplices almost luminescent in the candlelight: a sight so affecting I knew immediately my life might be changed. A priest touched me on my shoulder.

'May I help you?' he asked, observing me crying.

'No thank you, Father, I've just been robbed,' I said, and fled the building.

It was this same priest who married Harry and Stella Copeland at their wedding later that summer. I was Harry's best man. The priest did not recognize me from the night God had so nearly entered my heart, for it had been dark and my face not clearly visible.

In London I received a hand-delivered letter from Harry's mother, the first I had heard from her since leaving school. After deliberating upon its contents for several days, I finally replied suggesting she visit me, knowing this would place her at an initial disadvantage. I had rooms in Wimbledon, and my life was beginning to settle into the comfortable pattern I had long been seeking, with my work at the hospital during the day and social rendezvous amongst my new conservative friends in the evening. Whilst a love affair did not appear to be in the offing, I had no doubt one would materialize sooner or later.

If Mrs Treffgarne's letter had been a surprise, then she herself was even more so. I expected to greet an ashen woman, imagining the events of recent years must have aged her, but she was as composed as ever I remember.

'You have a friend in the Home Office,' she said. 'Sir Christopher was kind enough to give me your address. Thank you for seeing me, Daniel.'

'It is my pleasure. Please do sit down, Mrs Treffgarne.' I poured the Earl Grey, recalling this was her favourite tea. 'I didn't know you were a friend of Christopher's?'

'An acquaintance, yes. He tells me you are looking for a seat in the House of Commons?'

I wondered if she might be going on to question me about the secret and about whether I would ever let slip her version of the truth. 'Christopher is being very kind,' I said. 'I was sorry to learn of your husband's death.'

'We all must pass away. I am happiest by myself.'

'You look radiant, Mrs Treffgarne.'

'I will come straight to the point, Daniel. I have had a private detective investigate this woman Harry has married. It seems from his enquiries she may be married already and the marriage bigamous.'

I was thunderstruck. 'I know nothing of such things.'

'It seems from his inquiries she is married to an Italian who, at best, can only be described as a rogue. He is in prison for persistent thieving. Apparently he stole from her and instead of taking umbrage she married him. All in three weeks, I gather.'

'She can be a little eccentric,' I said.

'It seems more than eccentric. If this were true, would it surprise you, Daniel?'

'No, it would not, Mrs Treffgarne.'

'I gather this Italian lives the life of a saint because the guards are bribed to protect him. He treats the prison as if it were an hotel of which he is the owner.

'She is extremely wealthy.'

'And throws her money away by the reports of it.'

'What do you want from me, Mrs Treffgarne?'

'I will come to that. I wished to see if you could shed any light on the situation.'

'I cannot. How long is this Italian in prison?' I asked.

'Well, this is my point, Daniel. He is to be released next week.'

I swallowed hard. 'And Harry knows nothing of this?'

'I came here to ask that of you.'

I refilled our Dresden china tea cups, which had been a gift from Giles Salisbury and his father on my twenty-first birthday, thinking of the gold pendant Stella had shown me in New Orleans and her story of the young man on the Ponte Vecchio in Florence whose intimacy she had courted. 'What will this Italian do now?' I asked.

'Goodness knows,' she said. 'If he has any sense he'll stay in Italy, but I expect, being a thief, he has greater cunning, don't you?'

'Mrs Treffgarne, you never cared for Harry. Why interfere?'

She looked away towards the window where outside on Wimbledon Common the elms were losing their leaves. It is only as adults we can fully comprehend the regrets of others, for as children we are penitent momentarily, not yet aware of the longevity of guilt. I saw she was discomforted.

'I have never wanted to see Harry hurt,' she said. 'Now Mr Treffgarne is no longer here, the full consequences of our action fall squarely upon me. I cannot sleep at night. I imagine my son eventually told you the truth?'

'Yes, he did.'

'I'm so pleased he has a friend in you, Daniel.'

The sunlight was fading so I stood to draw the blind. Nannies with their charges were strolling across the common.

'I'm not sure I deserve your praise,' I said. 'Harry and I have a strange relationship. Part love, part hatred, Mrs Treffgarne. Although probably both those emotions come from me more than him. In New Orleans this summer I found him difficult to talk to. In fact, I can barely remember now what we spoke about. He has become distant in many ways, preoccupied elsewhere. But he is content, and that is all which should concern us.'

'I agree,' she said.

'Has he still not written to you?' I asked.

'No, Daniel. But the woman he has married writes regularly.'

'She is passionate and caring, quite un-American in her benevolence,' I said, sitting down on a small stool which had been a gift from my parents the last time I visited them in Yorkshire. 'I think eventually he will forgive you, Mrs Treffgarne, but it may take a little while longer.'

We talked on for a further two hours, and so it was that she persuaded me to travel to Italy to see what might be achieved on Harry's behalf. Once again I felt embraced by the Treffgarne falsehood, as if I were forever picking up the detritus of their affairs. I had tried breaking from Harry since leaving New Orleans and had not corresponded, but as my train rattled onwards from Paris it occurred to me for the first time my destiny might always lie in others' hands, for I realized I was essentially a follower, not a leader. Of course not many of us ever will achieve greatness, our names quite lost in the infinity of history. But I do believe the human race to be inherently good, which is why kindness is important, for it is the only influence we have, and the individual or political system which ignores this simple truth is heading for ruin. It is not an accident that man has developed a social conscience, cares for his neighbour, and desires his free spirit to triumph over avarice or dogma.

I was travelling through a Europe which in the next two decades would see the rise and defeat of Fascism, which among its many other consequences would lead, so unceremoniously, to Harry's death in a field in Yorkshire. I only wish I had accepted then the small place I have in history now, for instead, as the locomotive clattered across France, I allowed the anguish of being a follower to needle its way into my brain, which was beginning to hatch my own particular authoritarian ideology. I thought much on the journey. New landscapes have always made me melancholy.

At the Italian border there was a hiccough over passports. Mussolini's guards were running amok all over the carriage until we were shunted into a siding where we had to leave the train in order to be searched. I was given only a cursory glance by a young lieutenant with ginger hair who practised his English, telling me of Florence when I explained my destination, and of Siena where his father was a banker. This over, he ambled with me towards the smoking car, until his captain reprimanded him, at which the young lieutenant turned smartly on his heels, leaving me alone by the railway tracks. I had thought him polite, middle-class like myself and it seemed disdainful to treat him in this off-hand fashion. I turned to the captain but he had pushed me down into the mud before I could tell him so. It ought to have been a salutary lesson in the exercise of power: as it was, back in the smoking carriage with an American cigarette between my lips, I fantasized ways of exerting power over him until his body was beaten and broken. Revenge is sweet, often desirable, but seldom morally justifiable even in the imagination, for there begins the reality. I did not, as a young man, fully understand the complicated relationship between thought and deed.

I alighted at Florence in the early evening. The air was unusually cool and I needed the calfskin placed around my knees in the pony and trap to the Hotel Galileo. It had rained for the last hour of my journey so the streets were damp. The coachman chattered on in Italian and broken English about the sombre look of the city, which he seemed to imply was a rare phenomenon, although I have subsequently returned many times and often seen this self-same sombreness during inclement weather. He had a long scar across his cheek, which alarmed my girlish sensibility, so I was pleased to escape into my hotel. A bellboy carried my portmanteau to the reception desk; the Galileo's elegance was comforting after three days on the train and two nights in a sleeping berth. I had money to spare and requested their best room.

In my pocket I had the address of Stella Treffgarne's Italian 'husband' and the name of the prison he was to be released from the following day. I had thought much of Stella on my journey from London and left the hotel, walking casually past the occasional market stall selling leather goods, to the Ponte Vecchio hoping to imagine her with a sneak-thief amidst the goldsmiths' shops on the city's oldest bridge, built, I think, in the fourteenth century and little changed. In the centre of the bridge, below the three arches where one may look out over the river, is a statue by Romanelli of Benvenuto Cellini, whose work in gold greatly enhanced the commercial reputation of the city in the sixteenth century. It was here I saw Sir Christopher Salisbury. At first I could not believe it was he, thinking I must be mistaken.

'Christopher,' I said.

He turned towards me and his countenance fell, as if I were the last person he expected or wished to meet.

'Daniel, why on earth are you in Florence?'

'I'm here on a mission for Elizabeth Treffgarne, whom I believe you know.'

'I knew her husband. He often asked my advice about Asian affairs when I was at Trinity. We enjoyed one another's confidence.'

'It is odd how an aspect of a friendship can be missed, Christopher, because I know the family well. I was at school with Harry Treffgarne.'

'The boy with the unfortunate temper,' he said, as if he had greater knowledge and were questioning my own.

'Yes, the boy with the regrettable tantrums,' I replied, my face ungiving.

'Good, good,' he repeated as if desiring to leave.

'What brings you to Florence?' I asked.

'Oh, work. Work for the party, work for the Government.'

'But you're at the Home Office now. Does this mean you may still travel?'

'Oh, occasionally there may be a conference which requires my attendance. I prefer my presence to be little noticed, especially by the newspapers.'

'There is no privacy in Parliament,' I told him.

'When one has something personal one wishes to achieve, it is best to be alone in the venture. One has few colleagues in politics,

Daniel, who can be completely trusted. Loyalty is slippery. I preferred the academic milieu of Cambridge, where ideas could be freely discussed in private, away from public scrutiny. Newspapers simplify and ridicule.'

'You look tired,' I said.

'Yes, I am today.'

We strolled from the bridge along the Via dei Calzaiuoli towards the Cathedral of Santa Maria del Fiore and upon my suggestion went inside to view Michelangelo's unfinished Pieta with its figure of Christ descending the cross. But it was Mary Magdalene, added later by Tiberio Calcagni, which caught my imagination. The building was chilly, illuminated by candlelight; Christopher was growing restless. He paced back and forth across the transept as if deeply troubled.

'Look at Mary Magdalene,' I said. 'She wants to help the other two with the body of Jesus, but is in the way. She must really have loved Him. Isn't life incongruous? I'm in the way with Stella Treffgarne, yet here I am in Florence in another cathedral on her behalf. I'm beginning to wonder how much control we have over our destinies.'

I lighted a candle, and then we walked out onto the flat stones of the Piazza del Duomo.

'What were you saying inside?' Christopher asked.

'Nothing really. I was talking to myself, thinking aloud.'

'The ordinary person has little control over his life. Have you only recently understood that?'

'Yes, the feeling grows,' I said. 'I'm a follower. I follow people everywhere and do as they wish. I'm not a leader because I'm too easily influenced.'

'Don't belittle yourself, Daniel.'

'I have only recently understood how lost many people are. Including myself. This is perhaps why religion is so powerful, with its simple explanations.'

'Ordinary people are not listened to, Daniel.'

'You're an academic,' I said, rather unkindly. 'Why should I or anyone else listen to you?'

'I'm a politician. The Great War changed so much, the suffering experienced there has informed a kind of freedom. People no longer blindly accept the world as they used to, they want a say in its future. If not, what was the suffering in the trenches for?'

Two lovers were drifting arm in arm across the piazza, both coated against the drizzle which had begun falling.

'The world is becoming smaller,' I said, recalling a remark Stella Treffgarne had made when still Mrs Copeland. 'The increase in trade, commerce, travel –'

'I want to give people these opportunities, Daniel,' he interrupted me. 'I want to offer them this say in their future.'

We slipped into a restaurant and ordered a meal.

'I agree with you, Christopher,' I said. 'All this is adding to experience and heightening expectation. But what do we do?'

'Parliament cannot answer every question,' he replied. 'It's too slow, too democratic. I've decided to return to academic life where I'll have greater freedom to speak. I'm a man of ideas, not practice. I won't be tied to one particular line of thought, or rhetoric. Parliament is too emotional. I'm no good at carrying an argument in that way. I'll get no further within the party.'

'Why don't you resign the whip?' I asked. 'And speak from the backbenches?'

'Yes, it's a course of action I've considered.'

'Become an Independent MP, Christopher?'

'I'd lose my seat at the next election, and I'd be looked upon as a failure. If I resign my seat now I'd be thought honourable. I'd be strong.'

The two lovers entered the restaurant joking and laughing, both wet from the heavy rain which was now drumming against the window, helping to mist the glass inside where Christopher and I were seated. I looked down and saw I had written Mussolini's name in the condensation without a recollection of having done so in the intensity of conversation. Christopher raised his eyebrow to our waiter and ordered a second bottle of chianti. He had earlier asked for claret without success.

'But I will need a voice in Parliament,' he told me.

'You know many people. Is there no one you trust?'

'Daniel, I admire your naivety and kindness, but in the House of Commons it will not be enough. Those traits, admirable as they are, are not the stuff of politics. I listened to your speeches in the Cambridge Union, they were second-hand, second-rate. You were there because of me. It was my influence, you must know that?'

I looked towards the lovers whose eyes were so locked in each other's that I knew them to be mentally undressing one another.

'I was elected to the Vice-presidency of the Union,' I said defensively.

'Yes, as you will be elected to Parliament with my influence.'

'Have I nothing original to offer?' I asked.

'What you yourself are, your personal qualities, are not at issue here, Daniel. But being 'nice', being 'well-liked', will not help you in the House. What will count will be the strength of your ideas in debate.'

'Politics must have a human face. Otherwise, what is it for?'

'Yes, of course. But it is our actions which matter, not our words. Being kind is an irrelevance. All the sympathies in the world will change nothing, if we do nothing. It's time to act.'

The lovers were kissing one another with their toes.

'What are you writing on the window?' Christopher asked.

'Nothing. I'm writing your name,' I said, scrubbing out both his and Mussolini's names with the back of my hand.

He replenished our wineglasses. I was beginning to be tipsy; the restaurant, the tables, the waiters, the lovers were turning cartwheels in slow motion.

'Have you been planning this since the day we first met?' I questioned. 'My destiny is not my own, is it?'

'You are weak, Daniel, but I can make you strong.'

'I think you must be weak to need someone as young, as pathetic, and as useless as me,' I said. 'I will do what you wish in Parliament, but if you ever speak to me again with this degree of candour, that will be an end to it. I need flattery, not admonishment, Christopher.'

I walked on my own back to the Hotel Galileo and fell asleep fully clothed in a soft chair outside on the covered balcony of my room. At some point during the night I must have moved, as I awoke next morning in bed. A girl was lying beside me. It was the first time I had ever awoken beside a girl, and I had no idea how she arrived there. I blinked, and slid out of bed as carefully as I could, hoping not to disturb her, putting on my clothes, which were in a heap where I must have dropped them, and sprinkling cold water on my face in the white-tiled bathroom. When I returned to the bedroom the girl had stirred a little, and I could see she was naked. I quietly packed my portmanteau and descended the stairway to reception, where I explained that my plans had altered but that I would pay the bill in full. I found another hotel, the Arno, and made doubly sure that it was more than a short walk from the Galileo. Here I stayed for the rest of the morning contemplating the momentous happenings of the last twelve hours, a headache numbing my skull.

In the late afternoon I took a pony and trap to the outskirts of the city, passing lemon-trees growing up from the pavements and the numerous beggars by the roadside. The sun was sinking towards the orange, slated rooftops of the houses, long shadows making the buildings look artificial as if they were painted on canvas. Across the streets ran gamin-like children with under-nourished dogs on lengths of flax. At one point the trap had to swerve to avoid a girl who then ran alongside us, until I gave her a coin and she was left behind. On one or two buildings, usually cafés or cheap eating-houses, were frescoes beneath which were seated groups of men playing a board game similar to dominoes, some gambling with cigarettes, others with parcels of green olives, yet more with packets of vegetables which I presumed must be grown on their small-holdings. It seemed the game was a relaxation, but also a quasi-bartering system.

There were moments on the journey when I felt frightened by these spectacles, so powerful a feeling did I have of being in another's territory; it was an alien world I found not in the least invigorating, for the homes were too shoddy and their inhabitants too violently down at heel. I ought to have understood with greater clarity why Mussolini had gained a foothold over these people and why Sir Christopher was in Florence.

As we approached the fringes of the city, the driver turned around and addressed me in Italian so that I was forced to show my ignorance of his language. We had halted by a building with a mosaic in chipped marble. It had an open entrance and ascending concrete steps. On many of the apartment balconies damp clothes were hanging. On another a woman was feeding her child. She covered herself as I stepped from the trap. Elsewhere a boy was crying, tears hurrying from his eyes. I made it clear that the cabman was to wait and picked my way across the open ground towards the steps, the slip of paper already in my hand, a little moist from perspiration but the number of the flat still legible. Thank goodness numbers, unlike language, are universal. I found the correct door and after waiting a few seconds to compose myself, knocked purposefully.

Sergio was polite. He was long-legged, with cropped hair and had the vespertine eyes of a person most active at night. I was struck immediately by his resemblance to Harry, so much so I stumbled over the introductory remarks I had so carefully learned in Italian, which were meant to explain my deficiencies in this regard together with a brief résumé of the reasons for my visit. I need not have worried, for this skeletal figure spoke almost perfect English with an American brogue. His mouth was intelligent, so that he looked self-aware enough to be conscious of his own faults, and I could see he appreciated another's beauty and had a sense of humour. Regret had not yet troubled him, nor reflection made him neurotic. I had no doubt he and Stella Treffgarne – or whatever her surname might now be – were indeed married and that the assumptions of the private eye would prove correct.

Sergio asked me into the parlour. I walked timidly across the ripped linoleum, noticing how crowded the space was by furniture. An infant of three or four wearing only a vest was playing with a wooden toy by a cupboard. A crucifix, together with a Madonna and child, was beside a looking-glass where I caught my features momentarily. The infant stood, his legs still podgy, and walked through a drape into what I presumed must be the kitchen, for I could smell cooking and taste oregano faintly on my tongue.

'My hair,' Sergio remarked casually touching the top of his head, 'was cut off in prison. It is not my character.'

It seemed from the way he spoke as if he knew already he had carved a niche for himself in the world and therefore needed no aggression to make his point.

'You will not remember me like this?' he asked.

It appeared as if pride might be the only emotion which would ever trouble him.

'No,' I said, 'of course not.'

The infant returned with a metal ladle in his hand. Sergio picked him up, but the boy struggled so he placed him on the floor by the toy.

'My new brother, Signor Hinton. I only meet him for the first time today.'

A woman entered, causing the drape to billow, and went

straight to the child, taking the utensil from him. The boy, deprived of his possession looked up and whooped, making the mother smack him across the leg, whereupon he crawled beneath the dresser. The two adults, for I judged Sergio an adult but only just, talked in their native language.

'My mother asks if you will share our supper, Signor Hinton?'

'Will you tell her that's very kind, but I have a cabman waiting.'

The two spoke and Sergio's mother left. She was a plump woman with a strong face, as if marriage and children had not yet ousted contentment and a lifetime of sympathy for others had yet to disillusion her. I saw from whom Sergio gained his bearing.

'My mother asks if you will not change your mind?'

In truth, I was humbled by this extraordinary household. Being humbled is a rare and pleasant experience when one is at ease with life and with oneself, but at the time I had much to learn.

'No, thank you,' I said, feeling real and passionate guilt for the first time.

Sergio invited me to sit which I did on one of the cotton-shrouded chairs. Underneath, the upholstery was dilapidated. I gave Sergio the letter, carefully translated, which I had carried from London, explaining every detail of my visit in the simplest possible terms.

'The money she offers is not enough,' he said, raising his eyes from the paper. He was calm, self-disciplined.

'Then I am empowered to bargain with you. I'm to do a deal which will be satisfactory to us both.'

'Nothing will be satisfactory, Signor Hinton. I am a rich man already.'

'I can offer you ten thousand pounds,' I said, underplaying the amount.

Sergio smiled and then laughed. I could see he was dis-enchanted, a little tired, but his sense of humour was coming to his aid. For my part I felt discomforted. Sergio saw the ridiculousness of our situation, when I should have done but did not.

The child crawled from beneath the dresser. This time he accepted Sergio's lap where he sat playing with a trouser button covered in fluff.

'I will tell you my story,' he said, clicking his tongue at the boy. 'I started to thieve when I was only eight years old. The pickings in the city were very, very rich.'

The boy peered cross-eyed for a moment at his elder brother, his eyes intent but watery. Sergio had lit a cigarette and the smoke gave distance to both their faces.

'When I was thirteen,' he continued, 'I was running the gauntlet of many tourists along the river in the evenings, and during the day around Michelangelo's David. I learned to pick the wealthy by their poise, and when I was fourteen to follow them back to their hotel rooms and wait until they went out again for their early evening pleasures. I stole silk underwear for our Mama.'

The boy giggled. He could not possibly understand what Sergio was saying but his brother's voice was amusing him. Sergio pretended to address him but was really speaking to me.

'Mama learned not to ask, Patrizio. I stole clothes for myself and changed into them there and then. I took watches and coins, and I became braver. I stole jewels when I could and jumped down from balconies. When I was caught for the first time, Signor Hinton,' he said without any self-recrimination, his face turning away from the boy towards me, 'the police led me off to a reformatory where I was beaten on the soles of my feet.'

His mother entered with a bowl of soup, which was placed on my lap together with a spoon for me to use. Sergio waited for his mother to leave.

'I was four years in the reformatory. By then I was more attractive to the women than the jewels I had once stolen. I still visited their hotel rooms, but for different reasons. I was wealthy in every possible way.'

I listened on, but Sergio did not reach the point where Stella arrived in his narrative, and I could not find the courage to mention her name myself. Instead I ate the cabbage soup, which had been thinned with chicken-stock and inexpensive wine.

We spent the following days together in Florence, as he showed me the places he had spoken about. Whenever I thought of the deal, it seemed an impossible intrusion, for I had been correct in my early assessment of his pride. He knew the galleries, the river, and where to sit in a piazza to gain discreet views of the holiday-makers, whom he talked of with reference to his own happiness as if their lives might shortly be a part of his own. Sergio often appeared downcast in his judgements like an actor playing a role he no longer enjoyed. It was as if the onset of maturity had brought him to a more sensible conclusion regarding his future; but commonsense was not a trait he admired. In my heart of hearts I recognized these symptoms and knew him to be in love. I understood, too, why he loved her. Stella was daring, reckless, provocative, and both of us enjoyed the excitement of the unpredictable. I no longer required the completion of his story in order to understand him, for Sergio and I had developed a tacit understanding in the few days we spent together, each of us knowing more of the other than was ever expressed, both comprehending an irony which Stella in her Americanness would never have appreciated – it was Stella herself who told me that Americans had no irony.

'She is a very simple woman,' he said, apropos of nothing, but somehow picking up on my thoughts as we were riding in a pony and trap back towards his home. 'She is very straightforward, very uncomplicated. Is this why you fell in love with her on your first journey to America?'

I said nothing but Sergio understood my reply.

'Is this why your friend fell in love with her also?' he asked.

'I hadn't thought of that but perhaps it is, yes.'

'She is very good at removing problems, Signor Hinton.'

'Or creating them,' I said, remembering why we were driving together.

'She does what she wants, says what she thinks,' he remarked smiling, his good humour allowing him to be objective.

The coachman picked up speed along a street I did not recall from our previous journeys where, round one corner, a whole family were flogging a mule which had clearly died between the shafts. I felt I was beginning to be absorbed into the aesthetic of Italy. Here, the wasted energies and enthusiasms of my so far friendless adult life mattered not quite so much to me. I found Italy both beautiful and vulgar, and amidst these two extremes felt less hunted and alone. It is a cliché to say that in Italy the closeness of family life is important, but this is what I found reassuring. Families eat together, sleep together, and, out of necessity, caring becomes inevitable. I was slowly seeing the splendour and loveliness of poverty.

At his block of flats – there were twelve flats in all – we stayed below on the grass for a few minutes sharing a cigarette, passing it between us until I became light-headed. Sergio told me there was a special weed inside whose drug relieved monotony. I had not told him I was a doctor, these ordinary details of our lives being less important than they might otherwise have been, but did so now. Nor had we spoken much of politics. Sergio had a great capacity, as do many people with natural wisdom, to make the power-broking shenanigans of politicians appear mundane, as if a larger philosophy existed which would slowly, but more accurately, inform the world and effect its changes.

'Today, I have a letter,' he said, 'from America.' He brought an envelope from his pocket and gave it to me. 'It is from my wife.'

I read the contents imploring him to remain in Italy and looked at the cheque for $100,000 made out in his name.

'Were you planning to go to New Orleans?' I asked, relieved by what I had just read.

'It was our idea I do that when I was freed,' he said like one who is tired of the mediocre.

The city about me swung to the left, to the right, to the left again. I focused my eyes upon a church tower and the descending sun reflecting from the bell inside.

'America is an intelligent country, Signor Hinton. All I want to do is learn.'

It was clear to me that he knew he would never travel there. We went up to his mother's apartment and sat on the balcony amidst the infant Patrizio's newly washed clothes. The cool of evening was almost a chill, but we stayed where we were. As the effects of the cigarette decreased, the coarseness and truth of Sergio's situation became clearer in my mind. We had not spoken for some little time when Sergio picked up the cheque and ripped it in half, throwing the two pieces, as if they were as unimportant as confetti, over the balcony. Without saying a word I went below and recovered both halves, for I knew evidence would be needed for a second cheque to be sought from New Orleans. Sergio was standing above me.

'I will take fifty thousand pounds from you and not a penny less,' he shouted. 'I want nothing more to do with my wife.'

'I don't know if Mrs Treffgarne will pay that much,' I shouted.

'She will have to, Signor Hinton.'

I placed the remains of Stella's cheque in my pocket. Sergio's mother arrived on the balcony, wondering at the commotion.

'All right,' I called. 'I will see what I can do.'

We ate a meal, after which I left and did not see Sergio for three days. Instead I travelled by railway into the Tuscan countryside, waiting all the while for a reply to the telegraph I had sent to Mrs Treffgarne in London. It was like journeying into the Middle Ages, with oxen ploughing the fields and sheep being milked on open hillsides. I walked from the various station platforms with a small pack on my back, taking circular routes along muddy, uneven tracks, only diverting my course when a hill appeared too challenging. I hoped the rewards of the view would negate the risks of trespass. I was not often disappointed, for the Tuscan countryside, with its forest, vineyards and olive groves, is amongst the most beautiful in the world, second only, I think, to Lancaster County in Pennsylvania where John Bell lives. Both are tranquil places which remind one of the insignificance of man, for landscape alone has this power to humble.

On the fourth day I met Sergio again, and we travelled together retracing my steps to a rise in the ground which had afforded the best view the day before. I wanted to show him the farmhouses looking like models. We ate the sandwiches I had brought and drank part of a flask of beer. It had been chilled in the hotel but had warmed against my back, so we replaced the stopper and left the flask in a stream to cool. A teenage girl was watching our every movement from behind a mud wall. I now knew Sergio so well we could enjoy being lonely together without any discomfort. His great strength was to know the pleasure of melancholy and allow it in others. Sergio talked little that afternoon, but I delighted in his friendship.

On the fifth day I went in a pony and trap to his mother's apartment as we had arranged. It took a little while for the door to be answered, and it was the boy Patrizio who eventually stood before me. He raised his arms aloft for me to pick him up, which I did. His mother was in tears. Sergio had gone. I never saw any of them again.

When Mrs Treffgarne's telegraph finally arrived from London agreeing to the fifty thousand pounds, it was completely superfluous.

5

In London I sat with Elizabeth Treffgarne in my drawing-room.

'I'm certain we'll hear nothing more from him,' I said, speaking of Sergio, whom she had come to Wimbledon to inquire about.

'Thank you, Daniel. I hope the sights of Italy were a reward for your pains.'

'I know it is a country I shall return to often,' I said.

'But you're going to be busy from now on, aren't you?'

It had been reported in that morning's newspaper that I had been selected as the prospective parliamentary candidate for the seat of Richmond in North Yorkshire.

'Yes, extremely busy,' I remarked. 'It's a safe seat but nothing must be taken for granted these days.'

I was twenty-six years old when my winning declaration was announced from Richmond Town Hall steps the following year, the year which began Ramsay MacDonald's second Labour government.

Harry wrote to congratulate me, doing his best to seem sincere, and Stella added a lengthy footnote about my new responsibilities, which I found hypocritical. I had told neither of them of my sojourn in Italy, despite my desire for any news of Sergio which I thought they might have.

John Bell also wrote from Pennsylvania, the first I had heard from him in almost a decade. It was clear he must still be in touch with Harry for this was the only way he could know of my election to Parliament and have my address. I had almost forgotten him, but his words on the paper brought the memories back. His letter, too, was admonishing in tone.

In every letter John has written to me over the years, and there have been many, he has talked at length about the Pennsylvanian landscape. He has never tired of it, as I have never tired of his descriptions. It is there in his first letter. He describes the rolling countryside, the small seventy-acre farms, the crops which are grown for family subsistence and community sharing, the hayfields worked by hand, the rivers and streams harnessed by age-old waterwheels for their limited power, the children feeding the hogs at dawn, the barn-raising where a whole community joins together to build a whole barn in one day, the covered bridges, the women quilting, the family cemeteries without walls, the Sunday rides in a horse and buggy to a neighbouring farm for the long religious service on God's rest day; but, above all, he describes the quality of the light which he says is clear and harsh, yet forgiving. Always, too, in John's letters is the word forgiveness, for he says landscape alone has this power of amnesty. It is God's gift we be humbled by beauty, and judge ourselves first before we judge others.

John had left New Orleans in 1925 with $50 in his pocket, a present from Stella. He later repaid the amount – John's punctiliousness is sometimes alarming – but, having no money of his own and with a desire to see William Penn's Quaker State, he had had no choice but to accept her generosity. In Lancaster County he happened upon the latterday followers of Jacob Ammann, an Anabaptist group who had suffered martyrdom for their deviation from the established Lutheran church in the seventeenth century, and who fled their homelands in German-speaking Europe a century later to settle in Penn's woods, or Pennsylvania, where their redemptive understanding and observance of the bible was allowed to continue in peace. Here John saw a church community without a church, for the sect believed in worshipping in each other's homes. He saw a farming community whose members practised simple, austere living; a life still shaped by the faith and struggle of their European past, and little changed in over two hundred years. He saw people highly sensitive to each other's needs, who would migrate to distant lands rather than take up arms or defend themselves. He saw a pacifist group whose belief in the family of God was truly reflected in the way they lived.

What follows is John's account of his journey from New Orleans written for his youngest grandson, then nine years old, a copy of which I begged from him the last time I visited his farm. As in all John's writing it takes the form of a letter, so that it will not seem artistic or decorative, but rather informative and practical which is the Amish way with everything. For John is an Amishman and must abide by the rules. The 'letter' was written as recently as 1985.

Dear Benj,

I am writing to say thank you for the beautiful picnic yesterday afternoon. Your mother told me it was your idea to give me such a treat on my birthday, although I secretly think you enjoyed it too. When you fished the roach my day was complete because your face was such a picture of loveliness.

Whilst you were busy in the stream I talked with your mother. She put an idea into my head which I had never thought of before. As you know, Benj, I was not born into our faith but arrived here in the dim and distant past in 1925, exactly sixty years ago. It took me a long time before I learnt to speak German and could understand the language we use every day in our homes. I only spoke English, the language you have to learn at school. It is important we read and write English because occasionally one of us must go to the bank, or order something from a store which might require our signature, or, when we are older, write to a friend whom we have not seen for a while. All these things are difficult if we have not tried at school and learnt to write our name. When the milk lorry comes to the farm, how will you fill in the man's simple form if you cannot read the questions? At an auction, how will you bid for a horse if you do not know what is being said by the English auctioneer? When a visitor asks you the way, how will you understand him?

Benj, I had these same problems in reverse and know how difficult it is. I nearly gave up many times, but was happy I persevered. In language we must learn to say what we mean and write a little; in arithmetic we must learn accuracy and not to cheat; in health we must learn cleanliness and thrift. Are you listening, Benj? Or are you still hiding with your guinea-pigs? In history we learn humanity; in geography we broaden our understanding of the world; and in the playground we must be honest, respectful and humble.

It has been at your mother's suggestion that I have penned these opening words in order to try and help you. But she also thought if I told you a little of my journey from New Orleans you might know how awkward I once felt.

I don't expect you to have heard of New Orleans because it is a city many miles from here. I was a teacher there for a while in a one-roomed classroom very similar to your own. Our schoolrooms are safe on dry land in the corner of a field, whereas the classroom in New Orleans was on stilts above a river and very rickety.

Benj, I can hear you ask: 'Did the children leave their muddy, outer shoes on the school porch as we do?'

Me: 'No, Benj, they didn't because the black children didn't have shoes.'

And you say: 'We sometimes go without shoes in summer.'

And I reply: 'This is because shoes are precious, and we must only wear them when they are necessary.'

A young man named Daniel came to the school one day. I thought he had more goodness about him than he himself apprehended. That afternoon the schoolroom toppled over, and Daniel thought himself to blame when it was not his fault. It is always better to accept the blame ourselves than to accuse another. He didn't realize how much his response had made me think about my own life.

Benj, you ask me: 'What happened to Daniel?'

And I say: 'Much later because of his fear of loneliness, he became a not very kind person when he was a politician (ask your teacher, Benj, what that word means, she may or may not know). And much later still, after the death of a mutual friend called Harry, we got to know one another properly, and I was able to thank him.'

I left the city on foot. At the end of my first day my feet were aching because I wasn't used to such arduous exercise. The shoes I'd bought with borrowed money were pinching my feet so badly I thought about throwing them away.

Benj, you're an impulsive child, and I hear you rebuke: 'Throw them away. We never throw anything away, Grandpa. I have nothing new because it's all passed down.'

The next morning I put them back on. Walking day after day is a lonely pursuit and I began to look for people to talk to. When I could find no one, I talked with God and He was my companion. God often makes us uncomfortable by telling us things we would rather not hear. He knows we are not perfect, and on my journey He talked more and more about the evil nature of men. Another friend, I wasn't sure about her nature at all, had given me $50, and I wondered about putting the money beneath a stone, because I felt so uneasy about taking what was not mine.

I gave the $50 to a woman with a very ill child. We are careful about taking medication from the outside world, but she bought a mixture for his cough. I think this satisfied God because He ceased talking to me about wealth in the form of money and instead talked about riches in the form of man's complex thoughts, both good and bad.

Benj, I hear you ask me: 'What did God teach you on your journey, Grandpa?'

And I reply: 'The Lord taught me that man cares more for his neighbour in his imagination than he does in reality.'

And you, if you were a little older might question: 'When you walk across the fields today, are you still pondering man's self-delusion?'

And I would answer: 'Wherever we go we journey for God and must not alter course just because it might be easier for us to do so.'

The other day I saw your elder brother Noah working with our family's horses around the farm. It's a sight I've tried not to take for granted. Noah has learnt well from your father, and the horses' pace was your brother's pace, and the two were the same. Speed and modern technology do not bring enlightenment. They push man upon his selfish self in fuelling his desire for equality of possession.

Benj, you ask me innocently: 'Why is this bad, Grandpa?'

Me: 'Because self-pity is the result. Self-pity from those that have because they want more, self-pity from those that have nothing because they have none.'

So, Benj, as I walked from the city my pace became slower. I put greater effort into trying to understand my surroundings. I'd given away my money, so where I could I took odd jobs. I cut tobacco. I picked strawberries and trimmed cauliflowers. I harvested sugarcane until my fingers were numb. I bagged wheat.

At one point in my travels I came across a woman with five children. Hers was a poor farm; her life as harsh as I'd ever witnessed. Dear Benj, I cannot spare you this detail: her husband had been killed in a local feud. The drainage ditch he'd cut from the river crossed another's farm, and this farmer had closed it off so that their soil was like sand. The hens picked what they could from it, but it was hardly enough even for them. The husband pleaded with the farmer, but the farmer would hear nothing of his cries and instead demanded money for the river water, which the family did not have. One night the husband tried to break down the barrier but the farmer heard him, and in the fight which resulted the husband lost his life. The woman's living was now so mean I was filled with pity for them all and ate at her table only with reluctance.

You: 'What food did she have?'

Me: 'Corn and a few oats.'

I thought if the farmer could see her children it would make a difference, so I took them with me, but the farmer saw what he knew already and offered the family a trifling sum of money for their barren land. I begged her to accept. Unfortunately, she would not.

Benj, you might ask: 'Why, Grandpa, wouldn't she take the money and move?'

And if you did, I would reply: 'It wasn't pride which kept her there until death, because the starving cannot afford pride: it was territory. Every conflict in this world is at heart about territory and the sooner we learn a territory is not ours, but given us on short tenure by God, the quicker all strife will be ended.'

Benjamin, this is our view of the world. It is why we'll move to other lands rather than answer back. So you see, although I didn't realize it at the time, my journey was an Amish journey.

But you persist: 'Grandfather, what did you do to help this poor woman and her children?'

It's a fair question and one I still puzzle over because God didn't have an easy answer for me. I asked the Lord to divert the path of the river so they all might share its plenty. I went to the farmer. I returned to the mother. I went back to the farmer again. But no one listened, including God. In the end the only course open to me was to face my own death by doing what the husband had done. I took a spade but on the journey to the blockage cowardice came upon me. I sat down in the dust and was weak.

Benj, you admonish: 'So you did not help this family?'

I say: 'The Lord spoke to me at last and explained my weakness by telling me that only in man's imagination is he strong, and that it is self-deluding arrogance which allows him to believe in his own power. When he is truly tested man is found wanting and he must sooner or later accept the fate of his own fallibility in order to be truly human. When man is humbled he knows forgiveness.'

I comforted the woman and her five children until they were all dead, burying them one by one in an unwalled cemetery I created in what had been the farm garden when the land was fertile. Without knowing it I had made an Amish cemetery, very like our own.

Benj, you are a lively child and inquire: 'Did the farmer know forgiveness?'

And I reply: 'No, I don't think he did.'

And you, if you had worldly experience might then ask: 'Is this why you believe in the evilness of men, Grandpa?'

And I would answer: 'Yes, it is.'

But without that worldly experience, you say simply: 'What has this got to do with reading, writing, and arithmetic?'

And I tell you: 'If only the farmer had known how much there is to learn in life, he would never have been so brutal.'

You ask me: 'Why, Grandfather?'

I say: 'Because learning is humility.'

You: 'Does this begin at school?'

Me: 'It is relevant at school, as it is relevant everywhere, but it is most important in life amongst your family. It is no good you hiding with your guinea-pigs when a problem to

99

be solved doesn't suit you. We must all face our weaknesses and learn to be humble.'

You: 'The farmer wasn't humble, was he?'

Me: 'The Lord doesn't judge our imperfections, he judges our honesty in trying to overcome them.'

And you ask: 'Didn't the farmer overcome his?'

And I answer: 'No, he did not.'

And you, losing some of your innocence, question: 'Was the farmer evil, Grandpa?'

And I, almost crying because I love your innocence, reply: 'Yes, he was. We all must guard against evil for it is in us all. The farmer was not unique but sinful like all mankind.'

And you want to know: 'Would clearing the blockage have been sinful, Grandfather?'

And I, in full knowledge of the consequences of this lack of action, say: 'Yes, it would.'

You: 'Is this because Jesus tells us we must always turn the other cheek?'

And I don't reply because the asking of the question has shown you know the answer and have learnt something.

I walked away from the cemetery. My heart was shrivelled as the earth. God was not being easy with me, but I was beginning to understand what I must do. I let Him show me the road and discarded my maps (maps are items we don't have, they are as informative of a route system in the countryside as a label is of the contents of a jam jar) and gave away my shoes because I didn't want to be superior to the other hobos travelling the country. I picked cabbages. I cut turnips. I joined a family moving their cattle north. I walked on.

When I saw the Amish landscape I knew I had found home. I saw the white farms with the people rising at dawn to work in the fields. I saw simplicity in their labour and Godliness. I saw how their clothes reflected this way of life with their lack of adornment. I saw houses without drapes, because drapes are not required when you live by the sun, but merely improve the look of a room, which isn't necessary. I saw buggies moving from farm to farm and boys working with their fathers, girls with their mothers. I saw you, Benj, although it wasn't you but a boy very similar, honouring his family. I saw how one day I might have a grandchild like him, and he in turn a grandchild and so on. I saw steadfastness in a people who would shun the technological world and still live by the Ten Commandments. I saw, in one thousand years' time, another boy named Benjamin who would understand his life because he knew God's teaching and had learnt the old lessons well.

Benj, you say: 'I see, Grandfather.'

I ask: 'Do you?'

You say slightly more quizzically: 'I'll still need to go to my guinea-pigs to look after them, but I won't hide any more.'

Now I must write of your brother Levi. Levi is at the heart of my letter.

But you take my hand and say: 'Why don't we walk across the fields together, Grandpa, because I know what you want to talk about. Walking might be very pleasant for us both.'

So we do and my letter becomes a dialogue set in the Amish landscape.

Me: 'Your brother Levi is seventeen and has his first buggy bought for him by his parents. You will receive a buggy when you are his age, Benj, because that is our custom. But your brother has bought a Hi-Fi system for his. He travels down our country roads with pop music playing. The poor horse in front must wonder what is happening, as do we all. It greatly troubles me.'

You: 'It isn't a Hi-Fi system, Grandpa, it's a tape recorder. It uses batteries and cassettes. He plays music by Billy Joel.'

Me: 'So he said when I asked him about it. We do know how hard it is to be a teenager in this modern world, Benj, and how difficult it is not to be influenced by worldly desire. Whilst we will be tolerant of him until he is an adult, baptized member of our faith, we must also let him know we don't approve. Which is what I did. If we didn't admonish him we'd be letting him down, wouldn't we?'

You: 'Why don't you come to the point, Grandpa. Is it because you've seen me listening to Levi's tapes?'

Me: 'I've also witnessed you eyeing his English clothes.

101

They are away from the farm hidden in a gully, aren't they?'

You: 'Yes, Grandfather. He has buttons on his shirt, which is forbidden, and a zip-fastener on his pants. He even takes his hat off when he goes out and wears his hair open to the sky.'

Me: 'When a teenager does this, Benj, even if it is your brother, it's wrong to be interested. Tell him you have more important things to be getting on with. Tell him you have your work about the farm. Tell him it is a phase he is going through like a worldly teenager, but a phase he will overcome. Remind him of his love for his parents, who must be obeyed in all matters. Inform him that independence from God is wrong. Benj, speak of your own weaknesses to him. And I will speak to him of mine.'

Your loving grandfather,

John adds his signature in Biro, so even he is changing a little with the times. The Amish take a moral position on change, often debating a new development for decades, and therefore progress more carefully than the rest of the world, which regards them as an island of so called 'old-fashionedness'. But it is wrong to think of them as a stagnating society. At the moment their view seems to be that nothing should be taken from the outside world which they themselves cannot physically bring to their farm. But even this leads to many incongruities. Thus, they are allowed bottled gas but not electricity, although electric pylons cross their land. By federal law their buggies must have lights for night-time travel so they transport batteries, but they cannot have an electric torch in the home. By recent changes in state law their cows must now be machine milked so they have installed diesel-electric generators, but again this power must not be taken elsewhere. Consequently, bottled gas runs the fridge and the summer cooker. In winter cooking is done on a wood-burning stove, which also heats the house, doors being left ajar for this purpose. The Amish have three sets of clothes, one for wearing, one for washing, and a Sunday best. The washing is done by hand. There are those Amish who will sit in the evenings in what little spare time they have trying to invent a washing machine which will work by gas, for despite the severity of their lives they are a people not without humour or

102

wryness. I know John's wife Rachel would secretly love a washing machine.

I found my seat in Parliament, and the day to day grind of a political career began. My decade in the House belonged to Germany and her new Chancellor, Hitler's ever-strengthening dictatorship and rearmament programme unfolding around me amidst a welter of constituency meetings and late night debates at which I did my best to be noticed. I spent long hours with Sir Christopher writing my speeches, polishing them vocally until they lacked spontaneity: I was never an orator. This would matter less today where the public meeting has been overtaken by the television interview but then it was pivotal to high office, so I accepted lessons from an actor I met at a Palace garden party. He took me to an empty theatre, placed me on the stage, seated himself in the rear stalls and attempted to teach me breath control. But the truth was that my abilities and passions lay elsewhere, and I could never feed Sir Christopher's excitement into my own voice. Sir Christopher would become dogmatic and paranoid when his words in my mouth were drowned by the rantings of my opponents, who had quickly learned that a joke or savage aside could throw me completely off course, so much so that I often had to sit down in mid-sentence. When Sir Christopher returned to Cambridge, it became an uneasy, unworkable alliance; whenever I saw him I understood the better why his wife's escape route had been her eccentric dreams of the circus, for Christopher pushed everyone around him to their outer limits and one's only hope of sanity was to elope into a folly even more extreme than Sir Christopher himself; he became larger than life, a grotesque caricature that grew progessively manic the more I was ridiculed. Even amongst his old academic circle in Cambridge he ceased to have friends or influence, and by the time he decided to leave for America he had dwindled into a minor figure whose departure provoked joy in only a few hearts because only a few even knew he had emigrated.

In the Parliamentary summer recess of 1936 Harry returned to England with his wife. They had planned a holiday in Tuscany but instead I persuaded them to travel with me to Yorkshire, where I had constituency business to attend to. This we did after three weeks in London. Elizabeth Treffgarne had died two months earlier and there was still much for Harry to sort through. I had given this to Harry as the reason they should stay in England, but the truth was that I did not want them in Florence at any cost. I had attended Elizabeth Treffgarne's funeral, and Harry appeared genuinely interested to hear the details of who had been present, the nature of the service and even which hymns had been sung. Stella seemed a bystander to all this; she would take herself off to the royal parks whilst her husband dealt with the lawyers. The reading of the will left Harry a millionaire, money he had no need of, while I, to my great surprise, was bequeathed £50,000, making me at last a wealthy man. I thought of Sergio, for it was the very sum that Mrs Treffgarne had telegraphed her acceptance of from London to Florence. The money rightfully belonged to him. I had met Elizabeth Treffgarne only infrequently during the intervening years but she had never once hinted at such generosity. It was only after Harry's death some years later that I learned the truth: the money had been Harry's, but he had passed it to me through his deceased mother's solicitors in this mendacious but kind way. He must have known my pride would never have allowed me to accept such a fortune from him.

We travelled to Yorkshire by train, and I worried a good deal of the journey whether there would be room for the four of us in my small house. Harry and Stella had with them their five-year-old daughter, who I thought the most beautiful child I had ever seen, with Stella's auburn hair and a cheerfulness which made one immediately acquiesce to her every desire. In the carriage she sat next to her mother, I opposite, and we played the 'smile at one another game' as the slow train stop-started through the Shire counties. The little girl looked away whenever her coquettish behaviour became too obvious and a little of her mystery vanished. She reminded me of Harry at school. At Doncaster she seated herself beside me, touching my knee occasionally with her small fingers and giggling, over-calculating, wondering which next trick might hold my attention. I was flattered but, not having children of my own, it never occurred to me then that what she was doing could be flirtatious.

'Please stop that now, Jenni,' her father said.

'Why, Daddy?' she asked innocently in her American brogue.

'Because I'm sure Uncle Daniel wants to sit peacefully for a few minutes.'

Jenni looked up at me for confirmation of this statement or preferably denial. The lineaments of her face prompted for a moment a memory of the sneak-thief who had stolen my billfold in New Orleans. 'I'm quite happy,' I said to her father, interrupting my reverie, 'Jenni doesn't bother me in the least.'

'May I show you something, Uncle Daniel?' she asked.

'Of course, Jenni, show me anything you wish.'

Jenni stepped from the seat and took a rag-doll from her mother's carpetbag.

'But the doll has no eyes,' I said after she had placed the toy on my lap.

'She's an Amish doll, Uncle Daniel.'

When I looked again I saw the doll had no mouth or nose either but the face was completely blank, with the head bonneted in black and, below, a simple turquoise dress and two tiny shoe-less feet.

'She has no face at all,' Jenni remarked as if this were quite usual.

'The Amish believe it a graven image to reproduce the likeness of a human being,' Harry told me. 'They follow the Commandment in Exodus twenty, verse four: "Thou shalt not make unto thee any graven image, or any likeness of any thing that is in heaven above, or that is in the earth beneath, or that is in the water under the earth".'

'Who gave her the doll?' I asked.

'John.'

'Uncle John gave her to me, Daddy.'

'That's what I was telling your new uncle,' he replied.

We had talked briefly of John in London but not in any detail, and I had neglected to mention the letter he had written when I had first entered Parliament admonishing me to be upright in my dealings.

'We went to John's christening, didn't we, Jenni,' Harry reminded her. 'In Pennsylvania. We saw him baptized. Don't you remember?'

'Yes.'

'Then we walked across the fields with him.'

'I had a letter from John,' I observed cautiously to Harry. We were two strangers rediscovering one another. 'He wrote some while ago. I had never heard of the Amish until then. I know very little about them.'

'John is the happiest I've seen him, Daniel.'

'Who are they?' I asked. 'What do they believe?'

'I could not possibly give you a complete answer, but they believe in setting an example by living rather than in religious conversion. In worldly terms they are not pleasure-conscious, so selfishness is largely avoided. It's a physical world of work and very unintellectual. Individual thought is not encouraged. Instead of asking how or why, they observe the testaments of the bible.'

'Wasn't John always happy?' I asked.

'And you know why, Daniel?'

'No,' I said.

'Because John always takes action. He doesn't brood, he doesn't weep. If something is wrong, he doesn't blame another but seeks to improve the situation. John learnt forgiveness very early in his life.'

Stella shifted in her seat; she had spoken little since our departure from King's Cross. It had not been made clear to me from the conversation whether she, too, had been at John's baptism. I perceived a tension between them on the subject.

'I admire John tremendously,' Harry continued. 'Forgiveness is something I'm still trying to learn.'

'Vis-à-vis your mother, Harry?'

'Yes, Daniel. And my father. They're both dead now, so much between us will forever remain unfinished.'

Once again, despite the passage of years, we had slipped easily into the Treffgarne falsehood.

Jenni fidgeted. Stella lifted the little girl onto her lap where they appeared incongruous together. I still had the Amish rag-doll sitting across my knee.

'One must find a way of hating the sin whilst loving the sinner,' Harry remarked almost casually. 'To forgive one must be actively involved. It is something you do and not a concept. Forgiveness is a form of love.'

'Did you ever write to your mother?' I asked, his relaxed behaviour disarming or intimidating me, I was not quite sure which. 'She so wanted a letter from you.'

'No, Daniel, to my shame I didn't. The first step towards

forgiving is to accept one's past. I couldn't do that whilst I was in New Orleans. It's only now I'm home I can see forgiveness should have been possible. It's the cleverest thing to do. I wish I had respected my mind.'

Stella whispered into Jenni's ear, pointing out to her the particularities of the English countryside, which was water-logged by the rain of the last few weeks. I saw a heron and placed my finger on the glass, showing them. Harry smiled, his face aged since I had last seen him but still boyish in his delight at being home. Old habits die hard and I looked again through the window, adjusting my focus to watch the family's reflection. I knew, as Harry ran his palm absent-mindedly along the creases of his suit, that he had at last reached the decisions which would bring him to adulthood. He had spoken of shame: to my shame, I felt all the old jealousies bubbling to the surface inside me. I knew these feelings to be wrong, that they were even incredible in a man thirty-three years old, but could do nothing to halt the tide of resentment. When Stella shifted her gaze from the window, I lowered my face towards my knees as if interested in the rag-doll.

'What's the matter, Daniel?' she asked. 'You're crying.'

'I don't know,' I replied half lying, half speaking the truth. 'It must be seeing you all again after so long. And Jenni. I never imagined you all as a family. A family is something I would like myself. That's all it is.'

'Don't make my doll wet, will you,' Jenni said. 'She doesn't like tears.'

'Is John married?' I asked, surprised myself by the question.

'He was baptized to be married,' Harry explained. 'The Amish have accepted him. He's to marry an Amish girl. They marry in the autumn when there's time and less work to be done about the farm, so next autumn it will be. John isn't perfect, Daniel. None of us is. The difference is, we know it and you don't. You still expect perfection from yourself when you're one of the least perfect people I know. It leads to cruelty; cruelty you inflict upon yourself and upon others.'

Harry had lost none of his ability to sting. I looked up, my eyes dry with anger.

'I should have learnt not to expect sympathy from you,' I said rather too roughly.

'I'll give you sympathy when you deserve it.' It was a reply he should have given me fifteen years earlier. 'All of us can be jealous. All of us can be guilty,' he continued. 'Those emotions are easy. It's changing and growing which is more difficult. Your problem, Daniel, is you don't know how good – purely good – you are. John told me that. He thought you had great capacity for goodness but would never realize it until you learnt there was evil in the world. He told me you were headed for evil because you didn't know it existed. Ignorance, I think, is the worst sin. Anyone with intelligence knows that power is something we cannot achieve ourselves, but must have it discerned in us by others. I discern none in you, yet I see a figure who expects it. Parliament has ruined you.'

'That is cruel, Harry,' Stella said.

'No, it's not. I'm speaking to Daniel with affection.'

'What evil have I committed?' I asked. 'What wrong have I done?'

'I knew Sir Christopher Salisbury,' he said quietly, matter-of-factly. 'I remember him coming to the house. He used my father as he uses everybody. He's psychotic. Clinically psychotic. I hear he's gone to America?'

'Yes,' I answered, picking up Harry's unemotional tone.

'My father graced him with vast amounts of money, which he used to buy his way into political office. They had this dream of a Utopia. It was a land where every man was to be rewarded according to his ability; a place where talent would win out; a golden Erewhon where the intelligent would receive the fruits of the earth because they contributed most towards it. And there might be some truth here, except that many people do not have the talent to contribute in that way. It doesn't make what they can do any less worthwhile. In fact, the only ability that Sir Christopher and my father were interested in was the ability to make money; the talent to create wealth. It was simply about power. Anyone whose dream leads them to dogmatism should never be trusted because they ignore the fact that man is essentially weak, and weakness is a good thing and should not be abused. Evil, Daniel, is the abuse of weakness by the privileged and by those who should know better. You are weak, which is why I love you, Daniel. Why won't you just accept that?'

'I suppose it's envy,' I said after thinking for a moment.

'Don't you see, at school you taught me that strength was not necessarily laudable.' His face was flushed with a passion I had not witnessed in him since those days. 'I remember the night you slipped out of your pyjamas,' he went on. 'It isn't possible to be more defenceless than you were that night. Please don't be ashamed. Please don't hide. Daniel, I was envious of you. I thought you were so honest and different.'

'I thought I was peculiar.'

'No. That's what Sir Christopher wants, he wants everybody to be the same. It's totalitarian – it whips those who are odd or strange, different or eccentric. Yet those qualities are the richness of people. You went to Europe with him, didn't you?'

I bowed my head, expecting him at any moment to mention Florence. To all appearances, he knew as much of my recent history as I did myself, although I had mentioned none of it in my letters to New Orleans.

'Haven't you been to Germany, Daniel?'

'Yes, I have. Well, I followed Sir Christopher there, more's the point. It was a charade. Sir Christopher loves cloak and dagger. It was all a game.' I looked up, relieved to be telling the truth but still making the movement appear as insignificant as possible. I did not want to let him in on the full extent of my guilt. 'I think he truly believed Herr Hitler would see him,' I went on. 'He'd had a conference, some years before, with Benito Mussolini in Florence, and he thought his name would be known. We marched up to the Reichstag and the guards arrested him. It was a farce. It was in Berlin that he finally went round the bend. I had to hush it all up with our consular officials, whilst Sir Christopher ranted and raved in a prison cell about how beautiful the world would be if he could be in charge. Put like this, it's absurd. But somehow a situation is not so absurd when you're in the middle of it. I went along with him to a large degree because it happened in stages, each imperceptible in its way. I've no real excuse – except to say, Sir Christopher has proved himself to be harmless just as, I think, Herr Hitler will in time. These people are mad, but with great ability to disguise their mania and to draw people along with them. The human being will always fall for a Utopian dream, Harry, because he's basically good and wishes to believe the world can reflect that goodness and be a happy place to live. In many ways your friend John is right, I don't believe in evil. Perhaps I will when I see it for myself. Until then, my world is what I experience.'

'May I have my doll back now?' Jenni asked.

I gave the rag-doll to her and she transferred herself to her father's lap, where she stayed for the last few minutes of our journey, until we alighted from the Pullman carriage beneath the glass domes of Stockton station. Here on one of the lesser-used platforms, we showed Jenni George Stephenson's 'Rocket' which had run in 1821 at the then remarkable speed of 35 m.p.h. on the first railway to Darlington. For a small donation towards the footplatemen's charity, young children were permitted to clamber on board. Jenni did so with obvious pleasure. In this way, she unwittingly helped to disperse the hypercriticism between her father and myself.

Once in Richmond, we fitted into my small house as best we could. Harry bathed Jenni and read her a bedtime story, whilst Stella helped me prepare supper in the kitchen. She was chopping endive as garnish for a tomato salad, but not being used to the activity her progress was meticulous but slow.

'Daniel, I didn't say much in the train this afternoon,' she said quietly after several moments of silence, as if she required this tranquillity before she could begin, 'but I can't let your conversation pass without notice. I'm sorry Harry was so harsh. He's more upset about his mother's death than he'll ever tell you. He's been going through one of his darker periods.'

'Please don't worry, Stella. I should be used to it by now.'

I was preparing the pork-fillet I had purchased earlier at the butcher's, making ready the Dijon mustard I intended to braise the meat in with melted butter.

'I'm not a political person, Daniel. I don't really understand notions or ideas.'

'Neither am I,' I said. 'I don't either. I think that's where I've gone wrong.'

'I'm only interested in people. People are fascinating and more complex than your discussion, they don't always behave to a set pattern. Harry certainly doesn't, which is why he belittles himself when he attacks. He means none of it.'

Stella appeared serene in the kitchen. She was as calm as I could ever remember her; the simple action of producing a meal creating detachment within her as it almost always did with me. There is equanimity and joy to be gained from the subtle layering of tastes.

'Does Harry often deal with Jenni?' I asked, finding a knife with which to peel and dice a half pound of mushrooms.

'Yes, usually. We had a nanny for a short while but Harry interfered too much. Nanny thought it very strange for a man, but Harry prefers it this way. We've lived a simple life. The school has grown, but that's about all. I never considered I would spend nearly ten years doing so little. Is this chicory for the salad?'

'No, I bought that for lunch tomorrow.'

'You're quite domestic, Daniel. I never realized.'

'Put the endive with the tomato but don't toss it. It looks better if it's just left. I'll show you how to make a lemon dressing.'

Stella hovered beside me, whilst I stirred the pork into a heavy metal skillet I had purchased in France a few summers before on a holiday alone in the Dordogne, where I walked the country-side much as I had done in Tuscany, taking in the breath-taking views, and in the evenings sitting with a glass of beer or wine in a pavement café where I shunned company, preferring instead my own solitude. I had observed the French aloofness bordering on arrogance and rather admired them for this characteristic.

'There's some wine-vinegar in the cupboard, Stella, and olive oil.'

'Harry's much better with Jenni than I am,' she said, dancing across the floor, taking the bottles from their appointed shelves. 'It's very neat in here. You are neat. I lose my temper with her. Isn't that a terrible admission?'

'Why? Perhaps parenthood is a skill one learns?'

'It was Harry who wanted a child, Daniel. I'd come to the con-clusion I could never conceive.'

'You'll need a lemon from the pantry; a garlic clove; salt and pepper.'

'Harry was not my first lover as you must be aware,' she remarked casually, seemingly unaware of the effect of her words.

'I always think about that first boat trip with great fondness. I must have been so naive?'

'Yes you were. And I adored you for it. I love the excitement of innocence; it's just that I can't find any in Jenni. I don't know why. It's maybe because she's my own flesh and blood. Or is it because she's female and I can already see what she's up to?' She opened the door and stepped down the single step into my pantry without waiting for a reply. 'Daniel,' she called from inside, 'I've found a lemon – what does garlic look like?'

'There should be a string above your head, hanging from a nail.'

I used her absence to take a break from the stove, pouring myself a glass of cold water from the tap; the house was newly plumbed into the mains supply and water on tap was still a novel experience. I could hear Jenni upstairs, splashing in the bathroom.

I thought it possible Stella was flirting with me, but could not be sure. I was certain of little these days, having lost the simple, intuitive reasoning I had possessed as a child. In my desire to prove my intelligence, I often misread an atmosphere, making the shades of difference more complex than was the case.

'You'd be a good father,' Stella pronounced, returning with far too much garlic, 'you're a good listener. Parents need the ability to listen. You're a sponge for other people's thoughts and emotions, aren't you?'

'Perhaps. Sometimes, Stella.'

'Without ever giving rip to your own. Harry's the same. It's very English. I'm the opposite, I let mine out, which is why I'm not a good mother. Or Harry's convincing me I'm not. Ours is not a good marriage, Daniel. I'm too temperamental. What must I do with this garlic?'

'You've too much to begin with. One clove is sufficient for a salad dressing.'

I placed my glass upside down on the draining-board, noticing the dust that had come from the house being unoccupied for several weeks. When I looked at the pork-fillet it was steaming, bleeding a little, almost ready for the mushrooms and black pepper.

'Yes, I thought that would shock you,' she said. 'The English are always appalled by the truth. I'm peeling this garlic, I hope that's right? Don't go quiet on me, Daniel.'

'I didn't realize.'

'Why not?'

'I suppose I wished to believe you were happy together.'

'Oh, we are in our way. It isn't a marriage though.'

I tossed in the mushrooms, helping to expel the final juices from the meat, and turned over the entire contents of the skillet with my spatula from Perigueux. Harry entered the kitchen, but deep in concentration I did not see or hear him.

'What does a marriage have which yours does not?' I asked.

'Someone who truly loves me, Daniel.'

'Jenni would like a goodnight kiss, Stella,' Harry said.

I turned and saw him, his sleeves rolled to his elbows from bathing the child, his fingers pink from the water. The moment was perpetual; had no transience.

'Was everything all right, Harry?' I remarked casually. 'The heating system's new. I hope Jenni's bath was warm enough?' The action of the spatula in my hand served to normalize my voice, so that it appeared I was hardly thinking.

'Yes, it was fine, thank you.'

'That garlic clove needs crushing,' I said to Stella as if Harry had not asked her to go upstairs and the status quo was to be maintained, 'then it should be added to the oil and vinegar with some lemon.'

'I'll do it,' Harry said. 'Do go to her, Stella, you know she won't settle until you do.'

'You'd better ask Daniel about this lemon dressing. I suspect I've been doing it all wrong.'

'I'll show Harry.'

Stella left the kitchen and I poured a quarter pint of double cream into the pork and mushrooms before it was necessary.

'The preparation of the salad is behind,' I said. 'Stella is so slow. The meat is nearly ready.'

'Is there an hors d'oeuvre?' he asked, cutting the ends off the clove of garlic.

'No, I thought we'd have this with a dessert. I'll do a soup for tomorrow. You'll need a garlic crush. It's in the drawer beside the sink.'

I stirred the cream and listened to Harry rummaging.

'I hope Jenni will be comfortable in that bed. It's a new one and I've not slept in it myself.'

'She'll be fine, Daniel, don't worry about us.'

'I hope you wouldn't have been more comfortable in an hotel?'

'No, this is much nicer and more homely.'

'It's costly having to have two homes,' I continued nonchalantly, still searching for a less-measured approach towards him, 'both here, and in Wimbledon. I'm still buying furniture. I could not have afforded all this on my own. Sir Christopher helped me financially, too. In a way, he bought me.'

'So my mother's small legacy will be of some help to you?'

'Yes, it will, enormous help. But small is not the right word: it's a fortune. I wish I could thank her.'

'She'll know in heaven what she's done, Daniel,' he said with the simplicity of a boy at Sunday school.

'I liked your mother. It isn't always fair to judge too harshly what we've seen when we were young. I wish I had known her better, Harry.'

He was crushing the garlic, revealing a dexterity far in excess of Stella's. His fingers were now white, as if cold, and his eyes were focused downwards in introspection upon the chopping-board. He raised his head briefly as I joined him at the table, and then resumed his activities after a smile of complicity. I mixed the oil, vinegar and lemon for the vinaigrette into an unsuitable pipkin, but it was the best vessel I had for the purpose.

'I expect you feel the same?'

'Yes, I do, very much so.'

'Harry,' I was finally able to say, 'it wasn't me who initiated the conversation you overheard just now.'

'I know it wasn't, Daniel. I've just told you not to worry about us, so please don't.'

As we worked together at the table, for these short moments prior to Stella's return, I knew that there was something tacit and understated between us, as there had been at school before the nightmare voyage to New Orleans had driven us apart; and I realized that our friendship had resumed. We both knew more about the other than either of us would ever need to articulate, and I could sense we would never again use this knowledge for advantage, or seek to manipulate by undervaluing the other's experience.

'Jenni loves the bed, Daniel,' Stella said, coming through the door. 'She still sleeps in a child's bed at home, doesn't she, Harry? She feels very adult tonight.'

We ate around the kitchen table, for I had yet to clear a space in my dining-room, which was inundated with papers. The pork was dry and overcooked, but tasted sweet on my tongue.

There were many incongruities and paradoxes about Stella, and every one of them, now I think back, has made a contribution to what little understanding I have of the world. She was first and foremost a free spirit, who, finally, refused to be tied to any one personality or doctrine, which might have made her selfish had she not always fallen for people of a like mind, Harry and Sergio included. She knew passion, she knew guilt, and both had kept her with Harry far longer than was wise for either of them.

Stella was of half-Italian parentage, a fact I learned that night after supper, when Harry and I sat on into the small hours, drinking cognac and gossiping. Her father had travelled penniless to the land of milk and honey, as had many, and the American dream had served him well. With the initiative of the hard-working pioneer he had made money in first one restaurant, and then another, and another, until his investments were sufficient to purchase land for a cotton plantation in the deep south, to which he moved from Chicago with the confidence in his own future which only Americans enjoy. Stella, an only child by a late marriage, inherited the fortune which allowed her to play the world, as few had the wealth or insight to do then. In one way, I see her as a figure of the twentieth century, for her innovativeness and desire for pleasure are quite representative of our age. But in my view, this will not be the century of space exploration, or the micro-chip computer, or even the cold war and the nuclear bomb – it will be the century in which many people found small kinds of freedom, realized how frightening these freedoms were and returned authority over their lives to those who loved power for its own sake, since this is always easier than accepting personal responsibility for one's actions. Stella once told me we no longer required politicians but were in desperate need of philosophers, and I believe her to be correct. Stella is not representative of our age in that she would never be controlled by fools. Whatever her failings, and there were many in her pleasure-seeking, she had considerable foresight and breadth of mind.

Stella had helped us to wash up – it had taken her fifteen minutes to get the burnt pork and cream off the rim of the skillet – and then gone up to bed. Throughout the hours that we were alone in my kitchen, I did not speak to Harry of Sergio. It pained me a good deal that I was unable to do so, for it felt as if I were cheating him of the one fact which, finally, would enable him to make a decision regarding his future with Stella; and her future, too, for

I half-suspected she was waiting for his permission to leave. At the same time, a contradictory feeling within me was extremely grateful for this cowardice because I knew it made me human.

We sat on until the bottle of cognac was almost finished, and the day beginning to be light. I suggested we go for a walk, which we did through the empty streets. I thought if we cut through the churchyard and walked the two miles to the petrol station where I had my car garaged for safekeeping, we could then drive back. Harry kept his hands in his trouser pockets, jiggling some coins, the sounds mingling with those of the sparrows on the roof guttering of the church.

'I'd like to have Jenni baptized,' he said. 'She's never been christened. If we did, would you be her godfather?'

I was tired and feeling sentimental. He spoke with such simplicity that a tear rolled across my cheek, which I managed to hide by finding a handkerchief and blowing my nose.

'Yes, I would,' I said.

'Stella joins in with most religious ceremonies for appearances' sake, but somehow we've never got round to Jenni.'

'Is Stella agnostic?'

'She's not bothered, so in that sense, yes.'

'What about you, Harry?'

He lifted the latch and we entered the church grounds by the cemetery gate.

'Jenni asked to be baptized when we saw John's christening in Pennsylvania,' he said. 'Jenni can be quite self-possessed. Stella wasn't there. It was a period we spent apart. Jenni and I stayed with John. I'm not answering your question, am I? I don't know a proper answer. I think Jenni should be christened, that's all, especially if we're going to stay in England.'

It was the first time he had hinted at such a possibility.

We strolled between the gravestones, half-searching for a polecat we had caught a glimpse of earlier, but mostly looking at the names and ages of people who had died.

'As you're aware, Daniel, I'm not an easy person to live with. I'm manic depressive in some ways. I wouldn't blame Stella, whatever she decides to do.'

On one of the older headstones was an inscription to a baby girl who had died aged five weeks. The death of a child is never easy, but this child's life had been long enough for her death to seem a punishment for the parents.

'Harry,' I said, 'I'm not sure it's Stella's decision. I suspect it's a decision she's waiting for you to make. Don't leave it until the only result can be frustration and anger.'

'What has she said to you?' he asked.

'Nothing. It's a guess, but I think an accurate one. Why keep her tied down if you are not certain?'

'I don't know what might be correct.'

'It seems to me you're answering your own question. Stella needs her liberty.'

We walked on across the sacred ground, the moisture in the grass darkening our leather shoes. I found a football which had obviously been lost by a group of children, and kicked it idly for a few paces before booting it across the low stone wall into the street. Here I hoped the boys might find it once they came out to play.

I felt pity for Harry, but dared not let him see my face, recalling his dislike of this emotion at school. The energy he had possessed then, which had always been capable of lifting him from his blackest moods, seemed to have dissipated in adulthood, so that I was left wondering where the vigour was to come from which would return his equilibrium to its balanced state. Doubts absorb energy, whilst decision-making creates it. The easy decisions of the child could not be made now, and he was being pushed lower than I had ever witnessed. His doubts fuelled my own. I prayed that my interpretations of Stella's character were correct. I quite literally prayed, looking at the bell tower of the church, for it seemed a bold move on my behalf to have spoken in the way that I had, and I worried I might be wrong. Indeed, as we walked from the cemetery into the street, passing the football, which I now saw was punctured, the more certain I became of my error.

'Harry,' I said, 'please don't listen to me. I'm hopeless.'

'No, you're not,' he replied, absent-mindedly kicking the mis-shapen football.

'I'm not even married. What right have I to make judgements?'

'Daniel, take responsibility for what you've said. You've spoken honestly, haven't you. It's up to me whether I take your advice, but advice must be fairly given. I don't mean this in the way it

117

will sound, but please don't push your insecurity onto me. I need your strength at the moment.'

I saw the polecat but Harry did not.

Only twelve hours earlier in the railway carriage, he had been accusing me of, and saying he admired, my weakness. As he kicked the football back amongst the gravestones, I thought my life, and the life of my best friend, were full of opposites and contradictions. The ball landed with a thud. Harry was the most human person I have ever known. I would sometimes like to believe I have been his second.

My home and constituency was in the Yorkshire Dales, a two-hour drive from the town where I had been born and brought up. The following day, I departed with Jenni in the car, the plan being to spend the afternoon with my parents, who, I knew, disappointedly longed for a grandchild of their own, so I was certain Jenni would bring them pleasure. A day together, away from me and the little girl, also gave Harry and Stella the space to talk, and they had both been enthusiastic when I had mooted the idea the previous evening. So, off I went with Jenni beside me in the passenger seat, first filling the Riley with petrol at the garage, where I talked briefly to the owner. He revered all forms of transport, hence the beautifully maintained condition of my own automobile, which was regularly left in his charge.

Jenni chatted about England and I answered her questions as patiently as I could. Occasionally, she talked about her mother and father, and the school in New Orleans which now had four classrooms, with a similar number of teachers, all of whom were black. Her mother had interviewed them, she said, at the house, and one of the maids had gone to college to become a teacher. One day, she went on to explain, it had rained so tempestuously all the glass had broken in the schoolroom windows. Her vocabulary made me smile, and I realized she had been told a protective untruth by her father, for Harry had already informed me of the problems they were having with the white population, who were jealous of the high educational standards at the school. He had said the scale, vindictiveness and hatred of the violence had frightened them all to the point where guards had had to be employed.

We drove in silence for a few minutes, Jenni with her face

pressed towards the window, studying the countryside. So composed did she seem in my presence that I remembered Harry saying what a self-possessed child she was. Her bearing and quiet confidence reminded me of Stella.

'Uncle Daniel, might we see another heron?' she asked intently, turning her face briefly towards my own.

I was so absorbed by her, was so busy thinking how neat, how unfidgety she appeared to be that I neglected to answer her question, until she brought me back to the present by sighing loudly and tapping the dashboard with her foot.

'I don't know, Jenni. There are many herons in England, so you might if you keep looking. We really need to pass a lake, but I don't think we shall on this journey.'

The passenger seat dwarfed her. She was obviously enjoying her day out, and it was giving me enormous contentment to see the ease with which she was accepting my company. I missed children. In fact, there were odd, crazy moments when I had to stop myself fantasizing that I was her father. I had never before been so close to a child, and this pretence of fatherhood was new to me.

After half an hour, we left the dales behind and I began, instead, to concentrate on the route we must take across the Tees valley. One direction would lead us through the centre of Middlesbrough, and the second, the way I most often drove because of its convenience, skirted the perimeter of the town in slightly circuitous fashion. I resolved, this time, to take the more interesting route, directly through Middlesbrough and to show Jenni the Transporter Bridge, a famous landmark of engineering, which I thought she might find amusing.

I had forgotten how poor the town was, with its back-to-back terraced housing and down-at-heel inhabitants, whose poverty and inadequate hygiene was shaming. The dust, from blast furnaces and steel rolling mills, fell everywhere, making cleanliness almost impossible. White bedsheets, hanging out to dry, quickly became rouge from the density of the iron oxides in the air. Children were perpetually dirty, and babies ill with respiratory problems.

I parked the Riley in a terrace close to the river, and Jenni let herself down from the car, holding up her hand for me to take when I joined her, as I had seen her do with her father whenever they walked together. Her fingers were so small within my own, like paper, and I comprehended for the first time, from the pleasure and warmth in her grip, how trusting a child has to be. I felt proud, and the malaise I had experienced at being childless was dissipated for a moment.

We set off, together, along the pavement.

'Are the people who live in this district poor, Uncle Daniel?' she asked without looking up at me.

'Yes, I think so.'

'Are they like the black girls and boys who go to school in New Orleans?'

'Some of them are, yes.'

A woman approached us from the opposite direction, pushing three toddlers in the one pram. One of its four wheels was a bicycle wheel without the tyre.

Once again, for some inextricable reason, I was reminded of my billfold and the piccaninny who had zigzagged across Jackson Square with me in pursuit.

'Oh, I see what you mean, Jenni,' I said, understanding her quizzical tone. 'These people are not black, no. They're white.'

'Why are white people poor?' she inquired innocently as if poverty were just a question of race.

'I don't know, Jenni,' I replied, any explanation being far too complex to embark upon with a child, even if I had had good reasons which I did not.

'It isn't fair, Uncle Daniel, is it?' she said, shrewdly and knowingly echoing her father.

'No, Jenni, it isn't fair. It hasn't been fair for a long time. We must all be made to look at poverty to remember how lucky we are. Memory is very good at creating a myth from something we imagine has vanished, when it has not. It happens as we get older and more comfortable.'

Jenni tugged at my coat sleeve, obviously bored by my portentousness. I thought of picking her up and carrying her, as I had done with the infant Patrizio in Florence on the day his brother Sergio had disappeared from their apartment, but she seemed content to skip along beside me now that, once again, she had my attention.

'I didn't know white people were poor,' she said.

'It's all a question of experience, Jenni. It's a question of what we observe with our eyes. It's very simple really.'

She freed her hand from my own, and ran ahead of me towards the metal gates of the iron foundry we were passing. There she stopped, her head small enough to fit through the bars of wrought iron which closed the entrance to the public.

Her temporary absence allowed me to remember Florence in greater detail: the girl who had accelerated beside the pony and trap until I had given her a coin; the quasi-bartering system of the men on the streets; the gamin-like children; the family flogging a mule which had clearly died; Sergio's marijuana cigarette; Patrizio in his vest, naked from the bottom down; their apartment overcrowded with furniture and his mother's weak, cabbage soup. It seemed arrogant that I could ever have thought I had been absorbed into the aesthetic of Italy, when all that had touched me was the romanticism of the dirt and squalor of another country.

I caught up with Jenni, and she took the hand I proferred with such alacrity that it made me smile.

Inside the gates, a hooter whistled and the early shift of, perhaps, five hundred men and older boys, began to leave the brick sheds housing blast furnaces and Bessemer Converters. The hangar doors now open, I could feel the intense heat of the molten steel and see the white flames in the reverberatory, where a crew of operatives, all stripped to the waist, were providing this fumarole with its power, shovelling coal from a handcart pushed along rails by a boy. The boy was blackened from head to foot and raven haired, the whiteness of his eyes vivid across the foundry yard, where a watchman, in navy-blue uniform, had arrived to open the gates. Those ending their shift filed through, each with a snap-tin, each with a milk or lemonade bottle now emptied of the cold tea it had been filled with at the beginning of the day. Some were talking together, others silent, some were in small family groups, others by themselves; some were walking home, purposefully, through the fuliginous streets where stragglers for the late shift were still making their way to the foundry, whilst others, now finished for the afternoon, were entering a nearby public house.

And yet again, I could not help but find the scene romantic.

Jenni, too, appeared to be captivated, leaning backwards into the crook of my knees, as if both excited and intimidated by the masculinity surrounding her.

Inside the shed, the boy was now hand-rolling a cigarette. I could see that his face, but not the agility of this fingers, was affected by my presence, and I could smell the escaping oxides frowsting the air about him. The boy lit his tobacco by lifting his boot and striking a match across the leather, without once taking his eyes from my own or distancing his stare. His smoke mingled with the blue and yellow gases pouring from the blast furnace vent, still open to receive the last of the coal from the operatives. They meanwhile had also ceased working, leaning their shovels against their legs in apparent mimicry of my own particular stance with Jenni. The boy laughed and raised his fist in a superior, dismissive gesture of defiance.

I swung Jenni by the elbows from her position against my knees and landed her on my shoulders with a thump.

'Where are we going?' she asked.

'I thought you wanted to see the Transporter Bridge,' I replied, walking impulsively through the crowd of labourers still leaving by the gate. 'It's wrong to stand and watch people for too long. It isn't fair. How would we like it if we were busy?'

'One of them thought we were very funny,' she said, kicking her legs as if I might be a pony.

I stilled her ankles, and made a mental note to avoid the foundry in future. My voyeurism was becoming a habit. As I calmed down, I remembered her father saying, recently, on the train journeying north with her mother, that to forgive one had to be actively involved and that forgiveness was not a concept. I now wondered if this, also, might be true of life, for it occurred to me that my desire to remain an observer had only ever served to place me at a distance from real experience. Life is not a concept, I thought, but a series of events in which one must take an active part. I had been holding myself aloof, deliberately preferring the bogus intellectualism of ideas, encouraged, originally, by Sir Christopher in his study at Cambridge. It was this remoteness from everyday life, I now realized, which was responsible for supporting and comforting my romanticism.

'Gee-up, Uncle Daniel,' she said happily, 'I want you to be a pony.'

'I'm too old, Jenni. I'm too weary,' I answered almost frivolously, releasing my grip on her ankles so that she could kick my flanks.

I could also see, as Jenni's father had pointed out in the railway carriage, that Sir Christopher, too, was an arch-romantic, whose concept of and belief in idealism had only ever succeeded in keeping the reality of the world at bay. His mental dishonesty had never faced the truth of human insecurity, or vulnerability, or helplessness. And neither had I, yet all these traits I displayed in abundance. The constant debate about ideas had been the mechanism we had both employed to disguise our weaknesses. I was hiding, terrified of what might be revealed should I be honest with myself at last.

'Is that the Transporter Bridge?' she inquired, stilling her jockeying movement.

'It probably is, Jenni. We must be very close. You're higher up than me. I can't see over this fence.'

'Why do you keep being quiet? Aren't you interested in the bridge anymore?'

'I was thinking, Jenni, that's all. I'll stop now.'

I lifted her from my shoulders, and we continued along the pavement now strewn with flotsam and jetsam from an overflowing high tide. Soon we turned a corner which afforded a full view of the river. Jenni halted in mid-step, as if alarmed by the enormity of the girdered steel construction before her.

Luckily, the bridge was in operation, carrying an army lorry, two industrial wagons, and a horse and cart towards our side of the river. A wind was blowing, rocking the cradle of steel wires.

'It isn't really a bridge, is it?' she asked intelligently.

'No, it isn't, you're quite right. It's a cross between a bridge and a ferry. This is what makes it almost unique.' I kneeled beside her so as not to be patronizing. 'The platform, which travels back and forth across the river, is suspended on steel cables from above. At the top, these cables are attached to four large wheels. Can you see?'

She nodded.

'The wheels run on a track, to and fro, between the docking berth on either bank. Can you see the horse and cart being ferried across at this moment?'

'Yes. I like horses.'

'The steel cables need to be very strong to support the platform and all that weight.'

'Was it built in the foundry we saw, Uncle Daniel?'

'I don't know. It could have been, yes.'

'They thought we were very funny,' she said.

'Well, I am funny sometimes, Jenni. I can't help it.'

Metal hit metal as the platform slowly docked, and the wheels above inched to a standstill. Sparks flew into the air, created by the side-pressure of friction from the transporter's final manoeuvre. The gatekeeper, with an action so familiar that he was able to gossip with the foot passengers at the same time, hoisted the barrier, and the vehicles disembarked towards the town.

Jenni asked to stroke the horse, so I beckoned the driver to stop.

'Who's that?' she asked after a moment.

The dray was cleverly stacked with a multiplicity of rag and bone, and a small boy, perhaps five or six years older than Jenni, was sitting, balanced precariously, on the apex of the scrap, looking about him as if he owned the world, his jaunty expression not at all affected by our presence.

'Who's that?' she asked again.

'It's a boy, Jenni. Please don't be rude.'

'What's he doing up there?'

'I don't know. He's sitting.'

'Why don't you climb up with him,' the driver said.

Jenni looked at me for consent.

'She shouldn't really, she's her best clothes on. Haven't you?'

Jenni nodded, but I took her by the elbows and placed her beside the boy, who remained oblivious, almost as if he had not seen us.

'He's blind,' the driver said. 'Get up beside me and I'll take you back to your car. I presume you have a motor.'

I climbed onto the seat and felt the rough straw padding of the cushion through my trousers. The driver gently clicked his tongue, and the horse obeyed him with a similar nonchalance, setting off along the street at less than walking pace.

'He started to go blind seven years ago.'

I tried not to feel the pity which Harry so loathed.

'Can nothing be done for him?' I asked.

'The doctor says not. We do what we can to help him, and he seems to be getting used to it. It's his education we worry about. I had none, but I had hoped he would learn to read and write.

Now it won't be, unfortunately.'

'Have you taken him to an eye specialist?'

'We did discuss it, the wife and me. But there's our other boy to think about. Because he's not blind, it doesn't mean he isn't equally important.'

'Why's that?' I asked.

'Money. I'm really talking about money. We don't have the money to go questioning one doctor against another. And I know so little about it. That's the problem with ignorance, it always means you have to trust someone else's word. I'd have liked my boys not to have to do that. I had hoped they would live more for themselves.'

'Have you approached the various charities?'

'It seems he's not a bad enough case. We were shocked by that, but that's what they say. Again, what can we do but take their word?'

'You've obviously done your best,' I said.

'Oh, yeh, I've done my best. I'm not a man who sits on his hands and does nothing. This is your motor, it must be your motor, it's the only one on the street. It's a wonder it's still in one piece, this is a rough area by the iron foundry.'

He clicked his tongue and the dray slowed to a halt by the Riley.

'Seven years is a long time,' I said. 'Did your son's blindness occur gradually?'

'Yeh, it did. It's the last three years where it's deteriorated to the point where now he sees nothing.'

I stepped from the dray and lifted Jenni from the scrap. Her dress was marked, as I had feared. The driver noticed my concern.

'I'm sorry about her dress,' he said.

'It's all right, it doesn't matter.'

'She looks as if she's going to a party.'

'We're going to see my parents.'

'They've a beautiful granddaughter. They must be very proud of her.'

'Yes,' I replied, compounding his false assumption with a further untruth.

'She's very quiet, isn't she?'

'She isn't usually. I don't know why she's so quiet at the

moment. Normally, she's a chatterbox. Aren't you?'

Jenni nodded obligingly.

'What's your son's name?' I asked him.

'Peter.'

'This is Jenni. Would you mind if I looked at your son myself?'

Peter's father raised one of his knees in a right angle across the seat. And again, as he turned back to face me, I thought of Harry's hatred of pity.

'I'm sorry,' I said, 'I didn't mean to patronize you. But I'm a doctor.'

'No, you surprised me, that's all. It's funny how people surprise you. Please do. Please do what you can.'

I picked up the little boy, who was lighter than I might have imagined, and seated him on the tailgate of the cart, legs dangling, so that his eyes were on a level with my own. His father joined me.

'Peter is how old?' I asked.

'He's twelve. He's very small for his age.'

'And your doctor. How old is your doctor?'

'That's very shrewd of you,' he said.

'I'd say your doctor is in his seventies. He's probably blind himself.'

The child's corneas were opaque. I rechecked both membranes to be certain I was not in error.

'Has he ever had problems with his teeth?' I asked.

'Yes, he has,' his father said. 'That's begun recently. How did you know that?'

It was pure fluke that, while I was a student, I had once seen another child in a similar condition, and could add credence to my diagnosis.

'Peter,' I said, 'would you please open your mouth for me.'

The boy did so without protest, the blindness dulling his senses to the point where his lethargy and stoicism seemed unworldly. I thought it unfair that a boy his age should be so meek.

His teeth were notched and peg-shaped as I had expected.

'Peter has Hutchinson's teeth,' I remarked, thinking but not meaning to speak this observation out loud.

'What is that?' his father asked.

126

'Well, it's a disease which results from the same infection.'

A cure for the boy would be relatively simple, but more troubling, particularly psychologically, for his mother and father. I knew the boy's sibling must be considerably younger, perhaps a toddler, and used this knowledge to check that the understanding I had reached was not mistaken.

'Peter's brother,' I asked, 'how old is he?'

'He's five, going on six.'

'Thank you, Peter, you may close your mouth now.'

Peter did so without losing his poker-faced expression. It was not an unreasonable guess that his brother would shortly be developing the same symptoms.

'Did your wife have a miscarriage before Peter was born?' I asked gently.

'Yes, she did.' His anodyne features were shedding their inscrutability. 'What do you know? What is it?'

'I think your son should see a specialist at once. It is worth challenging one doctor against another. Your own doctor is old-fashioned and a little out of date.'

Peter's father was staring at me.

'You must take your younger boy, too. In fact, all of you must go. It's imperative.'

'Why?' he asked.

I tried to stop myself being overwhelmed with pity for the family but, despite Harry's omnipresence, did not succeed in my efforts.

'Because Peter has congenital syphilis,' I said. 'Your wife is almost certainly affected, or has been in the past, and all of you need to be checked as soon as possible. Peter was infected in the womb.'

'You are always crying, Uncle Daniel,' Jenni said.

'She calls me uncle sometimes. She likes to be amusing. We're both funny, aren't we, Jenni?'

Jenni nodded.

'A treatment is possible with Atropine and sulphur-based drugs. I'll give you the name of a doctor I know in Middlesbrough. Here, I'll write his name down for you. And I'll speak to him myself. I'll get him to send me his bill. But you must go immediately. Do you understand?'

'Yes,' he said.

'It isn't too late for Peter, but it will be soon. It's never too late for any of us.'

I gave him the address, written on a discarded cigarette packet from the highway, and jumped into the Riley, first throwing Jenni ahead of me onto the passenger seat, bruising her leg on the steering-wheel in the process. She nursed her wound silently. We had driven past the iron foundry and the docks, before I realized her submissiveness was the result of fear.

'Jenni, have you wet yourself?'

'Yes,' she said meekly, her dulled senses and quietude reminding me of Peter.

'Oh, Jenni, I'm so sorry.'

She put her hand onto the leather where there was a pool of water, and lifted her fingers to examine them as if the liquid might be glutinous.

'Why are you a cry-baby, Uncle Daniel?' she asked without looking towards me, her voice impassive and incurious.

'I've really upset you, haven't I?'

She nodded. She was still playing with her fingers in the water, but distractedly, like one absorbing a hurt which would never be forgotten.

'I'm sorry I pushed you.'

'Why did we have to leave so quickly?'

'I was feeling claustrophobic. I had to escape and get away. I couldn't have stayed a moment longer.'

'Why couldn't that boy see anything?'

'I don't know, Jenni. Well, I do know why he was blind. I can't explain.'

I was defeated and exhausted by emotion. My control of the wheel was perilous.

'You won't hurt me again, will you?' she asked indifferently, unaware of the hazards of my driving.

'No, I won't, Jenni,' I said. 'I promise you.'

She raised her bottom and inched forwards, tortoise-like, towards the edge of the seat, leaving behind the pool of urine in the concavity of the leather, where it spilled to and fro with the car's movement.

'Uncle Daniel, I need a clean pair of underpants.'

'I know you do. Let me get a little further on the journey and then I'll help sort you out.'

'Where are we going?'

'I'm not sure, Jenni. We'll go somewhere. I'll make it up to you. Please don't worry.'

I drove onwards through my parent's home town without stopping and finally brought the Riley to a halt on the moor road. It was the same road Harry and I had bicycled as boys to Whitby, where we had eaten fish and chips and first encountered John Bell. I scooped Jenni's water from the seat with my hands and washed her pants in a stream. All the while she remained beside me, inactive and detached.

'Where would you like to go?' I asked, still feeling on a razor's edge between the past and the present.

'I'd like to go home,' she said, 'to Daddy.'

'I can't take you home at the moment.'

'Why not?'

I spread her pants on the warm engine of the motor to dry.

'Because I don't want to see your father at the moment.'

'Don't you want him to see you crying, Uncle Daniel? He doesn't like people who cry.'

'I know he doesn't, Jenni. I remember your father from school a long time ago. His depressions would never allow pity. But pity is a benevolent and honourable emotion. Your father is wrong. All I ever wanted to do was to feel sorry for his predicament, but he would never let me.'

Jenni kneeled by the roadside to pick the wild heather which had seeded there in profusion.

'Can I go home without you?' she asked.

'No, Jenni, you're coming with me.'

At Whitby, I turned south along the coast towards Scarborough and Bridlington, only pausing at a garage to buy petrol and a confectioner's to buy chocolate, until we were well into areas of countryside I did not recognize and towns I had no knowledge of. Jenni inquired politely as to our destination, and I could sense from her passivity that she was, once more, becoming increasingly alarmed, so I pulled the Riley onto the verge and allowed her to play amongst the grasses for a while. It seemed imperative I find a purpose for the journey, so opened my road atlas to search for one. We were travelling towards the chalk hills of north Lincolnshire, and I quickly resolved upon the flat lands of Norfolk as being the place where we might find peace. Later, after it was dark, I stopped at a secluded public house and asked the whisky-faced landlord if I might use his telephone, so as to inform Harry and Stella that my parents had invited us to stay the night and we would return to Richmond the following afternoon.

We spent the night at an hotel in Gainsborough. I had no night-clothes for Jenni and this proved an almost insurmountable problem, for she would not go to sleep without them. To assuage her many protestations, I was forced to descend the stairway and explain to the lady of the house that I had mislaid my daughter's baggage and would she please have a garment suitable for a child? Luckily, she found me a pair of boy's pyjamas which Jenni eventually seemed happy with. But the incident terrified me: I had had to compound my lies, and the woman's suspicions made me feel like a fugitive.

When Jenni had at last cleaned her teeth with her fingers and closed her eyes, I sat on the counterpane of my own bed, feeling nothing but hurt. My heart raced with incident after incident from the long day, yet, somehow, I knew I would not turn back, some inner compulsion within me being far too strong. I knew my actions were not transitory; they would have consequences. The worries and obsessions multipled inside my head until I was filled with blackness and despair, and the world seemed to be spinning so fast that I could no longer focus, yet all was real as if my cranium might soon explode, and splinter, and leave me bereft of anything I had previously thought of as normal, or commonplace, or ordinary.

In a moment of quietness, I realized I had neglected to telephone the doctor in Middlesbrough. This was another lie, another untruth, another commitment promised but not fulfilled.

My skull burst into a thousand tiny fragments, each spiralling outwards at speed into a vacuum where no reason or logic appeared to exist, and there they floated in a vast desolation of self-loathing and self-pity. Above all, self-pity. In the void that had been my morality, limitless pinpricks of conscience collided with one another, until my head in my hands was a ball of fire, and I knew I needed, but would not seek, the help of others.

Jenni was washed and dressed before dawn. Once in the Riley, she fell straight back to sleep with her hand pressed beside her cheek on the arm rest of the car door. A pale sunlight was filtering through the trees, and a ground mist dispersing across the fields of barley. The roads were empty: I was driving south again. At some point towards mid-afternoon I telephoned Harry from a public box and told him we would be spending another night with my parents.

'Is everything all right, Daniel? There's nothing troubling you?'

'No, we're fine. Jenni seems to be enjoying my parents, and my parents are certainly enjoying her company. Don't worry, nothing is wrong. We thought we might drive to Whitby and spend the day there.'

'Remember me to Whitby,' he said. 'Buy Jenni some fish and chips.'

'I will. How are you and Stella?'

'We're talking.'

'Arguing?'

'We never argue, Daniel, I thought you knew that.' There was humour in his voice. 'No, we're talking quite peaceably. Stella has gone for a walk, I'm preparing lunch. We've decided to part, Daniel. It seems to make the best sense to both of us. That probably sounds trivial, which I don't mean it to be. We're discussing Jenni.'

I could see the little girl sitting neatly in the motor.

'It's not a very good connection, Harry. What was that about Jenni?'

The line was crackly and his voice distant, which, initially, I had been thankful for.

'Stella and I are discussing Jenni's future. Can you hear me now?'

'Yes, I can.'

'Stella is returning to New Orleans. I've decided to remain in England. We'd prefer to offer Jenni the choice, but we both feel that is inappropriate for a child of her age. I hope she will stay with me, and Stella has agreed to this in principle.'

'You sound buoyant, Harry.'

'Yes, I am. My depression has lifted.'

'Harry?'

'What?'

I left a long pause, not certain of what it was that I wanted or needed to say.

131

'Are you still there, Daniel?'

'At school, Harry, why wouldn't you allow me to feel sorry for you?'

'Daniel, that's history. What on earth are you talking about?'

'You can sting when you're depressed. You can really hurt. I just require you to understand this.'

It was his turn to think and to leave a hole in the conversation.

'I know I can. I'm sorry.'

'Would you mind if I took Jenni to London?'

'London?'

'Yes. There's something I need to sort through. I'd like Jenni to accompany me. Don't you trust me, Harry?'

'Of course I do. It seems such a strange request. When will you be back?'

'The day after tomorrow.'

'What about Whitby?'

'The three of us can go to Whitby on another day. We could go together.'

'Are you sure you're all right?'

'I don't know, Harry. I'm not sure, no. I need to clear my desk at the House of Commons. I'm resigning.'

'Good for you.'

'Is that all you can say?'

'There's nothing else I want to say. It must be your parents making you see sense at last.'

'It's Jenni.'

'Jenni?' He sounded astonished. 'Why Jenni?'

'I can't really explain. Anything I say will only be pompous. But I understand for the first time how children are at the mercy of adults. As you were, Harry. I've seen how power is worthless and degrading. I'm talking about myself. Only myself. I'm confused at the moment. Jenni is with me and she's fine.'

There was a silence.

'Where are you, Daniel?'

'I'm at Bow in east London.'

He deadened his tongue. I could hear him thinking.

'Daniel, I'll take the railway. Wait for me. Meet me at King's Cross.'

'There's no need, Harry. I'll clear my desk at the Commons, and we'll begin driving back this evening.'

132

'Is Jenni there?'

'Yes. Would you like to speak to her?'

I had parked close to a market where street traders at their stalls were busily selling everything from cheese to kitchen curtains, apples to refined-paraffin, needlebooks to shrieking cockatoos. Awnings were raised to protect customers from the drizzle which was falling, so that the highway was a succession of canopies beneath which the shoppers had to dodge to keep dry.

A group of Jewish children in black habiliments were snaking between the Riley and a shooting-brake delivering millinery.

I beckoned Jenni from the motor, and heard these words as she talked with her father: 'Iron foundry . . . blast furnace . . . Transporter Bridge . . . army lorry . . . horse and cart . . . blind boy . . . steering wheel . . . underpants . . . Whitby . . . chocolate . . . Gainsborough.' And finally, but with most emphasis: 'pyjamas.'

'You have been having a strange time, Daniel,' her father laughed when she had finished and I had taken the receiver once more.

'Yes, I can only apologize for that.'

'She seems most concerned about having to spend another night in a pair of boy's pyjamas.'

'I know, I'm sorry. If I'd known I was going to set off on an escapade, I'd have packed.'

'At least you've got your sense of humour back now.'

I was rendered speechless for a second or two.

'It isn't deliberate, Harry, I feel terrible. I spent most of last night doubled up like a foetus with my head almost literally exploding.'

'Now you know how I used to feel at school,' he joked. 'Don't worry, you've done nothing wrong.'

I was relieved by his cheerfulness.

'It feels as if I have.'

'I know it does, but you haven't. At school you helped me by telling me I was innocent.' His voice was pert and resilient, waggish and jocular, flushed and exultant. 'Don't you remember?'

The absence of pity in his voice was providing me with energy.

'Vaguely, yes. I'm sure the memory will return when I'm better.'

'Are you ill? I thought you were being eccentric.'

A woman was hemming a petticoat beneath an umbrella on

133

her doorstep. With a scream of amazement and joy she embraced an admirer who had approached from amongst the crowd. A market trader gave them both an orange, and I realized the reunion had been expected.

'I'm not eccentric, Harry, so I must be unwell.'

A round of applause for the pair echoed from across the street towards the telephone kiosk.

'Daniel, what's that noise?'

'It's some barrow-men clapping. A wanderer has returned. It's a scene reminiscent of the Great War.'

Jenni left the kiosk to go and look closely at what was going on.

'I'm by a market with hawkers and pedlars. It's been raining so everything is filthy. There's rubbish everywhere. The lovers are lifting everyone's spirits.'

'Including your own, Daniel?'

'I don't know about my own.'

'What about King's Cross?'

'Well, travel if you want to, but I don't think it's worth it.'

'Give Jenni a kiss from me.'

'I will.'

I found Jenni, who had pushed herself to the front of the crowd where she was watching the continuing spectacle of reunion with a bemused, abstracted detachment, and waited beside her. She seemed her own happy self again, and it occurred to me how similar we were in the way we both observed an event without involvement, as if what was happening might be on a screen in a picture house.

The lovers bowed and went indoors.

'What was that all about?' she asked, reluctant to take my hand and leave.

'I'm not sure, Jenni. There are some stories we'll only ever know the middle of, unfortunately.'

We motored together through the narrow lanes of Bethnal Green and Shoreditch towards the City of London and Westminster. At Trafalgar Square I parked, briefly, in order to show her the lions, afterwards driving along Whitehall where I pointed out the Prime Minister's residence in Downing Street. It was clear she wished to see for herself, so I pulled the Riley into the side once more. The policeman on duty recognized me and offered to let Jenni wear his helmet, but she declined his invitation, saying 'No thank you' with a firm voice. And again I was struck by our similarity, for we both kept our distance from people who only wished to be kind. I saw how the little girl would not be patronized, as I had endeavoured not to be over the years, and understood how this failing had often removed me from simple pleasure. Jenni would not be cajoled. The policeman donned his helmet, and we said goodbye.

I parked, finally, by the Abbey and strolled with her across the road into the House of Commons, where I cleared my desk by throwing much of my now defunct paperwork into the waste-paper basket, left empty for the long recess. It amazed me, now that I had reached a decision, how little documentation I thought it necessary to retain. Journals and gazettes, dossiers and press-cuttings were quickly discarded, while I kept only the odd copy of Hansard. On the whole seven years of life and par-liamentary duty were dispatched with ease.

Whilst I rummaged to and fro, Jenni drew a picture at my desk in pencil on the back of one of the order-papers I had given her. She was a calming presence amidst the mounting chaos, and, registering that she might be feeling forgotten, I went across to see what she was doing. Her drawing was of the Palace of Westminster, or so she told me, and I thought it a pity that I had no crayons she could use, for, despite being childish, the picture had sufficient atmosphere to warrant colour. Selfishly, I wished to keep the drawing for myself as the best memento I could take from the building.

'This is the window of your office, here,' she said, putting her thumb nail on the paper, 'and this is us, standing looking out. We like looking, don't we, Uncle Daniel?'

I saw my second, London-kept address book which I had placed beside the Hansards a few moments earlier.

'Jenni, you were going to remind me of something.'

'What?' she asked quizzically.

'Don't you remember in the car? You were going to remind me to call a doctor in Middlesbrough. We're both as forgetful as each other when we get busy and involved with ourselves.'

I picked up the receiver and asked the telephonist to connect me with the number in Middlesbrough.

On our way out from parliament, Jenni stopped.

'What is through those doors?' she asked, as if behind every door there was a secret to be explored.

'That's the chamber itself,' I replied.

'Can I go and have a look?'

'You want to see everything, don't you?'

'Yes,' she said contentedly.

'It isn't permitted, Jenni. I think a person has to be elected to enter the chamber.'

'But who sweeps the floors?' she asked intelligently, tucking her pencil sketch beneath her arm.

'I don't know, it's a very good question, one I've never thought about.'

So we entered the chamber, where I instinctively bowed towards the empty speaker's chair, whilst Jenni ran ahead towards the mace and the despatch boxes, unconcerned about rules or protocol, her small feet echoing dully across the wooden floor. I had often taken part in debates with only a handful of members present, but the deserted chamber had a restfulness and melancholy, like a cathedral without worshippers, which surprised me to such an extent that I felt again the majesty I had experienced seven years earlier on first entering to take my seat. I stood for a moment looking at the ceiling with the copies of Hansard weighing heavy in my arms, hearing the voices once raised in anger, listening to the orators once speaking of injustice, and knew I was too simple a person ever to proclaim a cause, or defend myself from charges put against me. In a way my life had been lost in parliament, for the business of politics is not for those ordinary men and women whose insecurities ought to make them modest. For the first time, amidst this tranquillity and with only Jenni present, I felt the pleasure of being mundane, and understood how this personal lack of expectation might eventually lead to goodness; as John Bell, many years later, was so clearly to demonstrate in Pennsylvania.

But this is in the future, with much of my present self-awareness still to come, and the period of my continuing 'strangeness' yet to be lived through to its end.

I walked towards Jenni, who was sketching on the government's dispatch box with the pencil she had kept in her white sock, for her dress did not have a pocket, and seated myself behind her on the front bench, watching her elbows move to and fro as she drew another picture.

'That's where the Prime Minister speaks from,' I said.

'Who's the Prime Minister?' she replied, destroying my previous impression of her brightness.

'Jenni, I've already told you. He's the most important member of the government, if not the most important man in the country.'

'I know. I was being funny, Uncle Daniel.'

The chamber was silent but for her scribbling.

'I'd like to live in here,' she said.

'Would you?'

'I've just told you. Weren't you listening?'

'I must be tired, Jenni. Come on, let's go home.'

We spent the night at an hotel in Potters Bar, where Jenni wore the pyjamas – much to my surprise she refused a nightdress – I had bought her after we had left the House of Commons. It was nearing midnight the following day when we arrived in Richmond.

6

Home again in Richmond, with Jenni in bed, I remained awake
into the small hours of the next morning, determined to clear
my dining-room of papers much as I had my office at the House
of Commons. Harry joined me in his dressing-gown with two
glasses of Armagnac, as if my mania were making him restless.

'Sit down, Daniel.'

'Why?'

'Because you're exhausted. Sit down. This is silly at this time
of night. There is nothing that will not wait until tomorrow.'

'We've nowhere to dine. We're forever having to eat in the
kitchen.'

'I know, but this behaviour is manic. By all means throw away
your past, but do it in the morning when you're feeling sensible.'

'I'm sorry,' I said, doing as I was told.

'And stop apologizing.'

In a moment of avarice a few months earlier I had purchased
a Regency grandfather clock, which I could hear ticking as we
talked. Like many single men when in company, my inclination
was to talk about myself, but I was too fatigued to do so. Instead
I asked Harry about Stella.

'We're making love again, now that we're parting. Isn't that
odd? I find it odd. We haven't made love for years.' He seated
himself beside me on one of the cane chairs and appeared to
change the subject. 'We're very different cultures, America and
Great Britain. Our common language is deceptive. The American
still believes his dream is possible, whereas we in Europe do not.
And it's this consequent lack of cynicism which I find most
endearing, and naive, and irksome, all at the same time.' He

smiled, the contours of his face breaking into laugh-lines. 'The average American still believes he is right, which I find irksome, too, because actually they know very little of the rest of the world. It's a culture which encourages certainty. Not that I would accuse Stella of these traits.'

'I thought you'd made up your mind to stay in England?'

'Oh, I have. I'm trying to put my time in America into some perspective. Making love again with Stella has removed a burden I was carrying.'

I swallowed my Armagnac, too spent to apprehend a connection between his disparate trains of thought.

'I know I have let Stella down when it has come to sex between us. I'd hate to think our marriage had ended for this reason, but it hasn't, I can see that now. It's America. I'm very English, Daniel, more English than I ever realized. My loathing for my family had pushed me abroad, but I can see that was wrong.' He was speaking with a deep-centred positiveness I had not witnessed before in his character, as if he had no axe to grind or agenda to propose but was simply talking honestly about himself. 'I couldn't have remained in America. It's too competitive for me. I compete when I'm depressed, but Stella competes all the time. I find it so wearing. She flirts, which I don't mind too much, but I can't manage my life when even that becomes a competition. I'm probably being harsh, Daniel.'

'No.'

'The physical act of sex I can take or leave, but not love. The English love in secret, whereas in America love is open and passionate. I prefer the former with its irony and uncertainty.'

'Do you wish for a quiet life from now on?'

'Yes, I do. I wish to be unexceptional.'

It was my turn to smile, which Harry read as more than that.

'Why are you laughing?'

'I was thinking something similar with Jenni in the House of Commons two days ago.'

He produced the bottle of Armagnac which had been hidden in his dressing-gown pocket.

'Not tonight, Harry. I couldn't do a full bottle tonight.'

'One more before we go to bed?'

He refilled our glasses with two large measures, his eyes searching my own eyes, which for some reason had become nervous with my eyelids flickering.

'By the way, I've bought a motor, Daniel.' His voice was so placid his head might have been upon a pillow. 'A Mercedes. It's second-hand but in good condition. I don't know why I've bought second-hand. From the chappie at your local garage.'

'He's very reliable, you can trust him.'

My fingers were resting upon the table. Harry touched them with his own fingers. He stroked my thumb and forefinger tenderly.

'You wish to go to bed, don't you?'

'I am very tired, Harry.'

'I understand.' He nodded once and removed his hand. 'Go to bed.'

I climbed the stairs and left him in my dining-room, still surrounded by the mass of half-torn papers.

Stella returned to New Orleans a fortnight later. Because Harry preferred to stay in Yorkshire, where he was looking to buy a farm, I had accepted the responsibility of seeing her off from Southampton. They both thought it better for Jenni's sake if the goodbye were not a protracted one, so they parted without ceremony, Jenni in her new Wellington boots on my doorstep. I had not inquired what they had told the little girl, but she did not appear overly concerned, and waved to us as we drove away in the taxi as if we were going shopping and might be back within the hour.

I could tell it was the end for Stella, too, for she began the act of contrition which is my final memory of her.

'I'm sure I've said some very rude things to you, Daniel.'

Her desire to placate the past made me aware of her depth of feeling, and I saw how the decision to leave had not been an easy one.

'Not at all, Stella, quite the opposite. I've always listened to what you had to say. I'll always remember your kindness.'

'You never intrude, Daniel, I admire that. You never ask personal questions.'

'Don't I?'

'No, you prefer to rely on your imagination. I'm not like that at all, I ask questions, I'm not a brooder. You've never once asked me about my first husband?'

'Haven't I?'

'You see, you're not even going to ask when I invite you to. He died after being thrown from a horse in Louisiana. But I would have left him; this is the only point in my telling you about him now.' Her long legs were filling the well in the back seat of the taxi; to be beside such charm and grace was exquisite. 'I should always have taken greater care in deciding what to tell you.'

'The fault is equally mine for listening too much, for putting that pressure on you, Stella. It isn't fair when we listen to a person so much that they have to guard against every word they say.'

'At least we understand one another, Daniel.'

Through the window I glimpsed a farmer ploughing the upland of a hillside with a team of horses, his face concentrated against the chill in an end-of-summer breeze. The horses were stepping carefully down the incline, the farmer with the reins grasped between his hands further steadying their movement so that progress was deliberate and skilful. Behind the plough a flock of birds, mainly blackbirds and thrushes, scavenged for insects thrown up in the soil, until a rare peregrine falcon swooped from nowhere and we passed the point where I could see, my view obscured by a dip in the highway.

On the quay at Southampton, after a tiring but pleasant railway journey from Darlington, she said: 'Look after Harry and Jenni for me, won't you?'

Before I could reply she was gone amongst the crowds.

Three weeks later, at my local church, I was godfather at Jenni's baptism. In her hand she held the Amish doll which John Bell had given her at the time of his own christening in Pennsylvania. It was Harry who suggested she bring the doll to the ceremony: I know he wished John to be present.

In the summer of 1968, on the same holiday which found me in Shiprock in Arizona where I had so eccentrically taken off my clothes, I visited New Orleans, being determined to try and find Stella and resume the friendship which I had always missed. I arrived in the late evening on a flight from Albuquerque in New Mexico. After finding my hotel, I toured Bourbon Street with its blues-parlours, skiffle-clubs, and honky-tonks offering wild jazz, even wilder booze, and a life which drifted out onto the pavement into the small hours, where strip-joints, peep-shows, and topless bars swung their doors ajar to lure customers. It was so different from the scenes I remembered, but, wishing to sample every delight, I travelled from bar to bar drinking 'hurricanes', a cocktail which was rumoured to devastate entire populations and which certainly devastated me. The music of the black men was extraordinarily soulful, as if each calculated phrase or improvisation had the truth of the player's life behind it, so that nothing produced in the clarity of the sound was wasted or indulgent. Trumpets, clarinets, and saxophones reverberated with drums and doublebasses across the walls of the bar, enhancing the taste of the alcohol. By contrast, in the strip-joints where girls danced on the tables, all was seedy, and I rather enjoyed feeling disgraceful for an hour. On the street outside, groups of young boys wearing tap-shoes and little else were still out begging with cardboard boxes in front of them for money. The night was warm and the pavements sticky with heat. Up above, on the painted wrought-iron balconies, revellers ate the local oysters, or called to the bartender for another beer whilst awaiting their Creole dish of jambalaya, a fragrant stew of sea-food, tomatoes and rice: but whatever the pursuit, be it at street level or above, it was impossible to escape the jazz running from the unshuttered windows of each parlour. Inside, the jazzmen added excitement upon excitement, and walking outside was like listening to a constantly changing record. At two o'clock, the Salvation Army came along saving souls, filling the street with renewed merriment. I risked one last cocktail – an absinthe frappé, goodness knows what was in it – and crawled to bed at my hotel.

Next morning I found Stella's home in the Garden District with ease, but there was no trace of Stella herself. Her palace (as I had once thought the house) was now a private school, and the result of my inquiry was that I spent a pleasant afternoon talking with a class of bright girls about life in England. When I asked them about America, it transpired they had never heard of the Amish community in Pennsylvania, where I was to spend the final weeks of my holiday. I knew John would frown upon Bourbon Street, but for these children the life that went on there was part of their everyday experience. In their tee-shirts and sneakers they were so different from the children who walked barefooted across the fields in Lancaster County, their lives at such variance, it was no surprise to find that the ones had never learned of the others. Modern, white, middle-class America, in the shape of these girls, could not understand why a community should wish to make moral choices about progress, this despite their country's atrocities in Vietnam being at their worst; and the Amish, in the guise of John, would never have seen how these girls were ordinary, decent, and fair-minded. I enjoyed our discussion, being sorry when it was time to leave.

The next day, I hired a car and drove along the delta of the Mississippi, eventually taking a small steam boat through the brackish water into the shallow creeks, where I found a very different kind of school, its pupils as black as I remembered, but its stone buildings far superior with eleven classrooms and a full complement of teachers. The headmistress, knowing something of the history of the institution, had heard of Stella Treffgarne and her influence in the area, but they had never met. I talked with her staff, and again spoke to the children, this time of my memories: one or two had been told a similar story by their grandparents of the day a shack toppled over, upended, and floated down river in the afternoon sunlight. They were an idyllic few hours, ones I will always treasure.

Stella may still be alive, although I suspect this is now unlikely for she was several years older than me. I would like to hope she returned to Florence, rediscovered Sergio, and that this is why I have never seen him either, although I have searched in the streets around the Hotel Arno whenever I have been in the city; and that at some point, somewhere in the world, they enjoyed a peaceful life together.

The two hundred acre farm Harry bought at auction almost a year after I had seen Stella off from Southampton was an easy fifteen minute drive from my home in Richmond. On the day he took possession, my mother died. It was fortunate the farmhouse contained a telephone or I might not have known for some hours, for I had had in mind to spend the day with him and stay on into the evening should I be asked. My housekeeper instructed my father as to our whereabouts and the telephone rang as we were looking over the property. It was Harry's first telephone call.

My mother's funeral was a dismal, lonely affair. The shop, which when I was a child had seemed the cornerstone of the High Street, had obviously not made the same impression upon others, for only a handful of regular customers were in the church and by her graveside, or so my father explained to me in a moment of quiet solicitude. The largest contingent was a group from the Women's Institute, who mourned as if it might be their profession in a tight, self-important circle. I had been to several funerals, but this was the first where I truly cared about the person who had died, and I experienced the common feeling of regret that her life and our relationship had not both been happier. I felt light-headed, sad, disjointed, somehow removed from the ceremony as I had been from my mother in life. As her coffin was lowered into the earth, I almost laughed because the pretence at bereavement from all those present seemed so ridiculous, with no one daring to be sufficiently anarchic to reveal their true sensibilities, including myself.

When it was time to throw soil upon the coffin, I did so, taking the responsibility from my father because he, too, appeared distracted, uncertain, unaware. I nudged his elbow, and he removed his glove to pick up some earth, which went the same way as my own with a dull thud onto the brass plate engraved with her name. Harry followed our example, and I was thankful once again for his being there, for his seeing me through these hours, for his taking my father's aged hand as the liturgy finished, when he could have been busy on his farm. As they ambled towards my car talking with one another, I walked beside them trying to listen to their words but hearing only their footfalls on the pavement, imagining the conversation I would have with my father at the day's end, feeling very peculiar indeed, dreading the occasion, knowing my mother's death had left me with a stranger who required my solace.

Harry drove us through the town in my car, leaving the taxis free for others; something my father had suggested earlier in the day. We rode in the back seat. As we travelled the streets and passed the market cross, my father kept looking at his pocket watch, as if this Friday might sooner be over if he knew the exact time. It was a short journey, but he must have consulted his old timepiece, given him by my mother many years before, at least fifteen times. Finally, he squeezed my arm to relieve his anxiety, and Harry pulled into the road where neighbours were standing watching.

I had organised a caterer from the town to be ready at the

house upon our arrival. Two maids, in absurdly old-fashioned black pinafore dresses with white collars, served us with sandwiches and over-rich sugar pastries, the kind of coquettish food I generally disliked, but it was the form on these occasions, and my father had wanted nothing out of the ordinary. It was the first time I had known him express a desire to be common-place, as if for once he seemed unable to tolerate the idea of his own eccentricity. But he had, unknown to me, purchased a firkin of beer as some small act of rebellion, which I could see annoyed the women of the Institute, who were throwing up their noses like lemmings without a cliff, drinking stewed tea from a samovar-like urn on the starched linen-covered table, eating their delicately glazed pastries. As he offered the ladies half-pints of ale, I suddenly saw the joke: even at the moment of my mother's death, he was getting his own back on her pretensions and snobbishness. The ladies declined with polite sobriety, which is what my father had expected, but his face never once betrayed a smile. I was proud of his courage.

When the guests were gone and the caterers dismissed, Harry volunteered to straighten the house, since my father had never been domestically minded, whilst I was left alone with him in the room where I had often played chess as a boy. I thought of taking the pieces from the sideboard but did not, being happy to accept a cigarette from his packet. He lit a spill from the fire, and we smoked in silence for some minutes.

I knew my father was perturbed because his one-time business partner, now the full owner of the shop which my father only managed, had not bothered to attend the funeral, and my father had once counted this chap amongst his closest friends. The man had made money in a succession of grocery stores, every five years buying another, whereas my father was now an employee with little or no say in how the business was run.

'I was never very lucky in the shop, Daniel,' he said, the cigarette burning towards his fingers. 'I was once lucky in love, but your mother changed. I had my little joke this afternoon. I hope you didn't mind?'

'No, father, I thought it was very funny. I'd been wanting to laugh all day and that gave me the excuse.'

'It's my fault I was never lucky in business: I don't have a business brain. Unfortunately, your mother would never forgive me.

You have to be able to envisage what you want in this world, in order to get it. I couldn't do that, so I mustn't have wanted it enough. Love is the same. That has to be visualized too for it to be successful. In marriage, when one of you loses that vision, it's the end.' Nicotine was yellowing his moustache. 'The Treffgarnes, Harry's parents, must always have been able to see their success. That's the only difference between us. They were just business people like ourselves. They went up in the world, we came down.'

'They weren't lucky in love, Father.'

'I know. I still like Harry. I still think he's the best friend a person could ever wish for.'

I stood and poured two beers from the firkin.

'Thank you,' he said as I gave him his glass. 'When you were a boy I wanted a motor. I don't regret it, though it ruined me financially, Daniel. In life, you regret what you should have done, not what you actually did. That's why it's better to be active, and to always take the risk. There's nothing worse than brooding on what might have been. Cheers.'

'Cheers, Father.'

'I think your mother would have been pleased with today. Apart from the beer. I think you're non-conformist, Daniel, aren't you? I don't know you very well. I think you might be a rebel if you'd let yourself go. All this political nonsense has made you hold yourself in. The Women's Institute came to see you, you know. You probably didn't realize that? Your mother made sure they were impressed. But you hurt her by never coming home, by promising and then never turning up. How often did that happen? Quite often, Daniel.'

'I know. I'm sorry.'

'Dear me, I didn't mean to attack you. She used to go to her gatherings, proud as Lady Muck, and never let on that she hadn't seen you. I felt sad for her, I'm not really complaining for myself. Or I'm complaining a little, but only because I wish to know you better.'

'I've been going through an unhappy time.'

'Harry told me.'

'I don't know why, Father. Well, I do know why but it's hard to explain. It's to do with the past, it's to do with the present, and it's to do with the future. I haven't behaved badly in the past, perhaps misguidedly is a better word. It's been making me very self-pitying in the present, and I can't see a future with that emotion. But I believe pity for others to be honourable. I somehow can't separate the two. The Fascists, Sir Christopher Salisbury, Oswald Mosley, all those people, I think they're somehow self-pitying. I suspect that anyone with absolute dogma is, because they believe themselves to be the only ones who are right. They are never wrong. They never apologize. They will pretend something is not the case rather than admit their mistake. I believe them to be weak, whereas those of us who admit our weaknesses are strong, because we have doubt, and therefore some breadth of mind, sympathy, and compassion. It's the more difficult position to hold. I can't explain it more than this at the moment. Perhaps I will be able to one day? I have been very unhappy.'

'Why haven't you told me before now?' He lit a second cigarette from the butt-end of the first: it was the first time I had known him do this. 'Why have you been leaving me to guess?'

'May I have another cigarette?'

He gave me the packet and I followed his example. His hair was tousled from the exertions of the day; his face thinning and gaunt but still lively, like a man whose humour has been held at bay far too many years. He picked up his book from the floor and began to read.

'Father, that's rude, we're talking.'

'If you're not going to answer my question, I might as well learn from this.'

'What are you reading?'

He held the spine aloft: he was reading a novel by D.H. Lawrence, which surprised me. I had read his travel book, *Twilight in Italy*, whilst in Florence, but had not bothered with the stories.

'Oh, I suppose I was afraid,' I said. 'I suppose I wanted you to think of me as perfect.'

He lowered *The White Peacock* and spoke with the cigarette between his lips. 'Who wants to be perfect? Perfection is for fools. What must you think of me if you believe in that?'

'I don't think anything. It's rather the opposite, I rather admire you. Particularly today. That's why I laughed so much at the beer.'

147

'Get me another one, would you.'

I took his empty glass and poured a beer.

'Daniel, the woman who came and talked to you this afternoon as we were leaving the church: she's very nice, don't you agree?'

'Which woman is that? I can't remember.'

'Yes, you can. She came and said hello to you as we were walking towards the grave. She was the only woman without a hat, you commented upon the fact. That was my idea. Oh, do stop looking so prudish when I surprise you.'

My lips must have puckered. I placed the beer on the small table by his chair.

'You were surprised by my reading D.H. Lawrence, and now you're surprised by my having a lady friend. Actually, the two are the same: she gave me this book to read. Do sit down and close your mouth, you look absurd standing there.'

I did as I was told.

'You must be more innocent than I thought if you're surprised this often,' he said.

'I suppose I am innocent, yes.'

'What is it about you that always has to be priggish?'

'Perhaps I'm my mother's child, Father.'

'Perhaps you are. Daniel, Mrs Smith has been my mistress for some while.'

My head exploded into a thousand fragments as it had done the year before with Jenni in the hotel room in Gainsborough.

'Your mother never knew,' I heard him say through the void. 'I never hurt her. Mrs Smith was content to know your mother must always come first.' His voice was distancing itself from me as an echo will across a valley. 'I would have hurt your mother unless I'd had some place to go for comfort. I don't care who we are, we all need that. I'm an ordinary man in my appetites.'

'Is she married, too?' I heard myself ask, my voice fast in my skull as if my ears were waxed or blocked.

'She's a widow. As I am now. We shall leave a decent interval, but I wish you to know I have every intention of asking her to marry me. I'm sure she'll accept.'

'I'm pleased for you, Father,' I lied. 'I'm really very pleased for you both,' I continued adding further untruths but trying to be generous, still knowing this was the solace he required from me. I picked up my beer. 'Here's to you both. Thank you for being so honest.'

Some months later I received two letters, I think in the same post but cannot be certain. One read:

Dear Daniel,
Why do you not reply to my correspondence? Why do you put down the telephone when I ring? Why, yesterday, would you not answer the door when I knocked? Harry tells me you are ill and have no wish to see me. I am hurt and deeply worried.
Father.

The second was from someone called Wilfred Cole, whose name I did not at first recognize, but the underlinings in the letter slowly began to make sense.

Dear Dr Hinton,
We called at your house the other day. Peter thought he saw someone moving about through the window. No one bothered to open the door. He wondered why you would not let us in. Peter wants to <u>see</u> you in person because he can really <u>see</u> now, and he wants to thank you for his <u>sight</u> which is really very good. We think it is a miracle what has happened to us. I can't write, so have told this letter to a woman across the street who can. Peter will one day write to you himself, he will be able to learn now with his good <u>eyes</u>, because he will never forget your generosity. We think you are the kindest person on this earth.

III

Harry's will

7

I was sitting at the desk in my study re-reading the two letters, when, a few moments ago, someone rang my doorbell, and I was forced to put away my thoughts for a short while. It was Peter Cole: it seemed an odd but delightful coincidence that he should choose to visit just as I was about to begin to describe his contribution to the changes in my life. It was partly his idea that I begin this conversation-piece, and, as it turned out, he had called to see how my story was progressing. Peter is my closest, dearest friend, and he worries about me more than is necessary, so I spent a few minutes reassuring him that my story was moving forward reasonably well and that my silence of the last few weeks was for no other reason than that I had been busy. Since he lives twelve miles from me on the outskirts of Richmond and is careful about drinking alcohol when he has to drive, I poured two mugs of Earl Grey tea, still my favourite, and we came through into my study where we sat amongst my shelves of books and talked for an hour. Peter is an enchanting conversationalist, with that special ability to find the humour in almost any serious topic: being with him is to be reminded of the ridiculousness of pessimism. I have known him for over forty years – he is now in his mid-sixties – and never once have I seen him less than optimistic. He is the first to admit that his whole life is a testament to a belief in miracles.

Whilst we were talking together, I could not fully shake my writing from my mind, and I began in some vague way to realize just what a subjective account this is. It ignores much that would be important if I had taken a more objective approach. Memory is selective, and I can flash through my life quite quickly. It is the

153

people I remember and think about most; my mother; my father; Harry; Stella; John in Pennsylvania; and now Peter.

My memory of Peter's first visit to the house with his father is extremely hazy, unfocused as if I were standing a few inches from a large oil painting where only a few brush strokes are visible, and at variance with the facts: not that I think this matters very much. I have Wilfred Cole's letter in front of me now, and it definitely implies that I did not open the door. I can recall being fearful of the strangeness of others, but my memory is of lifting the latch and of seeing them before me in my front garden.

'Do you remember us?' they had said.

'You must forgive me,' I had replied, 'I don't think so.'

'This is my son Peter. You have given him back his sight.'

'No, you must have the wrong house. Try along the street. It's nothing to do with me.'

And with that I had shut the door.

I have a further memory of them waiting a minute or two on the cinderpath looking baffled, before leaving in the van in which they had arrived. It seems reasonable to expect I was in tears.

Whilst he was here, Peter offered me a cigarette to complement the Earl Grey. This is one of his several excuses for not giving up. I often think he comes to my house mainly for a quiet smoke. I am eighty-six years old and beginning to worry about the effect smoking is having on my health, but I accepted his mild Silk Cut. We are a dying breed, and friends must stick together. Left to myself I will still smoke Park Drive, which I keep hidden in a kitchen cupboard because people who mean well are inclined to become angry.

'It isn't surprising your memories are hazy, Daniel,' he said, lighting both cigarettes with his clipper lighter. 'You had a nervous breakdown.'

'Yes, logically I know I did. It's just everything is a jumble and so vague, there's no detail in my recollection. I can recall feeling really ill, just as I can remember feeling healthy and happy in another part of my life. On those many days when I was happy, I can visualize entire moments. Pain is like that, isn't it? We can recall we were in pain, but the specifics are dulled. Thank goodness we have a human mechanism which protects us.'

'Can you remember what finally tipped you over the edge?'

'Yes, that's very clear. It wasn't you or your blindness. It was learning of my father's mistress. I was so naive then, Peter, it was such a shock. It was the last thing I ever expected in this world. Now, of course, I think it's rather jolly, but then it altered my whole perception of him when it shouldn't have done. He was still my father, he was still the father I'd always known, but with a woman whom he loved and wished to marry. Who amongst us would choose to be alone? It was very simple and not complicated at all.'

'It's like all our lives, Daniel, what we are is in our silence, in what we never say, in what we choose not to reveal of ourselves.'

'Yes, I've been realizing that. It's funny, but I've learnt so much these last few weeks as I've been sitting at my desk. I never expected to learn quite so much about myself.'

'Are you pleased?'

'It's certainly keeping me young. I'm more content than when I began. I've revealed parts of myself that so far I've shown to very few people. I've even put in the episode in Arizona where I took my clothes off. You're the only one I've ever told about that. Boring people may think I'm odd or untruthful, but I don't care anymore.'

Peter drew on his cigarette and spoke with such nonchalance that I knew his next question would be personal. He stammers a little when he speaks in disguise.

'Have you r-reached the point in the s-story where I re-enter as an adult, D-Daniel?'

'Peter, you're being vain,' I laughed. 'It's not often you're conceited.'

'W-well, I'm looking f-forward to r-reading about myself. I can't wait. Am I still a boy?'

'You're still a boy.'

'Oh, what a pity. I was such a vacant child. I never said very much. I became interesting as I got older.'

Peter left me a few minutes ago and I am once again alone with my thoughts. It is nearing ten o'clock. In the light from my window I can see the vixen who calls regularly at this hour to take the dog food which I leave out on my patio. Every night I worry about the wisdom of this, for it only encourages her forays into the town, but I can see she is in cub and her visits must cease shortly in any case. She eats greedily from the dog bowl I bought at the pet shop, with her head tossed upwards between mouthfuls so that I can see the full length of her neck, which is blood-marked from some recent scrap or fight, her fur knotted where she cannot twist to reach and lick her wound. Momentarily, she darts away into the shadows at the sound of my neighbour who is carrying a box of rubbish to his dustbin with a torch, unaware of my vixen's nightly vigil. A few weeks ago, she would have been off across my garden wall, but now she stays quietly where she is by the rhododendrons until the neighbour goes back inside. I could no longer live such a worried life, which is why I admire her.

On my desk is a photograph of Harry and Jenni, in an antique silver frame, taken when Jenni was thirteen at her grammar school during the second war. Every year in June her school held a sports day, and every year I went along with my camera to snap pictures on the playing field. Those girls who were not athletic, including Jenni, ran novelty races as their contribution to the afternoon's entertainment. In my photograph she is holding an egg and spoon. Harry is beside her on the long jump running track where he was helping to officiate with a tape measure. I have managed to catch them at a moment of giggling, unposed spontaneity. It is the last photograph I took of Harry.

I am slowly reaching that point in my story when I must begin to describe his death, and I am dreading it. He died in a hole in a wheat field, with the spilled blood running from his mouth, and his hands twisted beyond recognition because he must have raised them to protect himself from the shrapnel of the bomb. So much is fluke that my friend should die in this way. So much is not fluke that the world should war war war, and end the life of one who was devoted to peace.

When Harry bought the farm, I had naively imagined he might wish to cultivate the land following Amish practice, but this proved not to be the case at all. He travelled the length of the country visiting almost every agricultural show, looking at invention upon invention, until his farm became a model of innovation, and people travelled long distances to see the new machinery at work in his fields. He was one of the first in the North Riding to buy a tractor, and the very first to plant corn with a new seed-drill employing the tractor's hydraulics. In his second summer, he cut his wheat with a combine harvester, which stopped the traffic on nearby roads because no one had seen one before. The horses became superfluous, so much so that Jenni insisted they be treated as pets with a field of their own. When harvest was over, he flew to Holland to meet a pig breeder who was developing a revolutionary method of raising pigs outdoors in small corrugated metal huts. Harry kept his own pigs in conventional sties, and he wished to see how his system might be changed. On his return, the farm was completely re-planned, reorganized, the land re-fenced, and an additional hundred sows purchased. The idea was to shepherd the pigs around the farm on an annual basis, so that pasture fertilized organically one year would, the following year, be suitable for a crop of barley, wheat, or oats. In this way there was a natural continuity to the husbandry of the land. As with all Harry's undertakings, he set about his endeavours with an energy bordering on fanaticism, working tirelessly, and expecting his employees to do likewise. He paid his men one and a half times the average wage, plus a six monthly bonus, and even flew each of them to Holland with their families so they might see what they were trying to achieve. It was remarkable, anarchic behaviour from a man whose lunacy appeared to know no limit. When his fellow landowners became malicious and spiteful, he shunned them without regret, turning his back on the local pub, the local hunt, and finally the local church. They were alarmed by his egalitarianism, and wondered how it could be that he was not making massive losses. But, unlike them, he was not interested in money and did not need to return a profit: the farm was simply his hobby.

I saw little of the farm myself at this time, but learned of the changes from an ebullient Harry, who called regularly at my home. He was the only person I would allow into my house, and we developed a secret knock, at my instigation, so that I might know it was him. He accepted my 'strangeness' without complaint, but always pointed out my paranoia. He insisted on normality, and would prepare a simple meal from food he had brought, or make a hot drink for us to have together in front of the fire. In summer, when the weather was clement and he was frequently delayed by the long hours of work required in the fields, we would drink iced lemonade in my garden, where we would sit beneath the oak tree mostly in silence, because there was little I wanted to say and he was tired. His face was often ashen despite the sun. On those nights when the summer heat was unbearable, he would fall asleep, and I would leave him in the deckchair with his head resting upon a pillow throughout the early hours, waking him at dawn to return to the farm without his having slept in his bed. He would cook breakfast for us both at the stove, improvising from my inadequate larder, and wash the dishes by himself at the sink before leaving. We ate unusual combinations of eggs and cold chicken, bacon and pears, peas and creamed cheese which he said was Hindu from Madras. He wore an apron. On all these occasions, he laid the table with cutlery from the drawer as if my kitchen were his own. One morning, as he was sweeping breadcrumbs from the table-cloth with his hands, he turned and kissed me lightly on my forehead. I found pleasure in his domesticity, and thought his peaceful home-keeping such a contrast to his excited stories of the changes taking place on his farm.

But the eighteen months I spent indoors or in my garden is almost a complete blank.

At some point towards the end of summer, I heard the usual confidential knock on my door. It was midday and the sound caught me by surprise because Harry called according to the light, always as it was getting dark. My immediate reaction was that something must be wrong. I panicked, hearing the crazy screams in my head which, until that moment, had begun to ease. In the seconds it took me to open the door, my head exploded with all its old rage and anger. It was Jenni in a duffle-coat and a pair of over-large Wellingtons. At first I did not recognize her because her hair had been cut short like a boy's. Her face had lost some of its puppy fat; her cheek bones seemed higher and thinner. She took my hand. I hid my tears as best I could, expecting her habitual comment on my crying, but she had grown up a little and kept her observations to herself.

I ushered her in and we stood for a minute or two in my sitting-room with a glass of lemonade each and a bar of choco-late I had managed to find. I felt uncomfortable. Jenni talked non-stop about how pleasant it was to see me – she was then nine years old – which put me even more on edge. I shuffled to and fro in my stockinged feet, looking through the bay window where I could see her father's Mercedes parked with a mysterious driver in overalls sitting at the wheel reading a newspaper. Jenni sensed my restlessness and was confident enough to explain that he was one of the farm workers. So, when the lemonade was finished, I put my shoes on and went with her to the farm.

The roads were quiet apart from a long succession of army trucks travelling to Catterick Camp a few miles away. The Daily Sketch, which the farm worker had tossed onto the back seat beside me, headlined the German invasion of Poland. It was the first newspaper I had seen in almost two years, and the first I knew of impending war.

At the farm, Harry was waiting for me by the new lean-to barn. We walked together across the fields amidst the rows of corrugated pig huts, which were not quite what I had imagined from his description: each small hut was an upturned semicircle with wooden planking at the back to protect the sow from the weather; the front was similarly enclosed but with a small opening onto the field. Inside each hut, I could see a bale of scattered straw and the sow's nest.

'I thought you might come if I sent Jenni,' he said. 'I always feel you're frightened of her.'

'She got me here, so I suppose I must be, yes.'

'How's your anxiety?'

'Well, it's quite high,' I said catching my breath. 'I'm not used to being outdoors.'

'You've been looking better lately, Daniel. There's colour in your cheeks, both literally and metaphorically. You've begun talking at last.'

'Have I?'

'It's time you began to change now.'

'Are you going to be tough with me?'

'Yes, I am. This behaviour of yours is no longer reasonable. We're becoming like Darby and Joan, you and me at your house. I'm beginning to feel like your wife.' He was jovial. 'I know I'm cheery about it, but there's no longer any excuse.'

Pig huts dotted the field. Sows roamed between them and the wooden feeding troughs placed at a central point, where the surrounding pasture had been denuded of grass and was baked with dried mud. Each sow had a metal ring shaped like a curtain hook through its nose.

'The sows congregate by the troughs,' he said, 'and root. Whatever pain we induce in their noses we can't stop them completely. It isn't too bad at the moment because the weather's been reasonably dry. But in the winter it will be a problem, so we've decided to move the troughs around the field once a week to stop areas becoming too muddy.'

'I'm sorry if you've been feeling like my wife, Harry.'

'Oh, I don't particularly mind for myself.' He smiled once again, and stopped to scratch one of the sows behind the ears: small particles of dust flew up into the air from her skin. 'Actually, I quite enjoy it. But it isn't fair on Jenni my never being there. And it certainly isn't good for you to become dependent.'

'Do the sows like being petted?'

'This one does. She's quite tame. Pigs are highly intelligent animals.' The sow leaned into his legs and tried to scratch an itch on her neck with a movement upwards and downwards rather than sideways. 'Stroke her, Daniel. Pigs are great therapy.'

I ran my hand along the arch of her back where the skin was brittle, tougher than I might have imagined. Beneath my fingers I felt the layer of coarse hair which was hardly visible to the eye, but which lay like a succession of needles towards her tail. I stroked my hand backwards and thought I might cut myself.

'I've been answering your correspondence for you, Daniel. Not that there's been very much of that lately. It's time you began replying for yourself.'

'Have you been planning this, Harry?' The sow was now leaning against my own legs, almost forcing me over into a water trough. 'Is this another of your schemes?'

'Let's walk on and I'll tell you what my ideas were to have been.'

We climbed the fence into a stubble field of cut wheat, immediately disturbing a hare, which darted left and then right into the pig field, where it looked even more disorientated, zigzagging amongst the sows. The wheat field was dry, as the skin on the sow's hindquarters had been, so that the stubble crunched beneath our feet as we flattened the straw with our shoes, taking with us the odd stray head of corn which caught between our shoe laces. We walked slowly and Harry adjusted his natural, keener pace to suit my own. I began to relax, allowing the air to fill my lungs for the first time in many months, permitting the iron grip of my chest to ease a little.

'You won't have seen a newspaper, Daniel?'

'I have as a matter-of-fact. In your Mercedes coming here. The Fascists are on the march. Hitler has invaded Poland.'

'Then you'll know war is about to be declared.'

'I suppose it must be, yes.'

The corn field was on an incline which from the top afforded a full panoramic view of the surrounding landscape. It was the highest point on his farm: hills and fields stretched before us as far as the eye could see. In the distance, farmers were still completing their harvests with binders and teams of horses in a scene reminiscent of Constable. Harry, whose own harvest was over, had left a small, circular grassy area which he had not cultivated or planted with wheat, to grow wild, and here he had built a wooden bench so that he might sit in peace and look out over the countryside. His 'garden' looked incongruous, but it was somehow typical of the man. On the bench was a bottle of beer for us both.

'You have been planning this, Harry. We didn't stroll this way by accident.'

'I wanted a disorderly area of the farm for myself. I love it up here. This is perfect. There can be too much order in the world. It reminds me how lucky I am.'

We opened the bottles and drank from the necks without glasses.

'It's time you had a drink again,' he said. 'There was a time when I worried you were becoming an alcoholic. Don't you remember all the brandy you were drinking?'

'No, I don't, not at all.'

'Well, you were, so I removed all the bottles from your house. It was partly my fault. I encouraged you when Stella and I were parting company.'

We sat down side by side on the bench. A warming breeze was getting up so I opened my coat. I ran my eyes over the small area of unfenced wilderness. It was no larger than an acre, and the notion for its existence could only have come from someone as unorthodox as Harry.

'Are you depressed?' I asked.

'Why, should I be? No, not particularly. A little melancholic. The thought of war disturbs me. You know I shall refuse to have anything to do with it.'

'Yes, I might have guessed.'

'Then you are beginning to be better because you're right.' He chuckled as if this affirmation of his pacifism was the cause of his present sunniness. 'But I didn't bring you up here to talk about war, although it now affects, unfortunately, what I have to say. One of the letters you didn't answer was from John. I wrote to him on your behalf, asking him to invite you to Pennsylvania.'

'I don't remember receiving a letter.'

'I even read it to you, Daniel. I have it with me in my pocket. I kept it.'

He gave me the letter and I read John's politely couched invitation to the Amish farm just as Harry had said. It was written in pencil, with the words carefully chosen so as not to imply superiority. Harry must have read the letter to me several times, for the lead was smudged across the page where he had re-folded the paper.

'It's been on my mind for some while that John is the person you ought to see, Daniel.'

'I'm not disagreeing with you, but why?'

Harry waited a moment to order his thoughts.

'Because John would understand the need you have to forgive yourself,' he said. 'I don't understand you completely, but you feel your behaviour has been Fascist in character, don't you?'

'I'm beginning to see I could never be authoritarian. I don't know enough about the world.'

'I think it's the opposite. In a funny way, you know too much to be a tyrant. I'm the one who cuts myself off. Look at this little garden I've created, it's like an island of peace.'

The bench had no support at the back, so we leaned forwards with our elbows resting on our knees. Harry blew across the top of his half-empty bottle making a whistling sound, and I copied him.

'Over the years, I've probably helped to reinforce the false view you have of yourself,' he went on. 'I remember criticizing your desire for elitism at that crummy school. I remember always attacking your naivety, yet praising your weakness. I remember John, whom you weren't sure about to begin with. I remember manipulating you to New Orleans when you were doubtful. On so many occasions I attacked your snobbery, and later your self-righteousness. I've so many memories of saying what a fool you'd become.'

'But all that is true. I did become those things.'

'Perhaps you did in some ways. Daniel, it was wrong of me to manipulate your insecurity in order to cover and hide my own deficiencies in the same regard.'

'Not at all. Where would I be now if you hadn't?'

'It's time the past no longer mattered. I suppose I brought you up here to tell you that. In a way, I'm manipulating you at this moment. Why don't we walk on and I'll show you the rest of the farm?'

We strolled down the hillside towards another field of sows, our empty bottles swinging by our sides. Harry, three or four times, blew across the top of his, as if he were distracted and still had much he wished to say but was biding his time. We climbed a wire fence by one of the upright stakes and jumped down the other side. The young sows immediately began to nuzzle about us, one of them biting at my shoes until Harry slapped her on the rump with his hand. She went away briefly to the water trough but came back and continued where she had left off.

'These are young sows,' he said. 'They've not learnt restraint. They've yet to farrow and raise a litter. They're gilts. Spell it the other way and it would be an appropriate word in the circumstances.'

I scratched the gilt's neck behind her ear. She had unfastened my shoelaces and was eating them. Her white saliva was all over the bottom of my trousers.

'How many are there?' I asked.

'Thirty-five. They're in-pig. They'll farrow this autumn.'

'It's incredible. I've never seen anything like it.'

We were surrounded by a writhing mass of pigs, all pushing to get close to us. I could feel their collective weight against my legs and could not move. One was tugging at the sleeve of my coat, so I raised my arms shoulder high as if I were tiptoeing into a cold sea and tried to inch my way forward, but the wave of pigs made progress almost impossible.

'Are they hungry, Harry?'

'Pigs are always hungry. They'll chew on anything. Push them with your feet.'

'I don't like to. I'm quite enjoying it.'

'You won't hurt them. Kick them on their snouts by the ring.'

I did so, gently.

'I said kick, Daniel, not caress.'

He came towards me slapping the pigs out of the way with the toe of his shoe, and we strolled on across the field between two lines of huts. The pigs trailed behind us, still yelping for attention.

'How many boars do you have?' I asked.

'Four.'

'They have a happy life.'

His face broke into an impish grin. He looked as boyish as I had seen him since our days at school, with his black hair uncombed as it always had been then. I thought of those summer afternoons when we had bicycled to the river and lain without our clothes in a hidden gully. It seemed a long time ago: an innocent memory of a bygone age, which indeed it was. It seemed possible that our naivety had been dissipated at a similar pace to that of the century itself, and that a war might clear the air.

'It's time you forgave your father,' he said quietly. 'The poor man's done nothing wrong.'

'I know.'

'We've both reached that point in our lives where we must forgive our respective parents, Daniel. Although he's dead, I must seek a way to forgive my father for blaming me for a murder I didn't do. Your father took a mistress, that is all.'

'I promise I'll write this evening.'

'I'd be grateful if you would. I've always liked your father.'

'Have you seen him?'

'Mmm, once or twice. He's remarried. I went to the wedding.'

My shoelaces were missing where the sow had chewed them away. I tripped over, falling straight onto my face. Harry waited whilst I picked myself up, a broad grin enlivening his eyes.

'That wasn't a trip to cover my embarrassment,' I said. 'I genuinely fell over. The pigs have wrecked my clothes.'

'You look like Charlie Chaplin in rags.'

'Harry, he's thin, I'm little and rotund.'

'Oliver Hardy then.'

'He's big and fat.'

'Jenni says we're like Laurel and Hardy. I think it's a compliment.'

I found my beer bottle which had flown towards one of the huts, and Harry opened a gate in the hedge which took us

164

through into the adjoining field where a small herd of cows were grazing quietly.

'These are heifers,' he said. 'I'm keeping a few to raise some beef cattle, but I prefer the pigs.'

The young cows backed away as though nervous of our presence. Unlike the sows, who had been delighted to see us, the heifers gave me the impression that we had invaded their territory.

'It was a modest wedding, Daniel. You would have enjoyed it.'

'I'm really pleased for them both. There was a time I'd have been lying if I'd said that, but I'm not now. Tell me about my stepmother?'

'She's very nice, very ordinary. I don't mean that to be patronizing either. She's good fun and down to earth. There's nothing snooty or precious about her. She wants to be merry and happy, which I truly admire.'

The heifers, overcoming some of their initial shyness, had slowly advanced towards us, and Harry stopped to count them because the previous day several had broken a hole in the hedge. I could see where their exit, into a field of boars, had been repaired with fencing posts and barbed-wire. I listened as he counted to fifteen. My hands were dirty with pig muck from my fall, so I took the opportunity to clean them on the grass.

'Daniel, one of them's got your bottle,' he yelled.

'I put it down to wipe my hands.'

'Get it off her. She'll eat it.'

The heifer, about a yard away, had the bottle in her open mouth and was licking it with her long, curved tongue. Her head was up and her eyes glazed with pleasure. I lunged forward, putting my fingers into her mouth, grabbing the bottle from between her lips. With a strong flick of her neck she darted sideways, panic-stricken. Immediately, her forelegs buckled beneath her so that her nose collided with the earth, almost somersaulting her onto her back, scattering the rest of the herd across the field towards the repair in the hedge. The heifer retrieved her balance, looked bemused and exhaled a snort of air through her nostrils, dug her hindlegs deep into the couch-grass, jumped high, and escaped to her left with such speed I thought she might never stop.

'You were lucky,' Harry said calmly as if nothing untoward had occurred.

'I don't think I've ever moved so fast in my life, Harry.' My heart was beating against my ribs. My fingers were bruised from where, in my haste, I had caught the heifer on her jaw. 'I thought cows were shy animals.'

'Oh, they're suspicious of strangers to begin with. You did well. She probably wouldn't have swallowed it, but it was best to be certain.'

I held the bottle in my hand, which was covered with her thick, milky-white saliva.

'Daniel, you've landed in some cow shit. I'm afraid that's very Oliver Hardy. Jenni will be delighted.'

'I don't care what we do now,' I said, wiping the cowpat from my coat with the edge of the bottle, making the mess even worse, 'but I am not walking through those boars. They look vicious. Goodness knows what might happen.'

'The heifers are all here so we can go on.'

The field was undulating: I kept losing my footing and even my shoes.

'My father is happy?' I asked, doing my best to walk normally.

'Of course he is.'

The heifers, recovered from their ordeal, were following us at a safe distance, as the sows had done earlier.

'I don't mean to embarrass you, and whatever you do don't trip over again,' he said carefully so that I knew a non-sequitur was coming, 'but I've often wondered about your own sexuality.' He blew across the top of his bottle. 'Have you had many girl friends, Daniel?'

It seemed no indignity was to be spared me, so I answered him truthfully, although it took me a moment to find the correct words.

'I'm almost a virgin, Harry. I think I might have had sex once with a woman in Italy, but I can't remember because I was drunk at the time. The answer is no, but I'm not homosexual. I know you've thought I might be in the past?'

'It is something I've considered, yes. I finally dismissed the notion when I saw you were jealous of your father. I don't think a homosexual would be envious of his father taking a mistress. You were envious, weren't you?'

'Yes, I was. My life is a mess regarding sex.'

'Don't be self-pitying. I thought you were over that?'

'I was simply being honest.'

166

We climbed a stile into a field where barley had been growing before it was harvested, and we walked along the ruts created by a tractor's wheels in the soft earth. The afternoon light was beginning to fade across the lower-lying farms in front of us, lengthening the shadows of trees and hedgerows, fashioning the dales into a sepia-like photograph with the autumn browns in prominence. It was so still, as if this moment would never be so again, as if I somehow knew a catastrophe would one day befall us. The premonition was so powerful that I forgot about the ruin of my clothes, the muddle of my life, and instead concentrated upon my friend.

'I often seek a schoolboy's relief,' I said. 'I was jealous of my father finding a lady. It didn't seem fair that he should enjoy a sex life. I know that's silly, but many things we feel are silly. It doesn't help us not to feel them, as you once remarked many years ago in the dormitory at school when you were talking about your father and a murder you didn't commit. I really understand you now. I didn't then. I can see how you believed yourself to be guilty, although you were innocent. Guilt is such a destructive emotion, isn't it? But a necessary one in some ways. It's the check on our avaricious desire. It's a control on our baser instincts. I distrust people with no guilt at all.'

'They are dangerous people, Daniel. People like my father.' He drew his arm across my shoulder as if we might be two boys on a day's ramble together. 'He thought he was guilty of nothing, and yet he was always in the wrong.'

'Goodness, I could no longer be hectoring or self-righteous,' I said. 'I know so little. It is thanks to you that I'm sane. Your patience these last two years has been remarkable. I'd have lost my temper with someone like me.'

'What would have been the point?'

'No point, of course.'

'I learnt patience from John. He taught me that to wait is one of the greatest virtues, which is why you must go and see him. I don't always follow his instructions, but it's good to know them.'

The field descended towards a hollow where our vista of the dales was cut off by the rising land ahead of us. Harry stopped in the dip at the bottom and looked at the sky which was beginning to be starlit. It was like standing in a bowl. I could see Orion to the east and the Plough to the north, taking shape through the thin layer of cloud.

'Occasionally, I'm reminded of Pennsylvania,' he said. 'The stars in Pennsylvania are magnificent. When you go, go out at night alone along the dirt roads and look at the sky. The Amish live surrounded by the most idyllic countryside in the world, and at night it becomes so peaceful that it really is heaven on earth. I understand why they know God, Daniel. There's nothing that disturbs: there's no violence, no anger, no pettiness. It's unique in my experience. John is very wise.'

'You love him, don't you, Harry?'

'Oh, not in the way that I love you. I love John as an ideal. He's someone I greatly admire. When you go, you'll see that he's a difficult man to love in a conventional way.'

'Why is that?' I asked.

'The Amish believe in collective thought, which doesn't suit my temperament. John sometimes has to subordinate his intelligence to the will of the majority. I could never do that.' He walked on up the slope without waiting for me. 'Are you coming?' he called.

'Yes,' I said catching him up.

He tossed his beer bottle high into the air as if energizing himself and then caught it with a slap between his palms. He was aware he had not fully answered my question.

'I learnt to juggle in New Orleans,' he said. 'Give me your bottle.' I did so and he juggled the two bottles from hand to hand. 'John can be very stern and uncompromising. He's austere and will not suffer a fool. I am a fool. I'm a clown, Daniel.' He dropped a bottle into the rut of the tractor wheel and picked it up. 'A not very good clown at that.'

He continued to juggle as we followed the wheel markings uphill towards the crest of the ridge, where the horizon was clear once more. The farmers, who had earlier been harvesting, were leading their teams of horses home in the remaining daylight. Harry, with his tractors and expensive new machinery, had completed his harvest the day before.

'But as clowning is serious, so am I,' he said. 'It's the money which makes me a clown, Daniel. I've the money to do anything I want. It's very un-John, very non-Amish.' He juggled the bottles high into the evening air. 'I can fail and it doesn't matter. There's nothing at stake for me.' The bottles turned gracefully at their apex in mid-flight. Occasionally, he arched his stomach and caught one behind his back. 'I have to create my own excitement all the time. I'm the sort of person who needs excitement in order to feel alive.' The bottles were going higher and higher. 'I need danger. I should really give the money away, but I haven't the courage.' He caught both bottles with a final flourish and put them into his jacket pockets. 'My lack of courage will be the story of my life, Daniel.'

'I don't think so, Harry.'

'When you go to Pennsylvania, you'll see that John has true courage. I play at life from a position of safety. John doesn't have that. He would never allow himself my luxury. It would be too comfortable for him, too soft, too ungodly. The Amish can be so strict that it is frightening. They have no ornaments in their homes, no photographs of their children, no blinds at their windows to shut out the night.' He chortled. 'You'll love it, Daniel, you can play Peeping Tom for hours on end. But watch for the dogs. They all have dogs, and they bark.'

'A war is going to make it difficult for me to travel,' I said.

'I know. Are you too old to travel on a banana boat, as John did all those years ago?'

'I think I am, Harry, yes.'

'I want your promise that you will travel as soon as war is ended.'

'What a funny way of putting it,' I said.

'Why?'

'Because it sounds as if you don't expect to be here.' I was reminded of my premonition. A chill inched the length of my spine, making me shiver. 'Of course I'll promise if that's what you want, but I rather hoped you'd be coming with me.'

'My impressions of Pennsylvania are my own. You'll enjoy being by yourself with John.'

The land fell away before us so that we were following a gentle gradient almost continually downhill. In the far distance, through the haze of the moon, I could see the pinprick lights of his farmhouse, where I presumed Jenni was having her supper with the housekeeper before bedtime. The farmhouse had been built as a monastery for a Franciscan order of monks, the Capuchins, but for the last two hundred years had been home to the families who had taken over and farmed the surrounding land some time after the monastery was dissolved. Harry had once told me he could still see the Franciscans walking from room to room with lighted tallows, wearing their dark-brown cowls, girdles and sandals. On a number of occasions he had heard their prayers emanating from the stone walls. If Harry found the austerity of these monks romantic, in the same way that he found the strictures of the Amish romantic too, it had not stopped him being the first occupant to re-design the interior, so that the house now had every modern luxury available, including central heating and mains electricity. Harry could afford to indulge his taste, and his taste was exquisite. The house was beautifully furnished throughout, with restored oak beams in the ceilings, Indian carpets on the floors and a marble fireplace as the centrepiece of the sitting-room. The furniture had been made to his own specifications in Northumberland. I understood what he meant when he said he played at life from a position of safety.

'Is supper in your new kitchen on the itinerary?' I asked, abandoning any idea I had of mentioning my foreboding.

'Yes, it is.'

He took a torch from his pocket to light our path.

'Have you ever heard from Stella, Harry?'

'No, I haven't.'

'Would you like to hear from her?'

'Not particularly. I'd like Jenni to have a normal life.' He lifted the beam of the torch so that I could see his face was close to laughter. 'There's a bedroom at the house for you. It's yours whenever you feel like staying. Make it your own. Furnish it as you please. When I'm depressed, ignore me. When I'm happy, be my company.'

'Yes, I will.'

'Should you ever need money, just take it. Don't even ask. I'll give you some signed cheques.'

'I've no need of money, Harry. I still have the fifty thousand pounds your mother left me in her will. I haven't even spent the interest.'

A few yards in front of us I could see the low, dark outline of what I presumed must be a hedge. Harry directed the torch away from his face, lighting a metal gate which he opened for us to pass through. On the other side was a rough track leading towards the farm buildings. Two deep ruts, cut by the persistence of the tractor's wheels, ran either side of a grassy ridge in the centre. I kept stumbling, losing my footing on the sharp stones which protruded through the dried mud in the bottom of the furrow in which I was walking. Harry, in the other furrow, shone the torch on the grass so that we both benefited from the light.

'You're slowing down, Daniel.'

'I'm beginning to be weary. We've walked a long way.'

'About ten miles. I'll read Jenni her bedtime story and then I'll cook us both a meal. I learnt cooking from you. You've always enjoyed your food, haven't you?'

'Yes, I have,' I said smiling, but I knew he could not possibly see my face through the darkness.

'The only person I ask you to be careful with is Jenni. I'm doing my best not to spoil her. She gets pocket money, but only as much as the other children on the farm. I don't want her thinking she is superior to them.'

'I would never interfere in your decisions. Children are a mystery to me.'

'Oh, I'm probably being silly, but it's why I'm sending her to the local school. She goes on the bus every morning with the other children. It's why I'm hoping she'll pass her tests and go to the grammar school when she's older. I've no intention of sending her away, as we were sent away. I want to go with her to founder's day, sports days, and be a normal father. I want to help out at the school in an ordinary way. I'd like her to know that I'm no better or worse than all the other fathers.'

'I understand.'

'Do you?' he asked, his voice questioning me across the density of the night as if I had told an untruth.

'Of course I do. It was a bloody terrible life you had in that house in Mayfair. You want Jenni to be happy. I do too, just as I wanted you to be happy as a child.'

There was a silence. The farm track stretched before us in the beam of his torchlight. As the silence lengthened, my heartbeat increased with the uncertainty of what was to come, for I knew instinctively he was going to say something he had never said before.

'Thank you for feeling pity for me, Daniel, when no one else

171

ever did. I think as parents we have to teach our children pity for others. I do not believe that love is natural. That is my subjective experience. My parents taught me nothing of what it is to be kind or sympathetic. I just want Jenni to be those things, if those things are possible for her, which I'm certain they are. She's a self-possessed little girl, but I'm fighting that. She's stubborn, rather awkward at times, and knows her own mind. I suppose she gets it all from me.'

He had stopped and was looking at the night sky as he had earlier when talking about John and the Amish. I waited, expecting our journey to continue, for our walk and conversation had become a journey, but instead he switched off the torch so that the stars were clearly visible.

'She knows I'm rich, but I've never told her how rich,' he said as if something else were at the front of his mind. 'I'd rather she never knew, Daniel. I can't spend the money. It's still growing. There's money in bonds and investments that I still hardly know about. Apparently, I own gold in South Africa. It's crazy. I've just refused to take an interest.' He switched the torch back on and shone the light onto his face. 'Do I look like the sort of person who knows what to do with money?'

'No, you don't, Harry, but I've always thought that.'

He walked the few feet towards me, and we continued on our way.

'What were you thinking about just now?' I asked.

'John. John is my conscience. I'd have liked to have given Jenni an Amish childhood, with all its purity and innocence. You'll see what I mean by that when you go.'

We were soon at the farmhouse, where Jenni, bathed and in her nightdress, was waiting to be read a bedtime story by her father.

'Uncle Daniel, it's Jenni.'

'Hello, Jenni,' I said into the telephone. 'How's tricks? I thought I might pop over tomorrow evening with some photographs I've taken. There are one or two of you and Daddy on the sports field at school. Would you like to see them?'

'I've been ringing you for nearly an hour.'

I had returned late from the hospital in Middlesbrough where for the previous year, after three years as a house officer, I had been working as a registrar in the orthopaedic department, and was just unbuttoning my jacket when the telephone had begun ringing.

'Yes, I'm sorry but I've been delayed,' I said. 'We've had the Luftwaffe bombing Middlesbrough again this evening. I've been operating. Fortunately, there weren't too many casualties.'

'Uncle Daniel, he's dead.'

Jenni often telephoned me with her news if I had been busy and had not seen her for a few days. I thought at first she was referring to one of the horses who were growing old and obese in their retirement paddock at the farm.

'Where's Daddy? Isn't he there to help you?'

'Uncle Daniel, you're not listening to me.' Her voice was beginning to choke and take on a staccato rhythm. 'Please listen to me. I don't know what to do.'

'It's all right, Jenni, calm down. What are you saying? Who is dead?'

'Daddy is.'

My jacket was hanging loosely from my shoulders, neither on nor off as a consequence of the haste with which I had picked up the telephone receiver. I manoeuvred my arms from the sleeves. The jacket fell down my legs to the carpet.

'I was sitting in my bedroom doing my chemistry homework when I heard an explosion. I knew Daddy was outside with his telescope looking at the planets.'

'I'm with you, Jenni. I'm just bending down trying to find my cigarettes in my pocket. I think I smoked the last one driving home. Are you there?'

'Yes.'

'I can't find them, it doesn't matter.'

'When he didn't come in, I went out to look for him. He's in a field. There's a big hole. I've told the farm men to go away. Please come quickly.'

'Jenni, stay inside the house. I've some cigarettes in the kitchen. I'll be with you in a few minutes.'

His body was as Jenni had described, in a field where the wheat was tall but still green, for it was early summer and the sun had yet to ripen the emerging heads of corn. I first saw the jagged crater, where the wheat was flattened as if by a strong wind, in the beam of my torch and kneeled down to check the pulse in his neck, but I could see from the way the explosion had caught his body that there would be no pulse to find. I did very little else, apart from pull his legs from behind his back and lay them as straight as I could in a normal, human position. His hands had been blown away by the shrapnel lying scattered across the crater's edge. He had been dead for about an hour and a half.

'Don't look, Jenni. There's nothing to be gained by looking.'

'I've seen already,' she said. 'He liked walking at night, watching the sky. I came running but couldn't get close because of the flames. When I arrived here the wheat was on fire. It's all burned, you can smell it. The farm men smothered them with their coats. I could see he was dead so I told them to go home.'

I turned the beam of my torch away from his face, but Jenni kept hers directed towards his torso where the blood from his mouth had dried on his waistcoat and shirt. Carefully, without asking her permission, I took the torch from her palm and switched it off. I played my own light along the edge of the field looking for the wreckage of an aeroplane but could see nothing apart from the blackened wheat and the charred remains of a sapling which had caught fire.

A German Dornier Do 217 bomber, having completed its raid on the iron foundries in Middlesbrough twenty miles away, had dropped its one remaining bomb over Harry's farm in order to lighten the load for its journey home across the North Sea.

I did not like to hurry her, but, after a few moments of stillness, I suggested to Jenni that we walk back towards the farmhouse to find a bedsheet to place over his body and that we telephone the authorities. Jenni continued to talk to me as an adult for the first time. She was almost fourteen years old.

'Didn't you have any cigarettes? Why aren't you smoking?'

'I thought I had but I must have been mistaken.'

'Daddy has some at the house. I'll find you them.'

'Would you, Jenni? Thank you.'

'I would have put the flames out myself but the farm men wouldn't let me.'

'You can't do everything on your own.'

'I felt dirty having them there watching.'

'Don't be silly, they were only helping.'

'I know but I couldn't stop myself feeling that way. I shouted at them.'

174

I put my hand in my pocket and played with the box of matches that was there, sliding open and shutting the drawer between my thumb and index finger.

'You're not crying,' she went on. 'I still remember when you used to cry rather a lot.'

'I do too. And your father would tell me off for it. Perhaps that is what I'm remembering now. Your father was unique, Jenni.'

'He wished to be like every other father, but he could never be because he was too much of an individual for that. I think he was frightened I'd inherit his depressions. I'm right, aren't I?'

'Yes, there's a lot of truth in what you say.'

'He was depressed today. He often went out with his telescope when he was depressed. The stars helped him to remember Pennsylvania.'

'I know.'

'Why did he buy the farm? Was it his wish to be like John in some way?'

'I think it was, Jenni, yes.'

And then she asked me her most mature question so far.

'How well did you know Daddy, Uncle Daniel.'

'I knew him very well, Jenni. As well as two people can know one another. There were many things which remained unspoken between us, but we always understood what lay beneath the silence. We didn't score off or hurt one another, but reached an acceptance of each other's values. I think that is what true friendship is.' I had almost used the word love instead of friendship and decided to do so. 'That is what love is, Jenni.'

'There were events in his childhood which he never mentioned. Did he talk about them to you?'

'Oh, occasionally. Only occasionally.' I began to protect her from the truth. 'There was no single event which was large enough, or of sufficient importance to be the sole cause of his depressions.'

'Yes, perhaps,' she said, 'perhaps not. Did nothing happen between him and his father, my grandfather, to make him feel unhappy?'

'Beyond their general dislike of one another, I don't think so. He wouldn't want us to remember the past at a moment like this.'

'No,' she said. 'Thank you. He didn't want to see me upset, did he, Uncle Daniel?'

'No, Jenni, he didn't.'

I looked at her face where a solitary tear had rolled the length of her cheek and thought my instinct to protect her from the discomfort of the truth had been correct. I knew that her father had told her little of his family's history, but it appeared from the tenor of our conversation that he had mentioned even less than I had presumed. I did not think it my place to enlighten her further and resolved there and then never to do so, just as some years earlier I had obeyed Harry's request never to talk about his wealth. Silence is often the easier option, but I was acting from the purest of motives: I, too, had no wish to see Jenni hurt, especially at a moment such as this.

At the farmhouse we found a clean bedsheet in one of the attics, which Harry had converted into a linen room. It was here that the housekeeper had often done their ironing before she had become ill and Harry had replaced her with a woman from the village who no longer needed to live in because Jenni could take care of herself. My room in the house was directly below, and I had frequently ascended the stairs to find sheets for myself, when I had decided to stay the night rather than travel home. Harry and I would spend the evening listening to the wireless, or playing canasta at the card-table with Jenni and her school friend, or Harry would play nocturnes at the piano whilst I rummaged through my medical textbooks for the exams I was still sitting. In some ways those gentle evenings had helped the war to pass us by, even though I witnessed suffering of one kind or another almost daily at the hospital, where the casualties were mostly civilian from the fire-bombing of Middlesbrough. Harry had registered early on as a conscientious objector but had been spared the indignity of a tribunal, for work on the land was automatically a reserved occupation. I had thought about his decision for some days and then followed his example, knowing that I too would escape compulsory conscription because of my medical qualifications. For both of us pacifism had become a principle, and we supported those Quakers who were going to jail, although we realized that our position in the comfort of our homes was by far the easier one. In this idyll of demanding but rewarding work during the day and relaxation at night, I had forgotten all about my earlier premonition. It had never again occurred to me that Harry might one day no longer be here, or that as Tommy Handley's ITMA came to an end on the radio he would not offer me a beer and inquire if I were staying the night. Despite the war, I was a decade too young for such thoughts of mortality.

Jenni waited beside me in the hall, patiently clasping the bedsheet we had taken from upstairs, whilst I spoke on the telephone to all the relevant people in Richmond. I knew I could sign the death certificate myself but could not tolerate the idea of ending our friendship in so clinical a fashion, so my final call was to a local GP, who agreed, after a little persuasion, to deal with the formalities for me. It was three o'clock in the morning by the time we carried Harry's body into the house. Jenni looked exhausted but would not go to bed. I had spent the intervening hours encouraging her to take the initiative and it was her suggestion that we place his body not in his bedroom, as I had anticipated, but in the library where her father had liked to sit and read on those winter evenings when he would come in earlier than was usual from the farm. It was in the library that he had read Freud and Jung and become bored by the human excuses of psychoanalysis, no longer believing in the relevance of this cerebral propaganda, as he called it. He thought Freud had made unacceptable behaviour acceptable by providing us with the intellectual rationale with which to defend our abhorrent actions, as if we as individuals were no longer responsible for our motives but were accorded the psychological justification to behave in any way we might choose. Harry saw life as practical, where a person's hands were more important than his mind, and where every decision was a choice between good and evil. This had been an argument we had returned to regularly, for I strongly disagreed with him that life could be this simple; to my mind the passage of Harry's life seemed to confirm, rather than contradict, the accuracy of Freud's opinions and my own views. Harry refused to accept that Freud did not motivate our actions, but merely interpreted them for us. For Harry the two were the same because knowledge was all-powerful and always led to change.

'What are you thinking about, Uncle Daniel?' Jenni asked.

'Oh, nothing, nothing in particular. A premonition that I'd forgotten about. A discussion that I once had with your father. They're like snapshots, like the photographs a camera takes.'

We were in the sitting-room, where Jenni was rocking in the rocking-chair.

'I was thinking about the time I went with you to London and we spoke to Daddy on the telephone, and went round parliament.'

'Why were you thinking about that?'

'I don't know.'

'Go to bed, Jenni. The tireder we become the less control we have over our thoughts.'

'I've never stayed up all night before. I'm wide awake now. I'm glad he's in the library. If he were on his bed I could imagine he were asleep.'

'That's a curious thing to say.'

'Why?'

'Wouldn't you rather he were sleeping?'

Jenni stilled her chair, and I could see that she felt caught out in some way, as if a superior mind had got the better of her. This had not been my intention so her reaction surprised me.

'Who are you to criticize?' she asked, her lips puckering in disbelief at what she was imagining was my challenge.

'Jenni, I'm not criticizing. I thought it was a curious remark to make.'

'Uncle Daniel, I made an interesting remark,' she said regaining much of her composure and rocking once more in her chair. 'The word "curious" implies a judgement, and I will not be judged.'

'We're both tired,' I said. 'But let me apologize if I've offended you.'

'I thought you were referring to the fact that I haven't burst into tears.'

'Oh, you were upset on the telephone, and I saw a tear in your eye as we were walking back here to find a sheet a few hours ago. I do know what you must be feeling.'

'The girls at school would cry. I shall refuse to do that.' She laid her head back into the chair with her eyes piercing my own. 'Tears are weak and weedy and silly. I agree with Daddy.'

Her words were carefully chosen and delivered quietly in the full knowledge of their effect. For the first time she was displaying a manipulative understanding of the history of our relationship, with her memories of my tears being used to her advantage.

'That isn't actually what your father thought, Jenni. I know he often said that tears were weak, but he didn't mean it in quite the way you presume.'

'That's too clever for me, Uncle Daniel. I believe what people tell me. Anything else is far too complicated. People must learn to say what they mean, as I'm doing now.'

I was shocked by the tranquil arrogance with which she had spoken and could not let her remarks pass without comment. As I was working on my reply, my eyes fell on her thin legs with their white ankle socks, and this gave me the courage to treat her as a child.

'Well, that is easy for those who have your confidence, Jenni. For those of us who haven't a great deal of confidence, it is far harder. On the whole, I prefer those people without confidence, who find it difficult to say what they mean. You've a great deal to learn, little girl.'

She rocked to and fro with her face turned downwards, her eyes partially hidden in the shadow of her neck, where her tendons protruded as a sign of her suppressed rage. I immediately felt guilty for what I had said but not so guilty as to apologize. As often happens when one is caught in such a dilemma and decides not to be contrite, I attacked further.

'It's no good sulking, Jenni.'

'I'm not.'

'Yes, you are. If people are always to say what they mean, then they must always speak the truth, and you're sulking, so admit it. Your philosophy is fine, but you must follow it to the end. It's no good fibbing when it doesn't suit you.'

She was rocking so vigorously that her chair was moving across the carpet.

'I'm not sulking.'

'Then why are you hiding your face in that exaggerated fashion. I recognize pity for oneself because it's how I used to be.'

She stopped rocking with such abruptness that I expected her to leap up and slap me on the cheek, but instead she raised her eyes to my own with a look of contempt which slowly dissipated until her expression was neutral, betraying nothing of what an ordinary person might be feeling. Finally, she grinned, but her face lacked humour.

'We're both tired as you remarked earlier, Uncle Daniel. This argument has come from nowhere, and it's going nowhere.'

I was chilled by her sophistication.

'Well, that is often the way with arguments, Jenni, when they become personal. They grow out of our sensitivity. And it is because of our sensitivity that we don't always say what we mean.'

'Yes,' she said quietly. 'I think I will go to bed.'

And with that indifferent comment she left the room before I could invite her to stay. The chair rocked to and fro with the movement of her getting up and leaving.

'Bugger it,' I said out loud, so annoyed with myself that the choice of the word did not surprise me.

Jenni's judgement of the argument was correct: it had come from nowhere, but, having begun, both of us were fully aware of the consequences of what we were saying. As with many arguments of this kind, it had become a battle between egos, not ideas. I felt ashamed of myself, for I was the one who should have known better, who should have had the dignity to rise above his baser instincts, who should have swallowed his pride in deference to a young girl who had just lost her father in the most horrific and macabre circumstances. I could hear Harry's voice shouting, rebuking, admonishing me to grow up. It was only when I remembered that I could hardly ever recall Harry shouting that I began to calm down and feel easier in my mind. His voice became my conscience and ceased to be my judge.

'Oh, damn,' I said towards the fireplace, where the coal had burned itself out hours ago so that the room was becoming chilly. 'This is Jenni's home, not yours. What gives you the right to speak to her in those lofty moral tones?' I could not answer my own question. 'No, of course you can't answer, Daniel, you're a fool.'

I opened the sitting-room door, which Jenni had snapped closed, and slowly climbed the stairs towards her bedroom, working on my apology with every step. I would have begged her to forgive me, I would have gone down onto one knee, but she was not there. At first I thought she was simply refusing to acknowledge my knock, and it is a measure of the contrition I felt that this did not annoy me. I called her name and, when there was still no reply, opened the door. Her bed was empty, her bath dry, her clothes absent from the chair where they were usually thrown, her homework not put into her satchel ready for school the next morning. I imagined she was hiding as I would have done at her age, in her situation: I would have wished to manipulate further, as she was doing, and bring as much hurt as possible upon my oppressor. But the wardrobe, her bathroom, the space between the bed and the carpet, the wall behind her taffeta curtains were all empty, even deserted. I switched off the electric light, with the energy for my apology draining from my body.

As I was descending the stairs, I heard a muffled sound from the library and knew immediately where she had gone. In her bedroom, it had occurred to me that she might well have walked towards the crater to be alone there. But I was not prepared for what I found when I opened the library door. Jenni had taken a bowl of warm water and a cloth from the kitchen. The white bedsheet was removed and her father almost naked in his underwear. Jenni was washing the dried blood from the cadaver.

'If you've come to apologize, don't bother,' she said.

'Jenni, I was going to do that. I've been waiting for you to go to bed. I didn't want to upset you.'

'With an argument, or with the sight of his body?' she asked.

'Both, Jenni.'

'I can manage, Daniel.'

'Am I no longer your uncle?'

She had put his clothes across a chair. The body looked so thin, like a newspaper lying on a table, and the skin was bruised where the life had drained away to leave him black and cold. His chest hair was full of small grains of wheat which had somehow penetrated his shirt. Jenni now had an ordinary head comb and was combing them through so that the corn was gathering in a tiny heap by his navel.

'This isn't fair on you, Jenni. Won't you let me help you?'

She continued combing silently with great concentration, her tongue between her lips. I caught her wrist, by her watch, and held her arm gently for a moment within my fingers before letting her go. After a few more seconds had passed, without really looking at me, she handed me the comb, and I put it down on the wooden trestle where her father was lying.

'He had a thing about being clean, Uncle Daniel.'

'I know,' I said calmly, but my heart was racing.

'He liked to bath every day. I do, too. The girls at school bath once a week, if that. They think I'm peculiar. I remember Daddy bathing me many times when I was a child.'

'He caught the habit in America. When I first knew him at school, he was not like that at all. Except we liked to swim together.'

'I've cleaned some of the blood from his body. It feels as if I'm going to tear his skin. It felt as if I were touching a chicken. His skin is so loose.'

She cupped her hands and scooped the grains of wheat into the bowl created by her palms, and then dropped the corn into the black water.

'Let me do the rest, Jenni.'

'Why do you want to protect me, Uncle Daniel? Did Daddy ask you to protect me?'

'I wasn't protecting you a few minutes ago when we were fighting.'

'That wasn't a fight. I enjoy an argument.'

'I used to. I don't any more. Now I just feel really terrible afterwards.'

I picked up the white bedsheet and placed it neatly across the corpse. Jenni helped me by taking hold of two of the corners. I thought, wrongly, that if we covered his body she might then take herself to bed.

'How rich was Daddy, Uncle Daniel?'

It was the question I was dreading. She asked me so simply that her inquiry demanded a truthful reply.

'I don't know, Jenni. He very rarely talked about money.'

'He was far richer than an ordinary farmer, wasn't he? None of the other farmers have a house like this, with four bathrooms. Or have tractors and a combine harvester. The money came from his father, my grandfather, didn't it?'

I straightened the bedsheet where she had left it ruffled and untidy by his swollen ankles.

'In effect, yes, Jenni. Although your grandfather died before your grandmother, so he inherited the money from her. I never knew the details of the will.'

'What was my grandfather like?'

I could, at last, answer one of her questions unambiguously, without hedging, or searching for a physical distraction to cover

182

my unease.

'I never met him so I don't know.'

'What happened between my father and grandfather to create so much bitterness?' she asked once again.

'Well, as I've already explained, they had little in common and did not care for one another.'

'You're fibbing, Daniel, you're going bright red. You know exactly what took place and you're never going to tell me, are you?'

I searched the library for something to do but could find nothing to hand. Inadvertently, I lifted the bedsheet to reveal her father's face, where his eyes were closed and still.

'You're correct, Jenni,' I said after a second or two. 'I shall never tell you what took place because it should die now along with your father.'

And over the intervening years, for almost fifty years now, until I began writing this account a few weeks ago, I have remained faithful to that statement. I was wrong, of course, not to tell her the truth when the truth demanded to be heard, but then so much of my life has been in error. I have done what I thought was right at the time and this, I believe, is the best most of us can achieve. My life has been no better or worse than any other life. I am too old for apologies.

'Richmond 319. Daniel Hinton speaking.'

'This is Philip Pennycott of Pennycott and Driscol, solicitors in Richmond,' I heard from the telephone receiver.

'Oh, yes, Mr Pennycott, I remember, we've met on a number of occasions.'

'I'm telephoning about the late Mr Treffgarne's will. As you know, you and we are the executors of his estate. And very surprised and flattered we were too, being a small provincial office and not in London.'

'Mr Treffgarne wanted his affairs to be dealt with locally.'

'It caused a stink with his old lawyers in Mayfair,' he gossiped.

'How can I help you, Mr Pennycott?'

'Yes, so sorry. I'm speaking somewhat confidentially because I have his daughter in an outer office and she is demanding to know every last detail of the various settlements. She is quite formidable, Dr Hinton, not to say terrifying. I have a daughter the same age who is in the same class at the grammar school, and I can only agree that Jenni Treffgarne's reputation is true. I've pooh-poohed it up to now. Christine, my daughter, has in the past come home with all sorts of stories about her being argumentative and difficult. If I were being asked, which of course I'm not, I'd have had to say that I don't think it's very proper for a girl her age to be so forward.'

I knew that Harry had made me an executor of his will but had no idea of the details.

'Yes, she told me she might come and see you,' I said bluntly. 'I did ask her not to. She's going against my instructions and being very naughty.'

'She's being quite obtuse about leaving, Doctor. Neither do I want to upset her. The will is actually very straightforward. What should I say to her?'

I had naturally assumed that Jenni would be the main beneficiary of her father's estate.

'Well, seeing as she's with you, you might as well begin to explain.'

The line went quiet for a moment, and then he stammered, as my friend Peter Cole sometimes stammers when put under pressure. Peter has often told me, with an impish twinkle in his eyes, that to be afflicted by a stammer is far preferable to being blind.

'I'd r-rather you w-were h-here, Dr Hinton. She's g-going to b-be extremely upset.'

'Why?' I asked naively.

'Her l-legacy is v-very s-small. It amounts to no m-more than a f-few thousand p-pounds.'

I was astonished and thought that amidst the jumble of sounds, I must have misheard him.

'I can t-tell y-your re-reaction is very similar to m-my own,' he went on. 'Not that a f-few thousand p-pounds to an ordinary p-person is n-not a s-small f-fortune. But Mr Treffgarne was adamant on the p-point. I q-questioned him myself to ensure that he w-was not m-making a mistake.'

'Mr Pennycott, who are the beneficiaries?' I asked, annoyed at his slowness.

'N-not you either, I'm a-afraid. There are instructions f-for you w-which he asks y-you to c-carry out, and a l-little m-money f-for you t-to fulfil th-these v-various d-duties.'

'Mr Pennycott, please do stop stammering.'

'The main d-duty he asks you to un-undertake is to bring up his d-daughter as your own. There is a small c-cash settlement for this purpose. B-but as for the b-beneficiaries, there are r-really only two. One far larger than the other. The b-bulk of the estate goes to America, to Pennsylvania, to a p-person who is named as John Bell. He w-will receive a sum well in excess of three and a half million pounds.'

This time the line went quiet because of me. All I could hear was a faint hum from the telegraph wires.

'Are you st-still there, Dr Hinton? Or have we been c-cut off?'

'I'm still here.'

'I don't like t-talking like this on the t-telephone. Agnes Follet, at the exchange, listens in. Are you there, Agnes?'

There was a click on the line as if someone were replacing a telephone receiver.

'Who is the other beneficiary?' I asked.

'The farm, together with some cash and bonds amounting to about seventy-five thousand pounds, goes to an address in Keir Hardie Street, Middlesbrough. To a Peter Cole. But he cannot inherit until his twenty-eighth birthday, and there are one or two other codicils which he added in the week that war was declared.'

He had stopped stammering, but I still thought I must have misheard or imagined the name.

'Did you say Peter Cole?'

'That is correct, Dr Hinton.'

'Is Keir Hardie Street close to the iron foundry?'

'That I don't know. We travel to Linthorpe in Middlesbrough quite regularly because my wife has relatives there. I say quite regularly, much less regularly these days because of petrol rationing being what it is.'

'Pennycott, please do stick to the point.'

'Yes, so sorry.'

I heard the click as Agnes Follet re-connected her line into ours.

'Agnes, go away,' I said.

A second click followed the first in rapid succession.

'It's hopeless trying to be private in this town,' I found myself saying. 'I don't know why Harry transferred his affairs up here. I know he wanted to be ordinary, but this is madness.'

There followed a short silence with no clicks at all.

'We would like to believe that we've dealt with Mr Treffgarne's affairs very satisfactorily, Dr Hinton,' Pennycott said apologetically. 'So far that is. I would hope that good relationship might now continue with you?'

'Mr Pennycott, I'll be with you shortly. Say nothing to Jenni Treffgarne until I arrive.'

Pennycott's office was on the High Street, a brisk ten-minute walk from my own home. It was market day, with the stalls severely depleted because of the war. Pennycott was waiting for me on the pavement amidst the women hunting for bargains. After a few nervous pleasantries, which were especially jittery from him, we went through into his office where Jenni was sitting peaceably with a glass of dandelion fizz. He shambled through the will clause by clause. I learned little that he had not told me already on the telephone. Jenni remained impassive throughout, listening as his voice returned occasionally to its stammer.

'You mentioned codicils,' I said, 'the codicils to Peter Cole's inheritance of the farm.'

'Yes, I was coming to those. Once again, they appear to involve you, sir. The will seems to be asking a great deal of you, Dr Hinton. Mr Treffgarne has given you several discretionary powers. The c-codicil is h-here somewhere.'

'Why don't you tell us what it is?'

'Yes, so sorry.' He consulted the papers and dropped one of them to the floor, where it lay out of place on the red matting. 'I've already mentioned that he cannot inherit the farm until his twenty-eighth birthday –'

'Is that it by your feet, Mr Pennycott?'

'Yes, so it is. Th-thank you. The codicil is that you accompany him to Pennsylvania, and that he spend time there working on an Amish farm under the tutelage of Mr John Bell. He leaves the length of time at your discretion, Doctor, but suggests that it be not less than one hundred days. Now, I don't know what an Amish farm is. We can try and find out for you.'

'Do not trouble yourself, Mr Pennycott, I know already.'

'When those conditions are met, he may inherit the farm.

186

There is an amount of cash for your expenses. He asks finally that you implement his will according to its spirit.'

'And Jenni? What might Jenni's expectations be?'

He consulted the papers but I could tell he did not need to and knew Jenni's bequest by heart.

'It's a simple cash settlement. F-f-f-f-five thousand pounds, which cannot be touched until she is twenty-one. It's the same amount as all the farm labourers shall receive. I'm very sorry, Miss Treffgarne.'

Jenni picked up her glass of dandelion fizz.

'Would you have a straw, Mr Pennycott?' she asked placidly, much as if we might be having a picnic in a harvest field with the farm workers. 'If I'm to be treated like a child, I might as well behave like one.'

Pennycott rang the bell on his desk and a secretary entered.

'I think Jenni was joking,' I said. 'There's no need to bother yourselves further.'

The secretary left, but Jenni's eyes had become like steel.

'I never joke, Uncle Daniel. This will is a charade. I refuse to accept it.'

'Is there no explanation?' I inquired of Mr Pennycott. 'Does he nowhere explain his decisions?'

Once more Pennycott consulted the papers but I could see it was yet another fruitless exercise to cover his nervousness.

'There is no explanation whatsoever,' he said after a few seconds of pretending to search for one. 'I can only reiterate, because he does so several times, that you are to implement the will in the spirit in which he intends it.'

'Is that all?'

'That is all, apart from one or two requests for his funeral which I haven't yet mentioned. He asks to be buried in an unmarked grave in what he refers to as his garden. He says you will know what he means, Dr Hinton. He asks that the garden then be ploughed over, left without any decorative plaque or ornament, and the field farmed normally. I remember the expression because 'ornament' seemed such a funny word to use.'

'It's Amish, Mr Pennycott. As far as I know, the Amish do not believe in decoration. I suspect he's asking for an Amish funeral.'

187

'He's not getting one,' Jenni said without a pause. 'It's ridiculous. How can he be buried in that silly wilderness. He's mad, quite mad. You know what he was like, Uncle Daniel, when he was depressed, he was far from sane. The whole will was written when he was depressed. It must all be challenged.'

'I do understand, Jenni.'

'Do something about it then. He asks you to implement the spirit. The spirit must be that I should receive more than five thousand pounds. The smelly farm workers are getting that amount. I know I've always had to travel on the same school bus with their smelly children, but he can't have meant me to receive the same as them. That's not the spirit of a sane man.'

I remained silent, not being certain of what I thought and in a dilemma as to what I should say. I did not know how to explain my reticence to her.

'Do something about it,' she said again, before I had a confident opinion to offer her.

'Smelly is a very pejorative word,' I found myself saying. 'It says as much about you as your father's request regarding his funeral does about him. I need a few days to think, Jenni. I need time to sit and read through the will on my own. I will do my best to see that you're not hurt by any of this, either financially or otherwise. But I must tell you, I believe your father to be the sanest man I've ever met. It may not seem it now, but one day it will all be for the best.'

'Go to hell, Uncle Daniel,' she said.

I knew that Jenni had every right to be angry and that her father's fortune rightfully belonged to her. I so wanted to take her side, to agree with her that the whole charade of the will was a mistake, but I could not bring myself to do so. I wanted to cosset and hug her but felt repulsed by her lack of understanding and vulnerability.

'One more unpleasant word, Jenni, and I'll smack you. Have I made myself clear?' The words were tumbling from my mouth without my having control over them. 'You are not too old to be given a smack across the leg, little girl.'

Pennycott was looking at the matting on the floor. He stood up from his chair and left the office.

'Now look what we've done,' I said.

'Who cares? He rambles on like the farts on a lavatory.'

'I know he can be verbose, but that's no excuse for an expression like that.' In truth, I was shocked by her rudeness: I tried not to show my surprise for it would have meant fulfilling my promise to smack her leg, which I had threatened in haste and had no intention of carrying out. 'I've heard words like those before, they are meaningless words, Jenni.'

'Fuck off,' she said with her eyes, like ice, on a level with my own.

'Yes, I've heard that word before, too,' I said. 'It is just forgivable when it rises from the gutter, unforgivable from the lips of someone like you. I won't hit you, Jenni, not because I don't want to, but because I can't. It is everything your father was against. But if you think that's weak of me, think again. I'm stronger than you. I'll fight you with everything apart from violence.'

Pennycott entered with a straw which he placed into the glass of dandelion fizz on his desk. The straw bobbled up and down and then dropped out onto the matting. His action almost turned the seriousness of what I had just said into a farce, so much so that I nearly laughed.

'I'll fight you,' she said. 'Haven't I every right to be angry and upset? I think I have. It was his family's money, not money to be given away. It was my grandfather's fortune and it should be mine. My grandfather would want me to have every penny of it.'

'Jenni, I think your father's will is his last message to us both. We should listen. I think we should both try and understand what he has to say before we criticize him.'

'This is not the message of the father I knew, Uncle Daniel. This is not Daddy, this is not the Daddy who used to put me in the bath and read me stories. This is not the Daddy who came to sports days at school and was proud of me. This is not the Daddy who used to love me.' She was close to tears. 'If it is and I'm wrong, then I've no interest in knowing him. He obviously had no interest in me, as his will shows. Yes, I want what is rightfully mine, but who doesn't from their Dad?'

'It is the Dad who used to love you, Jenni, and who used to put you into the bath,' I said.

Jenni came with me in the car to Keir Hardie Street where I hoped to find Peter Cole. The day was damp, with a low mist

189

clinging to the banks of the river Tees. We parked by the Transporter Bridge, which was showing its age and had suffered from the frequent night bombing of the iron foundries in the vicinity, almost a weekly occurrence at this stage of the war. Our quarrel had lasted well into the following day, but had abated a little, and I persuaded her to take a walk with me along the river so that we might, finally, clear the air between us. As well as being damp, the day was chilly, with low cloud hugging those factory chimneys that had escaped the strafing and remained standing. It was early July, but it could have been the middle of winter. Jenni walked with her gabardine pulled tightly across her breast bone, looking downwards at the path and speaking little, as if she were in my presence under sufferance and were registering a protest, even though it had been her request that she accompany me to Middlesbrough. She would not leave my side, and had not done so for two days, but was always by herself. It was a tension I was beginning to accept.

The river towpath was pockmarked with puddles, which were frequently too large for us to jump, so we had to skirt into the muddy grass, by the factory walls, to keep our shoes dry. Having suggested we take a walk to clear the air, I was happy to remain silent. At least we were on the move, and this in itself was helping to ease the tension. The strain between us was palpable but had eased from the previous day when Jenni had threatened to contact the old lawyers in London, in an attempt to have the will declared null and void. It had taken me all afternoon to pacify her, and even this relative peace had only been achieved by my agreeing to telephone the lawyers myself and have her stand at my elbow whilst I spoke to them. This I had done: there had been no other will. Jenni had taken herself into my sitting-room, where she had sucked her thumb until it was raw. I felt so sorry for her. I saw the child that she was and wanted to cherish her. I was fully aware of the youthful vulnerability that she would not admit to. It was later in the evening, after she had refused to eat the pork casserole I had prepared, that my sympathy for her grievances began to wane once more. I tried to explain this to her at the dinner table, but she would not, or could not, listen. Later still, when I had closed the curtains for the night, I realized she was becoming depressed, just as her father used to, with the same symptoms of fatigue. I put my arm rather awkwardly

190

across her shoulders, which she did not resist, but by then it was hopeless; her depression was too severe to be comforted by affection.

We walked further along the towpath than I had intended, until the far bank of the river was lost to the mist, and the broadening marshland of the estuary began to appear. Dunlin and curlew sandpiper were feeding on the mud-flats being revealed by the outgoing tide. Their activity was all bustle, as if their chance of finding food was increased by their speed. Jenni walked ahead of me on her own. So much had occurred during the last few days that I was grateful for these brief moments of peace. A redshank joined the flock of dunlin running along the water's edge, and I left the birds behind to catch her up, feeling guilty because I had let her get so far ahead on her own. I longed for a few hours of quiet contemplation, without action or talk, but where the silence might be the silence between friends and not a form of torture.

It was Jenni, who, finally, suggested that we turn round and walk back towards the town. I was overjoyed by the sound of her voice and the fact that she had spoken to me without my having to prompt her. I immediately tried to engage her in further conversation, but her eyes were lost across the river, where a small fishing boat was emerging from the mist, its blue hull sliding across the calm waters of the estuary. A foghorn, from the lighthouse at the point, mingled with the rattle of the boat's engines. The engine sounded loose, as if it might shortly cut out and the boat be left to drift.

'Jenni,' I said, 'money is a funny thing. There are some families who make money, and some who don't. Take my own family for instance; we will never be rich. My father somehow knows he will never be affluent, and therefore he isn't. That's not a choice he's made, it's simply the way it is. His belief that he can be wealthy is not strong enough to make it happen. Your family is the reverse of that. Your family has always had absolute belief in their right to money. Even your father had that. He couldn't escape it. He didn't want the money, but it was always there should he need it. He could only give it away when he was dead. That is the blunt truth, Jenni. He's actually telling you that he loves you, because he wants you to start again on your own. He wants you to do what he knows he should have done but was

191

too weak or frightened to have done himself. He knows you are not weak or frightened, Jenni. He's given you his strength. Your family has always made money. You will make money, too. But it will be money you've earned yourself. And the power you will gain from that money will be your own power, not his.'

Jenni listened to what I had to say but she did not reply, nor did her expression change by way of comment. Her eyes remained downcast towards the towpath, which was cindered at this point to prevent the puddles becoming too large. Every day the fishermen used the path to reach their small boats, moored to the wooden jetties in the shallow creeks, and it was they who repaired the path when the weather was inclement, or the reach of the tide made off-shore currents too dangerous for fishing. Jenni kicked the toes of her open, leather sandals at the loose cinders, taken from the residue of burnt-out coal in the blast-furnaces a few miles away. She was destroying their hard worked for endeavour, but I could not be annoyed because her actions proved that she was thinking about what I had just said. I so wished to appease her anger and depression that nothing would have annoyed me. I was relieved to have spoken in such a straightforward manner, for the sentiments I expressed had been running through my head for the last forty-eight hours, and I was pleased to be rid of them from my mind, just as we are delighted to be rid of many obsessions which inhibit the rest of our thoughts. More importantly, I was convinced that my words were the truth, and that Jenni would, in time, achieve everything she might desire. The ability to make money and to discharge power does run in families. There are certain families whose belief in their right to money and power is so inherent that their success is never in doubt: Jenni's family amongst them.

As we continued to stroll back, with my mind now freed a little, I first thought of Philip Pennycott's office and then Richmond, a town whose affluence and architecture was so removed from the poverty of the traditional back-to-back terraced housing of Middlesbrough, which we were beginning to approach once more along the towpath. The events with Pennycott had been so concentrated, and our conversation so intense, that I realized the details of his old-fashioned, wood-panelled, Victorian office had hardly registered in my imagination. I had missed the peculiarities of his world. It was a staid, musty, provincial office:

an office not used to dealing with millions of pounds, but with the affairs of the vicars and doctors, schoolmasters and shopkeepers of a small Yorkshire market town. It was not at all surprising that Pennycott had been nervous and in awe of Harry's patronage, which, I half-suspected, he had hoped never to have to deal with so personally, certainly not in death. Pennycott was in his mid-sixties, with a daughter Jenni's age, which ought to have explained why the poor man was petrified by Jenni's presence; but my thoughts had been elsewhere. I had listened to the will with increasing astonishment. That John Bell should receive a legacy of some kind was not unexpected, that he should be the major beneficiary of such a fortune was a revelation, but Peter Cole's name, often repeated by Pennycott as the reading of the deed progressed, was the mystery. It was a name I had almost forgotten. I had no idea that there had been contact between Peter and Harry, let alone an intimacy which might result in such generosity. Harry had kept faith with his enigma to the end.

By the time we reached Keir Hardie Street for the second time the mist had become a fog. The air was so still, and the whiteness so complete, that it felt as if the world had stopped. Keir Hardie Street was deserted, with no boys playing football or girls skipping, with no cats asleep on the window ledges, with no washing hanging on the lines which stretched above the road between the houses on either side, with no men repairing the battered bicycles they travelled to work on, or women gossiping on their doorsteps whilst they darned their children's jumpers. It was July, when, in the summer heat, the street should have been at its most attractive, but instead the fog had drawn a veil and revealed the road for what it was: poor and depressed, down at heel and neglected. The paint was chipped on the window ledges where the cats should have been purring; the washing lines were snapped, trailing into the puddles; a boy, the only boy we saw, was shuffling along the pavement in his father's old shoes; a girl, her face partially hidden by the jagged, broken glass in a window, was crying. Three or four houses, it was difficult to tell the exact number, had been bombed to extinction. It was a scene I had witnessed many times, but today, with Jenni beside me in the ever thickening fog, it was somehow different, and not at all romantic.

It took us a minute or two of searching to find the correct door. I had no idea why I was so frightened, beyond being nervous because it felt as if I were intruding on a part of Harry's mystery. I had reasoned that there must be something entirely personal in his legacy to Peter Cole, which he had not wished me to know about, but which I was shortly to discover. I expect I was frightened of a revelation which might alter my whole perception of my friend. The only fact I knew for certain was that Peter Cole must now be about eighteen years old.

It was Wilfred, Peter's father, who opened the door. He was in his stockinged feet and had obviously just arrived home from work because his hands were black. I noticed these simple details in the few seconds it took him to recognize me: they were seconds in which I had remained speechless.

'Dr Hinton,' he said, 'we always hoped you would call round eventually. Please, come in.'

There was no hall or entrance-way into the house, so we stepped straight from the pavement into the living-room, where a dining-table was laid with cutlery for tea. The table was pushed beneath the window ledge, and on each of the three free sides was a chair. An oval mirror, hanging from a hook above the empty fireplace, reflected the light onto the opposite wall, against which there was a sideboard, whose weight had created holes in the lino on the floor. The room was so small that the three of us immediately filled the whole space.

'Please, sit down,' he said, sensitive to our discomfort at taking in the smallness of the room.

Jenni seated herself on the settee by the open doorway to the kitchen, whilst I picked one of the chairs at the table. She took a handkerchief from her pocket and placed it to her nose, as if disgusted by the smell of iron-oxides from his clothes which were frowsting the air. If looks could kill, mine would have killed her, and she quickly put the handkerchief away.

In the kitchen, at a metal bowl on the draining-board, was a teenage boy who was stripped to the waist. He was washing the upper half of his body, stained black with soot, with a large cloth and an even larger bar of soap. The cloth, probably once a shirt, ran across his shoulders and down the small of his back as he wiped away the dirt. His hands were big but not clumsy, as if his fingers were used to this routine of cleaning, so that his actions were methodical and slow, almost sensual in some ways: he was enjoying the touch of his own skin. He found a towel and first dried his face, afterwards raising his arms to dry beneath them, where the underarm hair was bushy and thick. He turned towards me and smiled. I lowered my eyes, suddenly feeling incredibly shy. Then he dried his arms, his chest, and finally, his back, as if there were no hurry in the world and he had all the time he required.

'At least with this fog we'll have no bombing tonight,' his father said. 'That's one good thing.'

'Yes,' I replied, but my mind was elsewhere, for I had already realized what Harry had seen in the boy and why he wished him to have the farm.

Harry's daughter, meanwhile, was sucking at her thumb. She was annoyed with me because of the incident with the handkerchief.

The boy entered from the kitchen, still without a shirt and with the odd droplet of water colouring his skin.

'This is Peter,' his father said. 'This is the boy who you were kind enough to help.'

'Hello, Dr Hinton,' he said shyly. 'Thank you very much.'

'That's all right,' I replied, standing up from my chair to be polite. 'I'm sorry I was so rude a few years ago when you called at the house.'

Peter took a shirt from a drawer in the sideboard and began to dress.

'Mr Treffgarne told us you were ill,' he said.

'Yes, I was, but I'm fully recovered now.'

The room was so small that I could see Peter's eyes clearly. The membranes, which had once been opaque, were luminous and so vivid they even reflected the light, like the mirror on the wall.

'How are your eyes?' I asked.

'They're fine,' he remarked calmly, fastening the buttons on his shirt. 'Nearly perfect, but not quite perfect enough for the army. Mr Treffgarne said that was a blessing in disguise.'

He spoke with such quiet assurance that it was like listening to a storyteller. Indeed, there was a story emerging with every word he uttered, for it was clear that he and Harry had had contact with one another.

Peter tucked his shirt into his trousers, which he had not changed from work. Two pairs of working boots were by the street door through which we had just entered.

'We both work at the iron foundry, Dr Hinton,' he went on with the same quiet dignity and poise, any lingering shyness now over. 'My father gave up rag and bone when the war began. I'm working at the foundry for the summer months. Please, do sit down again.'

His voice, cultured and authoritative, was wholly at odds with the comparative poverty of his surroundings. The room was washed in thin white paint, but the adjoining walls had absorbed damp from the neighbouring houses, so that, in many places, the paint was stained with a black fungus, which was growing in ever larger circles towards the skirting-boards. The only area to have escaped the damp was the chimney-breast above the fireplace. I sat down again on the dining chair at the table as he indicated I should.

'We were very sorry to hear you were ill,' he continued. 'Mr Treffgarne replied to the letter we sent you, and then some while later he was good enough to call at the house to explain you were still no better. Mr Treffgarne has been very kind.'

'Yes,' I said, hoping that he would go on, which he did.

'It's been very kind of him to pay for my education. St Peter's in York is one of the best schools in the country, with a wonderful reputation. I never dreamed that I might one day go to such a school, and be a boarder, with all that privilege at my disposal. My background is very different from all the other boys, as you can see.'

His father pulled a chair from beneath the table and seated himself close to me. Peter remained standing. He was speaking with such modesty that what he was saying had the quality of a myth or parable, as if his story did not quite involve him but had none the less happened. The changes, from the vacant child I remembered, did indeed deserve a place in mythology.

'If I pass my school certificate, which I hope to, Dr Hinton, I shall go to university in the autumn. Mr Treffgarne is right, my eyes are a blessing in disguise. I can continue my education. I shan't have to worry about joining one of the services.'

'It's all thanks to you,' his father said placidly, speaking without embarrassment at the giving of a compliment.

196

'I'm prepared to take the credit when it's due,' I said, 'but credit isn't due to me in this instance.' I raised my eyes towards his son. 'I didn't know of these events, Peter. Mr Treffgarne never told me.'

Peter looked surprised and pleased, like a child participating in a secret. His stoicism and poise vanished for a moment as his face displayed an involuntary, boyish youthfulness, which I was delighted to witness because stoicism and poise do not make a whole person.

'Why is that?' he asked innocently, his voice rising to an adolescent, higher register.

'I don't know why he should choose not to tell me,' I replied. 'Mr Treffgarne moved in a mysterious way. That's a religious expression, isn't it? Mr Treffgarne was a very religious man, although not at all orthodox. He was very human. Whatever his motivations, he only ever wished to be kind.'

I told him, as simply as I could, of Harry's death in the wheat field, doing my best to involve Jenni in the telling, but she remained seated on the settee with her hands twisting between her knees, where she stared silently at the lino on the floor. It must have been purgatory for her as I answered his questions. Peter's eyes fell downwards in Jenni's direction. The vivid contours of his cheeks were still pink from washing, and cherubic. I had begun to think him a young man, but he was still a child: he grinned because he could not help grinning; he giggled because he could not help giggling; and he shook his head in disbelief when I talked about the will and its codicils.

'Please don't worry about your education,' I said. 'He's made no provision for it to continue, but I'll see everything is taken care of.'

Peter was still standing. He seated himself beside Jenni. They were two children in an adult world, where decisions had been made over which neither of them had any control.

'Why are you giggling?' she asked him, her face brighter than it had been for some considerable time.

'I don't know,' he replied. 'I suppose I'm giggling because it's like being in the middle of someone else's dream, only it's my own. Are you Jenni? No one has introduced us.'

'Yes, I am,' she said taking her hands from between her knees and placing them on her lap, where her fingers remained still.

'I'm very sorry,' he added quickly. 'Gosh, I'm so sorry about your father.'

'It couldn't be helped. There was nothing I or Uncle Daniel could do. It was just a silly fluke, he was in the wrong place at the right time. You're lucky, I've got nothing from the will.'

'Really?' he said with astonishment. 'Why is that?'

'Uncle Daniel tells me it's because my father loved me and wished me to make my own way in the world.'

'You can have some of mine if you want.'

'No, thank you,' she said politely. 'I've decided I must do as my father wished and not complain.'

'Gosh, that's big of you,' he said with admiration. 'Which school do you go to?'

'Richmond Girl's High.'

'What's it like?'

'It's okay,' she replied brightly with music and spirit in her voice. 'It isn't too bad when you get used to it. I prefer the sciences and maths to the more arty subjects like history and geography.'

'I like maths, too.'

'Do you?' she asked, now fully arrested by his ease of conversation.

'Yes. But I like reading as well, so I spend a good deal of my time buried in books.'

'I should read more than I do. Daddy was a great reader.'

'Was he?' he inquired innocently, halting the flow of the conversation for a moment.

'He was when he found time from the farm,' she answered.

'Your dad liked to help the underdog, didn't he?'

The conversation had taken on a staccato rhythm, which was emphasized all the more by Jenni pausing to think.

'Yes. All his life he had sympathy for the disadvantaged,' she replied, 'but he never really told me why. I expect he wanted to ease his conscience about something, although I don't understand what that something might have been. I don't have his worries or guilts, so perhaps I'll never understand him.' She paused once more. 'I like talking to you, Peter, you don't make judgements, do you?'

'I try not to,' he said.

Jenni looked at me.

'Uncle Daniel makes judgements all the time. He's most

unfair. He thinks we all should fit into his view of the world, and when we don't he wants to change our opinions. But every opinion is valid if it is held honestly.'

I said nothing, but in my mind I agreed with her. She looked back towards Peter.

'Have you ever been to Pennsylvania?' he asked.

'Yes, when I was very small, so my memory is extremely hazy. I was born in New Orleans.'

'Really?' he said with his voice rising to its adolescent crescendo. 'Gosh. What on earth was that like?'

'It was good fun. I had the run of the school where my Dad was headmaster. The little piccaninnies would run about and splash in the Mississippi river. They were as black as soot, with little pink fingernails and palms. My Dad taught them arithmetic and basic reading.'

'He must have really believed in education.'

'Yes, he did. He thought everyone deserved their chance. He thought many people were more intelligent than they were given credit for. Whilst I don't agree with that opinion completely, I do know what he means. I think some people are fundamentally not very intelligent. Those of us who are clever must tell them what to do, in order for there to be civilisation. That's what Daddy was doing in New Orleans, amongst the black people. He was helping them to be civilised. He's done the same thing with you too, Peter, hasn't he?'

'I'm not sure it's quite that,' he said tolerantly. 'I think it's slightly more complex than you're implying. Certainly with regard to me.'

The small talk of the two teenagers continued, and beneath the apparent equanimity of their discussion, their differences in background, life-history, and philosophy were obvious. He, with his good temper and composure, had a humanity; whereas she, by comparison, was shallow in her understanding and had much living yet to do. Jenni had no story of her own from which to draw real strength.

Wilfred, Peter's father, had commented little during my recounting of the will with its codicils regarding his son's age and the necessity of his travelling to Pennsylvania. I had not yet formulated a plan as to how the visit to America might be accomplished, and it is a measure of Peter's youthfulness that he had not thought to ask. Like most young people he was at the mercy of adults and presumed arrangements would be made without his needing to be involved. Wilfred Cole had been embarrassed by the riches of his son's legacy, at one point even hiding his face in the folds of his shirt sleeves. He was a large, stocky, rotund man, with a round face, deep set eyes, and soft brown hair, whose huge bulk was completely at odds with the sensitivity of his personality. He leaned forward across the dining-table and touched my arm to distract my attention from the conversation of the two young people at the settee.

'Thank you for coming,' he said quietly. 'This must be an ordeal for you.'

'Yes, it is. I'm glad it's over.'

I must have smiled because he smiled in return.

'Peter is more upset than he's letting on, Dr Hinton. To look at him now, you'd think he was a small boy on Christmas Day, but what you're seeing is not the truth.'

'I know it isn't,' I said softly. 'Mr Treffgarne was not a fool, he didn't leave money to a fool either.'

'We didn't know Mr Treffgarne well. We would have liked to have known him better. I suppose we didn't like to ask him to be our friend. Peter wrote to him from school, and he came to the house once or twice to see how we all were. I tried to thank him in my own way, but Peter has received so much. I feel unhappy that we didn't do more.'

'Mr Cole, Harry's pleasure was in giving. He would expect nothing from you. He was a rich man, he's actually given you very little.'

Wilfred thought about what I had said for a few seconds, with his eyes traversing the low ceiling.

'Yes, I do understand what you're saying, Dr Hinton. It's very generous of you.'

I touched his arm in a similar fashion to the way he had touched my own a few moments earlier. I wanted to reassure him and assuage his worries. His skin was rough, like orange peel, and black from the iron oxides of the foundry. There was a long scar across the back of his hand, where the skin was tighter than normal because the wound had not been treated and stitched.

'It's just that what he's done for Peter is so extraordinary,' he said. 'What about this visit to America?'

'There is plenty of time for that,' I replied, continuing to keep my voice as low as possible. 'We must go before his twenty-eighth birthday. Harry would have wished him to complete his education. I suspect that is the reason for the codicil, he must have known that Peter was doing well at school.'

Wilfred nodded his head. His huge weight was sinking back into the dining chair. He looked across towards Peter and Jenni who were still talking animatedly on the threadbare settee. Jenni was helping to define some point she was making by tapping her fingers vigorously on Peter's knees. Peter was listening attentively, with his own fingers held together on his lap like a demure schoolboy. Jenni was a different person from the morose girl who had entered the house an hour before.

'She's changed a lot from the girl who used to like horses,' Wilfred said to me in a whisper. 'I'll never forget the day I lifted her onto the cart by the Transporter Bridge, and thought you were her father. Most people think they live ordinary lives, but nobody's life is ordinary, is it? Look at what's happened to us. People only have to look about them to know how unexpected life is. There's nothing ordinary or normal in the world if you think about it for long enough. That's what Mr Treffgarne has given Peter, he's given him the chance to know that life is extraordinary. That's the greatest gift you can give to anybody.'

'I'd like to enter politics,' Jenni was saying, her voice so loud that further conversation between Wilfred and myself had become impossible.

'Politics is for scoundrels,' Peter replied in a voice much quieter than Jenni's. 'Politics is about judgement. Parliament is a court of law. Only those with great knowledge of themselves are fit to pass judgement on others.' He paused. 'But those are the very people who least wish to pass judgement on others, because their self-knowledge gives them a broader sympathy and understanding of people.'

'You're being too clever, too ironical for me,' she said. 'I was born in New Orleans, I see things simply.'

'Their concerns become philosophical rather than practical,' he continued, ignoring her aside about America. 'The day to day grind of politics does not interest them. They become interested in truth, not in power, nor in manipulating the truth to hold onto that power. They know power comes from within and not from the ballot box.'

'Peter,' his father said, 'do stop going on. Miss Treffgarne doesn't want to listen to you all the time.'

It was the first time I had heard Jenni discussing politics, or heard her express a desire to be a politician, and I was sorry that Wilfred Cole had curtailed the conversation by reprimanding his son.

'I'm enjoying myself, Mr Cole,' she said politely to him. 'I've been the one doing most of the talking.' She turned to Peter and continued sympathetically in a quieter voice, but in a voice which we could all hear. 'I know I was rude a few minutes ago when we were talking about education, and I said my Dad had civilised you. I didn't mean to be rude in that way. It's the way I am sometimes. I'm envious of you, you've lived a life that must have taught you a lot. I've always been protected from the harsher truths around me. I don't know why that is. There is something in my father's past which no one wants me to know about. Something evil occurred. The will lays that evil to rest.'

She was right. I should have told her there and then but did not. There was her father's story to be told her, a story far more remarkable than Peter's, which might have given her the real strength she was searching for, and altered the course of her life. Peter's story was mundane by comparison. In remaining silent, I denied Jenni her family history; I denied her a parable from which to learn; I denied her her father's myth from which to increase her own understanding of the world; I denied her her father.

Outside in Keir Hardie Street, the fog was still thickening and I was beginning to worry about the drive home. It would be a slow journey over the hills if the fog continued inland, which it usually did for about fifteen miles. The air was so torpid that I could almost see individual droplets of water in the whiteness through Wilfred's living-room window: this was not a good sign, for the stiller the air here, the denser the fog would be in the dales. I explained this to Jenni, exaggerating my amateur understanding of the weather to give urgency to my case, but she was reluctant to leave. Her rapport with Peter was now so strong they might go on all evening. I talked with Wilfred for a further hour, glancing back and forth between Jenni and the window, but she had become adept at ignoring my signals. Eventually, I managed to persuade her to get up from the settee by promising her that Peter could come and stay with us for a few days at the house in Richmond, when she could then show him over the farm.

'You will be coming to the funeral?' she asked him finally.

'Oh, yes,' he replied matter-of-factly. 'We'd like to come very much.'

'He's to be buried in a simple grave without a headstone,' she said. 'He asked in his will to be buried in the middle of a field, which we're going to do. The field will then be ploughed over.' She turned towards me. 'Uncle Daniel will come and pick you up in the car, won't you, Uncle Daniel?'

'Yes, I will,' I replied, delighted that the fog between us appeared to have lifted, even if the fog outside was as dense as ever.

Harry was buried, two days later, in a grave not unlike an Amish grave as Jenni had described it to Peter, and in accordance with the instructions in his will.

I cried, and was alone when I watched the field being ploughed over the following afternoon.

A short while ago, two things happened almost simultaneously: my telephone rang, followed by the doorbell. I have one of these new-fangled telephones without an attaching cord, so that one may walk from room to room, or cook a meal, or even have a bath whilst speaking to the person on the other end. I tried this once, being excited by the novelty of such debauchery, but dropped the telephone into the soapy water and was incommunicado for a week until I could replace the instrument with a new one. Alas, I am too old, too slow for such hedonistic pleasures and must leave them to the young.

I was watching one of the many excellent wildlife programmes on the television, which I adore, when the telephone began its incessant bleeping. I dimmed the television sound with the remote control so that I could continue to watch the pictures. An edible dormouse was regurgitating moths to feed to her hungry youngsters, who were putting their mouths into her own, taking the moths from the back of her throat.

'Daniel, it's Jenni,' she said.

I was surprised to hear from her, for we had spoken on the telephone only a week before, and these days I am used to speaking to her about every three months, if that.

'Where are you?' I asked rather pointlessly. I was still thinking about the poor dormouse, for the narrator had just said they could be purchased for eighty pounds a brace from a butcher in Hertfordshire, being the new taste, apparently, of the nouveau-riche businessman who wishes to impress his mistress.

'Downing Street,' she replied. 'The BBC left an hour ago. They're making a programme celebrating the anniversary of my first year in office.' Her voice was slurred. She was tipsy. Not many people will believe that the Prime Minister of our country tipples whisky, because her public image is one of Victorian sobriety.

'The programme is a personal look at the Prime Minister's private life,' she went on. 'I had to make a cup of coffee in the kitchen here, and be ordinary.'

'That must have been quite difficult for you, Jenni,' I said dryly.

'Yes, it was as a matter-of-fact.'

Jenni has no sense of humour, so even my sarcasm is wasted on her. On the screen, the dormouse was now running across the tops of the trees, being watched, eagerly, by a kestrel from the distance. I turned the sound up a little, hoping that it was a different dormouse from the one who had the family.

'The camera lights were set up in the kitchen,' she continued. 'I came in through the door, filled the electric kettle with water and plugged it in, went to the cupboard above the sink but there was no jar of coffee. I don't know where we keep the coffee. I never make bloody coffee.'

The Prime Minister of our country also swears, which may surprise many people. On the television, the kestrel swooped and carried away the dormouse in its talons, but almost immediately the picture returned to the dormouse feeding her youngsters. I was relieved.

'Why didn't you use a bottle of whisky instead, Jenni?'

'It turned out, some little nobody of a research assistant from the BBC had put the coffee in the wrong cupboard by the sugar. I didn't know we had any sugar. We had to do the whole thing

204

again. The crew are sworn to secrecy, of course. If this gets into the newspapers there'll be hell. The Prime Minister in Downing Street not knowing her own kitchen, what would that look like? We'd already had to borrow a pint of milk from the Chancellor next door.

'It's no way to be running the nation,' I said wickedly.

It was then that my doorbell rang.

'Is Peter with you?' she asked.

'No, Jenni, he isn't.'

Nowadays, I dislike several events occurring at once and did my best not to become flustered by the various sounds, from the narrator on the television, from Jenni on the telephone, and now from the doorbell. I stood up with the telephone in my hand and walked out of the living-room towards my front door.

'He'll be with you shortly,' she said. 'I rang him before you. His wife told me he was popping round. I really rang to speak to him.'

I opened the door with my spare hand.

'Hello, Peter,' I said. I immediately raised my eyebrows so that he would know who I had on the other end of the line.

'Tell her I'm not here,' he whispered.

I have given up playing games, games require too much energy, and energy at my time of life is a precious commodity.

'Yes, he's just arrived,' I said loudly into the telephone, 'but he doesn't want to speak to you.'

Peter looked down at the Wilton carpet in my hall. He hates it when I am candid to the point of rudeness: he says that I lose my dignity and become artless, which is probably true.

'And why should he?' I continued. 'All you do is badger him. All you do is badger us both.' I put my hand over the mouth-piece. 'That's told her,' I said to him.

I knew exactly what she wished to speak to Peter about. Their discussion has been going on for almost a year, ever since she entered Downing Street, with Peter taking his lead from me in refusing to accede to her request. But Jenni has a persistence previously unknown to me, which is saying a great deal, and I know she will go on until she gets her own way.

I switched her off by sliding across the off button on my telephone.

'These new telephones are marvellous,' I said. 'One little button and everything is solved.' I was behaving like an ingénue, which embarrassed him.

'Daniel, I wish it was that easy.'

'It is that easy. You just turn her off, Peter. She's not important.'

We went through into the living-room. On the television screen, a crass, meretricious couple were eating a brace of dormice in a French restaurant, with the restaurateur explaining they tasted like guinea-pig, which was a description of no use to me or I imagine to anyone else.

'How often has she been ringing you?' I asked, when we were seated in the armchairs.

'Almost every day. Probably every third or fourth day, to be accurate.

'She's manic. She's mad. She's on a high at the moment. The power feeds her so she'll never come down, Peter. She's been on a high since she made that terrible speech on the steps of ten Downing Street, quoting her upbringing in a Franciscan monastery. She no more understands Francis of Assisi than you or I could fly to the moon.'

'I know, but what do we do?'

'You go on saying no, Peter. No no no, like that.'

'I can't, Daniel, she's wearing me down.'

On the television, the young dormice, looking not unlike a family of squirrels, were taking their first, faltering steps from their nest in the top of the tree, being encouraged by their mother, who was jumping the short distances from one branch to another, hoping they would follow her, which they were beginning to do.

'Turn off the television, Daniel. Let's just talk rationally for a moment.'

I switched off the set with the remote control and came through into my kitchen, where I opened a bottle of white wine and a bottle of mineral water, which I brought back into the living-room with some ice cubes. I mixed what I believe is called a spritzer, for us both.

Jenni wishes to have her father's body exhumed from the field where it was buried over forty years ago. Taking his body from the farm has become a major priority in her life. It is pure snobbery, for, twelve months ago when she first entered Downing

Street, one of the tabloid newspapers ridiculed her for having been the daughter of an eccentric, and if there is one thing Jenni cannot tolerate it is ridicule. Mockery brings out the iron will in her for which she is famous. Secretly, she also agrees with the newspaper that her father's behaviour was perverse, and she has never really defended him from the ignominy, either in public or otherwise, but she has set about, quietly, trying to have his coffin unearthed, and once that is achieved to have it re-buried in the local churchyard, here in Richmond, with a proper head-stone. I cannot forgive her for this: but Peter is the one who is bearing the ferocity of her attacks, for he still owns the farm where her father is interred. He has, up until now, refused to countenance her desires and give his permission for a search of the land to begin. I have been doing my best to give him what little strength I have left, which is a flimsy mixture of sarcasm and childish candidness, so that he might continue to say no. But I fear, tonight, that her persistence has finally worn him down.

To begin with, he tried to offer me solace by repeating the flippant comment I had made earlier: 'As you say, Daniel, Jenni is not important.'

'I wish that were true,' I said, contradicting myself not for the first time. I gave him his drink. 'When a person believes them-selves to be important, as Jenni does, it is very difficult to win an argument with them, let alone when they are also Prime Minister. I belittle her, Peter, because it gives me some pleasure to do so, but I shouldn't really. I know how powerful she is. I know how powerful her self-obsessions are. I understand her unwillingness to yield to anybody but herself. I understand it in her, because I was once like that myself. It pains me to say so but I was.' I added ice cubes to my own drink. 'Jenni herself would never accept this, but her stubbornness, her belief in argument and yet her refusal to accept when an argument is lost, or that she is in the wrong, are all based on self-pity. Jenni is, fundamentally, very self-pitying. She has to be the most important person and only ever thinks about herself. Why else does that look of cold steel come into her eye when she is challenged? It's actually the look of someone who cannot tolerate a challenge, of someone who considers her opponent beneath her, of someone so self-righteous that the only way she can deal with that challenge is to dismiss them, either in reality or from her mind. If that is not self-pitying, I don't know what is. She now wants to dismiss her father. She's all the pity in the world for herself, but no pity for history. She wants his body moved because she no longer wishes to believe that her father was as he was. In her mind, she's turned him into a different man, an image which his grave contradicts. She cannot tolerate that contradiction. She's a very simple woman, Peter.'

I took my drink to the armchair and sat down.

Peter was, by now, reclining into his own armchair with his legs outstretched towards my fireplace, looking more relaxed. 'Daniel, don't hate her,' he said to me quietly, after a few moments of silence, as if he could not bear to see me being so vindictive. 'Think about yourself. Think about your own dignity. Don't give her the pleasure of losing that.'

'You want to give in to her, don't you?' I said sadly.

He swivelled the ice cubes round and round his empty glass, like a much younger person than he is.

'If I thought she had some guilt, Peter, some guilt from somewhere, I don't care where, I wouldn't mind giving in to her. But she has no guilt. She thinks she's perfect. I wanted to make a stand and tell her she's not.'

'They are bones, Daniel,' he said gently. 'A pile of bones. Her father had what he wanted from life and from his funeral. We know what he meant to us both. Let her have the bones now. She is his daughter. What does it matter?'

It was then I realized that Peter had not stammered, as he normally would have done by now, because the pressure I had been putting upon him was considerable. His voice had been calm since his arrival. We know each other so well that the expression on my face told him what I was thinking.

'No, I've not stammered,' he went on in the same peaceful tones as before. 'I've made a bargain with myself. I came here tonight to suggest that we give Jenni everything she wants, but I've decided, if that is what we do, that I shall never stammer again. I'm looking for what is positive. It's why you must not lose your dignity. She's won if you do that. Let us both take courage from the decision.'

'Your myth continues,' I said.

'What myth is that?' he asked.

'Oh, it's nothing, Peter,' I replied, but then went on to tell him about this narrative. 'I've reached the point in my story where you enter as an adult. You were asking me about that the last time you called here. Don't worry, I've been very flattering. Probably too flattering,' I added mischievously. 'I've described your story as deserving a place in mythology, which I think it does in some ways. I've also said that Jenni has a story which is as extraordinary as your own. Unlike you, Peter, she has never realized that. That is the difference between your generosity and her meanness.'

I then went on to explain how I had begun this account for Jenni – it being the way I hoped to explain her own myth to her – but that, over the weeks of its writing, I have realized that the account is not about Jenni at all, but is about myself. Slowly, she has disappeared from the front of my mind and become a character in my life, like all the others. I had hoped to find the reasons for her callous behaviour, but fearing I would not succeed I have increasingly sought refuge in myself and my own motivations, which are complex enough on their own. I have often been wrong-headed in not telling her the truth.

'Peter,' I said, after I had spent an hour explaining this to him, 'a few weeks ago I would have asked you to delay giving her your decision. I would have asked you to wait until I'd completed my narrative. I won't now, because I don't think showing her what I have written will make any difference. I thought I might be able to liberate her, and explain to her why her father was unique, but I know I haven't succeeded. I've found it very hard to describe my own self-obsession and self-pity because it was buried deep in my heart, as hers is buried deep in her heart. I think what I've written so far will mean absolutely nothing to her.'

Peter left me a short while ago, and I have been depressed ever since returning from showing him to his car. I am sitting at the desk in my study, finishing the bottle of white wine, and still wondering where I went wrong with Jenni, for, in large part, her obduracy must be my fault. It is too late to speak to her of her grandfather, either in person or in writing. It is this which saddens me most because I have, up until now, believed that no one was beyond redemption, but I fear that Jenni is, for any atonement offered to her would only add succour to her wrong-

209

headedness. I have been wrong to imagine that I could change her opinions by presenting her with a story. I now realize that Jenni would find additional strength from my narrative, when I had meant her to discover the value of weakness. This is simply because we do not like each other, and she thinks I am a feeble-minded, gutless fool, an impression my story has done little to dispel.

IV

Elmer's nose

8

Peter and I arrived in Pennsylvania in the late spring of 1952, two years before he would inherit the farm on his twenty-eighth birthday. The previous summer, he had completed his education by receiving a doctorate in mathematics from Newcastle University.

In the intervening eight years, I had married my wife, Armanda, an Italian doctor, whom I met, by chance, one evening in Florence when we were both dining alone and our desire for companionship brought us together over coffee. Jenni was meeting a boy on the Ponte Vecchio: I was unable to control her even then. Armanda was a Catholic divorcee, which I was not unhappy about at all, but her family could not forgive her, so we married in England, away from any Italian limelight, in a simple ceremony at Richmond Registry Office. She helped me with the remaining years of Jenni's upbringing, coming to her final sports days at the high school, and taking her shopping when she required clothes for university. Armanda was skilful, adroit in her dealings with Jenni, much cleverer than I was, because she never kowtowed to her whims. Jenni complained frequently, but she nevertheless appreciated Armanda's forthrightness. The two of them liked one another. It was a relief and a weight off my mind. Jenni entered Cambridge to read chemistry, the year Peter began his doctorate at Newcastle, and we held a party for the two young people to celebrate their going. I cooked a goose, with celeriac, haricot beans, early turnips from the garden, parsnips and roasted potatoes, whilst Armanda made profiteroles for our dessert, which were exquisite with cream and black chocolate sauce.

With Jenni at Cambridge, our life together in the town settled down, and we began many of the ordinary, everyday friendships which have lasted until today. Sadly, Armanda died eleven years ago after a long illness, but she is remembered fondly by everyone she met, or at least by those of them who are still alive. Our retirement years were, without question, the most fulfilling years of my life, when we were free to explore England together, both by car and by train. We guffawed at the ridiculousness of old age, for we saw and experienced more in those few years than we had in the preceeding twenty-five when our busy timetables at work had often kept us apart. Armanda worked locally as a General Practitioner, whilst I continued at the hospital in Middlesbrough. In my early fifties, I was more or less offered a consultancy, but decided, after discussing it with Armanda, to maintain the status quo, for the added responsibility and burden of decision-making no longer interested me. By now, I was the senior registrar in the orthopaedic department, where I specialized in the lower arm and hand, operating on damaged tendons and nerves in palms and fingers. It was delicate surgery without much of the micro-technology of today.

I have Armanda's photograph in front of me now as I write at my desk, given prominence beside photographs of Harry and Jenni. If this account were about a different aspect of my life, of course Armanda's place in it would be far more important. She alone will understand that the small space given to her here is no reflection of the deep love I felt for her.

Peter and I spent three days in New York staying in an hotel close to Broadway and Times Square, exploring Manhattan by day and going to the theatre at night, before taking the mainline train service south from Penn Station. In Philadelphia we found rooms in a boarding-house, and the following afternoon caught the local railway service to Strasburg, which was the stop after Paradise. The line carried two passenger trains a day, one there and one back. The train rattled across the countryside so slowly that it was like travelling by mule.

It was evening by the time we arrived, with the descending sun bouncing off the parallel rails along which we had just ridden. Strasburg was the last stop on the line, so the single wooden carriage remained stationary, like an exhibit in a transport museum. We were the only two travellers, and there appeared to be no facilities whatsoever for us at the station, not even a plat-form to step down onto. As we lifted our bags to the ground, my eyes scanned the deserted space, looking for a station building or a sign of life. The whole area was so open that there was no natural meeting place. All I could see were the telegraph poles, which had run along the track since Philadelphia, and the open, cultivated fields, which stretched to the horizon like a quilt. There was no town of Strasburg even worth calling a ghost town. We waited a few minutes with our bags beside us on the loose gravel and cinder, with the intense sunlight shining directly into our eyes. I looked again, squinting at the fields which surrounded us, but could see no one. I felt a long way from home.

Then, standing on the vertex of the low, dusty incline which ran away from the track, I made out the shapes of a buggy and two human figures silhouetted against the light. One figure was clearly that of a man, the other a boy, recognizable by the differences in their height. They were side by side without quite touching one another, as if the inch of space between them might be important to both their dignities, and they were wait-ing so peaceably that I thought they must be playing a game to see which of them would remain immobile longest and be the last to move. It was as if the two people had been there all their lives. In the powerful, indistinct haze of back-light which en-circled them, both gave the impression of being undisturbed, quiescent, like two stoics who were used to waiting and who were now profitably using their time to examine the value of patience. Both appeared to be wearing black, with hats that had broad, prominent rims, so that even if the sun had been the other way, I might not have been able to see their faces. The darkness of their clothing, outlined against the brilliance of the light, created and added mystery to their unworldliness. Man and boy were clearly Amish.

They must have been able to see us, for they had the advan-tage of the angle of the sun and were looking in our direction, but still they did not move, nor even glance at one another to ask if we might be the people they were obviously expecting. The boy, both in posture and attitude, was a miniature replica of the man, and if it had not been for the differences in their size, they would have been identical. His disciplined, respectful manner could only be that of a child beside his father.

Peter and I picked up our bags and walked towards them.

The child's low crowned, wide-brimmed black hat was on a level with his father's elbow, which his father now raised to push his own hat further onto his head, where his hand remained as if the day might be windy, although not a breath of air was blowing. It was the first gesture of the pair to express doubt or concern. The boy, now also moving for the first time, imitated his father by tilting his head backwards in the same inquisitive fashion, and then, slowly, without looking at his father for permission but having the confidence of his action, he raised his arm in a simple wave which acknowledged our presence. The rest of his body was so quiet that this single, unaffected movement of his hand was beautiful. He waved once, before returning his arm to his side.

As we approached, the enigma created by their silhouettes began to decrease. They were wearing black, broadfall trousers with an unusual bib at the front where the fly buttons might have been, and purple shirts partially hidden by a waistcoat, which also had no buttons but were fastened by means of hooks and eyes. Neither was wearing shoes. The man had an uncut beard growing from his chin and wire glasses, which sat at the top of his nose making him look Jewish, but without the pathos Jews sometimes have. His face was inscrutable, reflecting the unhurried stance of his body, and his eyes were sober, almost grave. There was nothing poetic about his appearance, but rather he seemed unenthusiastic, spiritless, like a man who has laboured far too long in the hot sun. It was not the countenance of the tolerant, patient, submissive man that I had expected and which my initial impressions had confirmed. Now that I could see his features clearly, his insensitivity alarmed me, and I realized why it was that Peter and I were having to walk towards him, for there was nothing tender or compassionate in his manner which would have brought him towards us, thereby allowing us to meet on an equal footing. His stillness was born of arrogance, not of any purity or innocence.

It was a strange, frightening meeting, made even more disconcerting by the openness of our surroundings and the absence of a town from which to draw conclusions. I had not seen John for over thirty years but his greeting was cold and impersonal, as if my presence by his side was not welcome. He received Peter's hand with greater care than my own but the animosity was still present, for Peter was nervous and unsure. John ignored this by telling him straight away to lift our bags onto the buggy, without first allowing him the dignity of an introductory conversation. Nor did John inquire as to the comfort of his journey, which might have been polite when meeting a stranger. Peter did as John demanded by placing our bags on a ledge above the buggy's rear wheels. John hovered about him, plainly distrustful of what he saw as Peter's youth.

The last time I had seen John had been at the school in New Orleans on the afternoon when the shack had toppled over and Harry had swum in the Mississippi with the children, whilst John and myself, seated on the river bank, had talked at length about forgiveness. John was not as I remembered him, nor was his personality what I expected to find. The world turns without us having an influence upon it, and I had certainly had no influence upon John. His world was as foreign to me as any world I had ever encountered. I felt so sorry for Peter. At least I had the benefit of having corresponded with this abrupt, graceless Amishman, albeit in a largely practical way regarding the times and details of our visit, but Peter did not even have the comfort of this, never mind the solace of our shared history. I had tried to prepare Peter for the person we might find, beginning by telling him of the night in Whitby when John and Harry had fought in the tent, but John's letters were at such odds with the coldness we were now experiencing that I realized that it might have been preferable if I had said nothing. I had spoken of a kind, friendly, passionate man, but John seemed so remote that I could hardly believe it. I even wondered if we were not being met by the wrong Amishman or that someone else had not been sent in his place. The whole tenor of our meeting saddened and dispirited me.

The journey from Strasburg station to John's farm passed in almost complete silence. We travelled in the twin rear seats of the grey-topped, four-wheeled, horse-drawn buggy, which had enclosing canvas sides running from top to bottom. The effect was like riding in a box, and we saw little of the countryside of Pennsylvania. Our only view was above the heads of John and his son, who were seated at the front. I kept touching the canvas at my elbow, feeling certain it must be possible for it to be rolled up, and wondering why John seemed to be deliberately keeping us in the dark. The carriage was well sprung with steel elliptic springs, which made the ride far from uncomfortable despite the fact that the horse trotted along the narrow country lanes at a surprisingly brisk pace. We turned this way and that, taking a labyrinth of small roads which appeared to crisscross one another, and all of which were similar, with grass verges full of spring flowers, so that in no time at all I had completely lost my bearings. It was as if we had entered a maze with a complex network of crossroads and intersections. Whenever the buggy turned left or right at one of the many T-junctions, often without stopping, Peter and I were thrown together, for the centrifugal force created by the vehicle's cornering made it impossible for us to remain upright. The speed and agility of the carriage amazed me, as did John's handling of the horse, which was obedient to his every command without his once having to raise his voice. There was little gentility in the way he drove. Rather he was quick and workmanlike. I might have thought him reckless had he not appeared to be relaxed. It was obviously the usual practice of this Amishman to take the narrow lanes at breakneck speed, although thankfully at less speed down the hills, where he slowed the carriage to a walk; but on the flat he thundered along. The carriage had wooden wheels with metal rims, so the noise generated from the paved roads was considerable. It was not unlike continuous heavy rain falling on a tin roof, only much, much louder.

At the station, John had introduced us to his son, whose name was Elmer. Apart from a polite hello, spoken in English, the boy had said even less than his father. In the buggy, I was seated diagonally behind him to his right, so that occasionally when he turned to his father who was sitting directly in front of me, I caught the profile of his face, still slightly shadowed by the brim of his hat. I put the boy's age at between ten and eleven years old. His hair was distinctive, being parted in the middle and cut straight around the head at a length that covered approximately half of his ears, with a higher fringe cut above his eyes. It made him look like a young Renaissance fop or court dandy, which the quietness of his behaviour entirely contradicted. It was obviously the standard Amish haircut, done by his mother at home. It made no concessions to individuality, for his father's hair was cut in the same fashion, if a little shorter and neater. The boy's trousers had unelasticated, cloth braces, which ran straight up the front of his shirt and crossed over on his back, marking his back with a black X against his purple shirt. His hands were clean but not clean enough, as if he had washed them too quickly after an afternoon spent working in the fields. There was a purity and innocence about the child which was accentuated by the grubbiness of his fingernails, by the rough cut of his hair, and by the plainness of his simple clothing. I was reminded of the simplicity of his wave at the station, which had been so undramatic and unfussy that it was a reflection of the boy himself. Elmer had no vulgarity: he was not humdrum or commonplace.

As our journey progressed along the roads, which appeared to become narrower with every new junction, the boy and his father began, very occasionally, to speak to one another in German, or in the dialect of German known as Pennsylvania Dutch which Harry had once told me about. It was the language the settlers had brought from Europe centuries before. Harry had maintained that the language was little changed, and I did not doubt it. Elmer answered his father's questions patiently. At one point, he stretched out his arm to show his father a particular landmark or event which I could not see from my position in the rear seat, but whatever it was made them both chuckle. They were beginning to relax, so I relaxed too. Only once, when the horse slowed to a walk because of the steepness of the gradient did the carriage become quiet enough for me to attempt to make out the nature of their conversation. I had learned some German, but the richness of their dialect made understanding impossible. They spoke quietly, unfussily, without always making eye contact, as two people will who knew each other very well. There was certainly a discipline in the way they spoke, with no word wasted. I was sorry when they became tight-lipped again.

Three quarters of an hour after we had departed from the station, we crossed yet another of the wooden bridges which seemed common in the area and then ran along beside a stream for a few minutes, before John turned the buggy off the road and up a farm track. By now the sun was almost touching the horizon and the light going quickly, so that our view of the farm was further restricted: but, even so, I could just make out the warm colours of the landscape being exaggerated by the falling sun. I remembered Harry talking about the particular quality of the light and longed to see the sunset for myself but feared I had missed this first opportunity by ten minutes. The horse and carriage trotted along the rough track, with John taking little more care than he had on the public highway. The house, directly in front of us, was haloed by back-light and therefore shadowed in darkness, much as John and Elmer had been at the station. Disappointed at not being able to see the house clearly, I moved forwards in my seat trying to improve my view. Instantaneously, John cracked the whip which had lain dormant in his hand the whole journey. His action was that of a man pleased to be released from self-control. In the same movement of his wrist, he flicked the thong backwards and cracked the whip again, skilfully rapping the horse across the neck. The horse accelerated into a canter. I held on, gripping the seat in front of me, until John brought the carriage to a halt outside the house. The noise, from the speed of the carriage wheels on the dirt road, had been so deafening that the silence that followed our sudden stop was eerie.

Elmer jumped down from the buggy as if nothing untoward had occurred. John showed us into the house and left us almost immediately to go and unhitch the horse. Elmer went with him, duplicating his father's urgency. We did not see them for over an hour but were left in the hands of Rachel, John's wife, to whom John had (too briefly, I thought angrily) introduced us on the doorstep. Rachel was a petite, demure woman, whose hair was bonneted in a white cap tied with two strings beneath her chin. The cap was so thin that it was translucent, and I could see the full head of uncut hair partially hidden beneath it. She showed us straight away, without welcome or ceremony, to our room at the top of the house, which had two small beds and little else. The room was on the shadowed side of the house, so our only light was from her paraffin lamp, with which she pointed out a small chest for our clothes. She then left us to return downstairs as solemnly and brusquely as she had shown us up, having been with us for not a second more than was necessary. Her nervousness and agitation had made my spirits fall again. The unconventionality of our meeting was becoming more irregular with every moment that passed, for it was obvious these people did not wish us to be in their presence.

Peter chose the bed beneath the window whilst I lit a paraffin lamp which had been placed on the chest for our use. As the orange glow fizzed across the room, I was reminded of the dormitory at school where Harry, too, had chosen the bed by the window, and I felt almost as young and unsure as I had done then. I had become used to electricity. It was like being thrown back into an age and time which I thought had gone forever, but which once more surrounded me, bringing with it a myriad of buried memories. I had forgotten the unholy, spectral atmosphere created by a paraffin lamp in a small space. At school I had learned of Harry's family and his secret in such an atmosphere. His secret no longer seemed important, yet somehow I knew the final unravelling of its effect on his life was to be found here in Pennsylvania amongst the Amish and with John in particular. I knew nothing of the Amish way of life, but what little I had witnessed so far did not endear them to me, and that Harry had thought I might find solace amongst these people puzzled me, for the opposite was proving the case. As far as I could see they were rude, obtuse, aloof, uncaring, even slightly crazy, for John's escapade on the farm track with the horse and buggy could only be described as such. He had deliberately tried to frighten us. I was disappointed. We had travelled to his home with such high expectations of the love we should find, that banishing these uncharitable thoughts from my mind proved extremely difficult. I felt as childish and as selfish, as uncertain and doubtful, as frightened and alarmed as I had done in my youth, long before my nervous breakdown had brought me to my senses.

A little girl, younger than Elmer but similarly attired to her mother in a translucent white bonnet, eventually brought us water and a towel and we were able to wash. She said nothing, but carried the bowl of water carefully, spilling none, as if under instruction on both counts from her elders below. I tried speaking to her in pidgin German, which elicited a polite, embarrassed smile but nothing else. She was wearing a long, navy-blue dress fastened at the back with hooks and eyes, over which was a white pinafore made from the same material as her cap. The dress covered her completely so that only her face and her bare feet were visible. Like her mother she was shy and demure, and like her mother she left as quickly as she arrived, without squandering a second of her time.

The water was fresh and cold. Peter, who had spoken little

since our arrival at the station, washed first and then kneeled on his bed to look through the uncurtained window at the rising three-quarter moon. After washing myself, I kneeled beside him on the quilted bed covering. We must have looked like two children on Christmas Eve, eagerly awaiting Father Christmas, but neither of us felt excited. I could sense Peter's bitter disappointment, and recognized his listlessness because it was similar to my own. His eyes were staring vacantly through the glass, but all he could see was his reflection. The paraffin lamp behind us was providing just sufficient light to dull the effect of the moon on the landscape outside so that only the moon itself was observable through the window with any clarity. I turned down the lamp to darken the room. Peter opened the window and we leaned out with our elbows side by side on the windowsill. I felt as if I were back at school breaking some petty restriction for which I would shortly be punished, but I soon ceased to care, for the night air had such tranquillity, such peacefulness, such stillness and silence that it was like being in heaven on earth. Peter cupped his hands and leaned his chin between his palms. He, too, had sensed the deep peace of the landscape and noticed the activity along the country roads, for dotted here and there were the surprisingly fast moving lights of what could only be horses and buggies travelling from farm to farm. The lights were turning this way and that at the many road junctions, usually without pausing, creating the impression of a series of jagged shooting-stars. Occasionally two lights met on the same road and passed, or missed one another at a turning by seconds, but neither stopped. As one light left our field of view, another entered. I counted fifteen separate lights, each moving in a different direction, and then four came together at a crossroads and momentarily reduced their tally by three. It was a beguiling sight. The Amish were coming home from work or going out for the evening in considerable numbers, and at considerable speed. Their progress along the narrow lanes was far from sedate. I looked at Peter. Peter looked towards me. In that same moment we had both realized that John's handling of the horse and buggy was, perhaps, not as crazy or as unusual as we had first thought. Peter looked back to the horizon, whilst I listened to the silence. Intermittently, very faintly, I could hear the sound of a buggy's wheels speeding along a metalled road, but could not tell from which of the hard-driving lights the sound came, and I felt chastened by the experience.

I suggested to Peter that we brave the rest of the house by carrying the bowl of dirty water downstairs, and was relieved when he agreed with me that this was the best excuse available to us for joining whoever might be below. John and Elmer had not yet returned from the barn where their buggy was garaged. In the parlour at the foot of the stairway, the same little girl who had brought us the water, and who had just finished laying a table with cutlery, studiously accepted the metal bowl from me and went through a partition into what was obviously the kitchen, where she whispered to her mother. The partition was fully open so I could see her mother preparing a meal at the wood-burning stove. The room – it was really one large room which could be divided into two when necessary – was hot and the windows misted with steam from the boiling water in the cooking pans. The little girl, after being cajoled and appealed to, eventually came back into our half of the room and said, in English, that we might sit down if we wished. I smiled, but she did not smile at me. I asked her her name, but she did not reply, until her mother called to her from the kitchen in German, which made her say that her name was Anna. She was like a child nervously searching for a pocket in which to place her hands, but neither her dress nor her white pinafore had a pocket to find. Anna had been told to entertain us, but was too suspicious to do so. Her face was gaunt, with a prominent chin like her mother's, and her hair was pulled sideways from a centre parting into a bun, which sat at the nape of her neck partially hidden by her cap. The strictness of her hair style made her face look severe, giving the impression of a girl who seldom enjoyed herself. I asked her how old she was, but again she did not reply until prompted from the kitchen; she told me she was ten years old. She spoke politely, with a curious, old-fashioned seriousness and modesty.

I was about to explain that she had no need to be so respectful and could return to helping her mother at the stove if she wished, when the outside door crashed open and a boy came in. He did not see us, but Anna glared at him as if to tell him to behave. It was a look of reproach which he deliberately ignored by slamming the door closed with his foot. The boy had obviously forgotten that there would be strangers present. He was older than both Anna and Elmer but had the same implacability and was clearly their brother. When he did see us, his light-hearted teenage bravura switched to solemnity as he remembered and realized who we were. In an instant he ceased to be high spirited and became reserved. He copied, did not mimic, his sister's sternness. I attempted to begin a conversation with him by saying hello, but he went straight through into the kitchen where he, too, spoke to his mother in undertones. Anna remained in our presence, shuffling from one foot to the other, as though her brother's arrival had increased her discomfort, rather than lessening it as I might have expected. I asked her about him, and she nodded a shy acknowledgement to my inquiry, before the torment of being isolated drove her to her family in the other half of the room, where she began peeling some sweet potatoes.

The boy washed his hands and face in the metal bowl we had carried down from upstairs. His mother continued to speak to him in emphatic but muted tones. The change in the boy, from the gaiety of his entrance to the seriousness with which he listened to her whispers, was dispiriting and could not but confirm that we were an intrusion in the household, an interference which had completely upset its balance. His mother had done nothing to acknowledge our presence since leaving us after showing us to our room, although his sister Anna had spoken for her and I could sense that he was being instructed to do the same. When he had finished washing his face, he placed the bowl on the floor and diligently cleaned his bare feet. His mother began to help his sister chop the vegetables. He dried between his toes with a towel and then came through to where Peter and I were now sitting. His hands were pitted, their coarseness surprising in a child of his age. He was, perhaps, thirteen or fourteen years old; certainly his voice had not fully broken.

'My name's Emanuel,' he said. 'My mother has asked me to come and talk to you.' He spoke English with a slight American accent but with an even greater country lilt. It was not an accent I had heard before, in America or elsewhere.

'I'm Daniel and this is Peter.'

'Yes, I know,' he said. 'Have you come a long way?' It was a simple question simply put.

'We've come from England.'

Emanuel nodded his head: he was being courteous, but it was apparent from the vacancy of his nod that England meant little to him. His hair was cut on a level with the middle of his ears, in identical fashion to his younger brother, and his back was marked with the same X from his braces. Their simplicity and similarity was uncanny. I realized his hands were bruised from labouring in the fields.

'Have you been working today?' I asked. 'Where had you been before you came in just now?'

'Bird in Hand,' he replied matter-of-factly, with no awareness that he had left me with a puzzle, a quandary for which he accepted no responsibility. It was clear he thought I should know Bird in Hand because he knew it well. He was not being rude: he judged everyone's knowledge by his own.

'What is Bird in Hand?' I asked. 'Is it a place?'

'A town.'

'Ah, I see,' I said, 'so you've been into the town?'

'Yes.'

'How far is that?'

'Ten minutes in the buggy. Twenty minutes if I go on my scooter.' He then shrugged as if my question were ridiculous.

'And what have you been doing in the town?'

'Seeing Benj King in the harness shop,' he said.

'What does he do?'

'He makes harnesses.'

I chuckled at the pointlessness of our exchange, but he did not because to him all our exchanges were pointless. He saw no difference between my questions and did not spot my ineptitude. For him, asking if a harness shop made harnesses was no more silly a question than asking if Bird in Hand was a town.

'What was he doing for you at the harness shop?' I asked.

'Making blinders for the horse.'

'What do they do?'

'They stop it being frightened by objects behind it and to the sides of it.'

I thought his choice of words interesting because 'it' depersonalized the horse, in a way we would never have done in England. He could have been speaking of a machine with a mechanical fault. This, somehow, was at one with the plainness of his overall manner. Life for this adolescent boy was practical, with no romance. He was not embarrassed, he was not rude or offhand, he was not unsure or afraid, he was simply answering my questions as politely as he could, without any desire to court favour.

'Emanuel,' I said, 'did you drive back from the harness shop in the horse and buggy?'

'Yes.'

'What are the lights on the buggies? We saw quite a few lights through our bedroom window.'

'They are so we can see our way in the dark.'

'I understand that, but I thought you didn't have electricity.'

'They are not electricity, they are batteries.'

'Are batteries allowed in the buggies?'

'Yes.' He then offered a statement of his own, which showed him to be far from simple-minded. 'Our batteries make it less dangerous for the English, who have to drive along the same roads in their motorcars.'

'Who are the English?' I asked.

'You are English. English is anyone who ain't of our church. Americans is English.' He smiled at the irony in his joke. 'Do you know if you have electricity in England?'

'Yes, we do.'

'Do you use it for lights in the house?'

'Yes.'

I waited for his next question, but he had come to a halt.

'We use electricity for all sorts of things,' I said, 'not just for lights. We use it for vacuum cleaners, for cooking with, for heating, for powering the wireless.'

He nodded his head but it was clear that he had come to a halt because he did not know about vacuum cleaners, or electric cookers, or the wireless, and therefore did not have the knowledge to probe further.

'Jesus didn't use electricity,' he said. 'Jesus was born a long time before.' And then came a non-sequitur, which he asked with reverential wonder. 'Do you know if Bethlehem is near England?'

It was such a straightforward inquiry that it took me a moment to reply.

'Well, it's nearer England than the United States, yes.'

'Have you been to Bethlehem?'

'No, I haven't unfortunately.' His question had been asked with such awe and adoration that I was sorry to disillusion him. But he did not show the disappointment I had expected.

'Baby Jesus was born in a stable in the light from a star,' he said.

'Yes.'

'He was born in a manger.'

'Yes, he was.'

'The three wise men came to see him.'

'I haven't been to Bethlehem, but would you like to, Emanuel?'

He paused and I realized my inquiry had discomfited him. His face became perplexed as if he did not know the answer.

'King Herod ordered all the boy babies to be killed,' he said eventually.

I did not pursue the question because it was obvious that his travelling to Bethlehem was beyond his comprehension, and that he had answered in the only way that he could, by continuing the story of Jesus's birth. I was beginning to understand the smallness of his world.

Anna came through from the kitchen eating a slice of red pepper. She stood beside him running the pepper round her lips, like a child might a coloured Smartie in England. Her bonnet straps had become unfastened, making her face look less severe.

'This is my sister Anna,' he said brightly. I could see he was pleased by the diversion her entrance had caused.

'Yes, I know,' I said. 'Anna brought us some water for us to wash in.'

She placed her hand on to the small of her brother's back as though to reassure both him and herself. It was the action of an adult, undertaken with the nonchalance of a child. I was beginning to see her as a child, which I had not done before. Her lips were red from the pepper.

'Anna is shy,' he went on. 'She likes eating peppers, but she ain't very happy when she has to talk to someone. Are you, Anna?'

Anna nodded and then said something to him in German.

'We've to talk English,' he said to her without reproach. 'Daddy has told us we must talk English.'

Anna returned to the kitchen, where her mother pushed her straight back out into our half of the room. Her return was so swift that her mother could only have been prepared. Indeed, she must have been listening to our entire conversation, hidden, perhaps, behind the edge of the partition. This helped to explain why Anna had arrived so precipitously when her brother had become discomfited with our talk of his going to Bethlehem. Anna was being sent in as a distraction. It was all very curious.

'Anna don't talk at school, do you, Anna?' he said to her when she had resumed her position beside him. He put his arms across her shoulders, like a father might his daughter. 'Talking ain't everything, I say. Teacher says she good at her sums, and when I need something counted I go to Anna. Don't I, Anna?'

Anna nodded in agreement, the pepper held between her lips. Her brother pulled a wooden bench from beneath the dining-table. In the same movement of his sitting down, he lifted his younger sister onto his lap. She fidgeted for a few moments until she was comfortable. The boy then placed his arms around her waist.

'Are you the oldest in the family?' I asked him.

'No. My grandfather is the oldest.'

I smiled at his reply because it was so direct. He immediately looked quizzical. I worried that I had offended him.

'I was meaning of the children, Emanuel. Are you the eldest of the children?'

'No, I ain't.'

'Who is the eldest?'

'My brother Jacob.'

'How old is he?'

'How old is Jacob, Anna?' he asked her.

Anna began to count on her fingers. I counted with her until she had been one and a half times round her hands and stopped at sixteen. I must have smiled again at the simplicity of it all.

'Why do you keep smiling?' he asked me. 'Is we doing something wrong?' His confidence was returning, and he was speaking with bluntness, not rudeness.

'You're doing nothing wrong, Emanuel. I've smiled all my life. I always smile when I'm nervous. I'm a buffoon. I smile when I find people charming.'

He looked confused by the compliment I had tried to pay

him. Anna, indifferent to our conversation, offered him the red-pepper which he declined. He pulled his sister, who had slipped down, further onto his lap.

'Do you know if folk smile a lot in England?' It was the preface 'do you know' which gave him and his questions their innocence. He used it frequently.

'Yes, people do smile in England.'

'We smile when we make a joke. I ain't made a joke. Do you know if folk in England makes jokes?'

'Yes, they do.'

'Do you know if folks in England have farms?'

Before I could reply, Anna tilted her head backwards so that her face was slanted upwards towards her brother.

'Jacob makes jokes all the time,' she said to him in English. Her words were so unexpected that they were almost miraculous. 'Jacob is a bad boy.'

'He ain't a bad boy,' he said to her firmly, his manner still fatherly.

'Yes, he is,' she continued in English. 'Mummy has told us not to talk to him when he's bad.'

Emanuel reverted to German. His fatherliness disappeared and his tone of voice became admonishing.

'You says we is meant to talk English,' she said. 'Jacob makes jokes about the bible and Bethlehem.'

'Not in my presence, he don't,' her mother said entering from the kitchen. There was now no doubt that she had been listening to every word we had been saying. 'Come here, Anna. Come here this instant.'

Anna jumped from her brother's knee. Her mother knelt down in front of her so as to be at the same height.

'Trust you to speak when we don't want you to,' she said with greater cheerfulness than previously, making what followed less strict than it might otherwise have been. 'Jacob is older than you. He has his responsibilities about the farm, comes and goes more as he pleases, but he don't make jokes about the bible.'

Anna fidgeted. Her mother placed her hands on her daughter's waist to hold her still.

'Yes, Mama,' the little girl said.

'Jacob is a bad boy because he likes English ways. He wears shoes when he shouldn't, and hides his English clothes in a ditch. But no one makes jokes about the bible, Anna. No one. Not even English.'

'Yes, Mama.'

'Go and wash your mouth out.'

The little girl went into the kitchen where I could see her swilling her mouth with water. It occurred to me that her mother could have expressed herself in German, but had chosen not to. There was a tension between Jacob and the rest of the family which she had decided to make known. We would have found out sooner or later.

'I'm very sorry,' I said. 'It's my fault, I shouldn't have asked so many questions.'

'The children will answer you as best they can,' she said. 'I ask you not to bring your English ways to them. The children must learn from the bible, not from the evil doings of English, who don't try to understand us.'

'I understand.'

'Do you?' She questioned me with such force that it was like being winded by a punch to the stomach.

'Well, no, I don't understand,' I said after a moment. 'But I can try to. I can try and learn. You live a way of life quite unlike anything I have ever seen. I am the loser for that. I don't mean to patronize you.'

'You are curious like all English,' she said. 'We is not curious at all. We is a plain people. We believe in right and wrong. I ask you not to bring your wrong into this house.'

'I will try. I will do my best. I have been trying. We both have.' Peter had said nothing for over fifteen minutes. Her personality was so strong that I was beginning to wish he would. 'We neither of us want to be a nuisance. Neither of us will seek to influence your way of life. I think we both feel a little strange at the moment, but I'm sure that will pass. Peter is here because of the terms of his legacy.'

'Yes, I know,' she said. 'John will talk to you about his friend's will. We isn't happy with it. We isn't happy with it at all. We isn't happy with his evil money giving. You want to bring evil into this house.'

'No. No, we don't.'

I was so shocked by the inhumanity of her statements that that was all I could think of to say in reply. Her invective rendered

230

me speechless. We had done nothing to deserve such an onslaught. Her criticisms were based not upon us, but upon some false ideas of her own, and her judgements had clearly been made long before our arrival, so that Peter and I as individuals were irrelevant. We were outsiders and, as such to her, symbols of a hostile world.

That John and his family were enraged by Harry's will had never even been hinted at in the correspondence which had passed between us across the Atlantic. In only one of his letters could I now recall him passing comment on the magnitude of his legacy, and he had requested that the money not be transferred from England until we arrived, but he had expressed no doubt, as far as I could remember, as to his final acceptance of it. That he did have doubts and might disapprove of the inheritance was a bombshell. I could hardly believe what John's wife was saying. But it did help to explain their aloofness and her husband's attitude towards us at the railway station.

'I'm sure Mr Treffgarne had no wish to upset anyone,' Peter said straightforwardly, if quietly, 'let alone the friend whom he most admired. To call Mr Treffgarne evil, misrepresents his generosity completely.'

I was proud of him. Like many people who keep their own counsel in an argument, his words when they came were precise and soothing. His command of the situation had been worth the long wait. I relaxed a little.

'If Mr Treffgarne has made a mistake and upset you,' he went on, 'that is a different matter from his being evil. We all make mistakes, even you I expect. N-n-n-n-no one is perfect.' He stammered for the first time in his life. It was an indication of the tension in the room. The stammer was to remain with him for nearly forty years. 'I f-f-feel really t-terrible at this m-moment because we came h-here as f-f-friends and we are being t-treated as enemies. This is not w-what Mr Treffgarne w-w-would have w-w-wished at all.' His stammer was so bad that his words had ceased to be soothing and become embarrassing. In fact, it was hard to tell what he was saying.

'Mama, can I go to my guinea-pigs?' Emanuel asked, openly perturbed by the misunderstandings and tensions between us.

'No, you can't,' she said bluntly.

The boy neither remonstrated nor sulked, as an English child might have done, but accepted his mother's authority without complaint. I was relieved to hear her speak to him as plainly as she had done to us. I tried to imitate his reaction so as not to let her know my true feelings.

'Is there an hotel where we could find a room?' I asked her, almost stammering myself.

'Is what we have offered you no good?'

'No, it isn't that. Your children must need the space and we are in the way.' I appealed to every mother's worry concerning her child's education. 'Where do they do their homework from school for instance?'

'They don't do no homework,' she said, throwing my reasoning off balance.

I understood why Anna still counted to sixteen on her fingers, but resisted the temptation to comment – in truth, I would not have dared comment – so instead there was a brief silence, filled by the sounds of Anna at the stove in the kitchen. She had finished swilling her mouth and was now watching over the vegetables, testing them now and again in the boiling water with the point of a knife, like a Victorian orphan being made to slave: or so I thought because I was reminded of Oliver Twist in the workhouse. That I could think of Dickens is a measure of the suffering I imagined the children must be enduring. Anna seemed so small and the cooking pans so hot and large. I wanted to protect her.

'Jacob normally sleeps in the room you're in,' her mother said eventually. 'He demanded a room of his own, which is a sign of his English ways.' I could not imagine anyone demanding anything from this woman, let alone being successful as Jacob had obviously been. 'It is better we give in and try to understand him. Jacob must learn the error of his ways himself. He must see that English is not good. We must see that we are here when he needs us.' I thought I spotted a touch of sympathy in her voice, which shocked me almost as much as her sternness. 'He must see for himself that hiding his English clothes in a ditch is wrong. We can only guide him. A boy who is made to go in one direction by his parents is a boy who will change his mind. I ask you not to influence him with your English habits, but to let him see who you are so he can decide for himself.' I was right, there was indeed a detectable softening in her approach towards us. 'Jacob is happy to give you his room and to sleep with his brothers.

It will do him good. It will help him to see that we must all be humble before God. Won't it, Emanuel?'

'Yes, Mama,' the boy said.

'You must help him as well,' she went on to her son without pausing for breath. 'You must talk to your older brother about baby Jesus, and tell him how Jesus was born in a stable so that peace might come to all on earth.'

'Yes, Mama.'

'Jacob has no peace within himself. Giving up his room and sleeping with you will help him to find peace.'

These words to her son might have been smug had she not expressed herself so simply and calmly. She left us to return to the kitchen where she joined her daughter at the stove.

Once more I felt chastened. The feeling came upon me so quickly that I could not really pinpoint where it came from, or explain to myself the precise nature of its cause. Intellectually I found them a puzzle, and emotionally they caused me disquiet. It seemed to me to be a contrary world, but like it or not we were here to stay.

Emanuel remained silent for the next few minutes, as did Peter and myself, until John came in, from garaging the buggy, with Elmer and three other children, one of whom was clearly the troublesome Jacob, because he was by far the tallest and oldest. Apart from his height and age, he looked to be identical to his younger brothers and, despite his mother's fears, did not appear to be English in any way that I could see. His purple shirt sleeves were rolled up to his elbows, revealing surprisingly muscular forearms. The boy not only worked, but worked hard. I found it difficult to imagine him being idle, and in my wildest dreams I could not see him digging a ditch in which to hide a pair of denim jeans or a checked shirt. When he spoke to us, inquiring as to the comfort of our journey (which no other member of the family had done), it was with great deliberation, deference and old-world courteousness. But his statements and questions were as naive as Emanuel's had been ten minutes earlier.

There were so many children, six in all, that I worried about forgetting their names. Jacob appeared to be the one least troubled by our presence, whilst the other two new arrivals, a girl called Katie and a boy called Gideon, were far less willing to enter into the spirit of our meeting and mostly sheltered behind their father. Gideon, the smallest child, was under school age and spoke only German, but Katie, who I judged to be about eight years old, managed a few words with us before John ushered them all through into the kitchen where they washed their hands, faces and feet in water from the metal bowl.

Gideon washed himself without help, which I thought unfair because he was so young. He too had the distinctive black X formed by his trouser braces – for some reason this was one of the distinctive features of the boys – which on him looked even more unusual and unorthodox because of his small stature and tender age. Katie began to assist him, which pleased me, rolling up his shirt sleeves to stop the cuffs becoming wet. She too was wearing a white bonnet, covering her uncut hair, in the selfsame fashion as her mother and older sister, but her dress was a different colour from Anna's, being turquoise instead of navy-blue. As she washed Gideon's feet, the hook and eye fastenings on the back of her dress reflected the light from the paraffin lamp, hanging on a chain from the ceiling, with which the kitchen was now lit. I was struck by the religiosity of the scene, for the light was low and the little girl washed her brother's feet with devotion. He played with his shirt cuffs, which had slipped down from his elbows, and then put his hand on his sister's shoulder to balance himself. I gained the distinct impression that he was unhappy being helped, that he would have preferred to manage on his own. Then it dawned on me that Katie was using the activity as cover to watch us. Her head was constantly turning and her eyes moving in our direction. The scene was not religious at all. She, just like her sister and older brothers, was fascinated by the two strangers who had come to stay at her house. She was taciturn, but nevertheless as curious about us as we were about her.

Anna, too, was now watching us from the kitchen. The security afforded her by the rest of the family was giving her the courage to stare openly, whereas before she had been shy and clandestine.

'Are these all your brothers and sisters?' I asked Emanuel, who had been the one member of the household to sit with us throughout the hurly-burly of washing and cooking in the kitchen.

'Yes,' he said. 'My older, older brother was killed. My brother Levi is in heaven.'

John entered from the kitchen bringing Jacob with him. John

had spent much of the time, since drying his feet, listening to his wife. Whilst continuing to prepare the meal, she had spoken to him in whispers about all that had occurred between us during his hour-long absence.

'Levi went to Ohio,' John said, picking up straight away on what his son had just been saying, 'to spend a vacation there and to work on the farm with his cousins. There's a large community of Amish in Ohio, many of whom have travelled from here. They have built new farms and set up new homes. Levi had both legs cut off by a train running over him on the journey back. The conductor put him off while the train was in full speed. He lay there for several hours before some English found him and took him in, but he died.'

The whole room had fallen silent. Anna was standing in the middle of the partition beside her mother. Katie was drying her brother Gideon's feet with a towel. Elmer entered and stood between Jacob and Emanuel. I looked from one member of the family to the other, from the youngest to the oldest.

'Why?' I asked. 'Why did the conductor throw him off?'

'No one knows,' John said straightforwardly without emotion. 'He might have been cheeking the conductor, we don't know. The conductor might have thought his clothes funny, his looks odd, because our clothes are funny, our looks are odd. We are a community who make no compromises, we make no compromises when we travel, we travel as we are.'

In the kitchen, Katie lifted the metal bowl onto a ledge which was taller than her, and then she and Gideon came through into our half of the room, where they quickly joined the rest of the household in silence. They surrounded us. No member of the family moved. It was as though we were about to be accused of a crime.

'Children,' their father said, 'I would like you to meet a great friend of mine. We knew each other a long time ago, long before any of you were born. It isn't often that I talk to you about England, but I am going to now.' He looked towards his second oldest son. 'Yes, Emanuel, there are farms in England. I hope that answers the question you asked of our guest a short while ago. Your mother tells me you were interested to know. I'm sure Daniel will be pleased to talk to you about farming, whilst he is here, if you ask him again.' He ran his fingers along the length of his full-grown beard and looked from one child to the other. 'There are many questions you will all want to ask of both our guests, I hope you will be polite and listen attentively to their replies.'

Several of the children nodded their heads, including, most noticeably, Jacob. I feared the questions he would want to ask and any influence we might unwittingly exert.

'Daniel and Peter bring with them a very different way of life,' he went on. 'Always remember, children, that England is an evil place, full of evil people doing evil things. But we must try to forgive them. If we can find forgiveness in our hearts, then perhaps God can begin to forgive us for our sins. I want you to be honest with Peter and Daniel, and I'd like them to be honest with you.'

He was staring straight towards me. His eyes were piercing my conscience. My emotions ran from humility to anger and back again. I had never before felt so indecisive. I was impotent to act upon his use of the word evil, which had rattled me considerably.

'I'd like to tell you a story about Daniel. If Daniel will permit me?'

'Yes,' I said, expecting a story concerning New Orleans and relieved that the subject of evil appeared to have been changed.

'Daniel and I met in Whitby, one cold night in a tent. I was about your age, Jacob, and Daniel was a few months older than you, Emanuel. A tent is a canvas home which English use when they wish to sleep outside. Whitby is a town in England. I was breaking the law at the time because I had refused to fight in the English army, in an English war. Your uncle, my older brother, like your older brother Levi, had been killed in this war for reasons of pride. I was a pacifist and knew that to be the way to God. Daniel and his school friend, a different friend from Peter, invited me to spend the night with them in their tent. I could not sleep because I was fearful of Daniel going to the authorities to let them know where I was. I pretended to be asleep, which was wrong of me I know. Daniel got up, put on his shirt and trousers, and went out into the night. I did the same and followed him. This was wrong of me, too. I should have stopped and confronted him there and then, so that there would have been no mistaking our feelings. But I did not. I was weak and frightened. Daniel walked the streets as if still trying to decide what he should do. I shadowed him. The streets were empty, with everyone asleep in their beds. A few cats prowled around and Daniel bent down to stroke one of them. The cat raised its tail and purred. Daniel went to the police station. I hid behind a low wall and watched him. He kept looking at the police sign, wondering whether or not to go in. I could tell by the look on his face that he could hear voices from inside and was still undecided. They were the voices of the police, of authority, of the people who had power and influence. Daniel wanted to tell them about me, he wanted to add his own voice to theirs, but I could see from the worried look on his face that there was a stronger voice inside his head which was stopping him. He did not go in. He walked away.' He had spoken to the children, but now he was speaking directly to me, and I realized the whole speech had been for my benefit. 'Didn't you, Daniel?'

'Yes, I did.' I found his self-righteous presumptions extraordinary. The room was so still and he was being afforded such reverence that his words immediately became pompous. My emotions settled on anger. Any ambivalence I felt towards him and his family disappeared. My instincts were to get up and leave.

'Children,' their father went on, switching his eye line back to them, 'Daniel thought that his not going into the police station was an act of cowardice, and he hated himself for not doing his duty. He hated himself so much that his heart was filled with bitterness and envy. I should have caught him up, I should have talked to him about this bitterness, but I did not. I should have talked to him about envy, which is the ruin of this world, but I did not. I should have thanked him, but I did not do that either.'

I wanted to scream that I found his observations ugly, and his apology, if that is what it was, smug, but I kept my own counsel for the sake of the children. If they had not been present I might well have given full force to my rage.

'Children,' he continued with such surety it was as though the story were written down and he were reading from a book, 'it was not cowardice which stopped Daniel going into the police station to tell them about me, it was his goodness. Another boy might well have gone in, but Daniel did not. God had spoken to him, and God's authority was louder than the authority of the police. Daniel listened to God's authority, but did not realize it was God speaking. He shunned God and instead felt guilty for what he thought were his weaknesses, but he was not weak at all,

237

for God had given him His strength. Daniel's sin was not to recognize this. He thought he was more important than God and therefore blamed himself for his failings, when God had given him these failings in order to find strength and understanding. The weakest man is the strongest man in the eyes of the Lord, for he is the man who truly listens. That night Daniel felt such a coward that he refused to listen. He ceased to care and began to seek power for himself. He wanted a power that was greater than the Lord's power. He wanted influence that was greater than the Lord's influence. He felt so weak that he set about trying to change the world for his own selfish benefit, but he reckoned without the goodness which God constantly gave him. He sought power through speaking at the Cambridge Union, but God told him he was not clever enough to be original. He denied this and continued to seek influence by becoming a politician, but God told him that he was being led astray by fools. When he had almost found consolation with the devil, God spoke to him once more and made him ill. God told him that he was weak and ordinary, and that being weak and ordinary was his strength. God told him that he would never be the great man he had once hoped he might be, and that greatness in His eyes would come from accepting his failings like every ordinary human being. For two years Daniel listened to his failings, and he slowly recovered. The politicians who had manipulated him faded in his memory so that he found he could hardly remember them, and he realized they were not important to him anymore. Their faces became vague and their ideas shadowy and insubstantial, so that all that remained was the notion that he had behaved badly. He could not clearly recall why he had done what he had done, why he had almost entered into evil but had not quite succeeded, and why he had courted the influence of evil when he knew it to be wrong. He could not quite remember what this evil was, but he no longer doubted that evil existed. God had shown him and told him so.'

John came to a halt, closed the book as it were, and the silence which pervaded the room was almost tangible. It was a silence that was beyond being heard. Evil had become palpable too. He had spoken of evil as if it might be an insect flying through the air, which could be snatched into the palm of the hand, studied for signs of life, and then discarded. He had made the most complex

238

decade of my life appear simple, yet his interpretations were so accurate that I could not believe we had never spoken together about the events which had so dominated those years, but I was certain we had not. Neither had I written of such things in my letters to him. John had hit upon the truth without needing to know the exact nature of the facts. He was right, I viewed what I thought of as my potential Fascism through a haze, as though some other person had been responsible, and I could not recall with any clarity the faces of those who had manipulated me, or the bogus reasoning behind their ideas. I had closed the book on this chapter in my life, a chapter which John had reopened so succinctly.

I peered downwards towards the bare wooden planking on the floor, feeling insecure about catching John's eye. I could sense the entire family surrounding me but could see only their naked feet. The children were stock-still, their toes immobile. Even Gideon, who could not possibly have understood what had been said, was unmoving and patient. Rachel, John's wife, turned and went into the kitchen, where I could hear her emptying the pans of boiling water, obviously in preparation for serving the meal. Her clattering gave me courage.

'Did you really follow me to the police station?' I asked, peering upwards towards the children's knees, which was as far as my courage would allow.

'Yes.'

'Why?'

'I didn't trust you. I trusted Harry, but there was something about you, Daniel, which I couldn't quite put my finger on.'

My courage abandoned me, and I returned my eyes to their toes.

'I expected you to be angry,' he said, 'but I think you're more upset than angry. I've no right to be speaking to you in this way, but I wanted to set the ground rules for your visit. This is why I wanted the children to be present when I first spoke to you. I want there to be no misunderstanding or manipulation.'

He had spoken unequivocally, unambiguously, and was so sure of the correctness of his opinions that he did not wait for me to reply or to comment, but instead moved to the head of the table. I watched his feet change position as he seated himself. The whole family now moved in response. The meeting was clearly at an end. I could smell and taste the sweet aroma of the food being brought to the table by the two girls and their mother.

'Peter,' I heard John say, 'would you like to come to the table.'

'Daniel,' Peter whispered into my ear as he moved slowly past me, 'we're about to eat.'

I raised my eye line to see what was going on. John had taken off his glasses and was pinching the bridge of his nose between his thumb and forefinger. His long grey beard was growing untidily towards his chest, where his purple shirt was absorbing the light from the kerosene lamp hanging from the ceiling above his head. His trouser braces were slack, rising in un-elasticated humps above both his shoulders, and his eyes were watery, unmistakably focused upon the thumb and finger at the top of his nose, so that he appeared to be deep in thought, if not troubled. Despite the activity about him, of the boys moving the bench to sit down on, of the girls bringing the meal to the table, he was quite alone. No one bothered him, in fact everyone studiously ignored him, and it was this, more than his self-imposed loneliness, which made me aware of the burden he carried as head of the family.

'Daniel,' he said quietly without looking towards me, 'would you please sit beside Peter at the other end of the table opposite me.'

I was so lost in my own thoughts, I was so busy realizing what an effort it must have been for him to speak to me in such a forthright manner, that I did not move. His speech had been worked out, laboured over, planned from beginning to end, and now that it had been delivered, he was worried that he had made a mistake.

'Daniel,' he said again, 'we're waiting for you. We're waiting to say grace.'

It was the sight of the family seated around the long table, more than his words, which ended my reverie, and I went to the empty place beside Peter. Dinner was already upon the plates, having been served directly from the kitchen, doing away with the need for tureens or serving bowls. I was unprepared for the massive quantities of home-cured ham, cut in chunks from the bone, and the liberal portions of vegetables placed in front of everybody, even in front of Gideon, the youngest child. In the centre of the table were three or four jars of home-made sweet pickles, a pot of corn relish, chow-chow, and two loaves of bread with a dish of thick, yellow butter. We each had a tumbler for lemonade, of which there were two pitchers filled almost to overflowing. The family worked hard and ate accordingly.

'Daniel and Peter,' John said deliberately as though this were the beginning of yet another speech he had decided upon in advance, 'I wish to, and will seek to, influence you no more. It is up to you what you do from now on. We say grace silently before we eat.'

The family bowed their heads. Gideon could not quite manage the silence and mouthed the words of the prayer as he remembered them, occasionally becoming audible in German. At one point he must have made an error because his father quietly corrected him. Elmer, the boy who had met us at the station, smiled, but quickly averted his eyes so as not to be seen by his parents. There was less reverence, less seriousness in their prayers than I might have expected and it was not a pious minute and a half. In fact there was something very practical, very ordinary, in the laying of the meal on the table and the preparation for its eating. There was a sense of routine, of tradition about the whole affair, including its religious aspect, which prevented it from becoming sanctimonious. Grace was said far too often for it to be unctuous.

The seating pattern around the table was traditional. John was seated at the head of the table with the four boys to his right seated along one side going from the youngest to the oldest, so that Gideon was closest to him and Jacob farthest away. Rachel was seated opposite Gideon immediately to John's left, with Katie beside her and then Anna, following the same principle of age up the table. It made a curious sight to see the growth in their heights. If ever another child were to be born, depending on the sex, the girls or boys would all move down one place: it seemed a simple method of solving arguments at meal times about who had the most advantageous position.

Conversation for its own sake was not encouraged, and the meal was eaten without hubbub in a hushed atmosphere, interrupted by the occasional belch, which did not appear to be frowned upon. In any case it was John who belched first, followed by Jacob, followed by Anna, followed by Emanuel, followed by Rachel, followed by Katie, Elmer and finally Gideon, who was still perfecting the art and made several attempts, each one louder than the one before. I tried unsuccessfully to ask them about their lives, to inquire about the farm and the surrounding countryside, to request information regarding the hay fields which we had seen from the buggy on our journey from the station, but gave up when there was no response. In between the belching, one child or another talked formally, in as few sentences as possible, about his day: of work accomplished mucking out the hogs; of the cow whose lameness had improved; of the hay which had been gathered and stacked in the barn; of the second crop of hay which might be possible because the weather had been fine; of how her guinea-pigs were faring; and of the fifteen apple pies she had cooked which were now sitting in the larder waiting to be eaten. Inadvertently, in the most general terms, some of my questions were answered, but all this was spoken without reference to either Peter or myself, so that we felt like outsiders, and it was clear that no compromises were ever going to be made for our benefit. It was up to us to join in with the family as best we could, and not upset them by expecting anything else, or by wishing for hospitality which they were not prepared to give. The rules of both the house and our visit were straightforward and, in their way, satisfying, once I realized there were no psychological complications to worry about. The family were plain and ordinary: they were what they said and no more than they appeared. Their view of the world was not jaundiced.

'Elmer,' John said as two of Anna's apple pies were being brought from the larder to the table, 'what were you laughing at during grace? Was you laughing at Gideon trying to remember his prayers?'

'I isn't laughing,' the boy said defensively.

'I know you isn't laughing now, Elmer. I was asking what you was laughing at during grace.' His language became rougher when he spoke to the children. 'Was you laughing because you couldn't help it, or was you laughing because you wanted to be superior?'

Jacob, to my left, fidgeted in his chair as though his father's sternness were disturbing him. In doing this he was the first member of the household to comment upon the change in atmosphere, which had ceased to be tranquil but had not yet become hostile. The older boy was sensitive to discord.

'Was you laughing, Elmer, because you wanted to impress our

guests,' his father went on when the younger boy had not replied.

'I think he was laughing at me,' I said hoping to defuse the tension around the table which seemed to be growing with John's every word.

'If you don't mind, Daniel, I'd be pleased if you'd let me deal with this in my own way. No one minds laughing, but the boy must admit his mistake.'

'What mistake?' I asked. 'The boy smiled, that's all. He probably smiled because we're here and he's nervous. I caught his eye, it wasn't his fault. Blame me, don't blame him.'

'Daniel, please don't bring your English excuses into this house,' he said.

'They might be English, they might be American,' I found myself saying, 'I consider them human excuses.' I knew as soon as I began speaking that his family's affairs were none of my concern, but it was too late.

'I recognize and understand your passion, Daniel,' he said coldly, 'but it is misguided.'

'Yes, I shouldn't have spoken. If I understand your rules correctly, I've just broken them. Please forgive me.'

'He makes the rules,' Jacob said quietly, boldly, speaking to me of his father. 'They isn't everyone's rules. Other folks have rules which is just as good.' He turned towards the other end of the table. 'Only God can make rules, Daddy. We is here to try to live up to them.'

'I did laugh because I did want to be superior,' Elmer said to his father, copying his brother's daring. 'I did laugh because Gideon do make me laugh when he can't say his prayers. There ain't nothing wrong in that. Gideon don't mind.'

Rachel began to cut into the apple pies and I thought that this, together with Elmer's admission, despite his audacity, might signal a conclusion to the argument, but I was wrong. John asked Elmer to leave the table which he did without further drama; both of them went through into the kitchen, and John then disappeared outside. Elmer waited obediently for his father's return, with his hands by his sides, his thumbs playing a few inches along the seams of his black, broadfall trousers. His face was insouciant, but it was the movement of his thumbs which expressed his nervousness, his apprehension, and informed on the timidity which his nonchalance was trying to hide. The boy regretted laughing, but it was a measure of his determination that he was never going to admit the fact. An apology was required, which I could see he was never going to give. The boy knew he was about to be punished. I admired him enormously and would have gone over to him had I possessed the same courage, the same quiet strength of will.

'Thank you,' I said to Rachel as she gave me a dish of apple pie and cream. 'You must tell me how you cooked the ham. It was delicious. I enjoy cooking myself.'

'It ain't nothing,' she replied, 'the hog was roasted in his own fat.'

John did not return for some minutes. The kitchen light above Elmer's head began to flicker as the kerosene in the lamp ran out. When the light had died completely his face was left in shadow, the overspill from the lamp in our half of the room lighting his knees, ankles and feet. I ate the apple pie with growing despondency, for the protracted wait was punishing me along with the boy. There was a helping of apple pie in his empty place, which accentuated my dismay the more I looked at it. His mother had even placed a spoon in the bowl, so that it was ready for him to eat. It was the spoon, together with his patient, timid indifference, which made me realize that the beating I was about to witness was a regular occurrence. The boy had endured this experience many times before.

'Would you like some more apple pie?' Rachel asked me, already cutting the pie with a knife.

'Just a little piece. It's most agreeable. Thank you.' I felt hypocritical, partly because the pie was far from agreeable, tasting excessively of cloves, but mostly because I wished to support Elmer, and declining her offer would have been one method of doing so.

John returned with a horse-whip as she was spooning cream into my dish. In the half light of the kitchen it looked to be the same whip he had used on the horse to speed the buggy along the farm track on our journey from the station. I relaxed for a moment, sitting back into my chair, for the whip was far too long, far too clumsy to be used on a child and the leather switch at the end far too dangerous.

'Jacob,' he said bluntly, ignoring Elmer, 'come here.'

Jacob dutifully left the table and went through into the kitchen where he stood before his father, his chin raised in open disobedience so that he met his father's eyes. The boy, at sixteen, was still growing.

'Jacob,' he went on, 'I isn't able to find my strap. I've spent these five minutes searching for it. Where is it gone? Is it you who has taken it?'

'Yes, it is I,' the boy said. 'I've hidden it. You'll never find it. I isn't bothered neither.'

'There ain't no point in asking you again, is there?'

'There ain't no point in you asking me again, Daddy.'

'Hold out your hands.'

Jacob held out his hands with his fingernails upwards. His father thrashed him across both knuckles with the wooden end of the whip. Even in the shadows of the room I could see the boy's face reel with pain, although he did not cry out.

'Go and sit down,' his father said.

Jacob came to the table and resumed his place to my left. On his right hand I could see where the savagery of the blow had broken the skin. A thin line of blood was oozing from the cut. Both his hands were shaking gently, as though in shock, and already bruising. I had to deal with wounds like this in surgery and feared the damage the blows had done.

'Elmer,' their father continued from the kitchen, 'is you going to apologize?'

'Yes,' he said quietly, 'I is going to apologize.'

I did not blame the younger boy for changing his mind, for losing his defiance, for surrendering his spirit, and would have hugged him for his realism had I not been terrified myself.

'Go on then, Elmer, you is to do it now.'

Elmer came through the partition towards me, which I had not expected, and found a position so close to me that his knees were almost touching my own knees. He looked down into my eyes. His face was innocent, without guile. I could feel the apology emanating, like heat, from his body.

'I is sorry for laughing at Gideon during grace,' he said, 'and only do laugh to show off and be important. I is to be humble. I is to think of God. I is to not think about myself. I is to think of you and my family. I is to be honest.'

'I accept your apology,' I found myself saying when I knew

245

full well no apology was necessary, certainly not to me.

I hated John at that moment.

The insomnia, which had plagued me throughout my school-days and early manhood, that night returned with a vengeance unknown to me as an adult, and I could not sleep. John's brutality to his children seemed to know no limits. I tried hard to square this with his pacifism but could find no rationale. I saw only the violence of the whip, and the doggedness of his determination, which was so different from the gracious, amiable family man I had expected to find. Harry had spoken of John's love, of his kindness, of his understanding of the need for forgiveness, of his wisdom, none of which I could see. Instead I tossed and turned wishing myself at home with Armanda, praying for her level-headed guidance, wondering if it might be possible, even at this late hour, for her to travel to Pennsylvania. But I knew this to be absurd.

I crept out of bed and lit the paraffin lamp, keeping the wick as low as possible so as not to disturb Peter, who was snoring in the bed by the window, much as Harry had often snored at school. I had begun a letter to Armanda but had abandoned it when, earlier, after we had climbed the stairs to our room, Peter had wished to talk. His reactions had been much the same as my own, but his stammer was now so pronounced that his saying so had been almost more than I could endure. It was a relief, both for him and for me, when fatigue forced him into unconsciousness.

The night was chilly, so I sat up and pulled the quilt around my shoulders. I was so tired that occasionally I looked at Peter and saw Harry. The room, in its spartanness, lighted by the orange glow from the paraffin lamp, reminded me again of our room at school, and the shadows across the low furniture revived so many austere memories. I adjusted the quilt and thought about the night in London, thousands of miles away, when Harry had finally told me the truth about his father, the father who had killed his young son in a fit of adult rage. I had no accurate mental picture of Mr Treffgarne, for we had never met, but at that moment John's face was the nearest approximation I could find. In my head John became Mr Treffgarne. I even wondered if Harry had been drawn to John, had named him the main beneficiary of his will because of John's liking for violence, as if in some perverse way Harry had been drawn to violence too, but had subjugated the desire all his life. It seemed to me that Harry was returning his fortune to his father and that there must be an intelligible reason for his decision. I would have given anything to speak to Harry, to learn the truth, however unpalatable, and tried to imagine him coming into the room as a ghost, so that we might talk, but my imagination let me down. I was left in the continuing silence and instead saw his body buried deep in its Amish grave at the farm in Richmond, but could make no sense of why, before at last I fell asleep still sitting upright, as I had done once or twice at school when Harry's despair had been particularly black.

9

I learned that John and his family lived by the dictates of the sun. They rose before dawn, ate a substantial breakfast, like all their meals rich in fats and carbohydrates, consisting of eggs, fried scrapple or cornmeal mush, cooked cereal and fried potatoes, with bread, butter and home-made preserves, before leaving the house as it was getting light. Conversation at breakfast was typically about the work needing to be done that day, how and who should do it. Rachel would speak exclusively about her domain, of the necessity of preparing the new brooder house for her chicks, of the vegetables and fruits needing to be picked from the garden. John delegated such tasks to his two younger sons, directing that they be achieved after school or when there was time. At noon, the absence of the school-age children allowed more intimate conversations between the parents and the two older boys, Jacob and Emanuel, who worked solely on the farm. Over rivel soup and shoo-fly pie, the boys would report on work accomplished that morning, and all four would speak of the afternoon labour yet to come, exchanging ideas or suggestions. I was surprised that Emanuel was of an age to have left school, but it transpired that he had finished his education the previous autumn on his fourteenth birthday. Gideon, still too young for school, would listen attentively to their farming talk without understanding a word because they always spoke in English for our benefit. He had his jobs too, including helping his sisters mow the lawn every third day. At sunset, when work was over, the entire family would gather around the table where the hushed atmosphere of our first evening meal would be repeated, interrupted by the occasional belch, a question concerning farm life from one of the children, usually answered carefully and succinctly by John, or the bark of a dog, for the family had two which were kennelled outside. The food was generous and the flavour mostly excellent, although the overcooking and oversweetening were not always to my taste. I began to put on weight.

Our arrival in Pennsylvania coincided with Ascensiontide. The second Thursday of our visit was Ascension Day and was, therefore, one of the few days in the year, apart from Sundays, when the family could do no work. John had spent most of the previous three days cutting a second crop of hay with Jacob, whilst Emanuel worked elsewhere spreading muck onto the fields from which no second crop was to be taken that spring. Peter had helped Emanuel with the heaviest labour. Together they had shovelled muck and slurry from the cow barn onto the muck-spreader, which was horse-drawn like all the farm machinery, and which Emanuel then drove to the field standing upright on the muck-spreader's shaft. Emanuel was small for his age, but he possessed an adult's confidence in dealing with the team of four horses. I spent hours watching the effortless command with which he went about his duties, his natural authority dominating every problem as though he had been working all his life. I kept having to remind myself that his voice had not yet fully broken. Peter would follow Emanuel to the field, and I would go with him, occasionally leaving them both to return to the house, where Rachel would be busy cooking special pies and biscuits for the feast day to come. On one particular morning the kitchen was filled with the sweet smell of apple sauce. I left her to go to the hay field, where Jacob had the same command of the horses as Emanuel. He and John worked all day cutting swaths of grass with primitive, one-bladed scythes, their separate teams of horses moving back and forth across the field, until the field was cut and they moved on to another. In mid-afternoon when Elmer came home from school he would join them, taking over his father's position on the wooden shaft, standing upright between the horse and the scythe like his older brother. He would work the horse with the reins held in his right hand and the whip in his left hand, now and again flicking the whip towards her tail to encourage her forward. John would watch him begin and then walk back to the farm, where Peter and

Emanuel would have finished muck-spreading the hour before, so allowing the horses a short rest. Two of the horses would be harnessed to yet another machine, an ancient contraption with a large wheel used for turning the grass over, which John would take to a field cut the previous day, where he would work until sunset, anxious to achieve as much as possible before the enforced day of rest.

On Ascension Day all six children asked us if we would like to accompany them to the river where they were going to spend the afternoon fishing. The suggestion had clearly been made with John's permission, if not his collusion, for when we accepted the children became excited. It was as if an old joke had been told successfully once more. We set off from the farm after a convivial, festive lunch of pork and apples. Peter wore his Wellingtons, whilst I, not sensible enough to have brought boots with me, walked in my shoes across the fields which he and Emanuel had been spreading with muck. The children walked ahead of us with their fishing boxes, built from odds and ends of wood, swinging by their sides. Scrubbed clean from a bath the night before, in their one set of Sunday best clothes and freed from the responsibilities of work, they had become young again. I could not help but notice how carefree they were together away from John's tyranny.

The four boys tossed their hand lines in and out of the shallow stream as the two girls watched them from the bank. Only Jacob had the girls' patience to sit and wait. The two middle boys repeatedly baited their hooks with fresh earth worms, dug earlier from the garden, hardly ever giving the perch time to bite, so that Jacob soon became annoyed with them when they disturbed his own fishing, but his manner was too gentle to have influence. Finally he left them to find a place on his own further along the river. Elmer and Emanuel, always the liveliest pair, rolled up their trousers and began to paddle, at first taking their fishing lines with them to the centre of the current, where in no time they abandoned any pretence at fishing and, instead, began to build a dam with stones dislodged from the river bottom. Gideon tried his best to help them until he fell over and his two sisters were forced to rescue him. Their feet now wet as well, the girls hitched up their dresses and joined in, rolling boulders towards where the current was weakest, leaving the strongest, deepest water for the boys. Elmer organized his older brother as though their ages were the other way about, and together they soon had a line of boulders that stretched from one bank of the stream to the other. Gideon came and sat beside us, his best trousers and his best turquoise shirt so wet that I worried about the consequences when we returned to the farm. I even wondered about unfastening his braces and hanging his clothes from a tree to dry in the sun, but I had already learned, from their ritualistic bathing of the night before, how nudity, even amongst the smallest children, was frowned upon. In any case, his two brothers were becoming almost as soaked as he and their punishment would be shared. I decided to stop worrying.

Jacob, who had still not caught a fish, came back from his solitary position along the bank and, on behalf of his brothers and sisters, asked us if we would like to join in with the building of the dam. Peter surprised me by getting to his feet, but I stayed with Gideon, whilst the pair of them went off to the surrounding woods, where the others were now collecting fallen branches, which they were dragging back to the river and embedding in the soft mud between the boulders. The dam was taking shape but in the process their clothes were becoming ruined. Elmer's black trousers were covered in slime, his turquoise shirt streaked with finger marks from where he had repeatedly wiped his hands. Even his hat was damaged, for whenever he bent down to adjust a branch or to pick up a handful of small stones, it fell off his head into the water, several times nearly floating away and once almost disappearing over the lip of the dam, but thankfully he managed to grab it before it was lost to the faster current on the other side. All the boys made some kind of effort to remain clean by rolling up their trouser legs when they fell back down to their ankles, but the playfulness of their activity got the better of them, even of Jacob who quickly became as dirty as the other two. Only the girls showed restraint by staying where the river was at its shallowest. Gideon spent most of his time with me wishing to join them, conversing in Pennsylvania Dutch, seemingly unperturbed, but still determined to go to the river, when I replied in my few words of German. I finally managed to dissuade him with hand signals and shakes of my head, but I could see that he was annoyed at missing the fun, just as I was annoyed with Peter for encouraging it. Peter had slowly taken charge and was organising the children with his mathematical, worldly skills. The girls were opening up their side of the dam to let the pool of water out from the middle, where the boys were strengthening their section with yet more, larger boulders taken from upstream. Jacob's shirt was ripped along one side and his trouser braces had become unfastened.

It was only after Elmer had charged excitedly from the river that I noticed another group of children approaching through the elm trees on the farthest bank, as yet some distance away. I thought at first it might be John and was relieved when it was not. The impetus of Elmer's excitement carried him towards them. There were seven children in the group, four girls and three boys, the smallest being about Gideon's age and the tallest, I surmised, a little older than Jacob. Jacob tucked his torn shirt into his trousers and rearranged his braces before greeting the older of the girls, who responded shyly, coyly, her white translucent cap effulgent in the sun.

The children soon began to intermingle along the length of the dam. It was difficult to tell them apart, for they were all dressed alike, although the new boys were wearing blue shirts instead of turquoise. The girls were dressed in green, including Jacob's sweetheart, who busied herself not with Jacob, but with Katie and Anna. Occasionally she and Jacob looked towards one another. It seemed so old-fashioned, partly because the younger children had no idea of their entanglement.

Katie, Anna and the four new girls, closed their side of the dam where earlier they had opened it under Peter's instructions. The boys were still carrying rocks from upstream to add to the dam's height. Peter was shovelling grass and moss from the river bank with his hands, laying it between the boulders like cement. When the boys returned they joined him, mixing handfuls of grass with sediment from the river bottom as he told them to. I watched the twelve children and Peter, Peter out of place by his age, clothing and language, but not in spirit. I could see that they were delighted, were exhilarated by his company, and I prayed that John did not arrive to spoil their joy.

'They're the Lapp children,' a voice said behind me, 'they often come this way on rest days. I hope one of my children has introduced them?'

'Yes,' I lied, turning my head to see John towering above me.

If I had been aware of his coming, I would have called to the children to hide, which had been the plan in my head for some while. I knew, beyond doubt, that he would not leave us on our own all afternoon, but I had hoped to negate most of his anger by at least getting the children dry. He had not only pre-empted me by arriving sooner than I had expected, but the children were not even fishing. The dam was clear evidence of misdemeanour. I knew he would think their wanton enjoyment unholy. Their thrashing with the strap, or buggy whip, would be my fault for not calling them to heel when the fun became irreverent. I could see in my mind the terrified expressions on their faces and saw myself eavesdropping on the silence as their knuckles were beaten in the darkened kitchen. Only Gideon, still sitting patiently beside me because I had told him to, would be spared retribution.

John spoke to Gideon in Pennsylvania Dutch. Gideon jumped up and ran to the river where he joined his sisters and the Lapp girls, who were in the quagmire where the river had flooded, mixing mud and pebbles which they were depositing between the rocks.

'Why wouldn't you let Gideon enjoy himself?' John asked me severely. 'He tells me you've kept him sitting here all afternoon. Why is that?'

'I didn't want him to get wet,' I said instinctively, like an accused child. I was on the defensive all the time with John. It was a pattern I could not shake because I did not understand him. I had yet to find the logic in his rules.

'There's no harm done if he gets wet, Daniel,' he said. 'It does all the children good to be free for a few hours. They often build a dam. This one looks to be one of the best.'

'That's Peter's doing.' I began to rise to my feet so that we might be on an equal footing, but John stopped me.

'I'll sit with you for a few minutes,' he said, settling himself in the long grass to my left.

'I was worried about their clothes, John. They were pristine when we arrived.'

'You're such an old fuddy-duddy, Daniel. Clothes cover our bodies. They will wash. Why are clothes so important to you?

'They're not. I care about seeing the children hurt. They have one set of best clothes. I expected your anger. I hate it when you beat the children, John. It isn't fair.' These sentiments, which had preoccupied my thoughts for the last ten days, had finally tripped off my tongue without my thinking. I was proud of the passion I had displayed and must have smiled.

'I detect a degree of pride in what you say, Daniel.'

'My pride might be selfish, John. My desire to see the children happy might be selfish. But that doesn't mean that I am wrong.'

'Do you think the children aren't happy?' he asked plainly, straightening his legs and leaning back onto his hands.

'Not when one of them has English clothes which you make him hide in a ditch,' I said. 'Not when you beat one of them so badly he can barely hold the reins of a horse. You are farmers. That seems to me stupid.'

'Do you expect me to be perfect, Daniel? I can't be perfect just for you. I know you'd like me to be perfect, but that is your problem, not mine. I do what I do as best I can. Please try to be more objective.'

He picked up a blade of grass which he ran between his thumb and forefinger as Harry had often done by the river at school. It immediately brought back memories of those afternoons when we had swum without our clothes. I wished now, on one afternoon at least, that we had built a dam together.

'Why won't you talk about Harry?' I asked. 'Why won't you talk about his will and your legacy?'

'Jacob has complained to the bishop,' he said. I thought at first he was changing the subject because he always had in the past on the few occasions when I had either mentioned Harry's name or the will, but this time I was wrong. 'I'll talk about the legacy in a few minutes, Daniel. The bishop knows I'm not perfect, as Harry knew I wasn't perfect. Jacob has complained that he is being treated unfairly. He's probably right. It is hard to lose one son in death and a second son to the English. I'm human. What do you think?'

I thought I had made my position clear, but his question was asked with such straightforward humility that for a moment I could not reply. I was also uncertain of the power of the bishop, for I knew little of their church or its hierarchy, only that each small farm district held a church service, lasting all morning, every other Sunday at which the bishop officiated.

'I don't know, John,' I said. 'I'm not the person to ask. All I do know is that Jacob was really hurt the evening you thrashed him.'

'Yes, I meant him to be hurt. I almost enjoyed it. I'm human.'

'Tell me about the bishop?' I asked after picking up a blade of grass to run between my own thumb and forefinger. I was embarrassed by his honesty and sought refuge in the screeching sound produced by the grass.

John looked towards the river where the children, including Jacob, were still playing happily. It was the first time we had exchanged confidences and I could see that he was nervous. He was timorous yet wary.

'There's nothing to say really,' he said, 'the bishop is no better or worse than you and me. I say Jacob has spoken to the bishop, I'm sure that's an exaggeration. Word gets about very easily amongst us, nothing stays quiet for long. I've been beating the children too much. We are a community. We comment on each other's behaviour. It is the first time I've been commented on in this way. I don't like it very much. I'm being scorned.' He looked from the river back towards me. 'Thank you for listening, Daniel. Yours is another voice. I can never be completely Amish. I have worldly experience that it is impossible to forget. Knowledge cannot be destroyed. It stays with us whether we want it to or not. I have travelled, I have memories, I have history which will never go away. Amish history is simpler.'

'Why do you never talk to the children about England?' I asked.

'I'm trying to explain. England is not important to us. It is irrelevant. I have my memories but they are worldly, and I shall not pass them on. I wish my children to be Amish. I told them enough about you for them to understand that you are an outsider. England is a country I no longer care about. It is not important that my children know where England is. When they talk to you, they are talking to a person from a different world. Yes, they are intrigued, but they make their judgements accordingly.'

'When you deny them your experience, aren't you denying them something rich and valuable?' I sucked the blade of grass.

'No. The greatest gift a parent can give his child is to make the world understandable, to make it clear, to free him of inner conflict. I see the world as a simple place, Daniel, without the complications that you believe in. I believe in right and wrong, good and evil. I know you don't. I know you see grey, where I see black and white. I am not denying my children experience, far from it, I am giving them a simplicity which will allow them to make judgements. Or so I hope. I want those judgements to be truthful and not based on self-interest.'

'Self-interest is truthful. That's the world we live in.'

'It is the world you live in,' he said pointedly. 'In any case I don't believe you, I don't believe you are self-interested any longer. You no longer seek power therefore you can't be.'

'You're very worldly for an Amishman, John,' I said smiling both to show him that I appreciated his compliment and was making a joke.

'I've tried to explain to you why I can never be completely Amish,' he said seriously. 'There are times when I have to subject my powers of reasoning to the more basic wish of the majority, but that is as it should be. All I want is for my children to be Amish.'

I looked towards the river where the dam was almost finished. John's children and the Lapp children were indistinguishable.

'You've been successful,' I said.

John picked up a fresh blade of grass which he ran between his teeth. The wire rims of his spectacles were reflecting the sun and his beard was white, its greyness bleached by the candescent light. He lifted his hand to his black hat and tipped it backwards from his forehead, as though delaying registering surprise at my complimenting him on his success.

'Do you think so?' he asked finally.

'Look at the children, John, it's impossible to tell them apart. They're Amish.'

'Thank you,' he said with some pride.

'Did Harry wish to be Amish?' I asked.

He removed the grass from his teeth and lifted his hat from his head, placing it on his outstretched knees, which I had never seen him do before outdoors. The Amish always wore their hats when outside, and, strictly speaking, he was breaking the rules.

'He certainly thought about it, Daniel. We talked a good deal. I did my best to dissuade him. Harry was too much of a free-thinker ever to accept the discipline of our governance. He believed in no one's authority but his own. In that sense he was nearly an atheist. He also had a cause. We don't believe in causes. He believed in conversion. We see conversion as wrong. Our faith is not a faith that seeks to influence. We are here as an example of God's will, that is all. Harry would never have accepted that. Harry wanted to change the world. I told him to come back when he had learnt to live a quiet life, when he had learnt to be wary of positions of influence, but he never did. I hope I was right?'

'Yes, you were right, John,' I said.

'Harry always talked about you, Daniel. Even in New Orleans you were the person he talked about. He was very upset when you returned to England and left him and me together at the school. He wanted you there. His selfishness and moodiness were extraordinary. I'm being very non-Amish. I've even taken off my hat. It is strange to be talking to you like this after so many years, about events which took place so many years ago. You can see now how I can never be completely Amish. Harry loved you. When you weren't there he pined for you like a lover. I'm speaking of the love of one man for another, of carnal love, not of the spiritual love which is given us by God. Harry was a homosexual, Daniel, as you know.'

'No, I didn't know,' I said, which was half truth and half lie. I remembered him first kissing me by the river at school; I remembered his jealousy of Mrs Copeland, as she then was before he married her, on the boat to New Orleans; I remembered Stella's initial doubts and her saying later that their marriage was not a proper marriage; I remembered him bathing Jenni; I remembered him asking me about my sexuality and my telling him of the naked girl in my bed in Italy; I remembered him kissing me on the cheek in my kitchen during my nervous breakdown; and I remembered the numerous ways in which he was always loving, always forgiving. I should have known of Harry's homosexuality all along, and actually did, but had never fully admitted to myself that I knew.

'He wanted a child, Daniel, that's why he married Stella. He was desperate for a child like Jenni. He wanted someone to love. When Jenni came along he wasn't bothered about the marriage any more. He and Jenni came here to my baptism. When Jenni was in bed, we spent long hours talking together. It was then that he asked me if his being homosexual might preclude him from becoming Amish. I'm surprised you didn't know. I told him that I thought it would. I told him that I thought homosexuality an evil. I know in England he was happy to live with you and Jenni and that he didn't bother to try and find a partner. I have

257

his letters. It breaks every rule to keep them but I can't bring myself to throw them away. I remember Harry like a brother.'

'Do you feel guilty for saying what you did?' I asked.

'No. He wished me to speak the truth as I saw it. He was free to take or leave whatever I said. I've already told you that I have no worldly cause and that I am not interested in conversion. If becoming Amish had been right for him, he would have done so. But he knew, and must have continued to know, that it wasn't.'

We talked of other matters. John told me how his baptism had been, in part, a consequence of his meeting and falling in love with Rachel. He explained to me how the Amish, being an Anabaptist faith, practised adult baptism. John, as a Quaker, had never been christened, so there were no biblical complications to overcome. His head had been anointed with water poured from a tin cup.

'Did no one convert you?' I asked.

'Daniel, conversion is a worldly pastime. No one said anything to me at all. I liked what I saw and I decided to stay. But it was far, far deeper than that. I saw a community of people who truly lived by the word of God.'

He chewed on his blade of grass and told me of his marriage to Rachel the autumn after he had been baptized in the spring. The wedding, like his baptism, had taken place in a barn at his in-laws' farm. Buggies had travelled from throughout the county to attend the long ceremony presided over by the bishop; many had left their homes at first light, not returning until after dark. He spoke of how attractive all the children were in their best clothes, and how they had played softball together in a field in the afternoon when the formalities of the morning were over. They had begun a family of their own straight away, but the child, a girl called Rebecca, had been stillborn. A boy who followed died in infancy from whooping-cough.

'I had so much to learn,' he said freeing a piece of grass which had caught between his teeth. 'I had to learn what my children are learning naturally. I had to master the handling of a horse and the cutting of a straight furrow with a plough. I had to assimilate the seasons. I had to be taught how to work the land so that it should prosper. These things my children see about them every day. They take part in our lives from an early age. We don't segregate them. They are treated properly and respectfully. We don't mollycoddle them. There is nothing worse than always seeing a child getting his own way.'

Elmer came stumbling from the river. By the time he reached us he was out of breath. The dam was now finished. A large pool had formed where the rest of the children, including the seven Lapp children, were beginning to fish. I found his excitability refreshing.

'Is you coming to the river?' he asked me. 'We is all of us wanting you to before we is to knock the stones over.'

John explained that we would both come to the river in a few minutes and help them to catch some flies, which might bring greater luck with the fish than the worms they were using.

'I'd like to talk about Harry's will,' I said when Elmer had departed.

'Yes, I know. This is very difficult for me, because I liked Harry.'

'John, you've been putting off the subject of Harry's will since I first wrote to you about it six years ago. I think six years is long enough.'

'Six years is no time at all,' he said firmly.

'I realize now that you cannot possibly accept it,' I said as though he had told me as much in a previous conversation when he had not. 'Why didn't you tell me? Why didn't you even hint to me that this might be the case?'

'I wanted you to see why for yourself, Daniel. I wanted you to see why I might think the money was evil.' He placed his hat on his head in preparation for going to the river. 'I know that for you six years is a long time, but for me it is five minutes, that is the difference between us. I don't have a cause to fight, which makes six years a long time.'

He rose to his feet and I followed him. There were two circular indentations in the grass where we had been sitting.

'The fortune rightfully belongs to Jenni,' I said flippantly. 'She might as well have it.'

We walked together towards the river.

Harry had given me a problem.

Elmer was fidgeting because of the pain, throwing his hands to his face while I was trying to look at his nose, which was clearly broken.

'Keep still, Elmer.'

'Get off me,' he shouted. Blood was dripping from both his nostrils onto his blue shirt.

'How on earth did you do this?' I asked holding his head and tilting it backwards towards the afternoon sunlight. The bleeding ceased and my view of the fracture, on the bridge of his nose, improved.

'Fighting.'

'Fighting who?'

'Fighting at school. Fighting English when they says we is funny. They says we is not proper folk 'cos we do things strange. I tells them our folk is better than their folk. Then we fight.'

We were standing on the edge of a corn field where the newly planted shoots were beginning to grow. Surrounding us were Anna, Katie and the younger Lapp children. A few minutes before, I had noticed them all walking home from school, slower than was usual, and had gone over to join them on the path. It was the hottest day so far, and I first thought their leisurely pace to be a consequence of the heat. But I was wrong. They were ambling because they were worried.

'Why didn't your teacher intervene?'

'What's intervene mean?' he asked gracelessly. Any shyness towards me had disappeared weeks ago. I had begun to realize how tough all the children were.

'Why didn't your teacher stop you fighting, Elmer?'

'Teacher is English.'

'You mean your teacher takes sides. I don't believe you.'

'Teacher is English,' he said again. 'We isn't good in class. We isn't good at learning their ways. We isn't good at taking in their evil doings. We sits there and we holds our tongues.'

'You don't,' Anna said, 'you is always answering back. That is why you is always in trouble. Daddy is going to be so angry with you it will be the buggy whip.'

'Who is I to care if I get the buggy whip, Anna? Buggy whip don't hurt.'

'Last time you is buggy whipped you is crying, Elmer.'

'That is to show him I is hurt so he don't go on. Buggy whipping is for girls. Boys is strong. Boys must tell teacher when she is talking wrong-doing.'

'We is to close our ears like Daddy tells us,' Katie said joining the discussion. 'We is to hear baby Jesus when teacher talks bad. We is not to pull faces.'

'Is you buggy whipped many times?' one of the Lapp boys

asked Elmer in English.

'We is buggy whipped no more than thee,' he replied.

'Do you know if you have money in England?' the boy asked turning towards me. 'I is getting a cent on my birthday to buy candy at the grocery stores in Bird in Hand.'

'I's already asked him that,' Elmer said. 'They is pounds in England not dollars.'

I thought of John who had refused a fortune.

Even the Lapp children had begun to take Peter and myself for granted. The whole family had walked across the fields one Sunday afternoon for a picnic, which Rachel had presented, with her customary diligence, on the lawn at the front of the house. We had all served ourselves to the feast. I had talked at length with Amos Lapp, the children's father, about England, whilst his older children had listened quietly in the background. Amos Lapp's interest, both in Peter and myself, had made our company acceptable and desirable. The Lapp children had become proud to know the foreigners, and they had begun to question us whenever they could. The point had been reached where they were asking questions sent by their friends. I marvelled at their lack of education and wondered about the quality of their schooling, for their questions were always so naive.

'What have you learnt at school today?' I asked. 'What lessons have you had?'

'Science,' the Lapp boy said. 'Science ain't right.'

'We is to put stuff in test-tubes,' Elmer continued. 'We is to learn what ain't the science of the farm. We is to learn what is worldly. It ain't right. I tells them. I pulls faces.'

'You isn't to throw your pencil at teacher,' Anna said. 'It ain't no wonder she grab you by the hair. It ain't no wonder she calls you trouble. It ain't no wonder English fight you.'

'What was the lesson about?' I asked Elmer.

'I ain't know. I ain't listen. I ain't going to be worldly like them.' His language was becoming rougher, like his physical appearance, which was beginning to be aggressive. I had let his head go so that his nose was forward and dripping blood.

'Calm down,' I said.

'I ain't calming down. I ain't going to school no more. Not with English. I's going to beat them.'

'I thought you were a peace-loving community, Elmer.'

261

'I ain't care. I's working on the farm. I's be like Emanuel and Jacob.'

'Do you know if you have candy in England?' the Lapp boy asked. 'On my birthday I is to buy a candy bar.'

'Yes, we have candy. We have chocolate and sweets. We have cakes and pies, vegetables and fruits just like you.' But I knew, although accurate, that what I was saying was far from the truth. I was giving him the impression that our worlds were the same, when they were completely different.

'Do you know if you have schools in England?' he went on with the same ignorance of his innocence.

'Yes, there are schools.'

'Do you know if children go to them?'

'Of course, that is what schools are for.'

'Do you know if there is boys like Elmer in England?'

'There are many boys like Elmer.'

'See,' Elmer said, 'I's told you. I's told you there is fighting and kicking in England. There's biting and punching. I's told you I was right.'

'There isn't a community quite like yours,' I said, trying to correct the impression I had given. 'I think it must be very difficult for you having to go to school with English, having to live alongside people whose beliefs are not your own. I admire you, but you shouldn't fight, Elmer. Fighting is wrong in England as it is wrong here. What I like about your community is the way you all act together. I like the way you help one another. You should act together at school.'

'Only Elmer is the one of us with courage,' the Lapp boys said. 'They tells us at home to block our ears. Our ears is hard to block.'

'You seem to block them successfully,' I said, not meaning to be quite so flippant. 'I admire the way you all learn nothing.'

'In our lesson today we is learned how to make gunpowder,' he continued. 'We is learned how to mix saltpetre, charcoal and sulphur. Do you know if you have explosives in England?'

'Yes, we do.'

'It ain't right what we learn. It ain't godly.'

The children began walking towards the farm. Elmer had to help Jacob milk the cows and he knew he was late. The Lapp boy, keen to walk beside me, pushed his younger brother and sisters ahead with Katie and Anna. I diverted his persistent questioning by asking him about his father, who John had told me was having financial problems. He was finding it difficult to pay the interest on a loan secured from the bank. The community had pulled together and were giving him pecuniary assistance, but this summer's harvest was critical. I thought it asinine that John could not accept Harry's money for the benefit of them all.

When the Lapp children had left us at a fork in the path, I called Elmer to me. His nose had stopped bleeding. I knew he would not willingly allow me to treat the fracture, so I offered him no choice. I held his head in one hand and cracked the bone back into place with the other before he realized what was happening. He yelped so loudly that at first I worried I had miscalculated the pressure required to pull the bone out and snap it upwards. I grabbed his head and forced it backwards into the sunlight. His nose was bleeding but straight.

That night I sat with John in the living-room when the rest of the household had retired to bed. He had waited for the two of us to be alone before reprimanding me. I had planned not to bother defending myself, but ended up doing so.

'John, if you can refuse Harry's will because of your beliefs, then I can treat Elmer's nose because of mine. I know I'm a guest in your house but I'm also a doctor. The boy's nose would have been misshapen forever.' I did not tell him I thought my success a small miracle. I had only once before treated a fractured nose and that was as a young houseman nearly thirty years previously.

'I wish you'd asked me,' he said.

'I know you well enough to know your answer. If the bone had mended across his nasal passages, he might well never have been able to breathe.' This was mostly a lie, but it tripped from my lips with the authority of truth.

'Was it badly broken?'

'Yes. Yes, it was.' I replied honestly.

'Those English boys must have really thumped him, Daniel.'

John was sitting on a bench with his back leaning against the wall. He had taken off his spectacles and was cleaning them on his shirt. He was tired, his face and voice weary, but I had never known him to be so patient. In the subdued light from the kerosene lamp, I was fully aware that he was happy to be in my company. He explained to me how the problems with the English at school had been getting worse, and how Elmer's broken nose was only one incident among many which had occurred recently. He seemed to forget that I had used English medicine to treat his son, and became concerned to know my views on modern education. I told him I thought it wrongheaded and unfair for the children to have to block their ears in class.

'I'm sorry if my not accepting Harry's will has caused you problems,' he said, standing up from the bench when our differing ideas on education had reached deadlock.

'John, you may not have a cause, but you believe in Utopia. Utopias are fine in literature and in the imagination, but in life they're disastrous. There is a world out there which your children must know about. Correct judgements can only be made with knowledge not with ignorance.'

'I understand what you say.'

'But you disagree with me?'

'Yes. I think it is you who have spent your life searching for Utopia, not me. Everything I say is based on the goodness of God, whereas everything you say is based on the goodness of man. I admire you, but I don't believe that man is always good. It is disastrous when man believes himself to be more important than God, for then he also believes himself to be more important than his neighbour. No man is better than any other man. If education taught this I would be pleased, but it doesn't, it teaches the strong to be stronger and leaves the weak to be weaker. We need to know how to read and write, we need to know how to add and subtract, we do not need to know how to make gunpowder.'

'Gunpowder will exist whether you want it to or not,' I said.

'You cannot fight evil with evil. Goodnight, Daniel.' He went into his and Rachel's bedroom on the ground floor saying nothing more, but making it clear that our discussion was far from finished and would continue another day.

Instead of following John to bed, I wrote two letters, first to Armanda and then to Philip Pennycott, Harry's solicitor, in Richmond. His reply came three weeks later.

Dear Dr Hinton,

I foresee many fewer problems than you imagine. If Mr Bell has no wish to be the beneficiary of his legacy then so be it. In such circumstances Mr Treffgarne makes it clear in his will that you are to have absolute power of attorney.

Miss Treffgarne will be delighted. She will get what she wanted all along.

In the first instance, I suggest that Mr Bell consults his own lawyer. I shall require confirmation of his decision from them both. Meanwhile, I will prepare an oath of judicial proof, which Mr Bell should then sign and his lawyer witness. Once I have this affidavit in my possession, I will await your instructions.

Pennycott, unable to exercise his legal succinctness any further and being at heart a rambler, then goes on to repeat and explain himself twice.

I decided to show the letter to John. I knew, without asking him, that he had no lawyer and would refuse to appoint one, but he did, after prolonged discussion, grant me permission to seek legal representation on his behalf. He wrote his own letter to Pennycott, which the postman collected the next day as the children were leaving for school.

The Amish do not believe in churches, but worship in one another's homes every other Sunday. This is a collective affair, with the families from each small farm district gathering together for the long, traditional service. It is held on each farm by rotation, so that the twenty-six families, or thereabouts, hold the service once a year. In smaller districts, or where a district has grown too large and has been divided, some families may receive their neighbours twice during the year. In summer, when the weather is clement, the service is often held outside in the barn. Be it inside or out, each congregation has its own set of wooden benches and hymnals that are taken to the appointed farm on Saturday afternoon in a specially built wagon. The man of the house secures the church benches and supervises the seating arrangements, whilst the burden of the work falls on the woman, since it is she who must clean the house, rearrange the furniture, blacken the stoves, and wash the ornamental china. Neighbouring women come to the farm to bake pies and prepare the other food that will be served after the preaching service is finished to a congregation which can sometimes number over two hundred.

Preaching Sunday is a day of anticipation on an Amish farm. The cows are milked and by eight o'clock the family are on their way. Father always drives the horse and buggy, with mother and the youngest child beside him. The older children sit on the seat at the back. If there is not room for them all, the eldest son may drive the springwagon, an open carriage used for market, taking two of his brothers with him on the single seat. He will follow his father along the hard-surface road, where other carriages, from other families, will join him. No driver would dream of passing another. The spectacle of two dozen carriages turning single-file into a rutted farm lane, and the sound of yet more horses' hooves trotting on the metalled road over the brow of a hill, evokes a deep sense of remembrance amongst the gathering community. The Amish are mindful of history and their sentiments run deep. Sunday morning is a morning without triviality.

Upon arrival at the farm of worship, the buggy halts in the barnyard, where mother and the girls dismount. They will be wearing shoes, so he will try to pick a spot which is dry. Father and sons drive to a suitable resting place, where they are greeted by hostlers, usually sons of the host household, who help unhitch the buggy and find a convenient pen for the horse, often in the barn. There may be as many as fifty horses by the time this process is complete. Meanwhile the men, bearded if they are married, clean-shaven if they are not, cluster in small groups in the stable yard. They meet one another with a handshake and talk in subdued voices.

Those living nearby usually walk to the preaching service and join the growing congregation at this point, which was what John and his family planned to do on the Sunday that Amos Lapp was host. It seemed the final reconciliation of our differences that John should ask both Peter and myself to attend as well. I was hugely flattered, and had begun to appreciate the Amish doctrine which believes that first comes self-discipline and then comes understanding. I had tried to comprehend the richness of their world whilst forgiving their many contradictions. Far too often thinking only succeeds in re-ordering existing prejudices, and I had done my best to avoid this. My reward was an invitation into the heart of the Amish.

Rachel and the girls left us to hang their shawls and bonnets in the wash-house, where they remained, spilling over into the kitchen, with the rest of the women until it was time to join the assembly. The four boys left us to join their friends in the barn, whilst we went to the stable yard. Amos Lapp was talking quietly with a group of older men, but when he saw us he came away to shake our hands, and then John ushered us towards them to be introduced. The men were immediately familiar, as all Amishmen are familiar by their clothing· and bearing, but within their similarities were the schisms which nourished their community. They were talking about the business of the day, and when the preachers declared that it was time to withdraw to the house, they took off their coats and hung them in the barn on the same pegs where the buggy harnesses were hanging. It seemed the practical thing to do, for Amish homes have no closets and during the service the day would grow hotter. A ground mist was still evaporating from the fields and the small river which I could see in the distance. I could hear the constant tick of the waterwheel pumping water to the house and farm from a well, and see the wire cable attached to the pump handle running quarter of a mile to the wheel at the stream.

Amish homes are specially built to accommodate the number of people who gather for worship, and I soon learned the true purpose of the partition between the living-room and the kitchen. It created a space large enough, although cramped, for the whole congregation. The order in which the worshippers entered was governed by sex and age. The ordained men entered first, followed by the oldest men, followed by the middle-aged including myself. The women then entered in a similar line, one behind the other, each shaking hands with the ordained ministers as we had done. They were followed by the baptized single women and the girls. Then came Peter with the unmarried older boys in order of seniority, Peter at their head looking flushed with embarrassment, followed by Gideon and the youngest males.

We all entered in single file and found our places on the backless benches. Men and women were seated separately, although not in separate halves of the room. Several rows of unmarried women occupied the sitting-room with the men, whilst mothers and infants were in the kitchen. Being present at the service is important and there were a number of babies, some as young as a month old. Gideon had seated himself beside his father, close to me, and the girls with their mother. The teenage boys had three rows of benches of their own. Older men had taken benches next to the wall so that they had some-

267

thing to lean against, but the frail, those with walking-sticks, had been given rocking chairs. Chairs were also given to the ministers' wives and the older women. Everyone had a view of the four chairs in the centre of the room, set in a line between the partition, reserved for the two preachers, a deacon and the bishop.

When everyone was settled, an old man rose to his feet and announced a hymn number in German. In unison the men and boys removed their hats and placed them beneath the benches. It was such a uniform swoop of their hands that it almost made me laugh. John caught my eye, but his own eyes were stony-faced. The old man began to sing solo in a trembling falsetto. He sang the opening syllables of each new line of the hymn, after which the entire congregation joined in. The tune was slow, more of a dirge or a chant, with the voices of the old joining those of the young. Gideon's voice was one of the highest and strongest. He sang from memory because he could not read.

With the singing of this first hymn, the ordained men withdrew, the oldest going first, to a room upstairs, where together they planned the preaching of the sermons. It was not quite nine o'clock. Below, the chanting of the hymns continued, interspersed with long periods of silence. I could see Katie and Anna with their mother in the kitchen. Katie got the giggles whenever she saw me and she did her best not to look, but I must have appeared a strange sight in my English suit, waistcoat and tie, and she found it difficult, so to help her I began to stare away towards the walls. The walls were painted a uniform glossy blue, as were the walls in John's house, and I was struck by their similarities, for neither household had pictures or photographs of their children. I could see now why the walls in both homes were scuffed at a certain height, for the marks were where the old men were leaning their shoulders.

The preachers descended from upstairs and the singing of the hymns came to an end upon completion of the verse being sung. The return of their authority seemed to settle Katie, and I was able to look around the room once more. After shaking hands with a family of latecomers, the preachers went to their chairs in the centre of the room. One of them remained standing with his hands folded beneath his unkempt white beard. When the latecomers had taken their places on the benches, he began to mumble, his voice gradually rising in an ever increasing

268

crescendo to a full-throated, rhythmic flow of words, like a drum beating, in a mixture of Pennsylvania Dutch, German, and English. He was reminding the congregation of the word of God, pointing out the importance of obeying the commandments, and admonishing them to work out their own salvation with fear and trembling. It is important in this opening sermon that he mention the necessity of prayer and of trusting in God, which is what he went on to do, afterwards, as is also traditional, offering a few sentences of apology for his weaknesses, and explaining that he will take no more of the allotted time away from the brother who is to bring them the main sermon of the day. He then asks the assembly to kneel together in silent prayer.

Prayer is ended by the preacher rising from his knees. Those who hear his foot tapping the floor rise with him, while those who are further away and the hard of hearing follow the visual signal of the others getting to their feet. The congregation remains standing while the deacon reads the scripture. He speaks in a singsong, chant-like fashion, and he may, or may not, offer a few comments of his own on the scripture when he has finished reading, but he will certainly admonish the assembly to be obedient to the Lord. He always ends with the words: 'So weit hat die Schrift sich ersteckt', meaning, 'Thus far extendeth the Scripture.' The assembly then sits for the interminable main sermon.

I have been to many preaching services and have studied its form, but its length never ceases to astonish me. On that first Sunday morning at Amos Lapp's farm I had no idea what the main preacher was sermonising about. He spoke in formal, old-fashioned German, and I had no translation. It was a long time before I was fully to understand the repetition of their services, and learn how the main sermon always begins with the greeting: 'Grace be with you and peace from God our Father.' He reminds his listeners that they have already been admonished several times this morning by the first brother, and goes on to talk about obedience to the vow of baptism, obedience to the bible, and obedience to parents. He talks of their community's separation from the world, the rules and disciplines of their church, and implores them to be mindful of strangers and pilgrims in an evil world. He talks about learning, saying the best learning is the learning from God, and that too much worldly knowledge will bring ruin. He speaks in a singsong chant, like

269

the preacher before him, his voice rising in pitch towards the culmination of each statement, whereupon he pauses for breath before starting again.

I watched Katie becoming bored by the tedious monotony of his speech and phrasing. She took a handkerchief from her mother's lap and began to twist it between her fingers, knotting the four corners and pulling the ends together as though she were making something. She caught my eye and showed me what she had done: it was a rabbit's head with two large ears. Anna, sitting beside her, had been given one of the babies to hold and was nursing it, her little finger in the baby's mouth, but the child was taken from her as the nursing mothers began to take their children upstairs to be fed properly. Katie, meanwhile, had unfolded the rabbit and was creating a mouse. Anna was given an older child and seemed content to allow the little girl to play on her lap with a toy. Gideon, beside me, leaned on his father's elbow, and John placed his arm around his son's shoulders so that he might fall asleep against his thigh. When Gideon began to snore, a few people smiled, and John changed position so that the boy became silent. Elmer was far from still and was shaking his legs. When he stood up to leave, five boys followed him outside towards the barn wall, where they peed in a line, each boy trying to get his pee higher than his neighbour. When they had finished they examined the wall to see who had won before ambling back towards the service, where Gideon had woken up and was sitting upright on his own, his face hot from sleep in the warm, stuffy atmosphere of the room.

Had I known that the sermon had only just started and would go on for a further two hours, I might have stolen outside for a pee or fallen asleep myself. As it was, the backless benches became harder and harder. One by one all but the oldest children became restless. Mary Lapp, Amos's wife, picked up a jar of cookies, which had been on the floor beside her since the beginning of the service, and passed it down the aisle to all the parents with youngsters at their side. The jar circulated between the rooms so that no child missed the treat. Glasses of water, poured by Mary Lapp from a pitcher, followed in the wake of the jar. If the speaker had thought to halt his flow of words and if the service had not been so orderly and reverential, it might have been like half-time at a football game.

By now the preacher will have finished recounting the Old Testament story from Adam to Abraham. He will, in all probability, have drunk a glass of water himself, and begun the account from John the Baptist to the end of Paul's missionary journeys. If the room is hot, as it was in Amos Lapp's house, his face will be beaded with sweat, and he will take his handkerchief from within his coat pocket to wipe his brow. The handkerchief will remain in his hand and be waved through the air to accentuate the illustration of a point. He will conclude the long sermon by reading a chapter from the bible. Then, with a groan, he will sit down and ask the other ordained men to give testimony to what he has just said, or to correct any mistakes he may have made. When these testimonies are over, the main preacher will rise to his feet and say he is thankful that the sermon can be taken as God's Word. He will admonish the assembly to give praise to God and not to man, and thank everyone for listening quietly. The whole assembly, except for those mothers holding sleeping babies, will then kneel for the closing prayer, which the minister will chant from a prayer book. This will be followed by the benediction, which he will recite from memory, and when he says the words 'Jesum Christum' at the very end, the entire congregation, who will now be standing, will bend their knees. This genuflection will take any visitors present by surprise, but for the gathered community it will be an all-embracing experience indicating full obedience to the Lord. It will be an expression of the unanimity within their faith.

'There is someone I'd like you to meet,' John said, picking up one of the benches and passing it through the opened window to another Amishman the other side. The service had just ended with the chanting of a hymn and the benches were being cleared by the men in preparation for the women serving the meal.

'Who?' I asked, having been dislocated by the service and feeling displaced amongst a group of people who I did not know.

'There was a family who arrived late, Daniel. They arrived whilst the preachers were upstairs planning their sermons. I'd like you to meet the grandfather of the family.'

When the benches were outside on the lawn, they were set together to form tables, and the women brought along the pies, homemade bread, butter, cheese, jam, pickles, red beets, and coffee from the larder. John's children, who would eat last, had scattered to the four corners of the farm buildings and were playing hide and seek with their friends. Peter had gone with them. Age and sex determines who eats first, beginning with the men, so I was soon to meet the grandfather of whom John had spoken. The pies were baked firm enough for us to hold them in our hands and for there not to be many crumbs.

The man was called Abraham Esh and was in his seventies. He was given a rocking chair, and because John and I were with him, we were given rocking chairs too. He wore dark glasses to help protect his eyes from the sun, and took them off when John suggested that we move beneath the shade of a tree.

'I is the first man to meet John,' he said in English when we were settled below the branches, a cup of coffee in his hand. 'I do see him wandering down our roads and do wonder where he is sleeping at night.'

'I do sleep in the hedgerows, Abe,' John said.

'You is a terrible sight to behold,' Abraham Esh went on. His eyes were rheumy with age but his white beard was still full-grown. His trousers were smeared with butter from where he had eaten from his lap. His concerns in life went beyond his appearance.

'Abe took me into his home, Daniel. He and his family looked after me. I wouldn't be here if it wasn't for Abe. He was kind.'

'God was kind to you, John,' he said after sipping his coffee, which by now was lukewarm, but he was still blowing across the surface before drinking. 'John is telling me you is interested in schooling, Daniel. Education is an interest of my own. I read a book or two about schooling. John and I frequently discuss the problem of it. I would like to know your ideas on the teaching of how to make an atom bomb, which will happen in our schools very soon.'

'Atom bombs exist,' I said picking up on the atmosphere of secrecy existing between us and speaking quietly, 'therefore not to know about them is foolish. It is ignorance which is dangerous, not knowledge.'

'Your ideas are liberal,' he said.

'Yes, they are,' I admitted.

'Do you have peace in England?' he asked.

'We do have bombs,' I replied after thinking for a moment. 'We have bombs that kill, but we're a peace-loving people.'

'Do you draw a distinction between yourself and the people

who make those bombs?' he continued.

'Yes, I suppose I do.'

'Then it is your knowledge which is dangerous because you enter into evil knowingly. Ignorance can be forgiven. I draw no distinction between the policy of a government and the individual who carries it out. I ain't a liberal.'

'Yes, I can see that, Abraham.'

'I am very concerned at the moment for the welfare of our children.'

'I can see that as well. I do understand how the education of your children must be of prime importance to your survival.' It was the first time I had thought this, but it tripped off my tongue as if it had been on my mind for a while. 'I can see how worldly knowledge will inevitably lead to your disintegration.'

'That is what we face,' he said. 'We face the end of our faith. It is about our right to live as we choose.'

'What sort of schools would you like?' I asked.

'Schools with one room,' John interrupted. 'A one-roomed schoolroom for each local community, where we can educate our children as we wish, with our own teachers. We would build them in the corners of fields and have them relevant to home and farm life.'

'Not on stilts?' I inquired, a smile on my face.

'Not on stilts, Daniel, no. Small rooms where children are free to learn the basics of life without the modern pressures of the world. We would teach writing, reading, and arithmetic. Writing enough to be able to write a letter, reading enough to be able to read the label on a jam jar, and enough arithmetic to be able to go to the bank.'

The sun had moved across the sky and was penetrating the branches, so Abraham rose to his feet and allowed John to move his rocking chair closer to the trunk, where the shadow remained dense. It was as though we were in a cabal from which the rest of the gathered community were excluded. The women were now eating and the men standing talking in small groups, but I gained the distinct impression that John thought our three-some the most important. It was dark under the hanging boughs of the tree and my eyes took a few moments to adjust to the shade. Abraham's eyes required even longer, so there was a pause whilst he focused on me before speaking again.

273

'Some folks in our community don't see the problem as clearly as we do,' he said finally. 'We do know it ain't fair on the children, it ain't fair to ask them to close their ears in class.' He wiped his eyes on his handkerchief and then put his empty cup of coffee down on the grass. His chair rocked with his movements. 'Our bishop is not the cleverest of men. He thinks our children will not learn when we ask them not to.'

'We know that those most seeking power are the least able to exercise it responsibly,' John said, beginning to explain their governmental system, 'so we elect our bishops by chance. Every adult, baptized male is eligible. All our names are written on slips of paper and placed into the bible, and one picked out by lot. It is a good system because fate bestows power on our leaders, but it does mean that sometimes we end up with the village idiot.'

'What do you do then?' I asked.

'We meet like this, Daniel. We talk amongst ourselves. The elders in our community then begin to exert their influence. It happens naturally. Look about you, we're all talking in small clusters.'

'Yes, I've noticed.'

'We all have our say and are free to make our point. That is why change takes a long time in our community. We discussed Harry's will for six years, and then decided it would be wrong to accept the money. Abe spoke against it. I spoke for acceptance and lost. We move slowly.' He twisted his fingers through his beard, clearly worried that the speed of their decision-making would not help them regarding their children's education. 'This is one occasion where we need a strong bishop.'

'But you can't move slowly on your children's schooling,' I said. 'If you wait fifty years for a consensus, it will be too late.'

'Yes, I know,' he replied, irritated by my stating the obvious.

'We have two options we is to put forward to the bishop,' Abraham went on in a calmer tone. He picked up his cup of coffee forgetting it was empty and looked disappointed when he saw there was none. 'One of our options is to move to another land. We is thinking South America might be a suitable place. We is hoping there might be good land there for us to farm, and good people who would let us live in peace.'

'You would move to South America?' I asked John, astounded by what I had heard.

'Yes, we would, Daniel. That is our way. We will move on

274

'rather than answer back,' he said without pathos or exaggerated pity for himself.

'Our only other option is that we do nothing,' Abraham continued. 'If the authorities here want to educate our children their way, then we must refuse to send them to their schools, and we must find another land in which to live. We is to suggest to the bishop that we send people to South America to see if they can find good farming land.'

'I think you're crazy,' I said bluntly, angrily, although why I was angry I was not quite sure. It might well have been because of the impotence I felt at their doggedness. I caught a glimpse of the tenacity the older man must have possessed in his youth, which had softened with age, but not sufficiently ever to make him change his mind, or stay in Pennsylvania if they could not have their own one-roomed schoolrooms.

I saw, at that precise moment, with a clarity so lucid it was exciting, exactly how I should act, and knew that I must keep my actions secret forever. There was business to be done which no other person must ever know about. The deception would require stealth and cunning.

John sipped the last of his coffee. One of the women, as if knowing that Abraham liked two cups, brought him another. John put his empty cup down upon his lap.

'You're not going to send Gideon to school, are you?' I asked him calmly, covering up my excitement, knowing what his reply would be.

'No, Daniel, I'm not, you're exactly right.'

'Will you go to prison?'

'Possibly. I don't know. Probably, yes, I think so. I'll be breaking the law.'

'What about Rachel?'

'She agrees with me that what I'm doing is right. I'm not a bully.'

'What if your family is broken up? What if they take Gideon away from you.'

'Until we can find another land in which to live peacefully, there is nothing I can do about that. I must face the consequence of my beliefs. Abe will support me. The community will support me. I will not be alone.'

John had, once more, spoken without self-pity. It was his straightforward honesty which convinced me that what I was

275

about to do was correct. I had at my disposal a large sum of money which might help him to remain in Pennsylvania.

John was right he was not alone, for when he went to prison the following year over five hundred other Amishmen from across the United States, all fathers of young children, went with him. At home in Richmond, as Armanda and I read Rachel's letters explaining her dilemmas, and telling me of the court cases being fought by sympathetic lawyers on their behalf, I was reminded of the afternoon I spent beneath an oak tree at Amos Lapp's farm, talking politics, talking religion, talking about a person's right to live in the way that they might choose.

As I write now at my desk, some thirty-eight years later, it is early evening and two yellow JCB diggers have just passed my window on the road outside, coming back from Peter's farm where Jenni has had them digging up the field searching for her father's coffin. Peter telephoned me a few minutes ago to tell me that they had found it, and that young men were now digging more carefully with spades. He wanted me to go along so that I might see for myself, but I shall not, for I know that the sight would be too painful. I no longer need to feel self-pity in order to feel alive. I shall leave the self-pity to Jenni.

This morning I received a long letter from Jacob in Chicago, where he is married and works as a motor mechanic. He eventually left the Amish, as his father had feared, but without the rancour that each expected from the other. He shouldered many of his family's burdens whilst his father was in prison, including taking his mother, in the old beaten-up car he bought, to see Gideon in the children's home, where Gideon was making his own protest by refusing to eat. Together they convinced him that God would want him to be healthy, at least when they were present, and he ate the homemade bread, pies and cookies they brought with them. But it was touch and go, and Gideon died before John was released. He died a starvelling in an English woman's arms, and when Jacob went to the press, at his lawyer's suggestions, it was Gideon's death which helped outrage the American nation. Television crews flocked to Pennsylvania and the other Amish communities throughout North America to see the strange, old-fashioned, Anabaptist people in their black, blue, and turquoise clothes who were going to prison and dying for their principles.

The Washington Post ran headlines across its front page when the first Amishmen began to be released from prison, and John was chased by journalists and television reporters, but he declined to speak to them, as he had to the lawyers in court, preferring instead to keep his own counsel. It was Jacob who answered the reporters' questions at the farm gate, and it was Jacob who referred them to the lawyers whenever there was a legal question he did not understand. The lawyers fought on, lodging appeal after appeal, despite Amish antipathy, in the local courts in Ohio, Indiana, Minnesota, Wisconsin, Nebraska, Kentucky, Missouri, Kansas, Michigan, Illinois, and in Pennsylvania, until in 1968, three Amish fathers were arrested in Wisconsin for failing to send their three daughters, aged fourteen and fifteen years old, to high school. Jacob, now married and living in Chicago, heard of the case and wrote to tell me that the National Committee for Amish Religious Freedom, of which he was a member, had employed an attorney, an expert in constitutional and religious law, to defend them. The local court, as in all previous cases, ruled that although the Amish were sincere in their beliefs and their religious views were undoubtedly being violated, the compelling interest must be that of the state. As usual, with little expectation of success, an appeal was lodged with the Wisconsin Supreme Court, which held, to everyone's surprise, that the state had failed to prove its case and ruled in favour of the Amish. It was the first victory for the lawyers. When the state of Wisconsin appealed to the Supreme Court in Washington, the lawyers fought on and won. The Chief Justice in his judgement said: 'States undoubtedly have the responsibility of improving the education of their citizens, but this interest must be measured against the legitimate claims of the free exercise of religion.' A small group of Amishmen waited on the steps outside the court, and one of them tossed his black hat high into the air when the lawyers came out and told them they could after all have their own one-roomed schoolrooms. It was not John, for he was at home on the farm in Pennsylvania with Rachel, Anna, Katie, Emanuel and Elmer, whose broken nose had grown straight, and who had married an Amish girl the previous autumn and was shortly to be a father himself.

I was interrupted in my writing about the Supreme Court by the insistent ringing of the doorbell. It was Peter, who had driven round in the Land Rover to see me because I would not go to him. As usual, he was concerned about my wellbeing and happiness.

'I'm busy,' I said rather brusquely on the doorstep, not meaning to be quite so fierce.

'Daniel, you can't spend all your time writing. It isn't good for you.'

'I preferred you when you stammered,' I said. 'That way it took you so much longer to interfere.'

'Give me a whisky and a cigarette,' he replied. 'I need a tumbler of whisky after the day I've had. Those diggers of Jenni's have torn the field to shreds.'

'I expect there wasn't much of a coffin left,' I said pouring whiskies for us both in my sitting-room.

'The coffin held together until they tried to lift it out, then it just broke apart. It was awful, Daniel. I could see his skull and his neck bone, and the bones of his hands and his feet. I'd forgotten how tall Harry was.'

'I haven't. He once likened us both to Laurel and Hardy because he was thin and I was fat. He always said I ate too much, which is still true. Peter, I shan't go and see his body, I shan't go to the cemetery when Jenni puts it there, I shan't acknowledge what she has done. I have my own memories of Harry, they are personal memories which I don't want to see spoiled.'

Peter has just left me and I must write, briefly, of Jacob's letter which arrived this morning from Chicago. He, his wife, and youngest child have just returned from visiting the farm in Pennsylvania. He tells me, in simple language reminiscent of his upbringing, that his father's health is no better and that he expects him to die very soon. He implores me to travel to the farm before it is too late, for he says his father has something on his mind that he wishes to speak to me about. I am worried that John has discovered my secret, for I never had any wish to offend him, and this lunch-time I have booked an air flight to Philadelphia, from where I shall take the small train as usual. I had planned to travel in a fortnight, but have brought forward my departure. If John asks me, I have decided to tell him the truth. I deceived him and have never told him of the way I spent Harry's fortune.

10

The evening after the preaching service at Amos Lapp's farm and our talk with Abraham Esh beneath the branches of the tree, I asked John if I might be left alone to go for a walk. The day was cooling towards nightfall, the orange sun a crescent on the yellow bar of the horizon, the sky free of cloud so that the light caught perfectly the insects and dust in the air. Midges swarmed about my head, and in my ears I could still hear Abraham Esh talking about education: 'We need maths to count fruit jars or corn shocks,' he had said, 'to measure baking powder or corn feed, figure out how much paint is needed to paint a room, the amount of seed corn for a ten acre field . . .' It was the simplicity of his ideas which disturbed me most, and made me realize how complex we make our world in order that we might feel knowledgeable, useful, powerful, and important. Harry, I thought, had understood this a long time ago. He knew that true generosity was not in giving, but in understanding. I walked on across the field with my memories of Jenni's father, but it was John and Abraham Esh who made me realize that it is man's generosity of spirit and understanding which might eventually free him from his neurosis. Abraham Esh was free; he was the most liberated man I had ever met.

The sun caught hold of the landscape, picking out the white farm houses and farm buildings. The light caught the edges of the barn walls, sending sharp, mirror-like reflections out into the darkening sky. It was as though children were playing with glass. The rooftops were black, their grey-green tiles absorbing the last of the day's heat, their weathercocks motionless for there was not a breath of wind. I could hear the metallic click of a waterwheel pumping water from a well, but it was the only sound.

I stood amongst the tall grasses at the edge of the path I had been following and watched the sun disappear below the horizon, taking with it the long stretch of rolling countryside which I had been able to see clearly only a few moments before. For a split second it was like a man with a torch, and then I realized it was a torch and that a figure was approaching me. It was Jacob wearing his black hat, his black broadfall trousers and blue shirt.

'The light goes quickly here,' I said. 'I've noticed it before. There's so much open space that it's like standing on the roof of the world. It's rare to find such peace.'

'What is you doing?' he asked me, taking the passivity of his environment for granted and not comprehending why I might enjoy the melancholy created by the darkness and by being alone. 'Is it my father who has sent you?'

'No, no one's sent me. I sometimes get pleasure from being by myself. Your farms are so beautiful in the late evening sunlight. I came out to take some photographs like a tourist.'

'Can I see your pictures?'

'I didn't take any, Jacob. I know your father is against cameras.'

'You can picture me if you want.'

'Perhaps another day,' I said, 'it's too dark now. Your father would disapprove. I took one or two of you on Ascension Day when you all built the dam by the river.'

'My father ain't the only person who is important,' he replied as though answering a question when I had not asked him one.

We walked together along the path as the rising moon began to improve our view, so that the torch beam became less prominent across the fields planted with sweetcorn and barley, tobacco and sweet-potato. A few days before, I had watched Jacob hoeing weeds from the field of barley, his bare feet working methodically along the rows up the incline of the shallow slope, his wood and iron hoe digging into the dry soil upending the weeds, red poppies, and clumps of daisies; but now he seemed changed, somehow older, as if the teenager who worked the fields during the day was not the teenager who slipped out of the house at night. His step was jaunty, reflecting the freedom the moonlight gave him.

The land we were walking across was un-fenced and, for the most part, un-hedged to make access between the fields easier. The countryside rolled in a series of gentle inclines, like the movement of dolphins through water: it was rich land, well-farmed and well-irrigated.

'Would you like to travel?' I asked him.

'Yes, one day I would.'

'Where would you like to go?'

'I don't know. I isn't bothered. The Holy Land, I'd like to go there.'

'Don't be too hard on your father, will you?'

'No,' he said, 'I won't.'

'We can learn as much from looking at one field as we can from looking at a country. I've travelled a lot, but travel is useless unless we have an open mind. I'm glad I've seen you, Jacob. There is something I wanted to ask you about.'

'What?' he asked innocently.

'I spent the afternoon with your father and Abraham Esh. You were playing hide and seek, and then you played softball.'

'I saw you talking.'

'Your father tells me that you're going to begin to look for new land in South America.'

'I've heard it said.'

'Your community does not believe in ownership. Tenure of an area is given to you by God, but it is not permanent. Am I correct?'

'Yes.'

'How long will it take your community to find these new lands?'

The field descended away from us towards the bottom of a small gully, and the path followed the shallow slope downwards. The panorama of the countryside stretched into the distance, where the moonlight was now picking out the numerous white farm houses and farm buildings. Instead of reflecting the light, the barn walls now appeared to be absorbing it, so that the capacious, broad landscape, silent and without people, was almost ghostly. The gully was in shadow. I stopped so that Jacob was forced to stop.

'I don't know,' he said. 'It could take as long as a hundred years.'

281

'Would you move to South America farm by farm?' I asked.

'Yes. It could take two hundred years. One family would start the settlement, and then another would follow when neighbouring land was free to be taken. It could take three hundred years.'

'It's taken you three hundred years to colonize this area,' I said.

'We move slowly, Daniel.' He had echoed his father's statement and, for the first time, used my Christian name. He had been too shy, too accepting of his youth and my middle-age to use it before. I saw, in his decision to change and be an adult, how one day he would find the courage to leave the Amish. I could not know then that he would become a motor mechanic in Chicago, have four children, all girls, and that his youngest daughter would become a doctor.

'I admire the way you will move on,' I said, 'but the world around you is going to move faster and faster. The leisurely pace of change in the last three hundred years has not dominated you, but it will, even in the next fifty years. Technology is going to bring with it a new morality. That morality may not even be Christian. One man is going to have little influence. He will have as much influence as his understanding, and his understanding may be limited because the science of technology is going to be so complex. We live in an age of specialists, when those specialists have to be trusted. I admire your lack of trust, I admire the way you live your lives as an example to others, but it will not be enough. Specialists are greedy, they take what they want and discard what they don't want, leaving the rest of us to live in a muddle. Greed is dangerous because it is self-satisfying and fosters ignorance. Greed for the few relies on the ignorance of the many. Your goodness and the goodness of your people, may not be enough, Jacob.'

'You know my father is going to prison,' he said.

'Yes, he told me. He told me that Gideon would receive no education unless it was to be at one of your own schools. I admire that too, but I fear his decision is ill-founded. I fear the struggle will be a long one.'

We set off down the incline towards the bottom of the gully. The thin kerosene lights shining dully from the farmhouse windows disappeared from view. At the bottom, Jacob kneeled down and scraped away the dusty topsoil with a stick he picked up. He worked at the ground methodically, and sensed my unease.

'You isn't to stay with me if you don't want to,' he said.

'When you've found what you're looking for, can we walk back up to the top? I feel cut off down here.'

'No one sees me.'

'I realize that. I'd like to look at the view.'

I had seen the children cross this way many times on their journeys home from school. Unbeknown to them they had trodden on the hole Jacob was now digging. After a few moments he found the parcel he was looking for. It was wrapped in paper and tied with string, the string frayed where it had been knotted and unfastened repeatedly, the paper dog-eared from folding and engrained with earth. The wrapping was old newspaper. He placed the parcel beneath his arm and we walked up the slope towards the moonlight. At the top I could see he looked embarrassed.

'I comes out here on Sunday nights,' he said. 'I tells my parents I am with the group. We teenagers is meant to meet together and sing songs. I no longer goes. They will be singing songs at the Lapp farm this evening. Do you know if you have gang pressure in England?'

'There is always pressure to conform, Jacob, no matter where we are. It's always difficult to be one against the crowd, but it mustn't stop us trying. We may be the one who is right.'

'I don't want to be right. I don't want to be wrong. I want to learn for myself. I don't want other folks telling me what I should know.'

'Your father would disagree with you.'

'All folks is different aren't they, Daniel? No two folk is the same. I think all folks should be free to make other suggestions about living if they want to.'

'Your father would attack your liberalism, Jacob, as he's attacked mine. It doesn't make him superior, or you inferior, it's just a point of view. All that matters is that we don't manipulate our cause for our own ends. When we manipulate those people who are weaker than ourselves, that is when we begin the long road into evil. That will never happen here, because you as a community understand that fact. When your father says he hasn't a cause, that is what he means. He means that you are all equal.'

The moonlight was whitening the landscape, making it look as though a frost had gathered on the grass and on the crops in the fields, but the air was warm. Jacob turned his back and unfastened his braces, next taking his trousers down to his ankles and stepping out of them. His legs were thin, like Harry's legs. He untied the string on the parcel and pulled on a pair of denim jeans, fastening the metal buckle on the leather belt at his waist. He took off his blue shirt, and put on a checked one which I could see was creased and needed washing. His skin was sweating in the humid air, causing the shirt to cling to his arms and shoulders, making it difficult for him to hurry into it, as he had done the pair of jeans.

'I should have left you,' I said, 'instead of causing you discomfort. Where do you go?'

'I do go to Bird in Hand to meet some English boys. One of them do have a car. We go car driving. Do you think I is odd to dress in this way?'

'Yes, I do,' I replied, 'but we're all odd. None of us is normal. Your shirt needs washing.'

'Do you think English boys is odd to dress in the way that they do?'

'No, I don't,' I said.

'I do wash my English clothes in a stream.'

He fastened his shirt, his large, clumsy fingers more used to hooks and eyes than buttons, and then tucked his shirt tails into his jeans. He next took off his black hat, which he threw down on top of his black trousers, which were lying flat and seamless on the grass like a piece of worn, uncut cloth. His jeans by comparison had shape and body, and I could understand why he changed before meeting his friends. I thought of Jacob in the car, where they might drive him to, and what, if anything, would be their pleasure when they arrived there. It seemed such a dull place to live unless you were Amish, for there were no amusement parks, no cafés and very few restaurants, no dance halls or slot-machine parlours, no beaches for miles on which to surf, as years later, after the Amish had won their battle for their own schools, I was to see the kids doing on Santa Monica and Venice beaches in California. The kids there were rich and fashion conscious, had all the consumer desirables and the latest streamlined surfboards, some listening to music through waterproofed headphones as they rode the waves, whilst other youngsters skateboarded along the promenade in coloured shorts. Even then, as Jacob put on a pair of socks, it was clear to me that the Amish had colonized an area, so different from the rest of America, and made it their own. There were no bars in which to buy alcohol, no cinemas in which to see the latest films, no theatres like the hundreds in New York, Los Angeles, and Boston. There were no Sunset or Hollywood Boulevards, where young men cruised in their open-topped cars, but instead the country lanes had names like Musser School Road, Mill Creek Road, Beechdale Road, Stumptown Road, Horseshoe Road, North Harvest Road, Colonial Road, Weavertown Road, and Scenic Road, all of which I had walked. Jacob could drive a buggy along these roads with his eyes shut, and I had been told stories of horses which knew the roads so well that their drivers often fell asleep, waking up to find themselves at home in the barn.

'What do you do when you get to where you're going to?' I asked.

'We do sit and talk,' he said. 'We do smoke cigarettes and drink beer.'

'Isn't there anything more exciting than that?'

'I do find it exciting, Daniel.' He put on his shoes and stood up to stamp his feet into them. 'They do buy the beer in the big town, or steal it from their father's refrigerators. English have beer in their ice-boxes.'

'Don't get drunk, will you?'

'No, I never do. I don't like beer so much.'

'Do you ever get lonely, Jacob?'

'I is too busy to be lonely. Sunday is my one night when I do what I want. I break the rules.'

'It's breaking the rules which is exciting, isn't it? I know just how you feel.'

He bent down onto his haunches to fasten his shoelaces, his fingers unused to such intricate activity so that the laces became thick and over-knotted, like the knots on the string which had been round the parcel of clothes. When he had finished he was ready to leave me and to join his friends for the night. I watched him go.

Some thirty years later I was in southern California. I had

travelled there after having spent a month with Jacob's father on the farm in Pennsylvania, almost three thousand miles and a different world away. It was sunset. I watched as the affluent, surfboarding kids deserted the beach at Santa Monica. They were leaving the sands to the homeless, to the destitute who would then occupy the shoreline for the night. Many of the down and outs had supermarket trolleys in which they pushed their belongings, and in which they hid their hypodermic syringes and narcotics. Santa Monica and Venice beaches are dangerous after dark and I could see why, for life amongst these drifters was cheap. Life does become cheaper the poorer we become. As I watched the setting sun melt into the Pacific Ocean, I thought of Jacob on the night he had changed his clothes in front of me, and the journey I was to make the following day to see him in Chicago. The lawyers fees had taken much of Harry's fortune, but there was still almost a million dollars left, which had remained untouched gaining interest in a bank account in Pennsylvania since the Supreme Court judgement. It seemed time to spend it, to give it to the poor in one last romantic gesture. If the money had been in my pocket I would have thrown it, in single dollar bills, over the cliff to the beach below, where the dispossessed were gathering in frightening numbers. Money is confetti unless we have none.

I flew United Airways from Los Angeles LAX, and Jacob met me in Chicago in his new car, a white Dodge which he quickly negotiated onto the freeway, where five lanes of traffic intermingled like dodgem-cars at a fair. I thought his car aptly named.

'I saw your father two weeks ago before leaving for California,' I said. 'Whenever I go to the farm, I'm always reminded of the night you changed out of your Amish clothes. Your English clothes were wrapped in newspaper. You probably don't remember, or do you?'

'I do remember, Daniel. I couldn't forget because you always remind me. Whenever we meet, it's usually one of the first things you mention.'

'Is it? Am I so predictable?'

He smiled and drove the freeway at speed, as he had always driven the horse and buggy along the Amish lanes, being incapable of slowness whatever the means of transport. I enjoyed

Jacob's company and had grown fonder of him over the years. We knew each other well enough to avoid too much badinage.

'Yes, you are predictable about that Sunday night,' he said. 'I was young and immature. I wanted to go to the movies. I wanted to go to the beach like any American kid, except I didn't know what a beach was. I wanted to play pinball. I wanted to go to the ball game. You still know America better than I do. I've still never been surfing in California, or gone to Hollywood, or been to Disneyland. I've still never seen the deserts of New Mexico and Arizona, nor walked along the Mississippi in New Orleans. But I've seen the rich colours of the trees in the New England fall, that is my America.'

'If I weren't slowly becoming too old for apologies, Jacob, I'd say I was sorry that I've seen so much. I know small parts of America, but I don't know Americans. You're all so different, so disparate. The night that you changed out of your Amish clothes in Pennsylvania haunts me like a recurrent dream. I want to talk to you about it. I should have talked years ago. I committed a sin that night.'

'When? What sin?' he asked, his cheeks hollow.

'After you left me to go and meet your friends at Bird in Hand, I returned to the farm. Your father was sitting looking over his farm accounts. He wanted everything in neat order for you, in case he should go to prison sooner than he expected. He was busy and tired, but I talked to him.'

As the car sped along the freeway towards Jacob's home, I told him everything that I had said to his father, and how the next day I had gone back to the lawyer. I reminded him that he had taken me in the horse and buggy. I explained to him how it had been on the tip of my tongue to let him know of my intentions that night by the gully, but that I had changed my mind when I saw him fastening his shirt buttons, having decided that to implicate him fully in my plan would be wrong. I agreed with him when he said he was young and immature, and explained how easy any manipulation on my part would have been, which is why I had let him go to his friends, his beer and cigarettes. I told him of the million dollars remaining in the bank account in Pennsylvania, and how I had had the idea of giving it to the poor of Santa Monica. I explained to him how I really wished to scatter the money over the cliff but had to admit that setting up a drug

287

dependency centre might be preferable and make more sense.

'I always knew the money came from somewhere, Daniel,' he said when I had finished. 'Was the National Committee for Amish Religious Freedom set up with money from the will?'

'Some of it, Jacob, yes. Other people began to contribute, which is why there is money left over. I asked the lawyers to ask you to be on the committee. I knew your father would look more kindly upon the whole thing if you were part of the decision making. I did manipulate you, but you were older by then. I'm not apologizing for what I did; I just wanted you to know the facts. It seemed time that you knew the truth. I had thought that I would remain silent, but that decision was wrong. I've decided that silence can be evil. Silence is certainly the first refuge of a coward.'

He turned the car right onto a sliproad and we left the freeway. His gloved hands were holding the steering-wheel, his actions so different from handling the reins of a horse. He was wearing oily dungarees, having met me at the airport from work. The rough cloth of his working clothes and the expensive leather of his driving gloves were incompatible, so that for a moment everything seemed incongruous, including the Chicago skyline which I had seen several times before. I was still thinking of the night by the gully and could not shake its images from my mind, although this should have been easy, for Jacob was well into his forties and our relationship had become adult years ago.

'Thank you for telling me,' he said. 'I'm glad I know. You're right, silence can be evil.'

'Gideon died partly because of me, Jacob.'

'Gideon didn't die because of you, Daniel. He died because of my father's stubbornness. He died because Gideon was Gideon and because he was a good Amish boy.'

'I often think about him. I often think about you all. You were the children I would have liked to have had myself, but never did. I think you are the children Harry would have liked, too. Jenni's understanding is as nothing compared to yours, Jacob, or Elmer's, or Emanuel's, or Katie's, or Anna's. You all possess a wisdom infinitely greater than hers. That is why I did what I did.'

On that night when Jacob left me to go and join his friends at Bird in Hand, I stepped over his discarded Amish clothes and walked around the perimeter of the gully back towards the farm. The moonlight was still whitening the landscape, so that the farm buildings in the distance looked like alabaster models. Kerosene lights were shining from the upstairs windows of the farmhouse, where I knew the children would be preparing for bed, leaving John and Rachel alone for an hour, before they too would go to sleep. Jacob would not arrive home until after midnight. As I approached the farmstead I saw the lights go out, including Peter's light in the room that we shared, which pleased me because I did not want Peter implicated in my conspiracy. He would know later, but not now.

I felt nervous, as I should have done as a younger man before lying to and attempting to manipulate another person, but I never had been afraid then.

John was working on his ledgers at the kitchen table as I entered through the door. He had two hardbacked notebooks in which he wrote down the figures in pencil, licking the pencil with his tongue each time he recorded a number because the graphite was blunt. He was surrounded by invoices and auctioneers' chits, some dating back decades and so old that the paper had become brittle. He was finalizing his affairs, like a dying man might settle his estate, as though he expected never to return. I knew that an individual Amishman would not make a will, or accept inherited wealth, but John was coming as close to that as his principles would allow. In the margins of the ledgers, adjacent to the columns of figures, he had written notes to Jacob explaining what he had done, and why. There were detailed descriptions of which English traders were the most honest, and which to avoid, together with statements of money owing or money owed to each.

'Jacob knows most of this,' he said, 'I'm just reminding him. It's best it's written down.'

'Has Rachel gone to bed?'

'Yes. Have you had a good walk, Daniel?'

'Mmm, very pleasant. I saw Jacob on his way to the Lapp farm for the singsong.'

I did not tell him where Jacob was really going, or that Jacob drank beer and smoked cigarettes, and was even more English than his father realized. I needed to keep John in ignorance of these matters, so that later I could use his trust of his son to my own ends. The greater the bond between them, the better was my chance of manoeuvring them both to the point where I could act as I wished with Harry's money.

John must have picked up on my nervousness. He put down his pencil and looked up at me for the first time since I had come through the door. He removed his spectacles and rubbed his eyes against his knuckles.

'You're hovering as if there's something you want to say,' he said. 'Don't make me doubt what I'm doing. It's hard enough as it is. Jacob will do his duty. He's not a Judas.'

He made my body shiver along the length of my spine because I was the one about to be Judas. To disguise my agitation I sat down on the backless bench opposite him.

'Jacob has just told me it could take you three hundred years to colonize new lands in South America,' I said.

'Yes, Daniel, it could.'

'It isn't my place to sow seeds of doubt, John. I think you're right to go to prison and to search for new lands elsewhere,' I lied. 'I wish you luck.'

John smiled, and I felt happier now that the first lie was over. I wanted him to think that I agreed with everything he was planning to do, when, in truth, I knew it to be naive and doomed to failure. His plans might have worked a century ago, but not today when the world was becoming ever smaller, and the influence of technology ever larger. But I knew it was pointless to continue this argument with him, and instead left him to believe that I lived in an England where nothing had changed since he had left during the Great War.

I prepared myself for the second lie. I did this by putting my elbows on the table and speaking nonchalantly.

'Do you remember the solicitor in England, John? You wrote to him a few weeks ago.'

'Yes, I remember.'

'I've had another letter from him.' This was untrue. I felt my stomach muscles tighten.

'I will have nothing to do with a lawyer, Daniel.'

'I'm not asking you to.'

'Has Jenni Treffgarne received her father's fortune?'

My stomach muscles contracted even further, and I belched loudly several times. Luckily John thought me Amish for doing this.

'Yes, she has,' I said. I swallowed the small amount of bitter fluid which had come into my mouth.

'Then the matter is settled, Daniel.'

'That is exactly what I was going to say. Pennycott has written that the matter is now closed, that all is well.' I paused. I swallowed again. 'John, I sometimes feel that you don't trust me. You're so quick to jump in and take umbrage, as if everything I do is wrong. I would never go against anything you said, and I would certainly never go to a lawyer behind your back. It isn't fair. You're quite hurtful sometimes. I've never been less than honest with you, but you behave as if I'm a cheat. I find your lack of trust in me quite offensive. It's offensive when you doubt my word. I deserve your respect, not your distrust. I have done nothing wrong.'

He ran his pencil downwards along a column of figures as though he might be adding the numbers together in his head, but I had spoken with sufficient emotional force to make him feel guilty and for the numbers to be a distraction.

'I thought you were going to try to persuade me to use a lawyer over the schools issue,' he said quietly, without looking up towards me.

'Why would I do that?' I asked him. 'Do you think I have no respect for your beliefs?'

'No, I know you do have respect, Daniel.'

'Exactly. I can't tell you, John, how much you upset me sometimes.' I went on to exonerate my manipulation of him. 'When we first arrived here, in those first weeks, we were treated despicably. We were treated with contempt and told that we were evil. On our first night, when you thrashed Jacob, it was you who was evil for creating such an atmosphere in this room that I wanted to go home. Don't accuse me of anything ever again, accuse yourself.'

He rested his elbows on the table with his forearms perpendicular, so that his open palms were together side by side. He leaned his forehead into the bowl created by his fingers.

'You must know that I didn't mean to be rude, Daniel.'

'I don't know anything, John. I know only what I see.'

The bitter, bile-like fluid had returned to my mouth. It was so strong that I could even taste it on my lips. I swallowed hard, but it would not go away completely.

291

'Why haven't you said this before?' he asked.

'Unlike you, I try to be kind. I haven't wanted to upset you.'

'Why do you wish to upset me now?'

'I don't.'

I sat back, but had to sit forward again when I remembered I was sitting on a bench. John lifted his face so that I could see his eyes.

'I would never pretend that my judgement was better than yours, John, but you do it to me constantly. It's superior, it's arrogant, and it's wrong of you.'

'I agree,' he said almost inaudibly. 'I agree with everything you say. I'm very sorry.'

The guilt I had engendered was now emanating from every pore of his body. It is easiest to deceive and play on the feelings of those who love us most. I had succeeded in getting John never to doubt my word, or mistrust my actions again.

I took a handkerchief from my pocket and needlessly blew my nose so as to appear completely relaxed. In fact, I spat some of the foul tasting bile from my mouth into it.

'I have to go and see the lawyer at some point this week,' I said conversationally. 'I wondered if Jacob could take me in the horse and buggy. I'd like Jacob to come with me. It would save me time walking.'

'I thought the matter of Harry's will was settled,' he said again.

'It is. John, you're being suspicious –'

'I'm not being suspicious. I'm trying to understand the complexities of the law.'

'Pennycott has sent me another document for him to sign, that is all.'

This was untrue and a further betrayal of John's trust in me, but I had successfully brought the conversation back to the kernel of my deceit. What I really wanted to do was to have Jacob meet the lawyer, at least informally. This way I had the most susceptible member of John's family introduced to the man who might eventually defend them in court. I had yet to speak to the lawyer of my plans, but I was certain he would do as I wished. I had met him twice, and he had seemed the soul of discretion on both occasions.

'Jacob can take you whenever you are ready, Daniel. Just let him know when you want to go.'

'I will,' I said.

John put his fingers down modestly into his lap, where they moved to and fro as though he might be playing catscradle, but he had no string. His face was ashen.

'You look tired, John. Why don't you go to bed.'

'Yes, I am tired. But I'm more worried that I've treated you really badly. I should have realized how sensitive you are, and not been so obdurate. I never meant to be unkind.'

'I know that, John,' I said.

He moved his fingers to his lips, where he pulled away a few straggling hairs of his beard. I looked away, for I knew that he was about to apologize once more, and I also knew that if I caught his eye I might well tell him the truth. We need to know the limits of our own deceit in order to live moral lives and to act ethically, but that Sunday night I was far from certain of what those limits should be. All I knew was that my own particular limit had been reached.

'Daniel, you're dribbling, what's the matter?'

'It's nothing,' I said, 'I feel a bit nauseous. I'm sorry I keep belching. I've just brought up some food into my mouth. It's gone. Don't worry about me.'

He went into the kitchen and fetched a pitcher of lemonade. He poured me a glass, which I drank slowly.

We talked on into the small hours about John's dreams for the one-roomed schoolrooms, and about the preaching service, its meanings and explanations, its teachings from the bible and their relevance to farm life. It was unusual for him to sit up so late, for his life was dominated by work and the necessity of sleep, but he wished to reward my friendship.

I said nothing more about Jacob or the lawyer, just as I have said nothing since.

We drank the lemonade until the pitcher was empty, and exhaustion, finally, drove John to bed.

I should go to bed myself, but I am wide awake, as I was that Sunday night in Pennsylvania. It is nearing midnight and the traffic has ceased on the road outside. The diggers from Peter's farm have long gone. Jenni will be in Downing Street working at her boxes. I began this account for Jenni, but as the days have passed she has become less important, both in my mind and to the story itself. The image of the diggers, digging up her father's coffin, is the final image that I shall leave of her. If I had been able to manipulate her, as I had successfully manipulated John, I would have done so. It was not any goodness on my part, or old age that led to my failure; it was her cussedness. John was not cussed. He finally accepted the help of the lawyer in court, although he refused to speak to him in person, and Jacob had to do the speaking on his behalf. John was sentenced to nine months in prison. When I told Jenni she smiled – at least I thought she smiled – for she was still bitter at John's wealth. To this day she does not know how her father's fortune was spent.

I have re-read Jacob's last letter, where he tells me John's health is no better and that he has something on his mind he wishes to speak to me about. I can only hope that all along John has had his suspicions, and that he now gives me the opportunity to let him know the truth. It would salve my conscience and ease the guilt I still feel.

Peter has just telephoned to wish me a good journey, and to ask me to give his love to John. I must go and finish packing. I leave for Pennsylvania early tomorrow morning.